FOR TWO MEN BOUND BY HONOR

AND RIPPED APART BY BETRAYAL,

THE LAST BATTLE HAS BEGUN....

P9-DWH-900

DIRTY WHITE BOYS

THE
SECOND
SALADIN

STEPHEN HUNTER

Island
B O O K S

ISLAND BOOKS
Published by
Dell Publishing
a division of
Bantam Doubleday Dell Publishing Group, Inc.
1540 Broadway
New York, New York 10036

The title line "Are There Really Any Cowboys Left in the Good Old U.S.A.?" is used in the epigraph with the permission of the Algee Music Corporation. Copyright © 1980 Algee Music Corporation.

ISBN: 0-440-22186-2

Reprinted by arrangement with William Morrow and Company, Inc.

Printed in the United States of America

Published simultaneously in Canada

May 1998

10 9 8 7 6 5 4 3 2 1

OPM

For Lucy

ACKNOWLEDGMENTS

The author would like to thank a great many friends for their assistance in the preparation of this manuscript. A. Michael Hill and Joseph Fanzone, Jr., were especially generous with time and good ideas. The others were Charles R. Hazard, Jack Dawson, Wayne J. Henkel, Richard C. Hageman, Timothy Hunter, Virginia Hunter, Tom and Bonnie Hasler, Allen H. Peacock, Nick Yengich, Lenne P. Miller, and David Petzal. My editor, Maria Guarnaschelli, provided, as usual, extraordinary counsel; so did my agent, Victoria Gould Pryor. My wife, Lucy, to whom the book is dedicated, did all the crap work which enabled me to write every night; for that alone she deserves a medal; for putting up with me she deserves a good deal more. And thanks also to the three Bread Loaf friends—Anne Eastman, Page Edwards, and Steve Corey—who nursed me through my reading.

Finally, special thanks to Margaret Kahn, "Khanim," author of *Children of the Jinn* and one of few Americans to meet the Kurds on their own terms, for reading and commenting on the manuscript.

We the suicide fighters,
heroes of the nation,
lions of black times

We shall sacrifice our
lives and our property
for the sake
of liberated Kurdistan.

We shall wreak vengeance
upon the many guilty hands
which sought
to destroy the Kurds

And that shall serve
as a lesson for the
generations to follow.

—HYMN OF THE KURDISH FIGHTERS

Are there really any cowboys left
in the good old U.S.A.?

—LACY J. DALTON

1

Reynoldo Ramirez, moderately prosperous by the standards of his time and place, imagined himself beyond surprise. He observed the world through calm brown eyes set wide apart in a calm brown face—an Aztec face, an Indian face, a peasant's face, a gangster's face, for he was all of them—and nothing of his considerable bulk suggested a capacity for astonishment; or foolishness, for that matter; or mercy. He felt he'd seen most things by now: he'd killed men in fights with knives or fists; he'd been shot twice, stabbed four times; he'd had three wives and eleven children, seven of whom still lived; he'd spent six years in three prisons; and he looked forward at forty-four to a tranquil future, as befitted the owner of El Palacio, a bar and brothel on the Calle de Buenos Aires in the northern Mexican city of Nogales, on the Arizona border.

Yet, by the Virgin and Her glory, Reynoldo Ramirez was astounded.

A feeling that the simple rhythms of the world had been profoundly upset crept through him as he sat with his closest associate, the ever-smiling Oscar Meza, at their usual Number 1 table well back from the bar at El Palacio. Yet he allowed no sign of concern to disturb the surface of his face as he regarded the man who now stood before him.

The man was American. Or again, was he? He stood in blue jeans, impatiently, his face sealed off behind sunglasses. He looked immensely muscular. He was tan and hawk-nosed. And he had something quite foreign to the usual pawing, grabbing, yakking, farting gringo: he had dignity, which Ramirez prized most in this world, having worked so assiduously to fashion his own.

"Why not just walk up the street and go through the gate?" asked Oscar Meza in English. It was Oscar's job to handle this sort of negotiation. "A simple matter. It's done ten thousand times a day. Then you are there, eh? In wonderful America. Why trouble us with illegal proposals?" Oscar turned to smile at Ramirez.

"Why not just answer my question?" said the American—or the maybe-American.

The maybe-American was tall too, and his hair was blondish, light from the bright sun; and though Ramirez could not see them, he gauged the eyes, from the skin coloring, to be blue.

Yellow hair and blue eyes: what could be more American?

"It's a dangerous trip," said Oscar, "this trip you propose. It would cost much money."

"I have money."

"You are a rich man? Why, I wonder, would a rich man—"

"Just talk the business."

Stung, Oscar recoiled. He had merely been sociable. Oscar always tried to be sociable.

"All right then. Three hundred U.S., cash. No credit cards—" Oscar turned, pleased with his joke, and smiled at Reynoldo. "Two hundred now. Then one hundred tomorrow morning when you are in Los Estados safe and sound.''

''A boy said it would be one hundred.''

''Boys lie,'' said Oscar Meza. ''It's a rule. When I was a boy I lied. All the time, about everything.'' He laughed again. ''Forget what this boy said.''

No flicker crossed the maybe-American's face.

''I think you are not happy,'' said Oscar Meza. ''We want you to be happy. Sit down. Look, have a drink, get a woman—there are some pretty ones here and not too expensive, although you say you are a rich man. Think it over. You must learn to relax. We want you to be happy. We can work something out.''

Behind his glasses the man remained impassive.

''I want a guarantee.''

''Life is too short for guarantees,'' Oscar said. ''Maybe we ought to make it four hundred, five hundred, a thousand? All this talking is making me weary. I cannot guarantee what I cannot control and I cannot control fate.''

''A guarantee,'' said the man.

''I said, no guarantees. Don't you hear so good, mister?''

Ramirez at last spoke.

''Once every twenty nights out, they get you, mister. That's a law. You may go thirty-eight nights clean, then they get you twice. Or they may get you twice, then you go thirty-eight. But one out of twenty. I can't control it. God himself, the Holy Father, He cannot control it. It's the law.''

Oscar said, ''You listen good, mister. It's the true law.''

''Send this stupid man away,'' the man said to Ramirez. ''He makes me want to hurt him.''

"I'll hurt *you,* mister," Oscar said. "I'll cut you up damn quick."

"No," Ramirez said. "Go away, Oscar. Get me another Carta Blanca."

Oscar scurried off.

"He's a stupid man," said Ramirez. "But useful in certain things. Now. Say your case."

"You go a special way. There's a special way you can go. High, in the mountains. The direction from here is west. A road to a mine which is old and no longer used gets you there. Is this not right?"

The maybe-American spoke an almost-English. It was passable but fractured. Even Ramirez could pick out the occasional discordant phrase.

Ramirez looked at him coldly.

"You go this route," the man continued. "Once, maybe twice a year, depending. Depending on what? Depending on the moon, which must be down. And depending on the drugs, which you take across to the Huerra family in Mexico City for delivery to certain American groups. You are paid five thousand American dollars each trip. And the last time the Huerras gave you some extra because it went so nice. And I hear it said you don't give one dollar to the priests of your church, because you are a greedy man."

Ramirez stared at him. He had known such a moment would one day come. A stranger, with information enough to kill him or own him forever. It could only mean the Huerras were done with him and had sold him out, or that the police had finally—

"The last run was January sixteenth," the man said. "And the next one will be tonight, moon or no moon, and that's the true law."

Ramirez fought his own breathing.

"Who sent you?"

"Nobody sent me."

"How do you know all this?"

"I have friends."

"Important men?"

"Very important. Very knowledgeable in certain areas."

"You should have come to me and explained. You are a special man. I can see this now."

The man said nothing.

"You better watch yourself, though. Somebody might put a bullet in your head."

"Sure, okay, somebody might. And then somebody might come looking for *him* and put a bullet in *his* head too."

Ramirez struggled to take stock. The man had not had anything to drink, he was not talking wildly, he was not a crazy man. He had much coolness, much presence. He was a man Ramirez could respect. You wouldn't fool him too easily. He wouldn't make mistakes. He would make others make the mistakes.

"All right," Ramirez said. "But it will cost you more. The distance is a factor, the increased risk, the danger to my way of doing business. This is no easy thing—it's not running illegals into Los Estados. You want to go the guaranteed way, you got to pay for it. Or go someplace else, to some man who'll cut your throat in the desert."

"Nobody cuts my throat. How much?"

"A thousand. Half now, half later."

"You are a thief as well as anything else."

"I am a man of business. Come on, damn you, pay up or go someplace else. I'm done with talking."

"As God wills it." He handed over the money, counting out the bills.

"Out back, at eleven. Beyond the sewer there's a small shop called La Argentina. Wait behind it in the yard with the trucks. A van will come. You'll be in Arizona tomorrow. Pay the man in America, or he'll give you to the Border Patrol.''

The man nodded.

"If nothing goes wrong," he said.

"Nothing will go wrong. I'll drive the damned truck myself."

The man nodded again, and then turned and left.

Oscar returned.

"A gringo pig," he said. "I'd like to cut him up."

Ramirez would have liked to have seen Oscar try to cut the man up. But he said nothing. He wiped his brow with a handkerchief scented with persimmon, took a sip from the new glass of Carta Blanca Oscar had brought him, and looked about.

"Did you notice?" he said to Oscar. "Even the whores left him alone."

But now at least he thought he knew why, and he guessed that tonight the man would have with him enough cocaine for all the noses in America.

The tall man crouched in the yard behind the small shop called La Argentina. The odor of human waste from the open sewer in a gully next to El Palacio was disagreeable and thick. He could hear the music the Mexicans like, all guitars and vibration. He could see poor Mexican men gathering in the pools of light along the cobbled street that curved up the hill behind him. The few minutes passed and a drunk and a whore wandered into the yard and came to rest not far from him. Their conversation, in English and Pidgin Spanish, was all of money. The act of sex that followed lasted but seconds.

The man listened to it dispassionately, the two rutting against the side of the shop, in the dim light of half a moon. There was a swift cry and they were done and then another argument. Finally a deal was struck. Contemptuously, the woman strode away.

"Whore!" the man called, as though he'd just learned it. Then he too left the yard.

A truck pulled into the yard; its lights flashed twice.

"Hey! Where are you?" called the fat Mexican.

The man waited, watching.

"Damn you. Tall one. Gringo. Where are you, damn you?"

At last he stepped out.

"Here."

"Jesus Mary, you made me jump. Make some noise next time."

"Get on with it."

"In back. There are others. Poor men, looking for work with Tio Sam."

"Others?"

"Just don't bother them. They know nothing of you and care nothing."

The man shook his head.

"Two hours now," Ramirez said. "Longer, because of the special route. Bad roads, much climbing. But it will go fine. Just don't make no trouble."

The tall man spat. He climbed into the back of the truck.

"No policemen," he warned.

The truck crawled up the dark and twisting roads through west Nogales. The shacks began to separate, giving way to wider spaces and the vehicle moved out of the edge of the city, into rough scrub country. Then it began to climb slowly and after a while the road became a track, jagged and brutal.

Ramirez had watched this progress many times; it did not interest him by now. He was thinking of the man in the back. Yes, the man had had a bundle with him, a pack of some sort. It could carry twenty pounds of cocaine. Twenty pounds? Close to a million dollars' worth. Ramirez reached inside his jacket and touched the butt of a Colt Python .357 magnum in blue steel, his favorite pistol.

Jesus Mary, it would be so simple.

The tall man comes out high in the mountains, dazed, probably trembling with the chill. He blinks, shivering. Perhaps he turns. Ramirez lifts the pistol, already cocked, and fires once into the center of the body. Then he'd go into the business himself: no more errand boy for the Huerras. He had the contacts too; he knew the people in Tucson.

Jesus Mary, it would be simple.

"Turn here?" Oscar Meza asked.

"No."

"Keep going?"

"Yes."

"Reynoldo, I—"

"Keep going."

"We are going into the mountains. I—"

"Keep straight."

Ramirez reached down and turned on the radio. He fiddled with the dial until he found a Tucson station. He left it on, thinking of Tucson, a flat new city on a plain surrounded by mountains. He thought of it as a city of money, full of Americans with money, full of blond women and swimming pools.

So simple.

The American country music rolled softly against his ear. The jarring in the cab was thunderous. He prodded his cowboy hat lower down his face, masking off his eyes, set his head against the seat back, and stretched and crossed his legs. He chewed a toothpick and thought of himself as a don, with a palatial estate in the hills outside

Mexico City like Don José Huerra. He thought of blond women and horses.

So how did he know so much? And who was he working for?

This was the crux of Ramirez's dilemma. In three or four sentences he had delivered up Ramirez's most closely held secret. If he knew of Ramirez's connection to the Huerras and the mountain route into America, then—

"Reynoldo, I can tell. This gringo scares you. Say the word and I'll go back and finish him. Nothing to worry about."

"Drive on, stupid one," Ramirez said. Oscar was really getting on his nerves this night. He'd found him five years ago driving an Exclusivo cab and pimping for American college boys down from Tucson; now the fool considered himself a right-hand man. Ramirez spat out the window.

"Lights. And go slower."

"Yes, Reynoldo."

The lights vanished.

"Keep the side lights on, idiot. Do you want to go over the side?"

Oscar immediately turned on the lower-powered orange lights.

Ramirez got out a stick of gum as the truck lurched forward. Soon they were on a ledge and the two Nogaleses were visible, the small and pretty American one and its larger, less neat brother, spilling awkwardly over the hills, spangles of light these many miles away. But Ramirez was not a man for views; in fact, he was looking now in the other direction.

"There," he said suddenly. "Jesus Mary, almost missed her. I'm too old for this."

Oscar stomped the brake and the van skidded for a breathtaking moment on the gravel and dirt as its treads failed. Ramirez shot a bad look toward the idiot Oscar, whose fingers whitely fought the wheel. But the van did not slide off. Ramirez, cursing, got out, pulling his jacket tight against him. Cold up here, so high. The men in back would have no coats; they'd shudder and whimper in the chill. But the gringo?

Ramirez's breath billowed before him. He fished in the brush with gloved hands until his finger closed on something taut; pulling, he opened a crude gate wrapped with an equally crude camouflage of brush to reveal a smaller road leading off the main track.

"She's ready," he called.

The truck eased through the gap, turning. It began to slip and drop. Oscar double-clutched as the vehicle tipped off; it seemed to fall, sliding down the incline in a shower of dust, coming at last to rest on an even narrower road. Ramirez swung the gate shut and scrambled down.

The truck picked its way down the switchback in the dark. Ramirez hung out of the cab, watching. It was tough work. Twice the fool Oscar almost killed them, halted by Ramirez's cry, *"No! No!* Jesus Mary," only inches before spilling them off into blank space. It was a younger man's game and Ramirez's heart beat heavily. Once he even walked ahead, aware of the dark peaks all around him, of the stars and the scalding cold air and the half-moon, whose presence unnerved him. He'd never been here before in the gray moonlight. He crossed himself and swore to light a candle at the shrine of the Virgin.

Finally he ordered, "Kill it."

Ramirez climbed out of the cab and went back to the rear doors.

If you're going to do it, here's the time.

He took out the pistol. He opened the doors. He could smell the men inside, dense and close.

"Let's go, little boys. Nothing but American money up

ahead," he joked in Spanish, and stood back to watch them clamber gingerly out. They came one by one—five youngsters and an older man—shivering in the piercing cold. Ramirez waited, not sure what he would do.

He backed off a little and whispered, "Hey, gringo. Come ahead. We're waiting. Cold out here."

There was no sound from the truck.

"Hey? You fall out? What's with this *hombre,* eh?" He leaned forward, into the interior, and could not quite make out if—

The blow smashed him to the earth. Before he could rise, the man was on him. He could feel a blade.

"Patrón, patrón!" shouted Oscar, rushing to them with a shotgun.

The pistol was pried from Ramirez's fingers; the man rose and stood back.

"Hey," called Ramirez. "Don't do nothing stupid. The gun is for your protection. From *federales.*"

"What should I do, *patrón?*" asked Oscar.

"Tell him to drop that shotgun," said the man.

"Drop it," yelled Ramirez. The gun fell to the dust.

"Now get up," the man said.

Ramirez climbed to his feet, shaking his head. He'd been hit with something heavy, something metal.

"I was just making sure you don't bounce out," he said. "Don't do nothing crazy with that gun."

The tall man tossed the pistol into the scrub. Ramirez marked its fall next to a saguaro cactus that looked like a crucifix. He could pick it up on the way back.

"Okay?" he asked. "No guns now. We're friends."

"Let's go," said the man.

Ramirez walked ahead, pushing through the knot of men. He didn't wait to see what the tall man would do. He walked ahead a short way down a path, hearing them shuffle into line behind him. The moon's soft light turned the landscape to the color of bone. Ramirez turned.

He spoke in Spanish, quickly and efficiently.

"Now say it for me," said the tall man. "I don't have that language."

"Just telling them how it goes from here. Two hundred meters down the slope. Then a flat place, over a dry creek, then through some trees. A gully, a last field to cross. Okay? No tricks. Just the truth, just a walk in the moon. Some *compadres* of mine wait on the other side. And you are with your Tio Sam, eh?"

"Then do it," said the man.

Ramirez led them down the incline, thinking of himself, *stupid! stupid!* and trying not to mourn excessively the lost fortune. This *hombre* was a smart one!

The ground was stony and treacherous, strewn with cactus and jumping cholla and other bitter little plants, leather things that caught and tore at him. The feathery moonlight fell, light as powder. Ramirez licked his dry lips. The trees, twisted little oaks, were widely spaced among tufts and rills of scrub and he guided the clumsy party until at last they passed between the last of the trees and came to a stream, dry now, leaped the bed, and gathered finally at the edge of a moon-flushed meadow.

"Hold up, *muchachos,*" he called. He could hear them breathing laboriously behind him.

He scurried ahead. Here was the guarantee: a geographic freak in the landscape, where the underlying sandstone had been drained away until the land itself collapsed, forming this depression, this sudden, unexpected, unmapped flat stretch in the heart of otherwise impassable mountains. Accessible only by the lost road, it was a place where a man could walk across, where no fences had yet been built, where no border patrolman had ever set foot. He'd discovered it in 1963 and had been guiding the drug shipments through since then, three, maybe four times a year, during the dark of the moon, and never been caught.

But never before in the moonlight. He glanced at the white thing above him, feeling its cold.

He crossed himself.

He peered ahead. A cool breeze pressed against his face.

He took a flashlight from his coat.

Out there, if the arrangements had worked, were two Americans awaiting his signal.

Holy Mother, let them be there. Let them be efficient, dedicated gringos who follow orders.

He blinked twice.

Come on, damn you. You had plenty of time to get ready. The money is good.

A minute passed.

Come on, damn you.

Two blinks in answer.

He scuttled back.

"Done," he said. "Another five hundred meters. Then you pay right, *amigos?* Then they'll take you to Arivaca by back roads. And you'll be in the American Nogales by sunup."

"Thank you, Virgin," somebody said.

"Hurry, damn you all. They won't wait. You too, gringo."

They filed past him, the *norteamericano* last, his pack across one shoulder.

Good-bye, strange man. I hope never to see you again.

They picked their way across the flat in the moonlight. In a little while Ramirez lost them, even with the moon. They'd made it, made it easily, and then the searchlight came on and a harsh voice was yelling over the loudspeaker, *"Manos arriba! Manos arriba!* Hands up, hands up, motherfuckers!"

They froze in the light. Ramirez watched.

Curse my mother, that whore, he thought.

The voice from above: "Don't move, *amigos.* Get those hands up. Get 'em up! *Manos arriba."*

They stood stiffly, hands high in the glare of the single beam.

Ramirez thought, I ought to get out of here. Jesus Mary.

For Christ Jesus' sake, run, he told himself. But he watched in sick fascination.

An American officer—in the deep green of the Border Patrol and a baseball cap and carrying a shotgun—came into the light.

"Face down. *Down,* goddammit. *Descendente pronto!"*

The men in the light looked at each other in panic. One young boy turned back to Ramirez. The gringo stood erect.

"Down, *down,"* screamed the policeman.

They went to their knees. The officer walked behind them and with his boot nudged one forward into the sand. The others followed.

"Jimmy, get that chopper on the horn again."

"It's coming," came a voice from back near the light.

Luck. Maniac luck, the true law of God. Ramirez cursed his mother for bearing him and himself for his selfishness to the Virgin. He made a vow to change all that, crossed himself quickly and spat into the dust.

Clearly this was no raid; he had not been betrayed. There would have been hundreds of them, with bullhorns, machine guns. And on his side *federales.* He'd seen it before, down below, and once had to run half the night with an American .38 in his side. But this was just two stupid gringos with a four-wheel-drive truck. They had been lucky; Ramirez had been unlucky; the stranger with a million dollars in his knapsack had been unlucky. Fate, a whore like his mother with clap and no teeth and ribbons in her filthy hair, laughed at him, spat his way.

The border patroman had walked around in front of them again and stood nervously with the shotgun, shifting his weight from leg to leg.

"Buzz him again, Jimmy."

"I just did. He's on his way."

They would wait for the helicopter, for more men, before searching and cuffing their captives.

Ramirez thought: If the tall man is going to do anything he'd better do it now.

If he'd had the Python, he could have fired for the light, or even the patrolman. But that was bad business, shooting *norteamericanos*. They were a crazy people; they'd get you for sure. Besides the range was over two hundred yards, a long shot for a pistol, even a big one.

Ramirez looked again. The long figure lay on the stony soil. His pack was inches beyond his fingers.

Gringo, do something, do it now. They'll put you away for a century if they catch you.

Ramirez rubbed his mouth nervously.

A sound of engines, low and pulsing, rose in the distance and began to build.

"There he is," yelled the one at the truck.

"Okay," yelled the one with the shotgun, easing back a step, half twisting. He turned his head toward the sound—

It happened with the speed of a snake's strike. The patrolman turned, the tall man seemed to elongate upon the earth, and in the same half-second he had in his hands a small gun with a blunt barrel, and a spurt of flash broke from the muzzle and the patrolman fell.

A machine gun! A small machine gun! thought Ramirez, astonished at the treasure.

The others began to flee the light. A hasty shot rang out to kick at the dust near the tall man. He stood, holding his weapon with two hands, the left cupped under the grip for support, and fired carefully into the vehicle on the ridge. Ramirez heard the glass shattering, the metal shuddering as the bullets tore through. The searchlight vanished. The tall man dropped to one knee and swiftly changed magazines in his weapon. He rose and fired again, and the truck detonated in an oily orange flash that filled the night with heat and color.

Ramirez blinked as the dust and gas from the blast pushed across him. He saw purple spinning circles before his eyes from the bright flash. He squinted them away and turned back to the spectacle before him. Rolling flames from the ridge illuminated the valley.

The tall man had moved to the fallen Border Patrol officer. Ramirez watched in astonishment as the tall man bent to the man he'd just slain, and seemed to close his eyes and a hanging jaw. Then with one hand he pushed the flattened body to its side and turned it toward Nogales. Then he grabbed his pack and ran into the darkness.

The roaring of the helicopter became huge. Dust began to whirl and rise and Ramirez could see the dark shape of it, lights blinking, start to settle out of the sky. A searchlight beam sprang from the port to play across the stones.

Ramirez drew back. He knew that inside an hour the *federales* would arrive, summoned by the Americans. He knew that more Americans would come, and more and more. He knew he'd better get the hell out of there. He prayed that the Americans wouldn't find his gringo *compadres,* who'd obviously been spooked by the passing patrol. If they found them and they talked and they told of Ramirez . . .

Ramirez crossed himself. Holy Virgin, I've lied and cheated and stolen and killed, but spare your sinning child. He prayed intently as he scurried through the moonlight up the hill. He saw his van ahead and knew he'd make it. He even paused by the cactus to fetch his pistol.

"What happened?" asked Oscar. "Mother of Jesus, it sounded like a war."

"Mother of Jesus, it *was* a war," Ramirez said, thinking of the tall one, for he suddenly realized he'd seen a kind of soldier.

2

Bill Speight pulled the Chevette to the side of the road, puzzled by what he saw. He must have lost track of the numbers a while back—some of these little houses out in the western Chicago suburbs were set so far back from the street you couldn't read the figures. He reached for and opened his briefcase and sifted through the papers.

Come on, come on, old fool, he told himself, and at last located the address. Yes, it *was* 1104 Old Elm Road. Could he have gotten off the expressway at the wrong town? But no, he'd seen the exit—he'd been careful, very careful so far. He was in the right place.

A Roman Catholic church? He searched his memory, yet he could unearth no remembrance of Paul Chardy that touched on any issue of religion. Had Chardy gone strange—the brave ones had more than a little craziness in them anyway—and joined the priesthood? Another priesthood. As if Special Operations wasn't religious order enough. Yet he could not imagine that famous temper hidden beneath a priest's habit, nor could he see a large-boned, impatient, athletic man like Chardy, a man of Chardy's peculiar gifts, listening in a dark booth to pimply teenagers telling tales on themselves.

But he looked at the church and saw it was one of those

modern things, more roof and glass than building. A spindly cross way up top stood out against the bright blue spring sky; otherwise the place could have been some new convention center. Speight's watery blue eyes tracked back to the sign and confronted it squarely: OUR LADY OF THE RESURRECTION ROMAN CATHOLIC CHURCH AND SCHOOL, the letters white and blocky, slotted onto a black background, and beneath them the legend: LEARN TO FORGIVE YOURSELF. Speight winced at the advice. Could he? Could Paul?

But the school part made some sense. He could imagine Chardy among children, not among nuns and priests. For Chardy had still a little of the athlete's boyishness, the gift for exhilaration which would captivate children. That was his best half, his mother's half; but what about the other side, his father's side, the Hungarian side, which was moody and sullen and turbulent?

At that moment a class of kids came spilling out from behind the church onto an adjacent blacktopped playground. So much energy; they made Speight feel his age. The panorama was raucous and vast and not a little violent, and the one bearded old geezer in a raincoat, who was supposedly in command, stood so meekly off to one side that Speight feared for him.

It was nearly noon. What lay ahead filled him with melancholy and unease; he wasn't sure he could bring it off. Sighing heavily, he pulled the car into the church's parking lot and found a place to park, marked VISITOR—he searched for it at some length, not wanting to break any rules—and began a long trudge to the buildings, his briefcase heavy in his hand.

His walk would take him through the playground, where balls sailed and bounced and kids hung like monkeys off the apparatus. All the boys wore scrawny ties, he saw—now that's not a bad idea; his own kids dressed like tramps—and the girls kilts. But the imposed formality didn't cut any ice with the little brutes. They still fought and shoved and screamed at each other, and at one point the supervisor had to bound over to break up a bad scuffle. Kids. Speight shook his head, but he wasn't really paying much attention.

He was worried about Chardy. You don't just go crashing back into somebody's life after seven years—or was it now eight?—and take up where you left off. And it was true that at the end, at the hearings, Bill hadn't done Paul much good. He'd just told the truth, and the truth hadn't helped Chardy at all, and maybe even now Chardy would hold it against him. Chardy had a famous temper; Chardy had once slugged a Head of Station.

Bill stopped in the middle of the playground. He felt a little queasy. He wished he had a Gelusil. The church building loomed above him; he was surrounded by children. He had to go to the bathroom suddenly. Maybe he could find a john and get settled down, get himself composed.

But then, maybe the best thing would be to get it over with. Get it over with fast. He'd come this far, quite a way.

He reached into his pocket, pulled out a Binaca canister, and squirted a blast of the mouthwash into his mouth. Its cool sweetness pepped him up considerably, burying that sour taste that had collected in his throat.

I'll just do it.

He turned as a basketball glanced off his knee and a horde of little jerks roared by in pursuit.

"Hey, excuse me." He hailed the old duffer, who was bent in conference with two sniffling children. "Is there an office around here? Where would I find an office?"

"Are you sure you're looking for the office, Bill?" asked Paul Chardy, rising.

It was the coat, cloaking the man's size. And it was the beard, surprisingly shot with gray, masking the dark half-Irish face, blurring that pugnacious chin. And the hair, longish, almost over the ears, where Paul's had always been short, after the military fashion, like Bill's own. And it was also the playground full of kids, the bright sun, the bouncing, sailing balls, the noise, the church: it was all so different. The last time Bill had seen Paul had been at an arms dump on the border. Chardy wore baggy khaki pants then, and an embroidered coat and a black-and-white turban and sunglasses and had magazine bandoliers criss-crossed on his chest like some kind of bandit and had been almost mahogany from the sun. He'd carried a Soviet assault rifle, the AK-47, and had a couple of rocket-propelled grenades in their launchers slung over his back, and a belt full of Russian F-1 grenades.

"I-I didn't recognize you, Paul. The beard—you look so different."

"Old Bill, Jesus. I saw you getting out of the car. They still make you rent cheap little Chevys, huh? How are you?" He took Bill's hand and shook it. "You're looking good, Bill."

"You're lying, Paul. I'm looking *old,* which is what I am. You're getting some gray yourself."

"It's these kids. I look a hundred. These damned kids, they took my youth." He laughed, and clapped Bill on the back.

"Paul, we had some trouble finding you."

"You were supposed to. That was the point."

"Well, anyway. It's some old business. Have you got a minute?"

Chardy looked at his watch, a big Rolex. He still had it. All the Special Operations people wore them.

"This is my most open period. They work you pretty hard in these joints. I'm off around five. Can it wait?"

"Ah." It couldn't. Get to it, they'd told Speight. Don't give him time to think about it, to nurse his furies. Plunge in.

I know, Speight had answered bitterly. I'm not a kid at this game either, you know; thinking, *you bastards.*

"Well," Speight started, feeling outpositioned in his first move, "it's only that—"

But Chardy darted off—he still had that old quickness—shouting, "Hey, hey, Mahoney, Mahoney," and leapt into some sort of ruckus, pulling apart two squalling, clawing boys. He shook the big one hard, once, and spoke to him in an earnest, deadly voice. Speight imagined Chardy speaking to *him* like that.

Chardy came back. "That little prick thinks he's tough. He likes to hit people," he said. "His father's a cop."

"Paul, I never would have imagined this kind of a life for you," said Speight, stalling.

"At the parochial schools," Chardy said, looking at him squarely with those dark eyes, "you don't need a degree in education. You just need to be willing to work like a horse for peanuts. A big-deal sports background helps. What about you, Bill? Still playing cowboy?"

"They put me in a different section. Over in Central Reference."

"Siberia."

"Just perfect for a harmless old geezer like me."

"You show 'em, Bill."

"Paul, about the Melman hearings. You're not mad? I just told them what I'd seen."

"Forget it. It doesn't matter."

Bill licked his lips.

"Thanks, Paul."

"Is that why you came?"

"Well, it's—"

But Chardy darted off again. Speight stood helpless and watched him handle another crisis. Was that all these kids did, fight? But that's all grown-ups did, wasn't it?

Presently Chardy returned. "They really keep you jumping," he said.

"They sure do."

"Well, Bill?"

So this would be it then. On the playground, full of kids, no time to sit down and work it out in a civilized fashion. Chardy was playing him, he could tell. It was a no-win situation, all the noise, all the distraction. He wouldn't handle it well. A presentiment of failure crossed his mind.

We should have sent somebody younger, they would say, back at Langley. They would say it to his face. They could be so cold these days.

"This," Bill said, lurching ahead. He drew from his pocket and offered Chardy—who accepted it reluctantly—his treasure, the thing that had them running in circles at Langley.

Chardy looked at it, rolling it in his palm.

"A seven-six-five-millimeter Czech auto pistol shell. Must be ten million of these things floating around the world."

"Look at that scratch on the rim, where the ejector rod popped it out of the breach," Bill said.

"It's a Skorpion shell. I can recognize a Skorpion shell. There're Skorps all over the world. African generals love the goddamned things."

"Let me give you the rest of it."

Chardy looked at him. Bill could never read Chardy. The dark eyes squinted; the mouth now lost in beard seemed to tighten.

"Go ahead."

"That particular shell is from a cache of stuff some boys from a battalion of the One-seventy-third Airborne liberated on a search-and-destroy in July 'sixty-seven, a big Charlie ammo dump out near Qui Nhon. Mostly AK-forty-sevens, and those mean-ass RPG rocket launchers. Some mortars, some light artillery. The usual. But also a Skorpion. Very unusual for 'Nam in 'sixty-seven because the Czech stuff didn't start showing up until much later. But there was a single mint Skorpion in this dump, still packed in grease, and thirty-five hundred rounds of seven-six-five."

"And you're telling me this is one of those thirty-five-hundred rounds?"

"Yep," Bill Speight said almost proudly. "The arsenal marks check out exactly. See here on the base. It's marked 'VZ-sixty-one.' That's their manufacturing code for the Brno Arsenal and that lot of seven-six-five was made in January 'sixty-six. Same lot as we found in 'Nam. It can't be coincidence. You know what happened to that ammo?"

Chardy said nothing.

"Well, sure you do, Paul," Bill said. "We took that Skorpion and twenty-five hundred of those rounds into Kurdistan with us in 'seventy-three. In the operation we called Saladin Two, the Kurdish show. My show, your show. Especially, at the end, your show. Along with the other stuff, the AKs, the RPGs. Enough to start a small war. And we did start a small war."

Bill knew all about gear. His specialty was logistics, clandestine resupply, and he had organized the distribution of arms to guerrilla operations all over the globe, back when he was one of the cowboys of the Special Operations Division. He had been through some hairy moments himself.

Chardy nodded, as if in memory of the small war and its hairy moments.

"And you recall that you gave Skorpion to a certain man?"

"I gave it to Ulu Beg," Chardy said. "Where'd you get it?"

Speight told him of the deaths of the two Border Patrol officers.

"That case was one of forty recovered on the site. He fired two magazines. Those officers were torn up pretty bad. You know what a Skorpion can do."

The Skorpion was a Czech VZ-61, a machine pistol. Ten inches long with its wire stock folded, it weighed three and a half pounds and fired at 840 rounds per minute, cyclical. It was one of the world's rare true machine pistols, smaller than a submachine gun and deadlier than an automatic pistol.

"Bill, it's just one shell. You're dreaming. You're building crazy cases from nothing. A shell, an arsenal mark, a scratch in the brass."

"And there's this, Paul," Bill said. He reached into his briefcase and after thumbing through the reports from Science and Technology, the airline tickets, the maps, he came up with a picture of a body in the desert.

Chardy looked at it.

"How was he facing?" Chardy asked.

"He was facing east. The report says the body was moved. They think the killer was searching for money or something. Yet the wallet was left untouched. They can't figure it. But you could figure it, couldn't you?"

"Sure," Chardy said. "He didn't mean to kill the guy. He didn't want to. He felt bad about it. So in the frenzy of the moment, he tries to help his soul to paradise. He turns him on his right side, and faces him toward Mecca, as the Kurds bury their dead."

"You saw enough of it, Paul."

"I guess I did. A Kurd is here. Maybe Ulu Beg himself."

"Yes, Paul. After all, we never got any confirmation of his death after Saladin Two went under. And if it's any of them, it's him. And you know how the Kurds feel about vengeance."

A bell rang.

Bill looked to Chardy. The moment was here; shouldn't Chardy be reacting? A man he'd trained and fought next to and lived with seven years ago in Kurdistan was here, with a gun, willing to kill.

The children began to collect in a riotous mass near a set of steel double doors. Nuns appeared. Small skirmishes broke out.

"Mr. Chardy—" a nun called from the doors.

"Paul, it's—"

"I know what it is, Bill," Chardy said. "Goddamn you, Bill, for bringing all this back." He turned and went inside with the kids.

So Bill had to wait after all. He found a bar, a seedy, quiet little place in the next town up the road, and killed the afternoon with rum-and-Cokes at a table near a pinball machine in an empty room. He smoked half a pack of Vantages. He set the glasses before him in a neat formation. He had five of them at the end.

He's got to come, he thought. He'll think it over; he'll see it's just as much his job as anybody's. Ulu Beg is a loose end of a Chardy operation, no matter that Chardy was kicked out, no matter that he's been hiding out here, playing schoolteacher all these years. He has to come, Bill thought, wobbly.

It's his legacy. He stood for something, all those years. He was one of the heroes, one of the cowboys, and the thing about the cowboys, they never said no. Nothing was too hairy for a cowboy. They were crazy, some people said, they were animals; and lots of the staff couldn't stand them. But when you needed a cowboy, he was there, he went in. He lived for going in; it's why he became a cowboy in the first place, wasn't it?

Bill tried to convince himself. He looked at his Seiko and had trouble reading the hands. He'd had too much to drink; he knew it.

"You okay, mister?" The waitress, looking down at him.

"Sure, I'm fine."

"You better call it quits," she said.

"Truer words," he said, laughing grandly, "was never spoke."

The traffic had gotten pretty thick and he didn't reach Our Lady of the Resurrection until 5:15. He parked again in the visitors' space and walked across the empty playground to the school and entered.

He blinked in the darkness. Children's paintings hung along the dim corridor. Speight thought them absurd, cows and barns and airplanes with both wings on the same side of the fuselage. The crucifixes made him nervous, too, all that agony up there on bland, pale green walls. He encountered a nun and overdid the smile, worried she'd smell the booze or pick up on the vagueness in his walk. But she only smiled back, a surprisingly young girl. Next he found a group of boys, scrawny and sweaty in gym clothes, herding into a locker room. They seemed so young, their bones so tiny, their faces so drawn, like child laborers in some Dickensian blacking factory. But one was bigger, a black boy, probably the star.

"Is Mr. Chardy around, son?" Speight asked him.

"Back there," the boy said, pointing down the hall.

The destination turned out to be an old gym, waxy

yellow under weak lights that hung in cages too low off the raftered ceiling. They must have built this place twenty years before they built their slick glass-and-brick cathedral. One end of it was an auditorium, with a stageful of amateurish props for what would be some dreadful production. Speight saw Chardy, in gray sweats, a wet double dark spot like Mickey Mouse ears growing splotchily across his chest, with some kind of bright band, like an Indian brave or something, around his head at the hairline. He wore white high-topped gym shoes and was methodically sinking one-handed jump shots from twenty or twenty-five feet out. He'd dribble once or twice, the sound of full, round leather against the wood echoing through the still air, then seize the ball and seem to weigh it. Then the ball rode his fingers up to his shoulders, paused, and was launched, even as Chardy himself left the floor. The ball rose perfectly, then fell and, more often than not as Speight watched, swished through. Occasionally it did miss, however, and then the bearded man would lazily gallop after it and scoop it off the bounce one-handed, and turn and rise and fire again, and he looked pretty good for a man—what, now?—nearly forty. He did not miss twice in a row in the ten silent minutes Bill stood in the doorway watching him.

At last Bill called, "You're still a star."

Chardy did not look over. He completed another shot, then answered, "Still got the touch."

His talent with a ball was one part of the legend. During his two stateside tours—disasters in other respects—he'd torn up the Langley gym league, where a surprisingly competitive level of basketball was played by ex-college jocks; Chardy had set scoring records that, for all Bill knew, still stood. Chardy had been some kind of All-American at the small college he'd gone to on a scholarship, and he'd had a tryout with a pro team.

He canned another jumper and then seemed to tire of the exercise. The ball rolled across the floor into darkness. Chardy retrieved a towel and came over to Bill.

"Well, Old Bill, I see I didn't wait you out."

"Did you really want to, Paul?"

Chardy only smiled at this interesting question.

Then he said, "I guess they want me. I guess I'm an asset again."

Why deny it? Speight thought. "They do. You are."

Chardy considered this.

"Who's running the show. Melman?"

"Melman's a big man now. Didn't you know? He's Deputy Director of the whole Operations Directorate. He'll be Director of it someday, maybe even DCI if they decide to stay in the shop."

Chardy snorted at the prospect of Sam Melman as Director of Central Intelligence, with his picture on the cover of *Time* and *Newsweek* as had been Helms's and Colby's and Turner's.

"We're not even running this thing out of Operations, Paul. We're running it out of Management and Services, their office of Security. So—"

"What the hell is this 'Operations'?" Chardy asked suddenly.

He really had been out of touch, Speight realized.

"I'm sorry. You were in the mountains, I guess, when they reorganized. I didn't learn until later myself. Plans is now called Operations."

"It sounds like a World War Two movie."

"Paul, forget Operations. Forget the old days, the old guys. Forget all that stuff. Forget Melman. He was just doing his job. He'll be a long way away from you. Think about Ulu Beg in America."

"All the stuff about Ulu Beg is in the reports, in the

files. The reports of the Melman inquiry. Tell them to dig that stuff out.''

''They already have, Paul. Paul, you know Ulu Beg, you trained him. You fought with him, you know his sons. You were like a brother to him. You—''

But talk of Ulu Beg seemed to hurt Chardy. He looked away, and Speight saw that he'd have to play his last card, the one he didn't care for, the one that smelled. But it had been explained to him in great detail how important all this was, how he could not fail.

''Paul—'' He paused, full of regret. Chardy deserved better than the shot he was about to get. ''Paul, we're going to have to bring Johanna Hull in too.''

Chardy said, ''I can't help you there. I wish I could. Look, I have to take a shower.''

''Paul, maybe I'd better make myself clearer.'' He wished he'd sucked down a few more rum-and-Cokes. ''These are very cold people, Paul, these people in Security. They're very cold about everything except results. They're going to have to bring Johanna under some kind of control—and they want you to do it—because they think Ulu Beg will go to her. She's about the only place he could go. But if you don't do it, believe me, they'll find somebody who will.''

Chardy looked at him with disgust.

''It's gone that far?''

''They're very frightened of Ulu Beg. They'll play rough on this one.''

''I guess they will,'' Chardy said, and Speight knew he'd won his little victory.

3

He assumed they would be hunting him, but it did not matter and did not particularly frighten him. He had been hunted before—by Iraqi soldiers and policemen, by Arabs, by Iranians, by Kurds even. Now Americans.

But what could they do? For he was in the mountains now. Ulu Beg felt almost comfortable here; he knew this place. He had been born and raised in mountains and fought in mountains and these, though in many ways different, were in just as many ways the same as his own.

They were known as the Sierritas, ranging northward from the border for twenty or thirty kilometers before panning out into cruel desert plain on the way to the American city of Tucson.

These mountains were perfect, a wilderness of bucking scrub foothills shot with oaks and bitter, brittle little plants poking through the stony ground; until, reaching the altitude of 5,000 feet, they exploded suddenly into stone, a cap, a head of pure rock, bare and raw and forbidding. The saying went, "Each mountain is a fortress," and he felt the security of a fortress up here.

Let them come. He'd learned his skills in a hundred hard places and tested them in a hundred more and would set his against anybody's in mountains. But he doubted

Americans would try him. They were said to be a people of pleasure, not bravery. Still, suppose they had a Jardi to send against him?

The Kurd paused on a ledge, staring at the peaks about him, dun-colored in the bright sun. Everywhere he looked it was still and silent, except for a push of wind against his face.

What if it were written above that a Jardi would be sent against him? What if that were God's will?

Who knew the will of God? What point was there in worrying about it? Yet, still . . .

But there was another advantage, beyond security, to the solitude in the higher altitudes. And that was privacy: he could still think like a Kurd, move like a Kurd, *be* a Kurd. There wasn't the press of maintaining a fictitious identity, which was as hard as anything he'd ever done.

"You must be one of them," he had been instructed. "But it won't be hard," they assured him. "Americans think only of themselves. They have no eyes for the man next to them. But of course, certain small adjustments must be made in your natural ways. Do you agree?"

"Yes," he said. "Teach me. I will make any sacrifice, pay any cost. My life is nothing. It has no meaning other than as the instrument of my vengeance."

"Excellent," they complimented him. "Your hate is very pure, and to be nourished. It will sustain you through many difficulties. Some men must be taught to hate. You come to it with a gift. You are holy. You make a holy war."

"This is not holy," he had said, glaring, and watched them show their discomfort at the force of his glare. "It is a blasphemy. I must defile myself. But it is no matter."

He moved northward through the mountains slowly, enjoying his journey. He crossed a dirt road late in the night in a low place. He skirted campsites, places where

Americans came to play. The sky was fiercely blue, angrily blue, and in it a sun of almost pure whiteness, a radiance, beat down. The clouds were thin and scattered. At the top of one mountain he could see nothing but other mountains. One spine of crests gave way to another. There was dust everywhere, carried by the wind, and even patches of snow, scaly and weak, that gave when he put his American boots through them. At twilight the mountains were at their richest and in the shadows and the soft air they seemed almost *kesk o sheen,* a certain blue-green shade close to the Kurdish heart which spoke of spring and, more deeply, of freedom to travel the passes, to move through what they held to be theirs by right of two thousand years of occupation: Kurdistan.

At one point he saw a vehicle. He ducked back, for just a second, terrified. The thing lurched up a gravel track, an ungainly beast. Something in the way it moved: sluggish yet determined. He felt his body tensing, and a feeling of nakedness—the nakedness of the prey—overwhelmed him.

The vehicle pulled to a level stretch. He saw it was almost a bus, gaudily painted, an expensive thing. Bicycles were lashed to its rear and the top was bulky with camping gear. He sat back, watching the thing move. It was obviously some kind of vacation truck for rich or fancy Americans, so that they could tour the wilderness in high style, never far from showers and hot water.

He watched it poke along beneath him, pulling a trail of dust, glinting absurdly, its bright colors flashing in the sunlight. It was almost a comical sight, a preposterous American invention. No other country but America could have produced such a thing. He wanted to smile at the idiocy of it.

America!

Land of wealthy fools!

Yet he continued to breathe heavily as the machine passed from view. Why? What frightens me about this monstrosity? You'll be among them soon, if things go well. Is this how you'll perform, frozen with terror at the sight of the outlandish?

You'll never make it.

I must make it.

But it had been terror in his heart. Why?

Was it the shooting at the border? Would there be a huge manhunt for him? Would his mission be endangered? These things troubled him, but not nearly so much as the killing of the two men.

It put a darkness on his journey, a bad beginning. Damn that fat Mexican! They had told him this Mexican knew the best way, the safest way. The Mexican would get him across.

What would happen to the Mexican now? He was glad he wasn't the Mexican, because he knew now the Mexican was expendable. They would have to take care of the Mexican, because of the stir the shooting would make.

Death, more death, still more death. It was a chain. Every little thing leading out of the past into the future: heavy with death.

The two policemen, dead, for being in the wrong place. The Mexican, dead. And he himself, ultimately, finally . . .

"If they catch you, you have failed. They will never free you. They will use you and use you. Do you understand this?"

"I do."

"It is not that in captivity you no longer can advance your cause; it is that you hurt it. You destroy it. Do you understand?"

"I do."

"Swear then. We will help and support you, but you must swear. You will not be taken alive. Do you swear?"

"Kurdistan ya naman," he swore. Kurdistan or death.

He lingered in the mountains a week, for in them he went unhunted. He lived on the flat Mexican bread in his pack and on jojoba nuts and mesquite beans, as he had been instructed. But the land began to flatten beneath him until on the eighth morning there were no mountains except the ones rimming the horizon, crusty brown in the distance, and to get there he had to cross the flatness wavering before him in the sun, sending off a smoky radiance of pure heat. It was the desert valley that led to Tucson, a journey too dangerous for the dark.

"Beware the desert," he'd been told. "If you have to cross the desert you are an unlucky man."

But beyond the desert lay Tucson and in Tucson lay a bus route into America and toward the Northeast, where his destiny was *ser nivisht,* written above.

He set out early. He found it a wilderness of needles, of things that could hurt. It was, in its cruel way, quite beautiful too, an abstract of the textures of death. Over each rise or gentle dip, through the crumbling rocky passes, down the easy glades, up the rock buttes, each shift yielded a new panorama. Yet what impressed him most in this long day's journey was not the danger or the beauty but something entirely else: the silence.

There is no silence in the mountains, for always there is wind, and always something to blow in its path. Here, on the bright floor of the earth, he could hear nothing. There was no wind, no noise, nothing but the sound of his own boots sloughing through the dust or across the fine rocks.

There was no water either, and the heat was suffocating. He thought only of water. But there was no water and no mercy, only the sense that he had to move ahead. Miles beyond stood a last escarpment of hills, and beyond that had to lie Tucson.

He hurried onward, the dust thick in his throat. The saguaro cactus towered above him, exotic and beckoning. And a hundred other needled monsters, some whose delicate flowers mocked their ugly spikes. Small tough leaves slashed at his boots. He raced ahead, exposed in the great undulating flatness. He knew he had only a day to make the journey, for he'd freeze out here at night, and the next day the sun would come and bake him.

"A day, if it comes to a desert crossing. You've got a day. Your body can take no more." They told him stories of Mexican illegals who'd been led into the desert by unscrupulous smugglers and abandoned and how they'd died in horrible agony in just hours at the hottest time of the day.

He pushed ahead, feeling the blood pulsing in his temples. The shirt off and wrapped about his head in the fashion of a turban gave some relief from the heat; he wore only an undershirt over his body. But at each rise he prayed the mountains had moved closer and at each rise he was disappointed.

Kurdistan ya naman.

The pack had become hugely heavy, yet he clung to it. He pushed ahead.

In the early afternoon, there was a helicopter, low off the horizon.

Always helicopters, he thought, always helicopters.

He ducked quickly into a ravine, opening his wrist on the knifelike leaves of some grotesque plant. The blood spurted. He listened to the roar of the machine, an almost liquid sloshing, the rising pulse.

He crouched into the side of the ravine as the noise grew. He reached inside the pack and touched the Skorpion.

But the noise died.

He climbed and faced the same bright frozen sea of sand and spiny vegetation. His head now ached and the wrist would not stop stinging. In all directions it was the same—the crests of sand, the cacti, the cruel scrub under a broad sky and a fierce sun. In the distance, the mountains. Ulu Beg rose and headed on, facing death.

By midafternoon he began to get groggy. He fell once and didn't remember falling, only finding himself on his knees at the bottom of a slope. He stood, his knees buckled, he went down again. He got up slowly, breathing hard, stopping to rest with his hands on his knees. He thought he saw that bus, that crazy bus pulling toward him, full of blond Americans, rich and well-fed, their children riding before them on bicycles.

He blinked and it was all gone.

Or was it? Caught in his mind was a memory of the vehicle, the awkwardness of a thing so huge. In its tentativeness, its absurdity—but also its determination — there'd been a memory.

He called it up before him.

They had marched for days down through the mountains to the foothills near Rawāndūz, and set the ambush well, with great patience and cunning. Jardi was with them. No, Jardi was one of them.

There had been thirty of them altogether, with Ulu Beg's own son Apo along because he'd begged to go. They had the new AKs that Jardi had brought and the RPG rockets that he'd shown them how to use, and a light machine gun; and Jardi had his dynamite, which he'd planted in the road.

They caught the Iraqi convoy in a narrow enfilade in the foothills, men of the 11th Mechanized Brigade who had not a week before razed a Kurdish village, killing everybody. Jardi exploded his dynamite on the lead truck and they'd all fired and thirty seconds later the road was jammed with broken, burning vehicles, mostly trucks.

"Keep firing," Jardi yelled, for the shooting had trailed off after the initial frenzy.

"But—"

"Keep firing!"

Jardi was a fierce man, crazy in action, a driven man. The Kurds had a phrase: a fool for war. He stood behind them, his eyes dark and angry, gesturing madly, screaming, exhorting them in a language only Ulu Beg could understand, communicating nevertheless out of sheer intensity. Standing now, striding up and down the line, howling like a dog, his turban pushed off so that his short American hair showed, oblivious totally to the bullets that had begun to fly up from the dying convoy at them.

He was in some ways more Kurdish than any of them, a Saladin himself, who could inspire them to heroic deeds by nothing greater than his own ruthless passion. He loved to destroy his enemies.

"Pour it on. Keep pouring it on," he yelled.

Ulu Beg, firing clip after clip of his AK-47 into the burning trucks and the huddled or fleeing figures, watched as the Kurdish fire devastated the convoy. He could see glass shattering, the canvas of the trucks shredding, the tires deflating. Now and then a smaller explosion and a puff of flame rolled up as one or another of the petrol tanks detonated. And soon no fire came from the trucks.

"Cut," Jardi yelled.

The Kurdish fire died down.

"Let's get 'em out of here," Jardi yelled to Ulu Beg.

"But, Jardi," Ulu Beg called, "there's weapons and booty down there."

"Not enough time," said Jardi. "Look, that scout car." He pointed to a Russian vehicle on its side at the head of the convoy. "Look at the aerial on that baby. The jets'll be here in a few minutes."

That was Jardi too: in the middle of battle, with bullets flying about, he was coolly noting which vehicles had radios—and estimating what their range was and how soon MiGs would respond to the ambush.

Ulu Beg stood.

"It's time to flee," Ulu Beg yelled.

But it was too late. Far down the line he saw three men break cover and begin to gallop toward the crippled vehicles, their weapons high over their heads in exultation.

"No," commanded Ulu Beg, "stop—"

But two more broke from the line and others turned back toward him, frozen in indecision.

"Back," he shouted.

"We must leave the others," Jardi said. "The jets'll be here in seconds."

But one of the men was Kamran Beg, a cousin, who had been bodyguard to the boy Apo.

Ulu Beg saw his own child rise from the gully and begin to run down the hill.

"What the hell," said Jardi. "Why the hell did you—"

"I did nothing. I—"

Then they saw the tank. It was a Russian T-54, huge as a dragon. It swung into the enfilade. Tanks had never come this high before. Ulu Beg watched as the creature swung along on its tracks, its turret cranking. It moved with awkwardness, tentative even, despite its weight.

"Down!" Jardi yelled, in the second before the tank fired.

The shell exploded under the first three running men. They were gone in the blast. Others raced up the hill. The machine gun in the turret cut them down.

The small boy lay still on the ground.

Ulu Beg rose to run to him, but something pressed him to the earth.

"No," somebody hissed in his ear.

Jardi vaulted free and raced down the slope. He had abandoned his rifle and held only a rocket-propelled grenade. He ran crazily, not bothering to veer or dodge. He ran right at the tank.

Its turret swung to him. Machine-gun bullets cut at the earth and Ulu Beg could see them reaching for Jardi, who seemed to slide in a shower of dust as the bullets kicked by him.

He lay still.

The tank began to heave up the ridge toward them.

Ulu Beg saw that they were finished. They couldn't get back up the slope; the tank would shoot them down. A tank. Where had it come from?

He tried to clear his brain. He could think only of his son, dead on the slope, the brave American, dead on the slope, his men, his tribe, dead on the slope.

But Jardi rose. He was not hit at all. He rose, sheathed in the dust he'd fallen through, and stood, one leg cocked insolently on a stone. A wind came and his jacket billowed. From down the slope they could hear Jardi cursing loudly, almost—the man was crazy—laughing.

The tank turret swung to him again. But Ulu Beg saw that Jardi was close enough now and that the big gun would never reach him in time, and as its barrel swung on to him Jardi fired the RPG one-handed, like a pistol.

The rocket left in a fury of flame, spitting fire as it flew, and struck the tank on the flat part of the hull, just beneath the turret.

The tank began to burn. It fell back on its treads and flames began to pour from its hatch and from its engines. Smoke rose and blew in the breeze.

Jardi threw away his spent launching tube and ran

quickly to the boy. He hoisted him and climbed up to them, but he had no smile.

"Come on, get these guys out of here," he said. "Come on," he turned to shout at them, "get going, Jesus, you guys, get *going!*"

The boy was crying.

Ulu Beg was crying.

"You have given my son his life back."

"Come on, get going," Jardi urged.

They climbed to the mountains and were over the crest when the first jets arrived.

Ulu Beg smiled in the memory of that day.

Ahead, the mountains loomed.

He reached them at twilight. Toward the end he'd crossed a road and ahead he could see another road, one that crawled up the side of the mountain, but he did not go near it. Cars moved along it. In the falling dark he climbed cold rocks. He found a trickle of water. He tracked it to a pool, and then found the spring. He drank deeply. He sat back. He ate a piece of his dry bread, and drank again. He was in the chill of a shadow but could look out and see the desert, still white and flat and dangerous.

He climbed up. At the top, the city of Tucson lay before him. He saw a city built on sand, on a plain, cupped on all sides by other mountains. A few tall buildings stood in its center but it was mostly a kind of ramshackle newness. It was nothing like Baghdad, which was very, very old, and on a huge river.

God willed it, he thought, and I have made it.

He thought of Jardi and the tank and his son and why he had come to America and he began to weep.

———

In the morning he rose with the sun. He opened his pack, pushed the machine pistol out of the way, and found his other shirt, a white thing with snap buttons. He pulled the shirt on.

They had prepared him well. But they had also warned him.

"America is like nothing you've ever seen. Women walk around with breasts and buttocks exposed. Food and lights everywhere, everywhere. Cars, more cars than you can imagine. And hurry. Americans all hurry. But they have no passion. Any Turk has passion. Among Turks and Mexicans and Arabs, passion runs high. But Americans are even lower, for they feel nothing. They move as though asleep. They do not care for their children or their women. They speak and talk only of themselves.

"In all this, you will be dazzled. Expect it. There is no way we can prepare you for the shock of it all. Even a small city in America is a spectacle. A large one is like a festival of all the peoples of earth. But remember also: the grotesque is common in America. Nobody will notice, nobody will care, nobody will pay you any attention. Nobody will ask you for papers if you are cautious. You need no permits, no licenses. Your face is your passport. You may go anywhere."

Ulu Beg reinstructed himself in these lessons as he came down the last hill in the dawn light to the road. He moved swiftly. The distance was but a few twisting miles and the cars that sped by paid him no attention. The houses quickly became thick: small places of cinderblock in the sand and scrub. At each house was a car and in some of them men were leaving for work. Ulu Beg walked along the street. He paused to read the sign: SPEEDWAY, it said. He came to a group of men waiting by a corner. A bus arrived and they climbed aboard. He walked another few blocks and again the same thing happened. At a third corner, he climbed aboard himself.

"Hey. Fifty cents," the driver said angrily. Ulu Beg searched his pockets. They had told him about this. Fifty cents was two quarters. He found the coins and dropped them in the box, and took a seat and rode down the Speedway toward the center of the city.

He got out near the bus station and looked for a hotel.

"Always stay near bus stations. Small places, dirty rooms, cheap. But a hotel, always a hotel. In a motel, they'll ask about an automobile. You'll have to explain that you don't have one. Why not? they'll ask. They'll think you're mad. In America it is exceedingly odd not to have an automobile. Everybody has an automobile."

He chose a place called the Congress—the name proclaimed proudly on a metal frame on the roof—across from a Mexican theater in a crumbling section of the city. It was a four-story building with a bookstore, a barbershop, and a place that sold gems in it, across from the train station and behind the bus station.

He walked into the dim brown lobby.

A fat lady looked up when he came to the desk.

"Yes?"

"A room. How much?"

"It's ten-forty, dear. You get your TV and a bath."

"Sure, okay."

"Just sign here."

He signed quickly.

"One night? Two? A week? I have to put it down." Her face was powdery and mild.

"Two, three maybe. I don't know."

"Oh, and hon? You forgot to say where you were from. Here, on the form."

"Ah," he said.

He knew what to put. He thought of the only American he knew. Jardi. Where had Jardi grown up?

"Chicago," he wrote.

"Chicago, now there's a nice town." She smiled. "Now I have to have that money, hon."

He gave her a twenty and got his change.

"You go on up. Those stairs there. Down the hall. It's in the back, away from all the traffic."

He climbed the stairs, went down the dark hall and found the room. He went in, locked the door. He pulled the Skorpion from his pack and set it before him on the bed and waited for the police.

Nobody came.

You did it, he thought.

Kurdistan ya naman.

4

Trewitt was nervous. First, so many big shots in the room at one time. The special men, the elect, some of them legends, who ran the place. Then, the equipment. He was not by nature mechanical. He was not good with *things*. Wouldn't it have been easier to have brought in some technical wizard to handle this aspect of it? Well, yes, under normal circumstances. But these were extraordinary circumstances. Therefore he'd just have to run the equipment himself.

"You'll get the hang of it," Yost Ver Steeg had said.

And then the slides. They were the key; they had to fall in the right order and he'd just got the last one down from Photographic a few minutes ago—it had been touch and go the whole way—and he wasn't sure he'd gotten it into the magazine right. He might have had it in backward, which would have had a humorous effect in less intense briefings, but this one was big and he didn't want to screw up in front of so many important people. And see Miles Lanahan snickering in his corner, removing one point from Trewitt's tally and awarding it to himself.

"Trewitt, are we ready?" It was Yost.

"Yessir, I *think* so," he called back, his voice booming through the room—he was miked, he'd forgotten.

He bent, switched on the projector, beaming a white, pure rectangle onto the wall. So far, so good. If he could just find . . . yes, there's the bastard; it was a kind of toggle switch mounted in a cylinder, in turn linked by cord to the projector. Now, if this just works like the instructions *say,* we'll be . . .

He punched the button and there was a sound like a .45 cocking.

A face came on the screen, young, tenderly young, say eighteen, eyes wild with joy, crewcut glinting with perspiration, two scrawny straps hooked over two scrawny shoulders.

"Chardy at eighteen," Trewitt said. "His high school had just won the Class B Chicago Catholic League championship. March twelfth, nineteen fifty-eight. The picture is from the next day's *Tribune.* This is a close-up; you can't see the trophy, a hideous thing. Anyway, Chardy scored . . . ah, I have it right here. . . ."

"Twenty-one points," Miles Lanahan called. "Including a free throw with time gone that gave St. Pete's a one-point win."

"Thanks, Miles," said Trewitt, thinking, *you bastard.*

"Anyway," Trewitt continued, "you can see he's a hero from way back."

Trewitt's problem was heroes. His vice, his consuming passion, heroism. His deepest secret was that when he walked through the streets and saw his own bland reflection thrown back at him in shopwindows he projected onto it certain extravagances of equipage and uniform: jungle camouflages, dappled and crinkly, bush hats, wicked knives; and the weapons, the implements by which the hardened professionals performed their jobs—the M-16 and AK-47, antagonists of a hundred thousand firefights of the sixties and seventies; or the Swedish K so favored by Agency cowboys in 'Nam; or the compact little MAC-10 or -11, other racy favorites.

"The real name is C-S-A-R-D-I," said Trewitt, "Hungarian. His dad was a doctor, an emigré in the thirties. His mom is Irish. A quiet woman who still lives in the apartment in Rogers Park. The dad was a little nuts. He was a drunk, his practice failed, he ended up a company doctor in a steel mill. He went into an institution after he retired, and died there. He was hard-core anticommunist though, and a staunch Catholic. He filled the kid's head with all kinds of stuff about the Reds. And he wanted him to be tough; he really put him through some hell to make him tough. He—"

"Jim, let's move it along." Yost's stern voice from out of the darkness.

"Sure, sorry," Trewitt said, convinced he heard Lanahan snicker.

Two quick clicks: Chardy the college athlete; Chardy, hair sheared off, in the denim utilities of a Marine boot.

"Marine officer training, after college," Trewitt announced.

Trewitt had known of Chardy for some time. His job on the Historical Staff, to which he'd so recently been attached, had been to edit the memoirs of retiring officers who were paid by the Agency to stay at Langley an extra year and write, the idea being, first, to allow any impulse toward literature to play itself out under controlled circumstances and second, to compile a history of the means and methods of the secret wars. Aspects or fragments of Chardy kept showing up in these accounts, memories of him echoing through a dozen different sources, sometimes under cryptonyms. He'd been pretty famous in his way.

"And here he is," Trewitt announced, clicking his button, "among the Nungs."

Chardy had been recruited out of the Marine Corps

in Vietnam in the early days, '63, '64, where he was for a time a platoon commander and then a company commander and finally, having extended his tour, an intelligence officer, coordinating with South Vietnamese Rangers and running (and occasionally accompanying) long-range recons up near the DMZ. But an Agency hotshot named Frenchy Short talked him into jumping to the Company, which at that time desperately needed jungle-qualified military types.

The slide on the wall now was a favorite of Trewitt's, for it seemed to express exactly a certain heroic posture—the two men, Paul and Frenchy, among Chinese mercenaries from the Vietnamese hill country whom they'd trained and led in a hit-and-run war way out in the deep, beyond the reach of law or civilization.

"He did two long stretches with the Nungs," Trewitt said to the men in the quiet briefing room in Langley, Virginia, "with a stay in between at our Special Warfare school in Panama."

The two of them, the younger, leaner Chardy, his black Irish face furious and pale, and the older Frenchy, a stumpy man with a crewcut, thick but not fat, his raw bulk speaking more of power than sluggishness. They wore those vividly spotted non-reg jungle camouflage outfits—called tiger suits—and were hatless. Paul had an AK-47 and a cigarette dangled insolently from his lip; Frenchy was equipped with a grease gun and a smile. They were surrounded by their crew of Chinese dwarfs, tiger-suited too, a collection of sullen Mongolian faces that in their impassive toughness seemed almost Apache. Wiry little men, with carbines, grenades, a Thompson or two, a gigantic BAR—this was before the fancy black plastic M-16s arrived in Vietnam. The picture had a nineteenth-century feel to it: the two white gods surrounded by their yellow killers, yet in subtle ways that the photograph managed to convey, the white men were turning wog themselves, going native in the worst possible way.

"God, old Frenchy Short," somebody said; Trewitt thought it might have been Sam Melman. "He was a piece of work, wasn't he? Jesus, I remember when he nailed Che in Bolivia. He went all the way back to Korea. He was one of the guys we had ashore at the Bay of Pigs, one of the first in and one of the last out."

"Frenchy was something," somebody else agreed, and Trewitt recognized Yost Ver Steeg's voice. "I had no idea he went so far back with Paul."

"It was Frenchy who got Paul reinstated after he punched Cy Brasher," another voice offered.

"Paul's finest moment in the Agency," somebody—Sam?—said, and there was laughter.

It's true, thought Trewitt. Chardy was thin-skinned as well as brave and tough, and especially vulnerable to pedants and bureaucratic snipers of the sort intelligence agencies tend to attract in great number. Both his stateside tours, routine administrative pit stops that all career-track officers are expected to pull, had been disasters. And in Hong Kong, Chardy came up against Cy Brasher (Harvard '49, as he was fond of telling people) in what was referred to still as the Six-Second War. This was 1971, when Chardy was coming off his second long, terrible tour among the Nungs.

Brasher was an imperious, lofty man, cursed with a need to correct everybody. He was widely loathed but exceedingly well connected (*the* Brashers) and had skated without apparent effort to Head of Station in Hong Kong. During the first three seconds of his war with Chardy, he suffered a broken nose and the loss of two teeth; in the second three seconds he took several savage body blows which broke two of his ribs.

"I still worry about this guy, Yost," somebody said.

"Lord knows I despised Cy Brasher as much as anybody. But junior personnel just can't go around slugging station chiefs, no matter how fatuous an ass the station chief is. And if we have to rely on a guy like Chardy, then we are in rather desperate straits."

"We *are* in rather desperate straits," said Yost. "Trewitt?"

Trewitt obediently tripped the button, and a picture of Joseph Danzig appeared on the screen.

"The year," Trewitt said, "is nineteen seventy-three. The year of the operation called Saladin Two."

Danzig's famous face filled the room. There's no reason to show it, really, thought Trewitt, for they all know what he looks like, and all of them will remember what the Agency was like in those days, those Danzig days.

It had been his fiefdom, his ego extension; it existed only to serve his will. He had repaid this fealty, this slavish obedience with contempt and derision.

All of the men in this room had felt his influence, worked in his shadow or under his supervision, tried to guess what he wanted. Joseph Danzig, formerly of Harvard University and then the Rockefeller Advisory Board on Foreign Affairs, had been, under a certain President, Secretary of State. He was almost as famous, in his own way, as that other paradigm of academic-cum-international kingmaker and unmaker, Henry Kissinger, his contemporary at Harvard and in many ways his rival and his equal. Their beginnings were even similar: Kissinger born a German Jew, Danzig, whose family name had been simplified from something unpronounceable to that of the city of his origin by an American Immigration officer, born a Polish one.

But Saladin II and Danzig are linked, Trewitt realized, just as tightly in their way as Saladin II and Chardy. Without Danzig there would have been no Saladin II. It was shaped to his specifications, blueprinted to his calculations, implemented at his whim, and aborted by his will.

"Most of you are aware of Saladin Two," said Yost Ver Steeg, the host of this meeting. "Those who aren't are shortly to be so. Everything that happens now happens because of what happened then. This crisis we've got comes to us courtesy of that famous gent up there."

"Famous gent"—an uncharacteristic attempt at levity by Yost, who is normally, Trewitt reflected, about as amusing as a fish. Perhaps it's his nervousness, for he's the man whose job it is to stop the Kurd from doing whatever the men in this room are so terrified he'll do. And they are plenty terrified, except for Miles, who isn't terrified of *anything*.

Yost began to summarize what Trewitt already knew. Saladin II was pressure. It was pressure here to tilt this *that* way and that *this* way, a Rube Goldberg contraption of stresses and springs and gizmos that had as its only real purpose the spirit of keeping the Soviet Union off balance. Not included in the higher calculus of the design—and this too was a Danzig trademark—was a cost in human lives.

Saladin II had its origins in a complaint to an American President by the late Shah of Iran about difficulties with his obstreperous Arab neighbor, the radically pro-Soviet regime of Ahmed Hassam al-Bakr in Iraq. What, wondered the Shah, could be done to put the squeeze on the aggressive Iraqis and their new T-54 tanks and SAMs and pesky Russian infantry and intelligence advisers?

Part of the answer lay in the fact that spread throughout much of the contested region of northern Iraq and northern Iran were a people called the Kurds, who dreamed of a mythical kingdom called Kurdistan. They are a fierce Indo-European race of great independence and cunning, descended from the fearsome Medes of antiquity and said also to carry the genes of Alexander's legions, which might explain the astonishing presence among them of blue eyes and upturned little noses and blond heads and freckles, an island of northern fairness in the swarthy sea of darker Mediterraneanness. The Kurds were forced to traffic with whoever would have them—they are a cynical people, expecting little of the world; one of their bleak proverbs is ''Kurds have no friends''—and their ambitions must be seen as pitifully tiny against the designs of the superpowers: they wanted only their own schools, their own language, their own literature, and to be ignored by the outside world. They wanted a country, in other words, of their very own, which they would call Kurdistan.

The Shah did not like them but he saw a use for them. The Kurds have a violent history of insurrection against— against nearly everybody. In their time they have fought Turk and Persian and Iraqi with equal vehemence.

The answer then to everybody's problems, as suggested by Joseph Danzig, American Secretary of State, and implemented at his specific request by the Special Operations Division of the Central Intelligence Agency, was, in the language of the trade, a ''covert action.'' In plainer words: a little war.

Trewitt clicked his button.

The new face was blurry, out of focus, taken from absolute zero angle without consideration of the esthetics. Its subject looked like a victim. The face, even with the startled eyes from the unexpected flash, was young and smooth. It sported a huge moustache, a batwing thing that pulled the features down tragically, and the Adam's apple was prominent. The eyes were sharp and bright and small.

''We think,'' said Trewitt, ''that this is Ulu Beg. Chardy will be able to confirm for us tomorrow. At any

rate, in one of Chardy's early Saladin Two reports he
mentioned that somebody had told him the Kurd had been
to the American University of Beirut. He evidently
learned his English at an American high school near the
Kirkūk oil fields—there was a good one there. This would
have been courtesy of an A.I.D. scholarship. In those days
A.I.D. educated half the Middle East.''

"And of course *we* fund A.I.D., so in effect *we* taught
him his English,'' Yost amplified.

"We believe this is Ulu Beg at nineteen, during his one
year at AUB. We went to a great deal of trouble to get this
photo—it's from Lebanese police files. He was arrested
late in his first year for membership in a Kurdish literary
club—for which you may substitute 'revolutionary organi-
zation.' This is the picture the Lebanese cops got of him,
at the request of Iraqi officials. He escaped the Lebanese
pretty easily, and nobody ever touched him again until
Saladin Two.''

The face glared at them.

Trewitt tried to read it. It did not look particularly Middle Eastern. It was just a passionate young man's face,
caught in the harsh light of a police strobe. He was probably scared when they got this; he didn't know what was
going on, what would happen. He looked a little spooked;
but he also looked mad. The cheekbones were so high—
they gave his face an almost Oriental look. And the nose
was a blade, even photographed straight on, a huge, bony
hunk.

"The key document,'' said Yost, "from this point
onward is 'AFTACT Report Number two-four-three-
three-five-two-B-slash Saladin Two.' I urge any of you
unfamiliar with it to check it out of the Operations
Archive. You can also call on your computer terminals if
you're Blue Level cleared.''

"It sounds familiar," said a well-modulated, cheerful voice, to a small whisper of laughter.

Trewitt recognized the voice of Sam Melman, who, in the dismal aftermath of Saladin II, had compiled "AFTACT 243352-B," when he was Director of the Missions and Programs Staff in the Operations Directorate and had therefore committed his name to the document, for it was known in the vernacular (by the few that knew *of* it) as "The Melman Report."

The men who laughed with Sam would be his current staff, an Agency elect themselves, for Sam was now Deputy Director of Operations.

Trewitt had seen the report himself. It was a sketchy thing, a few dismal sheets of typewritten red paper (to prevent photocopying), such a tiny artifact for what must have been an extraordinary occurrence.

"You're not going to read us the whole thing?" somebody in the dark wanted to know. "I agree we've got a crisis, but nothing is worth *that.*"

Sam's laughter was loudest.

"No," said Yost. "But we thought you should have the context at least available."

But Trewitt couldn't let it pass from consciousness so easily. It haunted him, just as Chardy, the fallen hero, in his way haunted him. Chardy's performance before Melman, for one thing, was so strange. Trewitt had read it over and over, trying to master its secrets, the secret weight of the messages between the words. But there were none. Poor Chardy: Melman just barbecued him. Chardy had so little to offer in his defense, and on the stand, under oath, was vague and apologetic, either deeply disturbed or quite stupid or . . . playing a deeper game than anybody could imagine.

He confessed so easily to all the operational sins, all

the mistakes, the failures in judgment, the follies in action. Trewitt could almost remember verbatim:

> M: And you actually crossed into Kurdistan and led combat operations? Against all orders, against all policies, against every written or unwritten rule of the Agency. You actually led combat operations, disguised as a Kurd?
>
> C: Uh. Yeah. I guess I did.
>
> M: Mr. Chardy, one source even places you at an ambush site deep in Iraq, near Rawānduz.
>
> C: Yeah. I got a tank that day. Really waxed that—
>
> M: Mr. Chardy. Did it ever occur to you, while you were playing cowboy, how humiliating it would have been to this country, how embarrassing, how degrading, to have one of its intelligence operatives captured deep within a Soviet-sponsored state with armed insurgents?
>
> C: Yeah. I just didn't think they'd get me. (Laughs)

"Trewitt. Trewitt!"

"Ah. Yessir." Caught dreaming again.

"The next slide."

"Oh. Sorry."

He punched the button and the Kurd disappeared.

Somebody whistled.

"Yes, she's a fine-looking woman, isn't she?" Yost said.

"Chardy wouldn't talk about her at the hearings," Melman said. "He said it was private; it wasn't our business."

The picture of Johanna was recent. Her face was strong, fair, and somehow bold. The nose a trifle large, the chin a trifle strong, the mouth a trifle straight. Her blond hair was a mess, and it didn't matter. She was all earnest angles. Her eyes were softened behind large circular horn-rims and a tendril of hair had fallen across her face. She looked a bit irritated, or late or just grumpy. She's also beautiful, Trewitt realized, in an odd, strong way, an un-conventional collection of peculiarities that come together in an unusual and appealing way. Jesus, she's good-look-ing.

"One of the Technical Services people got this just last week in Boston, where she teaches at Mr. Melman's alma mater," Yost said.

"The Harvard staff didn't look like that when *I* was there." Sam again.

"Somehow Miss Hull managed to get into Kurdistan," Yost continued. "We don't know how. She wouldn't speak to State Department debriefers when she finally got back. But she's the key to this whole thing. Chardy had a 'relationship' with her, in the mountains."

The word "relationship," coming at Trewitt through the vague dark in which Yost was just a shape up front, sounded odd in the man's voice; Yost didn't care, as a rule, to speculate on a certain range of human behavior involving sexual or emotional passion; he was a man of facts and numbers. Yet he said it anyway, seemed to force it out.

"Chardy will love her still," Miles Lanahan said. The sharpness of his voice cut through the air. "He's that kind of guy."

The woman on the wall regarded them with icy superi-ority. She was wearing a turtleneck and a tweed sports coat. The shot must have been taken from half a mile away through some giant secret lens, for the distance was foreshortened dramatically and behind her some turreted old hulk of a house, with keeps and ramparts and doz-ens of gables, all woven with a century's worth of vines, loomed dramatically. It's so Boston, so Cambridge, thought Trewitt.

"Chardy had no brief to cross into Kurdistan. This woman had no right. But they both were there, in the absolute middle of it, with Ulu Beg. They were there for the end. In a sense they *were* the end."

Yost is discreet in his summary, Trewitt thought. The prosaic truth is that sometime in March of 1975 the Shah of Iran, at Joseph Danzig's urging and sponsorship, signed a secret treaty with Ahmed Hassam al-Bakr of Iraq. The Kurdish revolution, which was proceeding so splendidly, became expendable. Danzig gave the order; the CIA obeyed it.

The Kurds were cut off, their matériel impounded; they were exiled from Iran.

Chardy, Beg, the woman Hull: they were caught on the wrong side of the wire.

Chardy was captured by Iraqi security forces; Beg and Hull and Beg's people fled extreme Iraqi military pressure. Fled to where? Fled to nowhere. Trewitt knew that Yost wouldn't mention it, that even the great Sam Melman wouldn't mention it. But one passage from Chardy's testimony before Melman came back to haunt him, now in this dark room among Agency elect, his own career suddenly accelerating, his own membership on the staff of an important operation suddenly achieved.

C: But what about the Kurds?

M: I'm sorry. The scope of this inquiry doesn't include the Kurds.

The last details are remote, Trewitt knew. Nobody has ever examined them, no books exist, no journalists have exhumed it. Only the Melman report exists, and its treatment is cursory. Joseph Danzig himself has not commented yet. In the first volume of his memoirs, *Missions for the White House,* he promised to deal with the Kurdish situation at some length; but he has not yet published his second volume and somebody has said he may never. He's making too much money giving speeches these days.

The fates of the three principals were, however, known: Chardy, captured, was taken to Baghdad and interrogated by a Russian KGB officer named Speshnev. His performance under pressure, Trewitt knew, was a matter of some debate. Some said he was a hero; some said he cracked wide open. He would not discuss it with Melman.

He was returned to the United States after six months in a Moscow prison.

Johanna Hull showed up in Rezā'iyeh by methods unknown in April of 1975 and returned to the United States, and her life at Harvard. She had lived quietly ever since. Except that three times she had tried to commit suicide.

Ulu Beg, one source reported, was finally captured by Iraqi security forces in May of 1975 and was last seen in a Baghdad prison.

The fate of his people—his tribe, his family, his sons—was unknown.

"Lights," Yost said.

Trewitt fumbled a second too long for the switch but finally clicked it on.

The brightness flooded the room and men blinked and stretched after so long in the dark.

Yost stood at the front of the room.

"Briefly, that's it," he said. "I wanted to keep you informed. Chardy arrives tomorrow."

"Lord, you're bringing him *here?*"

"No, not to the Agency. We're running this operation out of a sterile office in Rosslyn, just across the river from Georgetown."

"Yost, I hope you can control this Chardy. He can be a real wild man."

"I don't think you understand," Miles Lanahan said.

He smiled, showing dirty teeth. He was a small young man with a reputation for ruthless intelligence. He was no sentimentalist; the "old cowboy" stuff wouldn't cut anything for him. He'd started out as a computer analyst working in "the pit," Agency jargon for the video display terminal installation in the basement of Langley's main building, and worked his way out in a record two years. Everybody was a little afraid of him, especially Trewitt.

"All right, Miles," said Yost, "that's enough."

Down, boy, thought Trewitt.

But Miles had one more comment.

"The plan," he said, "is *not* to control him."

5

Chardy sometimes thought only the game had kept him sane. At the end of Saladin II, the worst time in the cellar, he thought not of Johanna or the Kurds or his country or his mission; they'd all ceased to sustain him. He thought of the game. He shot imaginary jumpers from all over a huge floor and willed them through the hoop. Magic, they floated and fell and never touched metal. The game expanded to fill his imagination, to push out all the dark corners, the cobwebs, the spooky little doubts. Later the game had become, if anything, bigger. Into it he poured all his energy, his natural fierceness, his frustrations and dissatisfactions, his resentment: his hate. The game, more loyal than any human or institution on this earth, absorbed them—and him.

And now, on the night before what he knew was the most important day of his life, the game was especially kind to him. For of late his shots would not fall, his legs had been thick and numb, his fingers clumsy. But all that was a memory: tonight he could not miss. From outside, inside, but usually from the baseline with no backboard for margin of error, he shot, the ball spinning to the rafters and dropping cleanly through. It was only a Y-league game, mostly ex-college jocks like himself, or black kids with no college to go to; and it took place in a dim old gym that smelled of sweat and varnish and sported a shadowy network of old iron girders across the ceiling.

But for Chardy there was nothing but basketball court, no outside world, no Speights or Melmans or Ulu Begs. It was an absolute place: you shot; it went in or it didn't. There was no appeal, no politics, no subtle shading of results. It was a bucket or it wasn't.

Toward the end even the cool black kids were working the ball to him, just to watch it fall.

"Man, you *hot*," one called.

"Put it *down*," another yelled.

He hated to see it end, but it did. The team he played for, which represented a manufacturer of surgical instruments, easily vanquished a team that represented a linoleum installer; the margin was twenty-eight points and could have been greater. A buzzer sounded and the bodies stopped hurtling about. Somebody slapped him on the ass and somebody clapped him on the back and somebody shook his hand.

"You had it tonight," somebody said.

"Couldn't miss, could I?"

"No way, man, no way."

Chardy took a last glance toward the floor—two other teams, the Gas Stations and the Ice Cream Stores, were warming up. It meant nothing, but Chardy hated to leave it. A ball came spinning his way and he bent to scoop it up. He held it, feeling its skin springy to his fingers. He looked at the hoop and saw that it was about fifty feet away.

Shoot it, he thought.

But a black man came galloping up to him and without a word Chardy tossed him the ball, and off he went. Chardy pulled on his jacket and headed for the doors and what lay beyond.

6

He stared at the picture. Yes. Ulu Beg. Years younger, but still Ulu Beg.

"Yeah," he said.

"Good. Getting it was no easy thing," said Trewitt, the young one, a wispy pseudo-academic type who was tall and thin and vague.

"Once upon a time," Chardy said. "Years and years ago."

"Okay," said Trewitt. "Now this one."

The projector clicked and projected upon the screen on the wall of a glum office in Rosslyn a plumpish face, prosperous, solid.

"I give up," said Chardy.

"Look carefully," said Yost Ver Steeg. "This is important."

I *know* it's important, Chardy thought irritably.

"I still don't—oh, yeah. Yeah."

"It's an artist's projection of Ulu Beg *now*. Twenty years later, a little heavier, 'Americanized.' "

"Maybe so," said Chardy. "But I last saw him seven years ago. He looked"—Chardy paused. Words were not his strong point; he could never get them to express quite what he wanted—"fiercer, somehow. This guy was in a war for twenty years. He was a guerrilla leader for nearly ten. You've got him looking like a Knight of Columbus.''

A harsh note of laughter came from the other young one, Miles something-Irish. It was a caustic squawk of a laugh; Miles was a kind of Irish dwarf, an oily little jerk, but he'd know what a Knight of Columbus was.

''Well,'' Trewitt said defensively, ''the artist had a lot of experience on this sort of thing. He worked all night. We just got the picture in yesterday. It's the only one of Ulu Beg extant.''

''Try this one, Paul,'' said Yost Ver Steeg.

Johanna. Chardy stared at her. The face could have been spliced out of any of a thousand of his recent nights' worth of dreams. It meshed perfectly with all those nights of memory and struck him with almost physical force.

''It's very recent,'' said Yost.

Chardy stared at the image projected against the wall. He felt as if he were in a peep-show booth for a quarter's worth of pointless thrill with other strange men in a dark place.

''A week ago, I think. Is that right, Miles?'' Yost said.

''Tuesday last.'' Miles's voice was sure and smug and had a recognizable Chicago tang to it.

''Has she changed much in seven years?''

''No,'' was all Chardy could think to say, offended by the ritual he knew the shot to represent: some seedy little man from Technical Services, up there with a motor-driven Nikon with a 200-millimeter lens, parked blocks away in his car or van, shooting through one-way glass after three days' stalk.

Chardy rubbed his dry palms together. He glanced over at the three shapes with whom he shared Johanna's image: Yost, almost a still life, a man of deadness, and the two younger fellows, dreamy Trewitt and the loathsome Miles What-was-it?, the dumpy little Irish guy from Chicago.

"Did you know"—Miles spoke from the corner—"that in the years she's been back she's tried to kill herself three times?"

A kind of pain that might have been grief seemed to work up through Chardy's knees. He swallowed once, feeling his heart beat hard, or seem to, at any rate. He clenched his fists together.

"I didn't know that. I don't know anything about what happened to her."

Chardy could almost feel Miles smile in the dark. He'd only glimpsed him in the hurried introductions—Speight had said something about a computer whiz—and remembered a short, dark, splotchy man, a boy really, not quite or just barely thirty, with unruly oily black hair. He had the look to him of a priest's boy, the one in every parish who'd seek a special relationship from the father or the mother superior and draw power off it for years. He'd seen it at Resurrection too, and maybe elsewhere; maybe it wasn't Catholic at all.

"Once in 'seventy-seven, wrists," Lanahan amplified, "once in 'seventy-nine, pills, and a real bad one last year, pills again. She almost went the distance."

Chardy nodded, keeping his eyes sealed on the woman's image before him.

Johanna, *why?*

But he knew why.

"The university has had her in and out of various shrink programs," Lanahan continued. "We got the records. It wasn't easy."

But Chardy was not listening. He looked at his own wrists. He'd cut them open in April of 1975 after his lengthy interrogation by the KGB. He knew the feeling of comfort: the blood draining away and with it all the problems of the world. An immense light-headedness fills you, seductive, gratifying. You think you're going to beat them.

He remembered screaming at the officer who had supervised his interrogation, "Speshnev, Speshnev, I'm going to *win.*" But they'd saved him.

"Is that it?" Trewitt asked.

"Yes," said Ver Steeg, and the image vanished. Trewitt pulled the curtains open and light flooded the room.

Chardy stared at the wall from which her image had disappeared. Then he turned back to the others.

"So—Paul. May I call you Paul?" Yost asked. Chardy could not see his eyes behind the pink-framed semi-academic glasses he wore, a style beloved of high-level government administrators.

"Please," Chardy said.

"Ulu Beg knows only two people in the United States. You and Johanna Hull. And it seems unlikely he'd come to you—for help."

Chardy nodded. Yes, it seemed unlikely Ulu Beg would come to him—for help.

"That leaves this woman."

"You think he'll go to her?"

"I don't think anything. I see only probabilities. It seems probable that he's aware how difficult it would be to operate in this country without some kind of base. It seems probable, then, that he'd try and obtain one. It seems probable that he'd be drawn to somebody he felt he could trust, somebody who shared his sentiments about the Kurds. It seems probable, finally, that he'd go to her. That's all."

"You could try and anticipate his target," said Chardy.

"You could. And if you anticipated wrong you might put yourself into a posture you'd never get out of. We have no data to operate on at this point as to his target; there are no probabilities. That may change; until it does I've decided to concentrate on the probabilities."

Chardy nodded.

"So we have to wonder, Paul," Yost continued. It was a freak of optics that kept his eyes hidden behind the twin pools of light reflected in his lenses. "You're our authority. You know them both. Is it feasible he'd approach her? To you, I mean. Does that *feel* right? And if so, how would she react? And finally, would she cooperate with *us?* Or, more to the point, with *you?*"

Miles spoke before Chardy could form an answer.

"She's not an activist type, we know. She's not affiliated with any zany political group, she's not a demonstrator, a kook. She doesn't sleep with fruity revolutionaries. She's quiet, she's solid—except for her head troubles. She doesn't have a history of doing screwy things."

He fingered through some pages before him—Johanna's dossier, probably. God, they knew so much about her, Chardy thought. The idea of this Miles's small fingers riffling through Johanna's life offended him. His damp hands on her picture, her documents.

Miles smiled, showing dirty teeth.

Who'll save you, Johanna, from these guys?

I will, he thought.

And then he thought of her only contact with him, an answer to the fifteen-page letter he'd sent her when he returned from the Soviet prison. It had been a postcard with a cheesy picture of the Doral Hotel in Miami Beach on it, and it had said, "No, Paul. You know why."

"Paul?"

"Sorry, I was—"

"The question," Yost said politely, "is: will he approach her? And, would she help him?"

"She'd help *us,*" Chardy said.

"Come on, Paul," said Miles . . . *Lanahan!* That was it. "For Christ's sakes, she was sold on the Kurds. If you look at her record the way we did, you cannot escape that conclusion. She went to Iran in 'sixty-nine with the

Peace Corps. She came back in 'seventy-three to teach at the college in Rezā'iyeh. She wrote her Ph.D. dissertation on Kirmanji, a Kurdish dialect. She made the pilgrimage to Mahābād, where they had their republic in 'forty-six, and one of her Peace Corps chums told us she wept at the Street of Four Lamps, where the Iranians hanged the Kurdish martyrs.''

"That's all true," said Chardy. "But it's also true she's too smart to get involved in anything stupid like you're talking about. This is a very smart woman. She's brilliant. She just wouldn't get mixed up in something goofy like this. Ulu Beg or no Ulu Beg.''

"If he approached her, she'd help us?''

"Yes. If we could tell her we wouldn't hurt him.''

"Paul, he's already killed two police officers.''

"A terrible accident. And the FBI and the Border Patrol haven't made the connection to Ulu Beg yet. Because you want to play this thing low-profile. You wouldn't have brought me in unless you wanted to play it low-profile, and I don't think you want the FBI nosing through some old Agency business.''

There was stifled silence in the room. Chardy had them, he knew he had them.

"Let me tell her we'll try and pick him up and let him walk on it. That's the key. If you say, 'We're going to throw this guy in the slammer for two hundred years,' then it's all over. But if you say, 'Look, it's terrible, but we can still deal with it,' then maybe you've got a chance.''

"You love them. Both. Still." It was the boy, Trewitt.

"No matter," said Yost Ver Steeg. "But I'm sure Paul understands"—he seemed to speak to the younger man but in reality talked by echo to Chardy—"no matter what his personal feelings are, just how potentially serious a problem this is. An Agency-trained Kurd with an Agency-provided automatic weapon. Suppose he commits some terrible act of random violence—like the Japanese terrorists at Lod Airport. Or kills an important public figure. The Agency doesn't need to be tied up in a scandal like that.''

Chardy nodded. They *were* scared. He could see the headlines, one of the Agency's secret little wars exploding in America's own backyard, American blood on American pavement for the first time. They *were* terrified—of what it would do to the Agency.

''You can see that, Paul, can't you?''

''Yes.''

''After all, it's your past, too. It was your operation originally. You have some responsibility.''

''Of course I do,'' Chardy said.

''What happened, in the end, to the Kurds was—well, you must take some responsibility for that, too.''

''Of course,'' said Chardy.

''So if this woman is the key, we have to find out. We have to know. And if you want to tell her something to help, you go ahead and tell her. But remember what's at stake.''

''Yes.''

The rest was unsaid, and would be represented on no paper: Ulu Beg must be stopped to spare the Agency grotesque embarrassment.

''You'll do it then? You'll see her. You'll bring her in, you'll help us. You'll work with us.''

''Yes,'' Chardy said. He wondered if he meant it, or if it mattered.

After that it was a matter of details. Who would accompany Chardy to Boston as backup, what approach would he take, how would he handle it, what could he expect? The answer to the first question was Lanahan, who'd done the preliminary work in "developing Johanna," in Yost's words, and that simply it was set. They would leave in two days; the hotel reservations were already made. But when Chardy was finally done with them and wanted nothing more than to go find a beer, he looked up to see he was not yet alone. The boy Trewitt, the one who had said so little, had waited in the foyer for him.

"Mr. Chardy?"

"What's up?" he asked.

"Trewitt. Jim Trewitt."

"Sure, I remember."

"They had me working on the Historical Staff—I'm actually a historian; I have my master's—before all this." He seemed a little nervous.

Chardy did not know what to make of this. There'd been no Historical Staff in his time, just as there'd been no Operations Directorate. "Uh-huh," he said.

"We work with a lot of the older men; they're asked to spend their last year working on a memoir. So I've picked up a lot of loose information on—well, on Agency people. Your career, the stuff you pulled, you and some of those other Special Operations guys. Tony Po, Willie Shidlovisky, Scamp Hughes, Walter Short—"

"Frenchy. Frenchy Short," said Chardy, warming at the sudden memory of his best and oldest Agency friend.

"You and Frenchy. You really *did* some things. All that time with the Nungs in Vietnam. Hunting guerrillas with the Peruvian Rangers." He shook his head in admiration, embarrassing Chardy with his own gaudy past.

"I just wanted you to know how glad I was that you're back with us. And I wanted to tell you that I think you got the shaft when Saladin Two fell apart."

"Somebody had to get it," Chardy said. But then he stupidly smiled at the boy, winning his loyalty forever. He just hoped the kid wouldn't get in the way. But then he saw a purpose for him, so perhaps this business would work out after all.

"By the way, maybe you can tell me: what have they got the Frenchman doing now?" he asked, and learned the answer instantly from the sudden stricken look on the boy's face.

"I thought you knew. I thought they told you, or you'd heard or something," Trewitt said.

"They didn't tell me anything," Chardy said.

"I'm sorry I brought it up. I apologize. Somebody should have told you. Frenchy Short was killed in 'seventy-five on a solo job. In Vienna. They found him floating in the Danube. You were off in Kurdistan."

Chardy nodded and said something to reassure Trewitt, who looked sick with grief. He told him it was all okay, not to worry.

"I just—I'm really sorry."

"No, don't worry. I should have known. I just thought he was overseas or something. I was out of contact for so long."

"Is there anything—"

"No, no. The Frenchman always figured to catch it on a job. It had to happen. He liked to play them close. Don't worry."

He finally sprung himself from the boy and walked in the gray gloom across a grassy field in the center of a traffic circle toward the Marriott Key Bridge Motel, where he was staying. He could see Georgetown at the far end of the bridge, and the far side of the river down to the Kennedy Center, a magnificent view of white buildings and monuments. But Chardy wanted only to find a bar. He reflected that he had loved three people in his life and now one of them, his friend and perfect master, Frenchy Short, who had taught him just about all there was to know about their kind of business, was dead and he hadn't even known it. And the other two, Johanna and Ulu Beg, were coming back into his life in almost the same instant after what seemed ages, as part of the same phenomenon, linked as before; and this necessarily evoked a complicated and melancholy response, not only because he was charged to hunt the one and control the other, but more terribly because just as surely as he had loved them both, he had in a cellar in Baghdad in 1975 betrayed them both.

7

Ramirez did not like them. He should have loved them, for they were throwing money around like American millionaires or Colombian cocaine merchants, yet they were neither American nor Colombian. Tips for all the poor girls. American whiskey only, and lots of it. Cigars, a foot long, for themselves and for anybody else.

But who were they?

Ramirez took another sip of his Carta Blanca, which was warm and flat from sitting so long in his glass, then set the drink before him on the table. The room was long and dark but he could see their profiles by looking across the room into a mirror which in turn looked into a second mirror. They had just ordered another bottle of Jack Daniel's and given the boy Roberto, who brought it, a five-dollar bill. Ramirez knew his clientele well: college boys down from Tucson for a night of whoring, lonely tourists, an occasional Mexican businessman or two. It was a prosperous enterprise but no gold mine, and it didn't draw the big spenders such as these two.

He knew he should feel safe. He had journeyed to Mexico City after the fiasco at the border to make personal amends to the Huerra family. He had waited patiently for an appointment and been finally escorted into the old man's office at the top of one of Mexico City's finest buildings and there apologized abjectly and cravenly for his errors in judgment on the evening in question and offered to do a penance. Could he pay a fine, make a donation? Could he offer a service, do a task?

And Huerra, the elder, the patriach, an old gentleman with the courtly manners of a Spanish grandee, had said, "Reynoldo, you have served our family well and long. Two old friends such as ourselves should feel love toward each other, not hate or distrust. It is good that you come and ask forgiveness and I grant it to you. You are forgiven. You owe us no penance."

"Thank you, Don José," Ramirez had said and had dropped swiftly to his knees and kissed the old man's hand.

"I would ask one thing," said Don José.

"Anything. Anything."

"It is said you are no longer a religious man. I hear you do not give to the Virgin, you do not talk to priests. This bothers me. As I get older, I see the importance of the religious life."

"I have sinned. I have been a vain and greedy man. I have lived a terrible life, Don José."

"Go back to God, Reynoldo. God will forgive you, just as I have. God loves you, just as I do. The Church is your mother; she will forgive you as well."

"It is done. I will light a candle every day. I will give half to the Mother Church."

"Not half, Reynoldo. I should think a quarter would be sufficient."

And so Reynoldo had taken up again the religious life. He lit candles, he wen to early mass, he made ostentatious donations. He became a changed man, a new man. It lasted about two days.

He took another sip of his Carta Blanca. He looked

about for Oscar Meza who had disappeared. Had he left? Where was Oscar Meza? He looked again into the mirror and saw the two men—one wore a fine cream suit, elegantly cut, the other a pale blue leisure suit with an open-collared shirt, after the American style, though both were Latins—and saw that they had lit another pair of cigars and were laughing madly at some private joke.

What was so funny?

An hour later, Ramirez glanced at his gold watch. It was nearly 3:00 A.M. Things would die soon; the quiet hours before dawn would arrive, when even a poor whore might sleep. Ramirez pulled his bulk from behind his table and walked through clouds of stale smoke, past a few lingering drunken college boys who were trying to decide which girl to give their business to, and went behind the bar.

Instantly, the youth Roberto appeared.

"Patrón?"

Ramirez threw open the register and made a big show of fingering through the bills. He counted them twice, then turned to the boy.

"Stealing again, Roberto?"

"No, *patrón.*"

"There should be at least a thousand here. I have watched carefully."

"A slow night, *patrón.*"

"Not that slow. Steal only a little, Roberto. If you steal too much at once, the big machine gets out of alignment and maybe you get caught in the gears and squashed."

"I—I steal nothing, *patrón,*" the youth said, but could not look into Ramirez's eyes.

Ramirez knew exactly how much Roberto stole each night and that it was within permissible limits, just as he knew how much Oscar stole—more and more lately—and how much the old lady who sat by the top of the stairs and checked peckers stole. Everyone stole; everybody took only a little for themselves, but by certain rules. There were rules. Nobody was allowed to break them.

"Just do not get so greedy, Roberto. I want to see you live a long, wonderful life and have fifty children. Be fruitful, populate the earth with your seed."

"Yes, *patrón.*"

He turned, edged his large body away from the register. He paused for a moment, then moved along. In the pause his fingers had touched a Colt Cobra .38 Special in a holster under the register; he plucked the little revolver out and slid it into the waistband of his trousers, thinking, I wish I had my big Python instead of this little lady's gun. And thinking, I wish I lit a candle this morning.

The two men in suits continued to drink steadily at their table.

"Roberto," Ramirez called.

The boy hurried over.

"Take a bottle of the finest American stuff to our two friends. Say it is a gift of the proprietor."

"Yes, *patrón.*"

Roberto fetched the bottle and took it to the table. The two looked up as he explained with his stiff little bow. The two men laughed warmly and asked where the proprietor was.

Roberto pointed.

"With great appreciation we accept the gift of the proprietor," the man in the cream suit called in Spanish.

Ramirez nodded. Oscar Meza should have been back by now. Where was he?

"You run a nice place, Señor Proprietor," called the man in the cream suit.

"Thanks much, my warm friend," called back Ramirez. "It is a humble place but honest and clean."

"An excellent prescription for success in any endeavor," said the man dreamily. He had slicked-back black hair and was pockmarked, yet he was handsome in a mean way that attracts certain women. His friend in blue was fatter and more solemn—the sort who speaks only when spoken to, and then curtly. Also, he needed a shave.

"Did you have a visit with my girls?" Ramirez asked. "They're the prettiest in Nogales. In all Sonora."

"They are flowers. Each and every one. They know tricks, too, all kinds of tricks. I suppose the proprietor taught them himself."

"These modern girls, you can't teach them a thing. They already know everything," he said. "There's a young one with a magnificent mouth. A mouth of uncompromising sweetness. She'll play you like a trumpet for only a little extra."

"Is that Rita? I had Rita. Rita, a most refined and gifted young lady."

"Rita is truly a rare bloom," Ramirez called, and kissed his fingertips in homage to her skills. Under the kiss his fingers seemed to blossom, grow light and float away. Rita was fifty and needed dental work.

"We ought to be going," said the man in the blue leisure suit. "It's getting late."

"You'll come back, I hope?"

"Sadly, no. Our business in Nogales is almost finished."

"A great pity. But I hope you'll remember our little establishment fondly."

"I have a great affection for it," the man in the cream suit said, rising enthusiastically. He had an automatic pistol in his hand and he brought it to bear on Ramirez's center, aiming carefully, and Ramirez shot through the table, hitting him in the chest, spinning him around. The report in the closed space was sharp and ugly, but it did not bother the man in blue, for he shot at Ramirez, hitting him under the heart and knocking him back off his chair.

Ramirez felt as though he'd been punched. He fought to get his breath back and to find feeling in his fingertips and when he looked he could see the man in blue tugging at his wounded partner, trying to bring him to his feet, but the man's limbs were floppy and indifferent and the body kept collapsing forward. Ramirez pushed himself to his knees and rushed a shot at the man in blue, missing, and fired again quickly, hitting him in the jaw. The man sat down stupidly next to his friend. He held his head in his hands and began to moan. He started to weep.

"Oh, it hurts," he said brokenly, with blood spilling from his mouth.

Ramirez climbed to his feet and walked over and shot him in the back of the neck, pitching him forward.

"Jesus Mary," said Roberto. "Who are they?"

"Evil men," said Ramirez. But who were they?

"Run," he said to Roberto, "go get the Madonna. Quickly, boy, before I bleed my life away."

The boy dashed off to get one of the prostitutes who claimed to have been a nurse.

Ramirez sat down on a chair. He still had the pistol in his hand. He dropped it.

The room began to flutter before his eyes. He wanted a priest, he hurt so bad. He looked at the two women on the couch, who stared at him in horror and shock.

"Get out of here, whores!" he bellowed. "Whores may not watch a man die." They scurried off.

He wished he'd lit a candle that morning. He wished he'd been to mass. He wished there was a priest.

Where was the Madonna?

8

The van had reached a suburb of Boston called Medford, up north of Boston, and pulled into a crowded parking lot—acres and acres of cars—surrounding a bar or something called Timmothy's, a single low building of unsurpassing modesty. The name, in red neon, was written in about fifty places: on the roof, above the doors, on a huge sign at the entrance to the lot: This Is It! The Original! TIMMOTHY'S!

"We are here," said Lanahan, "because it's Saturday night. And every Saturday night, this studious intellectual lady, this gifted, brave, strong woman"—Chardy's words, thrown back at him—"comes here, or one of several other similar institutions, and finds a man and leaves with him."

"Last weekend she didn't get home till Sunday afternoon," said the driver, a wizard from Technical Services.

Chardy wondered if that was a smirk on Lanahan's lumpy little face in the red glow of the neon. He felt like smacking him, but then the impulse vanished. Lanahan was nothing to him, not worth hitting.

"Nobody from Harvard would come way out here," said the man up front. "They stick to Cambridge and snottier places like The Casablanca or Thirty-three Dunster Street. This place is too tacky, too crass, your suburban crowd, polyester.''

"She's in there now," Lanahan said. "That's her car." He pointed to a green VW parked nearby.

The wizard said, "She always goes for the same type. I've seen three of them now. Dark Irish. Big, six two, two hundred pounds.''

"She's looking for some others off your assembly line," Lanahan said. "She's looking for *you.*''

"That's shit," Chardy said.

"We shall see. You all set? You ready? You still think you can handle it?''

"Uh-huh," Chardy said.

"You don't sound so convincing. Look, there are other ways of handling this.''

Chardy thought, you little bastard.

"Chardy. I have to answer to Ver Steeg on this one. Don't fuck it up, all right? Just play it cool, don't come on too strong. Don't spook this girl. You do it wrong, she goes to the newspapers, makes a big—''

"I can handle it.''

Chardy slid the van door open, stepping into the chilly, damp evening.

Spring had not yet reached Massachusetts and he walked through the ranks of cars in a fog of his own breath. At Timmothy's a short line formed and he ducked into it. They were all so pretty: the boys in their twenties had expensive haircuts, parted in the middle, that fell in glorious layered cascades; they wore rich, dark clothing, European almost. The girls all seemed small and dark and jocular and somehow Catholic; they would wear crucifixes on their delicate throats and not really believe what they were here for. He felt like some kind of grown-up among them, stiff and stupid, for he was easily a decade beyond the next oldest person in the line. He waited patiently in his drab suit for almost ten minutes, until at last he reached a set of doors that were opened to admit him. He took a last look at the van, far off, under a tall light, its windows impenetrable, and knew that Lanahan was watching, and by extension Yost Ver Steeg and the Central Intelligence Agency.

Entered, the bar was really a collection of bars, each to its own motif, each equally fraudulent. It took him a while to move through all these variations—each big room was jammed—but just as he was beginning to grow panicky, he found her.

She sat at a table with some guy. The room was tonier than the others, fashioned after the Victorian age, if the Victorians had discovered plastic. Chardy felt he'd stumbled on to a movie set. But there was Johanna, her flesh, her face, with some man: as the wizard had said, a big man, Chardy's size or larger, in a three-piece suit.

Chardy squeezed in at the bar a discreet distance from them and ordered a beer. He could see her in the mirror, but just barely, for smoke hung in the dark space near the ceiling like a rain squall. She was so intimate with this man. She touched his arm. She laughed at his jokes and listened with rapturous attention to his anecdotes. Sheer jealousy almost crippled Chardy. He watched as they ordered another round—bourbon for the man, white wine for Johanna.

Chardy watched, mesmerized. When was the last time he'd seen her? He could call it back with surprising accuracy, even now, even here. It had been the day of the ambush, the day of his capture. She'd dressed after the Kurdish fashion, a gushing print peasant's skirt, a black vest, several blouses and scarves, and her hair wrapped in a scarf. But not now. Now she wore dark slacks, a turtleneck under a tweed jacket. Her biggest glasses, to soften the slight angularity of her face. Her tawny hair pulled backward, though a sprig of it fell to her forehead. And when she smiled he could see her white teeth.

Chardy thought: Oh, Jesus, you look good. He could not take his eyes off her. If he had a plan in his head it abruptly vanished. He had some trouble breathing; she robbed him of air. Her hands were white and her fingers long and she reached and touched the man on the hand. He laughed, whispered something. They finished their drinks. They stood.

Chardy stood.

They walked through the crowd into the hall. The man had his arm around her. They got their coats from the checkroom and stepped out the door. Chardy followed and caught them in the parking lot under a fluorescent light as the man fumbled with the keys to his Porsche.

"Excuse me," Chardy said.

She turned, recognizing the voice instantly but perhaps not quite believing it.

"Johanna?" He stepped into the light so that the man could see him. "I'd like to talk to you. It's important."

"Oh, Paul," she finally said. "Oh, Paul."

"Do you know this guy?" the man asked, stepping forward.

"This doesn't concern you," Chardy said.

"Oh, it doesn't?" he said, taking another step forward. He turned to her. "Do you want to talk to this guy or not?"

She could not answer but only looked furiously at Chardy.

"Look," the man said, "I don't think this girl wants to talk to you. Why don't you just go on and get out of here?"

"Johanna, it's really important. It really is."

"Just go away, Paul," she said.

"Paul, you better get on out of here," the man said.

Chardy felt electric with sensation. So much current was whirling through him he thought he might blow. She was so close. He wanted to touch her. He felt physically weak, but he could not draw back. Terror also gripped him. He knew he'd done this all wrong, coming on like this.

He stepped forward another step. "Please, Johanna."

The man hit him in the ear, a sucker punch. He twisted his leg as he fell back on the asphalt. He felt for an instant as though a steeple bell had gonged through his skull, and found himself sitting oafishly in a puddle. He looked up, and murder boiled through his brain; but the man who'd thrown the blow looked absolutely stunned that he'd done such a thing.

"I didn't mean to," the man said. "But I told you to stay away. I warned you. You asked for it. You really did. You asked for it and I gave it to you."

Chardy climbed to his feet. "That was a stupid thing to do. You don't know who I am. Suppose I had a gun? Suppose I knew karate or something? Suppose I was just tough?"

"I-I told you to leave."

"Well, I'm not going to. You better not try that again."

"Wally," Johanna said. "It *was* stupid. He's a kind of soldier. He probably knows all kinds of dirty tricks. Anyway, I hate it when men fight. It's so pointless."

"Just don't hit me again, Wally," Chardy said, "and you'll come out of this okay."

"This is ridiculous," Wally said. "Are you leaving with me or not?"

"Oh, Wally."

"You certainly changed your tune in a hurry. Well, fuck you, and fuck your crazy boyfriend too. You two have fun; you really deserve each other.'' He climbed into his car, pulled out, and roared away in a scream of rubber.

''Johanna,'' Chardy said.

''Paul, stay away. Stay the fuck away. I don't need your kind of trouble.''

He watched her walk away, through the pools of light in the parking lot.

''Johanna. Please.''

''Paul.'' She turned. ''Go *away. Stay away.* I'll call the police—I swear I will.''

''Johanna. Ulu Beg is coming.''

They sat in her Volkswagen near a park. He could see the deserted playground equipment, a basketball court empty and dark, through some trees. He drank from a can of beer—he'd told her to stop at a grocery store and she'd silently obeyed—his third in twenty-five minutes. The car ticked occasionally and it occurred to him that this American thing, sitting in a car with a woman on a quiet night near a park, was as exotic to him as a Philippine courtship ritual. Moisture beaded the windshield, fogging it; the air was damp and the trees clicked together in a breeze. She had not yet spoken and then finally she said, ''You're working for them, aren't you?''

''Yes. Temporarily.''

''I thought they fired you.''

''They did. They needed me back.''

''You said in that letter you'd never work for them again. You said you were all done with it. Were you lying then too?''

''No. I came back because I didn't feel I had a choice.''

''Because of the Kurd?''

''Yes.''

''Isn't it a little late to be paying off your debts?''

"Maybe it is. I don't know. We'll see, won't we?"

"How can you do it? Work for them? How can you stomach it?"

"If I didn't there'd be another man here. He wouldn't care about you. He wouldn't care about Ulu Beg. These are cold people, from the Security Office. They want him dead."

"What do you want from me?"

"They think he'll come to you, because he has no other place to go. Or so they say. I'm not sure what they really think. But that's the official line. So I'm here to get your help."

"There was a time when I would have killed you. I thought about it. I thought about flying to Chicago, going to your door, knocking, and when you answered, shooting you. Right in the face."

"I'm sorry you hate me so much."

"You were part of it."

"I never—"

"Paul, you're lying. It's part of the fiber, the structure of your life. I've done some research on your employers: they train you to lie without thinking about it. You can do it calmly and naturally, as if you were discussing the weather."

"Agency people are just people. Anyway, I never did lie to you. The lying goes on at higher levels. They have specialists in it."

He emptied the beer can and reached into the sack for another one. He wished he'd gotten another six-pack. He popped the new top, took a long swallow.

He finally said, "There probably hasn't been a night in seven years that I haven't thought of you and hated what came between us. That's not a lie. But if you love *him*— and I think you do, and I think you should—then you've got to help me. Or he's dead."

"Don't overdo the nobility, Paul."

"Don't overdo the betrayed woman, Johanna. While you're busy feeling sorry for yourself, they're going to put a bullet in his head."

"Paul," she finally said, "I lied too. I said I loved you. I never loved you."

"All right. You never loved me."

"I loved the *idea* of you. Because you were fighting for the Kurds, and the Kurds needed fighters."

"Yes."

"I was so impressed with force. I thought it was a great secret."

"It's no secret at all."

"Do you know what happened? To us? After your mysterious disappearance?"

"Yes."

"You lie!" she screamed. "Goddamn you, *you lie.* Again. Again, you lie. You don't know. Nobody knows except—"

"A Russian told me. He doesn't run with your crowd."

"The details?"

"No. This Russian doesn't bother with details. He's too important to bother with the details. He told me the numbers."

"Well, I think it's important that you know the details. So that you can carry them around upstairs in that cold thing you call a brain."

Johanna was beautiful in the dark, now, here, after so much dreaming of her. He ached. He wanted her, wanted her love or her respect. So many things had come between them.

"Come with me." She got out.

He followed her. They crossed the street and stood before a big dark house. She led him up the walk into the foyer. She opened a second door with a key and they climbed three flights of stairs. He heard music coming from one of the floors. They reached the top, turned down a short hall. She opened another door. They stepped into her apartment.

"Sit down. Take your coat off. Get comfortable," she said coldly.

He sat on a couch. The apartment had high ceilings and tall old windows and was modestly furnished in books and potted plants and odd, angular pieces. It was white and cold. Johanna went to a table and returned with a thick sheaf of paper.

"Here," she said. "My memoirs. It turns out I'm not Lillian Hellman, but at least it's the truth." She paged through the messy manuscript and peeled off a batch of pages. "The last chapter. I want you to read it."

Chardy took the chapter from her and looked at the first page. It bore a simple title: *"Naman."*

"You didn't tap it?" said Lanahan in the van outside, looking at the hulking old house.

"I couldn't, Miles," said the wizard, irritation in his tone because an old hand like him had to show deference to someone as young and raw as Lanahan. "Yost won't let me. You get caught doing something like that and you got all kinds of troubles."

"I don't know how he expects us to bring this off if we can't play it hard," Miles said bitterly. "What about the other units? Are they in touch? Can we get in contact with them?"

"They're here, Miles. At least they should be. We've got Chardy nailed. But I didn't think we ought to have a radio linkup in this van. We knew we were going to be carrying Chardy around in this van. I bet if you wandered up the street you'd spot them."

"Just so Chardy doesn't spot them," Miles said.

"He won't. They're good boys, ex-cops, private eyes. I set it up just the way Yost says. Yost says keep Chardy in a sling, and in a sling he goes. If that's what Yost wants, that's what I'll give him."

"Screw Ver Steeg. Ver Steeg is so small he doesn't exist. He's a gofer. We're working for Sam Melman and don't you forget it."

Chardy read:

I did not have a great deal of time to feel grief over the sudden disappearance of Paul, because almost immediately our bad situation became much worse: we came under shell attack. In my seven months with Ulu Beg and his group we had never been fired upon. I had seen bombed-out villages, of course, but I had no experience to prepare me for the fury of a modern high-explosive barrage. There was no way to take cover and, really, no cover. Ulu Beg had made his camp in a high, flat place under a ridge. The black tents were lined up under the mouth of a cave. The explosions were so incredibly loud and came so quickly that in the first seconds I became totally disoriented. A few people made it to the cave but most of us fell to the earth. I have never been so scared. In the few seconds between the blasts I would look around and try to squirm into a safer position but it was very difficult because there was so much smoke and dust in the air.

I thought the shelling lasted for hours. When it let up I felt dizzy and disoriented. Additionally, I had breathed a lot of smoke. I could not stop trembling, and though I had seen many wounded men in my times in the mountains, nothing could prepare me for the shock of a firsthand view of what a high-powered shell can do to the human body. They could destroy it utterly.

I struggled to get some grip on myself, but even before the dust had settled Ulu Beg was running about. I had never seen him so desperate, yelling at people to move.

We ran chaotically through the dust. We ran up the sides of the hill and found a path along a ridge and ran along it, all of us, soldiers, their wives, all their children. I can still see that sight: over 100 men, women and children fleeing in abject panic. It looked like a scene from the beginning of World War II when the Germans bombed refugee columns in Poland. The women's dresses and scarves stood out gaudily in the clouds of dust and I could see the turbans of the men, and their khaki pantaloons billowing over their boots. Most pathetic, along that lonely track, were the children, several of whom had been separated from their parents (if indeed their parents had not been killed in the shelling).

That night we hid in caves but were afraid even to light fires. We tried the radio, using the special channel as Chardy had instructed. But there was nothing. I even tried, thinking my English might be recognized by listeners back in Rezā'iyeh, but there was nothing at all. We felt alone in the world. I looked at the mountains in new fright. They had been so beautiful to me once, and now they scared me. If the Iraqis closed in we could hardly defend ourselves. If snow came and sealed us in a pass, we would certainly starve, for we had no food except what we could carry. And several people were badly hurt, including the wife of Amir Tawfiq, the man who commanded after Ulu Beg.

We saw Iraqis the next morning but they were far beneath us. Still, Ulu Beg believed it to be a large formation in pursuit of us. He said it would take them hours to reach us, but by that time we'd be gone.

"Gone to where?" asked Amir Tawfiq.

"To the border," Ulu Beg said. He said the Shah would give us safety.

Amir Tawfiq spat into the dust. The cartridges on his chest rattled. He was about 25. Amir Tawfiq said that the Shah was a black pig who suckled jackals. Ulu Beg told him we had no choice, and that was the end of the discussion.

We marched through the mountains for four days. Twice more we were shelled. The first shelling was the worst and three of the group were killed and several more wounded. They screamed to go along with us. But we had no choice. We had to push ahead.

My memories are quite indistinct. At one time Russian jets seemed to hunt us. We crouched in a long ravine and hid behind rocks—over a hundred people. We could see the shadow of the airplane passing over the ground and hear its roar, but could not see it because the sun was so bright. Apo, Ulu Beg's oldest boy, hid with me.

The nights were very cold. We huddled together in caves or ravines and were still afraid to light fires. It was at these moments I felt the most alone. I wasn't really a Kurd. I was an American, a foolish one, caught where she had no business to be. I didn't think we really had a chance. We were on foot, running out of food and energy. There were no donkeys. We had come a terrible distance, we had a terrible distance to go and we were being pursued by men in machines who wanted to kill us.

I heard some men talking. They said we were doomed. It was all over. We'd never get out. Ulu Beg said no. He said we had friends. Jardi's friends. Jardi's friends would help us.

We were almost there. I asked Ulu Beg how much farther? He pointed to a gap just ahead between mountains.

Ulu Beg asked me to come with him to talk to the Iranians.

We went down the trail and over the dusty rock, the two of us. The trail began to rise to the pass and we climbed between the forbidding cliffs. I fought to keep up. I wondered how the children would make this last, hardest part of the climb.

We were so close! The nightmare would soon be over! But I was also terrified that something would happen, so late, so close to survival.

We came over the crest. The land here was scorched. Nothing grew. For miles and miles it looked dead. There was no vegetation, no anything. It was the defoliated zone where the Iraqis had poured chemical poisons on the earth to prevent border crossings and resupply from Iran. I looked and could see where a stream had been cemented over.

We went ahead. If a Russian plane or helicopter came and caught us in the open, we'd be killed. Still, we didn't have the luxury of waiting for nightfall. We picked our way through this wasteland until at last, several hours later, I could see the wire fence and the border station—and green plants again. The station was a low cinderblock building, with the Shah's flag billowing on a pole near it. There were several military vehicles parked there too.

We raced to the gate. They had seen us coming and were ready. The officer in charge was a young major of very stiff and correct bearing. His name was Major

Mejhati—he wore it proudly on a tag on the chest of his battle tunic. His uniform was heavily starched.

He asked me in Farsi if I was an American. I said yes. He thought I looked American, even though I was dressed like a Kurd. He had been in America for a year and knew what American women looked like.

I explained to him that 100 people would be coming shortly, that some were wounded, some were children and all were hungry and exhausted. They were being pursued by Iraqis in Russian tanks, I told him.

He asked me what part of America I was from. I don't know why he asked that. Anyway I told him.

He considered Boston a lovely town. He told me that he'd been to some Army college in Kansas. He told me he really liked America, America was a very great country and that he wished Iran was more like America.

I was afraid we'd be there for hours. Iranians love to talk and move slowly. They hate to be confronted with an actual reality.

Then he asked if these Kurds were of the Pesh Merga, the mountain fighters making a war against the Iraqis. I said yes. He said they could admit no Kurds. It was a new policy. He said he would be glad to have me come into his country but it was a new policy and the border was now closed to the Pesh Merga.

I wasn't sure I'd understood him. I thought I'd misheard. I wasn't sure what he was talking about. I tried to get my composure back.

"There's an arrangement," I said. "Between the governments. Between my government and your government and the Pesh Merga."

"There is no arrangement," he said. Several of his officers and soldiers had their guns out and came over to us. They looked at us rudely.

I pointed to Ulu Beg. I remember that I said, "This man is famous. This is the famous Ulu Beg. He is a high officer in the Pesh Merga."

Major Mejhati said the American lady was free to come into his country but that the Kurd was not. He said he'd have his men shoot if the Kurd didn't move away from the border.

I told him there had been an American officer with us, an important man, with high connections in Tehran. . . .

But they told us that all the Americans were gone.

Ulu Beg turned and began to walk back to his people.

I ran after him.

Chardy set the manuscript down. She was sitting across from him. She had not even taken her coat off.

"You should have crossed the border, Johanna. That was a foolish thing to do."

"I couldn't, Paul. Keep reading."

We ran all that day and most of the next. We headed north, farther into the mountains. Our new goal was Turkey, where the border was not heavily guarded. It was a bitter solution to our problem, since the Kurds—and most of the Middle East—hate nothing more than the Turks, who for centuries, in their Ottoman Empire, ruled in corrupt greed.

The plan was then to continue north, into Russia. I knew that in his mind Ulu Beg was retracing the journey of Mullah Mustafa Barzani, who fled Iran after the collapse of the Kurdish republic at Mahābād in 1947. Barzani had gone into exile for 11 years in the Soviet Union. The irony of fleeing the Iraqis—who were led and supplied by the Russians—for Turkey and then

Russia, did not strike me at the time. Now it seems to illustrate to me a basic principle of Middle Eastern history and politics: ideology means nothing.

Finally, it was the sixth day, in the morning. We had found some caves and at last dared light a fire. We had even found a spring that was not cemented over.

Somebody turned on the radio—it was a standard procedure, for Jardi, as the Kurds called him, had always tried to make his contact with Rezā'iyeh in the morning—and suddenly, where for five days there had been nothing, there was a signal.

There was, as I understand, a certain code sequence to be gotten through before communications commenced. I heard Ulu Beg speaking in his awkward English.

"Fred to Tom," he was saying. "Fred to Tom."

The radio, a Russian thing like all the equipment Paul had brought, hissed and crackled.

I heard English words—"Tom to Fred, Tom to Fred"—and recognized the voice. It was Paul Chardy's.

"Do you remember that part, Paul?" she asked.

It was so still in the room. Chardy looked over at her. At last he said, "Yes, I remember," and turned back to the pages.

We waited in the clearing. The helicopters would come at four, Paul Chardy had said. There would be six of them, and they'd have to make two or three sorties to get everybody out. It had to be orderly, he said, no panic, no crowding, and it would take some time but they'd get everybody out.

The men were praising Allah the Merciful for their

deliverance but Ulu Beg said to praise Jardi and his friends from America.

We seemed to wait a year. It was really only a few hours. By now the skies had cleared, and the sun was very hot. On higher peaks snowcaps reflected back at us. A few scrub oaks stood about in the clearing.

The people gathered in these few trees and I could see them laughing and lounging about, the bright colors of their clothes showing through the brown branches.

I had gone with Ulu Beg to a ridge above the clearing where we took some cover behind a group of rocks. I asked him if he was expecting trouble.

"I always expect trouble," he said.

His face was caked with dust. The lips were cracked and almost white, his eyes a tired blue. He had taken his turban off and I was struck by his hair, which was almost a brownish blond. He had very powerful eyes.

He told me to go down below to wait for the helicopters.

"I will stay," I said.

We heard the helicopters before we saw them. They rose over the crest of the hill. It was an extraordinary sight for me. I stared at them in almost dumb disbelief.

There were, as Paul had promised, six of them. They hovered in the sky. On the ground, Amir Tawfiq ignited a green smoke bomb. A pillar of green rose through the trees.

The helicopters were gray things, and had the bull's-eye Royal Iranian insignia on them. Their noses glittered in the sun because of all the glass or plastic. They were much bigger than I'd imagined. They generated a great deal of noise. They were in a formation of two lines, three each. They lowered themselves from the sky, dark and big. I could see the pilots in helmets and sunglasses behind the windshields.

Their rotors pulled up the dust, which spun and whirled. It rose and stung my eyes. Green smoke whipped through the air. Wind beat against us and I could see the leaves of the trees shaking off.

I could see the two little boys, Apo and Memed, sitting off to one side. I could see Amir Tawfiq and his wife, whose arm was heavily bandaged. I could see Kak Farzanda, the old man, waiting patiently. I could see Haji Ishmail, who had been a porter in Baghdad before leaving to join the fight in the mountains. I could see Sulheya, the old woman, in her black scarf, who had told me stories and myths that I had recorded, and her daughter Nasreen, who did the cooking. I could see . . . well, I could see them all, people I'd lived with for seven months and grown, as much as is possible for a foreigner, a foreign woman even, to love.

The helicopters hung over the trees and for a while I did not quite understand what was happening. I stood, quite stupidly. There was a commotion in the dust down below.

Ulu Beg had turned and I heard him say, "Russians."

Men in the helicopter doorways were shooting into the trees. Dust flew. I could see tree branches breaking. Links of color began to spit from the guns the men were shooting. It was as if they were hosing the trees with light. Sparks flew and fires started.

Beside me, Ulu Beg fired with his Russian gun. I could see a helicopter tilt as the glass of the windshield broke. *Kill them,* I felt myself thinking. The machine began to fall, tilting crazily. It broke up when it hit. Its blade thrashed at the earth. It exploded into a huge oily

wave of flame which spilled through the clearing. I was
knocked back.

The men in the helicopters were shooting at us. Bullets were hitting rocks and banging off. The stench of
burning gasoline reached my nose. I was so mixed up I
almost walked into the terrible panorama beneath us,
but Ulu Beg grabbed my arm and pulled me down the
far side of the ridge to a dark ravine. We tumbled down
its side, sliding through the rocks. In my sheer terror, I
did not feel any pain. We moved deeper along it until
pressed into a dark crevice. I could see a helicopter
overhead. It hung there for the longest time. Ulu Beg
had his Russian gun ready. But then the helicopter rose
from the sky and vanished. Two columns of smoke rose
in the sky, one huge and black and the other green.

"Did the Russian tell you about that?" Johanna asked
him as he laid down the last page.

"No," Chardy said. "Not the details."

"Was the ambush the part of the other thing? Was it
part of some larger betrayal? Were you under orders? All
those months when I loved you, when you fought with the
Kurds—did you know? Did you know how it would
end?"

"Of course not."

"But that *was* you on the radio?"

Chardy remembered it, but not very well. It was a Soviet LP-56 model, with double amplification and some
kind of frequency scanner thing, standard issue in Soviet
armored units. He remembered the microphone in his
hand, a heavy, blocky thing. They were way behind in
radios, he remembered thinking. He had felt so numb.

"What?" she said.

"Yes," he said.

He remembered the KGB colonel, Speshnev, had been pleased with his performance.

"Why, Paul?" she said quietly.

"I—it was very important to them to kill or capture Ulu Beg," he said.

"But why did you help them?"

"I didn't have any choice."

"Did they torture you?"

"They had some fun. But it wasn't that."

"Tell me, Paul. Why?"

"Johanna, I can't tell you. And I can't change a thing now. I guess I'm really here to try and make it up."

"Nobody made anything up for the Kurds."

"Johanna, he's here to kill. Suppose some more children get stuck in the crossfire? Suppose it's another massacre? Suppose somebody innocent—"

"*We* armed Ulu Beg. *We* supported him. *We* urged him on. Paul, nobody's innocent."

"Johanna—"

"Paul, get out of here. I can't help you, I won't help you. What's going to happen will happen. *Insha'allah:* God's will. The Kurds say, 'Do not hesitate to let the vengeance fall on the head of your enemy.' "

He looked at her.

She said, "Get out, Paul, I'm so tired."

He stood.

"Don't ever try to see me again. I swear I'll call the police."

Chardy stood outside her house in the cold. He wondered if they'd followed him and after a few minutes the van pulled up. He walked across the street and got into it.

"How did it go?" asked Lanahan.

"Terrible," he said, sitting across from the boy in

back. The van started and he looked out the window as lights and dark houses fled by.

"Who the fuck does she think she is? What the fuck does she think this is all about? Okay, she won't help us, we've got some tricks we can throw her way. We'll—"

Chardy had the boy by the thick lapels of his raincoat and rammed him against the side of the van, feeling the head slap hard against the glass of the window.

"Hey, *hey.*" The wizard in front turned, horrified. "Take it easy, you guys."

But Chardy planted a forearm against the boy's throat, pinning his neck against the seat, and told him to watch his fucking mouth. Then he released him and sat back.

The boy shook his head woozily and touched his throat. Fear showed in his wide eyes and trembling fingers, but the fear turned to rage.

"You *are* an animal," he said.

Chardy looked out the window, into the dark.

They returned to the hotel sullenly. It was nearly midnight. Chardy went to the bar and had a few more beers. He looked around the room—it was pretty packed—for the biggest man he could see, found him, and went to pick a fight. But the man turned out to be timid, and left quickly, and people stayed so far from Chardy after that that he finally decided to go to bed.

He slept poorly, thinking of helicopters.

The phone roused him early the next morning. He blinked awake in the gray light in a messy room. He had a headache and a sour taste in his mouth. He answered.

"Paul?"

"Yes?"

Her voice held promise of a question, but did not ask it. He gripped the phone so tight he thought he'd shatter the plastic.

She said, "I have to see you."

"Why?"

"Paul, you son of a bitch. Why didn't you stay in Chicago?"

He looked at his Rolex to discover it was 7:30.

"I haven't slept," she said. "I seem to be a little nuts. I did some speed a little while ago."

"Take a nap, for Christ's sakes. Then meet me someplace in the open. Outside."

"By the river. By the boathouse. Off Boylston. Anyone can tell you where it is. At noon."

"I'll see you then."

"Paul. Please come alone. Don't bring any little men in overcoats."

9

Ulu Beg sat next to a black man. He'd learned that the black men were best. Between El Paso and Fort Worth, an endless flat monotony, he had sat with a white man who talked and talked. The tales were filled with unknowable references—the Spurs, mortgage rates, gas prices, the Oilers, Johnny Carson, the PTA, waterfront lots, barking dogs—that troubled his brain. He kept a smile on his face and nodded eagerly for the hours of the journey, and when at last he was freed found himself waxen, shaky, slimy with perspiration.

So Ulu Beg looked for black men. You could sit next to a black man for hours and he would say nothing. He would not see you. He would sit encased in his own furious silence, absorbed and bitter. Ulu Beg was somehow drawn to them. Were they America's Kurds? For, like the Kurds, they were a manly and handsome people, intent upon preserving their own ways. They had a dignity, an Islamic stillness he could understand. And they were skeptical of the America around them, he could sense that too. Yet they had never retreated to the mountains to fight. He wondered why. He thought it might have to do with the music they always listened to, the huge radios they carried with them everywhere.

Beyond the glass of the bus window the state of Arkansas rolled past, flat and green.

The black man stirred. He was a large and silent man with small angry eyes in his huge face. He rattled the newspaper he was reading. Ulu Beg could see in black letters:

**MAN TAKEN BY UFO FOURTH TIME
SALLY, BURT: SECOND TIME AROUND?
CHERYL LADD: DAVID ABUSED ME**

Ulu Beg tried to get comfortable. He was not used to sitting for long periods of time. He'd sat still very seldom in his life. He shifted his pack, which he carried in his arms rather than storing on the overhead rack, squirming awkwardly. His elbow poked into the black man's outstretched newspaper.

"Sorry," he said, drawing into his seat even farther.

The black man made an elaborate ceremony of turning the page, claiming for himself even larger amounts of space.

Ulu Beg looked past him, out the window again.

Arkansas. After Arkansas, Kentucky, Tennessee. Then Ohio. Then . . .

They were strange names and stranger places. He almost didn't dare say them, even though the drilling had improved his English greatly; and he had memorized them, that curious, shambling route up through the middle of America, through dirty towns of no distinction that all looked the same. He'd been on the journey now for many days and would continue for many more.

"There is no hurry," they had told him. "Caution is better than risk. Three certain steps back are better than one risky step forward."

Little Rock upcoming. Memphis, then Bowling Green.

By bus, by train, but never by airplane. Americans were crazy with fear about airplane hijackers, terrorists, killers, and so there was no more dangerous place for a man with a gun in America than an airport.

Lexington, Huntington. Always the same. Roll into a city bus station late at night, or, if arriving in the day, wait till nightfall. Then, with certainty, there will be a small hotel that caters to travelers without much money, without pasts and futures—*transients,* the sign will say. Take a cheap room. Leave it only to eat. Eat only in small restaurants, where you do not have to order elaborate meals. Stay for several days. If you stay more than three, change hotels. Then move on.

Ulu Beg was becoming something of an expert on such a life, and the places required by it. The hotels were full of old men with bleak eyes who spat and smelled of liquor, who would talk to anyone or no one. This was no America of wealth and might; it was a mean place, like the slums in any country, especially for lonesome men with problems: no money, no homes, no job. Much hate. These men without women lived on and fed off their hate. They hated the blacks—who hated them in turn—and they hated the "others"—that mysterious remainder of the world which they did not fathom but which somehow seemed to have the skill to live nicely. They hated children, who had futures; and they hated women, for not seeing them; they hated each other; they hated themselves.

Yet they did not seem to notice Ulu Beg, or if they did, because he fit into no category, they could not hate him. They ignored him.

SURGEON SUED WHEN BREAST SLIPS
I KILLED MY BABY, CRIB-DEATH MOM SOBS
NEW CANCER CURE FOUND BY MEX DOCS

They were right. They could not prepare him for America. Nothing could prepare him for America. They had prepared him for much but they had not prepared him for the hate. It was as if he had never left the dangerous streets, the gun-haunted hills, the ugly free-fire zone of the Middle East. There was a war here too. The old men in the hotels that stank of disinfectant and had bugs that bit you in the night—as at home. The black men, in angry knots on the street corners: the young ones looked like tough young Hanafis in a Sunni area. Solitary old Negroes, who moved so slow you'd think they'd seen their own death waiting at the end of the block. The women, both inviting and hostile. Could they all be whores? Painted like Baghdad harlots for sure, thrusting their hips and breasts and fat mouths at you. Yet they were brittle with a kind of fear too. But worst of all he saw were the white men.

Masters of this world? Rulers, emperors? Conquerors of the moon?

He'd never seen masters so sullen and wan. It is worse to suffer dishonor in this world than death, the Kurds say. Kurdistan or death, the Kurds say. Life passes, honor remains, the Kurds say.

No white American could say such things. They were like the corrupt old Ottomans—America a tottering Ottoman empire, as Byzantine, as greedy, as muscleless. American men sweated because they were so fat. They did not seem to own their own streets but merely to lease them at exorbitant rates. God willed nothing for them, because God could not see them.

Or maybe it was the weather, or maybe it was the city. Whatever, the air seemed blue in the cities he passed through—blue with rising smoke, with rising steam, blue with the nighttime hues of huge lamps, blue with hate. At any moment it would break apart and the groups would begin to hunt each other in the streets. Beirut, Baghdad, Tehran, Tabriz: it had happened a hundred times in his part of the world, all the hate swirling madly until one red day it burst, spilling across the pavement. And it would happen here. Surely that was the message in all this. He saw no Jardis.

America had lost her Jardis. Sent them away, pushed them, driven them, murdered them, blasphemed them, for whatever mad reason.

In his travel he saw no Jardi—not the posture which had seemed to him in the mountains the very essence of America, which had been perhaps only the very essence of Jardi. Jardi always pushed them on.

But Jardi had betrayed him.

Jardi, Jardi: Why?

His head ached. Jardi's crime mocked him.

Jardi, you were my brother. Jardi, I loved you. You had honor, Jardi, you could not do such a thing.

Jardi, why? Who reached you, Jardi, who took you from us, who turned you against us? You would have died, Jardi, rather than betray us.

You once gave life, Jardi. You gave life to my son, Apo. Why would you then take it, my brother?

"Little Rock, folks. Municipal Station, 'bout ten minutes. Check the luggage rack overhead now."

The passengers stirred.

Ulu Beg looked out the window: in a mean blue city again.

" 'Bout motha-fuckin' *time,*" said the black man, turning another page in his newspaper.

MAGIC ENERGY PILLS RESTORE VITALITY
REDFORD TO DIRECT STREISAND
U.S. MUST SHOW SPINE, SAYS JOE DANZIG

10

Trewitt felt as if he were at an audience with Lyndon Johnson. This huge old man who carried a nickel Peacemaker in his holster, who never sweated through his mummified skin, who had hands like hams and eyes like razor slits and spouted laconic Texas justice, hellfire and brimstone: these *characters,* these essays in human charisma, they always meant trouble for Trewitt. They enchanted him and he stopped paying attention, which he knew to be both stupid and dangerous.

Vernon Tell was a supervisor in the U.S. Border Patrol, Agent in Charge of the Nogales, Arizona, station, and he was trying to explain to Trewitt and Bill Speight, who were sitting in his office under the weak fiction of being investigators for the Treasury Department's Bureau of Alcohol, Tobacco, and Firearms interested in an automatic-weapons violation, just how little there was to go on in the case of the death of his two officers, 11 March last. He wore gigantic yellow-tinted Bausch & Lomb shooting glasses and had the shortest crewcut Trewitt had ever seen. Trewitt blinked in the heat, trying to sort it all out. Evidently a climax in the conversation had been reached, for now the bulky old cop and Bill Speight rose. Trewitt felt the situation squirming out of control and wanted urgently to have it in his fingers again—if it had ever been so in the first place—but he felt himself rising too, drawn by Vernon Tell's creaky magnetism, and by the desire to demonstrate to a creep like Speight that he wasn't confused.

The old officer turned to him suddenly and said, "You in Vietnam, son?"

Trewitt, startled, felt he was being tested.

"No, sir," he said.

"Well," said Tell, whose forest-green uniform was crinkleless even though the air conditioning in his office was on the fritz and both Trewitt and Speight had wilted in their clothes, "reason I ask is most nights it's like Vietnam out there." He gestured to his window, through which, in blazing, cloudless radiance, could be seen a representative vista of the Southwest, miles and miles of scrub and desert and mountains and, incidentally, as Trewitt could see, a Dog 'n' Suds. "They come with dope and guns and they come just plain illegal. They come in planes and in Jeeps and on foot. It can get pretty wild and woolly."

"I'm sure it's a tough job," said Trewitt ineffectually.

"This-a-way," said Tell.

He took them down a glossy hall under the gaze of various official portraits and through a double set of green doors. Beyond lay a gate, which the old cop swiftly unlocked. This led into another hall and into an atmosphere that rose in thickness and discomfort in direct proportion to their penetration of it. Cells, empty, flanked them, but there was still another destination: at the end of the hall two uniformed men sat in a prim little office.

"How's our boy today?" Tell asked.

" 'Bout the same, sir."

"These gents come all the way from the East to see him."

Another door opened, a room, half cell and half not, a private little chamber. In the cell a single Mexican boy lounged on the cot, slim and sullen.

"This is what we drug up," said Tell. "His name is Hector Murillo. He's sixteen, from a village called Haitzo about a hundred miles south of Mexico City. Any of you speak Spanish?"

Trewitt and Speight shook their heads.

"We think Hector came over that night. The others are dead in the desert, or back on their side of the border, or got clean away. But from the tracks on the site, we know at least seven men went across. One of them, the man who did the shooting, in boots. We're still trying to track the make on the boots."

"What's his sorry story?" asked Bill Speight gruffly, mopping his face with a sodden handkerchief. Speight looked gray in the heat and his hair clung in lank strips to his forehead. Upstairs he'd been spry and folksy but the heat had finally gotten to him.

"Funny thing, he hasn't got one. We just found him wandering half-dead from thirst and craziness in the mountains a week after the shootings. Says he can't remember anything. Hector. *Cómo está la memoria?*"

"*Está nada.*"

"*Nada.* Nothing."

The sullen boy looked at them without interest, then turned and elegantly hawked a gob into a coffee tin and rolled to face the wall.

"These Mex kids, some of 'em are made out of steel," said Tell. "But unless we get some kind of break on the case, he's looking at Accessory to Murder One in the State Code and Violating the Civil Rights of my two men in the Federal."

"Jesus," blurted Trewitt, "he's only a boy," and saw

from the furious glare off Speight that he had made a mistake.

"They grow up fast on that side of the fence," Tell said.

"Any help coming from the Mexican authorities?" Speight wanted to know.

"The usual. Flowers to the widows and excuses. They'll kick down the doors of a few Nogales whorehouses."

"Any idea of who ran them across?"

"Mr. Speight, there's maybe two dozen coyote outfits in Mexican Nogales that move things—illegals or dope— into Los Estados. And there's hundreds of free-lancers, one-timers, amateurs, part-timers. Ask Hector."

But Hector would not look at them.

"In the old days, we'd have him talking. But that's all changed now," said Tell.

But Trewitt, studying the boy, who wore gym shoes, blue jeans, and a dirty T-shirt, did not think so. You could bang on that kid for a month and come up empty; a tough one; steel, the old cop had said. Trewitt shuddered at the hardness he sensed. He tried to imagine what made him so remote, tried to invent an image of childhood in some Mexican slum. But his imagination could not handle it beyond a few simpering visions of fat Mexican mamas and tortillas and everybody in white Mexican peasant suits. Yet he was moved by the boy.

"Well," said Speight, "thanks for your trouble, Mr. Tell." He probably wanted to head back to the motel bar for a rum-and-Coke. Trewitt had never seen a man drink so many rum-and-Cokes.

"Sooner or later Hector will decide to chat with us," the supervisor promised. "I'll give you a ring."

"Do you think you could let me run through your file on the border runners, the coyotes?" Speight asked.

"Don't see why not," said Tell.

They turned and left, and Trewitt made as if to follow. But his sense of poignancy for the rough, brave boy alone in an American jail, facing bad times, stormed over him. He paused, turned back.

The boy had perked up and sat on his bunk, eyeing Trewitt. His dark brown eyes were clear of emotion. In the office Trewitt heard the two old men enmeshed in some folksy conversation about the old days, the way things used to be. But Trewitt, in the cell, felt overwhelmed by the present, by the nowness of it all. He yearned to help the boy, soothe him somehow.

You should have been a social worker, he thought with disgust. This tough little prick would cut your throat for your wristwatch if he had the chance.

But an image came to him: Hector and the others in some kind of truck or van, prowling through the night on the way to something they must have only vaguely perceived as better. They would have been locked in with the Kurd for hours, with a strange tall man. What would they have made of him?

The boy looked at him coldly, and must have seen another gringo policeman. Trewitt felt he'd blundered again. He knew he should leave; he didn't belong in here. He felt vaguely unwholesome. He turned to leave—and then a terrific idea, from nowhere, detonated in his head.

"Hector," he said.

The boy's eyes stayed cold but came to focus on him. Speight's words boomed loudly behind him someplace and the supervisor and the guard laughed. Had they noticed his absence? His heart pounded.

He could see before him a picture: it floated, tantalizing him. It was a picture of a high-cheekboned, tall, bright-eyed man with a strong nose and blondish hair. It was on a wall. It was the picture an artist had projected from the old photo of Ulu Beg.

Blond. And tall. And strange.

Trewitt said, in the Spanish he had so recently denied knowing, "I'm a friend of the tall *norteamericano* with the yellow hair. The one with the gun. He is a big gangster. He thanks you for your silence."

The boy looked at him cautiously.

Trewitt could hear them laughing, old Speight and old Tell, two old men full of good humor. Would they miss him yet?

"You were betrayed," Trewitt invented. "Sold for money by the man who took you to the border. The tall man seeks vengeance." He hoped he had the right word for vengeance, *la venganza.*

"Tell him to cut the pig. Kill him. Make him bleed," the boy said coldly.

"The tall *norteamericano* gangster will see it happen," he said.

"Tell him to kill the pig Ramirez who let my brother die in the desert."

"It's done," said Trewitt, spinning to race out.

Ramirez!

He was so charged with ideas he was shaking. He couldn't stop thinking about it.

"Okay," he said, "I think we ought to bump something back to Ver Steeg. The hell with cables. I think we can call it in. Then we can open a link to Mexican Intelligence—I'm sure we have some guys in Mexico City who are in tight with them—and get a license to do some nosing around over there. *Then—*"

But Speight was not listening. He sat gazing thoughtfully into his rum-and-Coke. It wasn't even noon yet!

"Bill, I was saying—"

"I know, I know," said Speight, nodding. He took a long swallow. Trewitt knew he had once upon a time been a real comer, a man with a great future, though it was hard to believe it now. He looked so seedy and didn't want to be rushed into some mistake.

"You're probably right," he said. "That's a great idea, a fine idea. But maybe we ought to hold off on this one. Just for a while."

"But why?" Trewitt wanted to know. They sat in a dim bar, at last safe from the bright desert sun that seemed to bleach the color from the day almost instantly. They were not far from the border itself. Trewitt had glimpsed it just a few minutes ago; it looked like the Berlin wall, wire and gates and booths, and behind it he had seen shacks crusted on suddenly looming hills, a few packed, dirty streets—he had seen Mexico.

"Well . . ." Bill paused.

Trewitt waited.

"First, it never pays to make a big thing out of your own dope. Second, it never pays to rush in. Third, I am an old man and it's a hot day. Let's just sit on it, turn it around, see how it looks after the sun goes down."

"Well, the procedure is—"

"I know all the procedures, Jim."

"I just thought—"

"What I'd like to do—you can come along too, if you want; you might find it interesting—what I'd like to do is a little quiet nosing around. Let's just see what we can develop in a calm way."

"*Mexico?* You want to go to *Mexico?* We don't have any brief to—"

"Thousands of tourists go over there every day. You just walk across and walk back, it's that simple. It's done all the time."

"I don't know," said Trewitt. Mexico? It frightened him a little bit.

"We'll go as tourists. *Turistas.* We'll buy little curios and go to a few clubs and just have a fine time."

Trewitt finally nodded.

"*Turistas,*" Old Bill said again.

11

He waited by the huge old boathouse, a Victorian hulk; it was a clear, chill day, almost a fall day, and before him he could see the wind pushing rills across the water. Some Harvard clown was out in a scull working up a sweat and Chardy watched him propel himself down the river toward the next bridge, bending and exploding, bending, exploding. The rower developed surprising velocity and soon disappeared under the arches, but by that time Chardy's vision had locked on an approaching figure.

It seemed to take a great deal of time for her to cross the shelf of worn grass that separated the Georgian mansions of several Harvard houses from the cold Charles. She wore jeans over boots and her tweed jacket over a turtleneck. Her hair was hidden in a knit cap. She had on sunglasses and wore no makeup. She looked more severe, perhaps more bohemian, certainly more academic than last night.

Chardy walked to meet her.

"You get some sleep?"

"I'm fine," she said, without smiling.

"Let's go down to that bridge."

His head ached and he was a little nervous. A jogger, ears muffed against the cold, loped by and then, traveling the other direction, a cyclist on one of those jazzy, low-slung bikes. They reached the bridge at last, and walked to its center, passing between trees only a little open to the coming of spring.

Chardy leaned his elbows against the stone railing, feeling the cold wind bite; his ears stung. He had no gloves, he'd left them somewhere. Chardy could feel Johanna next to him. She had her arms closed around her body and looked cold.

He scanned the left bank, Memorial Drive, which ran through the trees. Cars sped along it. He looked off to the right, where the road was called Storrow Drive and studied the traffic on it, too.

"This should be all right," he said.

"What are you worried about?"

"They have parabolic mikes that can pick you up at two hundred feet. But you need a lot of gear to make it work, which means you need a van or a truck. I was looking for a van or a truck parked inconspicuously somewhere."

Chardy looked down at the water.

"I think," he said, "they've only let me see a little of the operation. I think it's much bigger than they've let me know. I haven't worked it out just yet—just what they're up to, just how much more they know than they say they know. They've got me working with some jerk without a human twitch in his body and an Ivy League drone and a dreamy kid. It's got to be bigger. I just know it is. And somebody's watching."

Sam, he thought. *Sam, I bet you're there.*

"It's safe to talk here?" she said.

"If they really want to nail you, they can do it, no matter what. But they don't have much respect for me now. So it's safe."

"You gave me such an awful night, Paul."

"I'm sorry."

"What choice do I really have?"

"None. If you care for him."

"I hate the fact we don't have a choice."

"I hate it too. But that's the game."

The wind was quite strong; he turned against it, looked the other way down the curving river. He could see the rower, fighting his way back to the boathouse.

"You hurt us so bad, Paul. Oh, you hurt us, Paul."

"Things happen," Chardy said. "You do your best and sometimes it's not nearly enough. I just got into something I couldn't handle. I'd give anything, my life, to have it to do over again. But I can't do anything about it."

The wind had really become strong now, and he could see it pushing up small waves in the river.

"Don't they believe in spring in Boston?" he said.

"Not till June."

"Has he gotten to you? Has anybody reached you?"

"No."

"Can you think of what he might do? Is there a Kurdish community, an exile community, where he might go? Are there people who might help him? Where can we look for him? What can we expect?"

"There's no Kurdish community, Paul. A few Kurds, I suppose. Paul, there's something I have to tell you. Something else. It was something I wanted to put into the book, but I couldn't. It's something I just wanted to forget, to bury away. But it comes back on me, Paul. It comes back at odd moments. I think it's made me a little crazy."

Chardy turned to look at her.

"Okay," he said. "Tell me."

"We went into the clearing after the helicopters left. We thought we could help people." She giggled in an odd way. "And we did. Most of them were . . . blown apart. You've been in wars; you'd know."

"It's—"

"It was like a meat shop. The bullet holes were burning, had burned through people. There was a smell of cooked meat. Paul, one of his boys was still alive. He had a bullet in his stomach that was burning. He was crying terribly. He was crying for his father. Ulu Beg knelt and told him that he loved him and kissed him on the lips and shot him through the temple with that gun you gave him. Then he walked around, shooting other people in pain. His own son, then maybe fifteen, maybe twenty others. They were all screaming."

Chardy was shaking his head slowly, breathing with difficulty.

"That was what it cost to become involved with the Americans, Paul. Not only the death of his family, his tribe, his way of life, but that he was required to kill his own child."

Chardy could say nothing.

"We've got to save him," she said.

"Somehow we'll do it," he said.

12

The pit is usually kept in half-dark and the supervisors, perhaps sensing they are not needed or wanted, look down on the analysts from a bank of brightly lit windows. They look like monks or angels, just pure dark silhouettes against the light. But down on the floor, nothing disturbs: by tradition there is no talking between the analysts—each sits in his or her cubicle, bent over a video display terminal, face illuminated in the weird glow of the screen, fingers clicking dryly.

It's a funny place for a war—or maybe not. Anyway, it *is* a war zone, a combat theater of operations: here the real battles are fought, the private Thermopylaes and Agincourts and Trafalgars of the Central Intelligence Agency, in electraglow (greenish) in sans serif letters on a TV screen plugged into an electric typewriter, observed by grim young men who rarely smile. Agents half the world away never dream that their shadow selves float in the currents of destiny in the great memory of the Langley computers.

It is a simple proposition: analysts are warriors. Given a terminal with access to the database, then given a mission by the upstairs people, they simply hunt for ways to make things happen. They look for links, oddities, chinks in armor; they look for irregularities, eccentricities, quirks, obsessions; they look for proofs, patterns, fates, tendencies. They comb, they cull, they sift and file. The good ones are calm and bright and, most importantly, literal-minded. They just have a brain for this kind of thing, a symbiosis with the software based on the sure knowledge that the machine is never ironic, never witty, never clever: it always says just what it means and does just what it is told; it has no quaint personality, but at the same time its etiquette is remorseless and its willingness to forgive nonexistent.

Down here also there are champions. Some men just do better than others, by gifts of genes or drive, by luck, by nerve. Miles Lanahan was one such. It was said he could do more with less data than any man in the pit. He became a kind of legend himself, and got so good, made them so scared of his talent, that he actually rose from the pit and entered the real world, the operational realm. It had not happened before in the pit's living memory. The current champion, however, was Michael Bluestein.

Michael Bluestein, twenty-four, had been a math major at MIT; he had the lazy genius, that unerring sureness of touch that scared everybody too. He also worked like a horse. On the same Sunday afternoon that Chardy struggled to come to terms with Johanna while evading Miles, Michael Bluestein sat in jeans and a polo shirt (Sunday shift cavalierly ignores the unstated dress code—another tradition) in the semidarkness in his cubicle in front of his VDT, nursing a sore left index finger—he played firstbase on a softball team (his teammates thought he worked at the Pentagon, which he encouraged because he caught such shit if he mentioned the Agency) and the day before, at practice, he had jammed it, pulling a low throw from the dirt. Now, stuff flowed across his screen, plucked up from the Ongoing Ops file on a random basis by the machine for his delectation, for his best effort. The stuff was Kurdish poetry.

Not that Bluestein was a fan of poetry: he didn't know T. S. Eliot from Elliot Maddox. But there was a big scam going on up at Security, and a sense of crisis had suffused the entire apparatus. Bluestein, not immune to these vibrations, could feel it. He didn't exactly know *what,* he didn't *have* to know exactly what. You just took so much on trust. Upstairs said: Kurdish, go through our data on Kurds, exhume our tangled relations, and look for traces of a particular Kurd, one Ulu Beg.

Funny, there wasn't much. Only the legendary Melman Report, the postmortem on Saladin II, and since Bluestein wasn't Blue Level cleared yet, he couldn't get the code to call it up. But there was very little else to go on; nobody knew much about the Kurds, or maybe some of the stuff was missing from the records. There was no pre-mission dope on Saladin II, none of the working papers or feasibility studies were there. Mildly odd, but not unheard of. There was also no critique scenario of the operation, pinpointing why it went sour. Again, mildly odd, but not unheard of. It wasn't that he *couldn't* get any more. If they gave you the codes, you could get anything and when they wanted you to check something, they gave you the codes. The dope just wasn't there.

But there were public documents, material acquired randomly, perhaps as part of Saladin II's planning, perhaps as part of the postmortem, and never examined terribly closely before. Political pamphlets, position papers, volumes of poetry (the Kurds are extremely poetic), posters, the text of an appeal to the U.N. in 1968 accusing the Iraqis of genocide, the notes of Baathist (reform party) meetings, Command Council decrees, hymns, the usual detritus of a failed political movement, all of it begrudgingly translated into English and programmed into the machine for textual examination.

Bluestein looked at the poem before him. Surely the translation was a poor one, for even allowing for his lack of enthusiasm for the material and even allowing for the Islamic tendency toward flowery, overstated rhetoric, it was simply awful.

> *We the suicide fighters,*
> *heroes of the nation,*
> *lions of black times*

ran one bit of doggerel.

> *We shall sacrifice our*
> *lives and our property*
> *for the sake*
> *of liberated Kurdistan.*

Just awful. Only one image arrested him: that "lions of black times" business, although it sounded something like a Roger Zelazny novel, sword and sorcery jazz. At any rate, it certainly was melodramatic.

> *Across our frontiers,*
> *we the suicide fighters,*
> *we shall wreak vengeance*
> *upon our enemy,*
> *the vengeance of the Kurds*
> *and of Kurdistan.*

Crazies. Wild-eyed Moslem fanatics. Imagine writing something so inflammatory, so pointlessly stupid.

We shall wreak vengeance
upon the many guilty hands
which sought
to destroy the Kurds . . .

Were the Kurds opening a terrorist franchise? Was that what this one was about? Bluestein shook his head. He tended to be moderate and orderly—he was a mathematician, after all—and the rawness of passion, its bald fury and literary artlessness somewhat offended him.

Bluestein had read enough. He cleared a line and typed EN on the screen, directing the computer to remove this one and pick out something new from the Kurdish file.

Another poem! They need an English major, not a math star, thought Bluestein. What was he supposed to make of it, anyhow? The preliminary note explained that this item was from a 1958 edition of *Roja Nu,* a letter-press literary, cultural, and political journal put out in Beirut by Celadet and Kamuran Bedir-Kahn between 1956 and 1963. Its author was identified in the note as— well, well, *well!*—U. Beg, later a Kurdish guerrilla. U. Beg?

Bluestein sighed heavily, and began to scroll the piece across his screen, trying to make sense of it. It's only words, he thought. He mistrusted words; give him numbers any time, and to hell with the Theory of Uncertainty. U. Beg is nothing special. More of the same: standard revolutionary garbage, full of flatulent zeal, outrage, the language soaring off into the realm of the ridiculous.

We the Kurds must be strong
and fight the masters of war
who would have us surrender.

We must fight the jackals of the night,
we must be lions.

We must fight the falcons of the sky,
we must be lions.

We must fight the merchants of honey
who offer sweet promises
and scents of delight
yet sell bitter, dead kernels
that become bones under the earth.
We must be lions.

And on and on it went. Spare me, please. Give me North Vietnamese agricultural production tables or Libyan import quotas or the price of oranges in Marrakech or the detonation sequence in Soviet intermediate range ballistic missiles. What can they want, what do they expect? Get an English major, for Christ's sakes; and Bluestein knew, because he dated one once, fierce and goofy and promiscuous and dramatic; she'd hurt him very badly.

He swiftly sent the item back into the computer memory and diddled up another from the Kurdish file, and while he waited for it to arrive he nursed his aching finger. His legs ached a little too; he was very tall, and they didn't quite fit in the cubicle without bending in places where they oughtn't bend. He wiggled the finger. Broken? No, probably not. He could bend it; it wasn't swollen too badly.

A new item trundled up across the screen. Poetry? Blessedly, no. The prelim note explained that it was an anonymous propaganda bulletin issuing from HEZ, a radical Kurdish underground group in Iraq, dated June of 1975, just a few months after Saladin II was closed down. It was predictably vitriolic, a torrent of abuse directed at the United States in general and one of its public figures in particular.

Bluestein had read a hundred of them and doubtless would read a hundred more. Pity the people in Translation who sit there all day long and work the stuff into English, so that it can be programmed into the computer memory. Don't they ever get *tired?* Bluestein supposed they did not; it was their job, after all. He knew they were all from the National Security Agency over at Fort Meade and must be grinds. Dreadful, uncreative work, and the way they were pouring it out meant somebody had lit a fire over there too, more evidence that this thing was big and that it had people worried. Yost Ver Steeg, the Security chief. It was his name on the system-time authorization forms, and he must have had some clout if he could get this stuff on-systemed this fast, and take up hundreds of pit hours in poring through it. But what could even this Yost Ver Steeg expect? Miracles? It didn't matter how hard you worked, how many computer hours were invested: the principle involved was the famous one involving poultry—i.e., chicken shit and chicken salad and the impossibility of transmogrifying one substance into the other. Like this grim denunciation he was reading—it proved only that there was hate in the world. We already knew that, thought Bluestein. That's why we're *here,* for God's sake. So the Third World hates the First. It should surprise nobody and it proves nothing.

Bluestein scanned the green letters, the columns of type flying across the screen. How long is this one, how long will it go on, what the hell is he looking for, why are they so scared, why is this so big, who is Yost Ver Steeg, why doesn't my finger stop hurting, why did Shelly Naskins dump me three years ago, when is *that* going to stop hurting and—

Bluestein halted.

Something just went click.

He looked very closely at the words before him, almost saying them aloud, feeling their weight, lipping their shape.

". . . a merchant of honey, who offered us sweet promises"—this was an American somebody in HEZ was describing—"and scents of delight. Yet he sold bitter, dead kernels that became bones under the earth."

Bluestein sat back.

It was the same.

Could it be a coincidence? No, not by any law of probability. Could it be a quote, an allusion? No, if this were a famous line, the preliminary note would have said so.

U. Beg, you bastard, he thought, you wrote the second version, too. You were *quoting* yourself.

And who was U. Beg talking about?

Bluestein checked, just to make sure, and then he began to dig through his directory for Yost Ver Steeg's emergency code. And a single image jumped into his head: it had nothing to do with Kurds or kernels or honey or bones. It was a picture of a huge, gleaming plate of chicken salad.

13

It was an awkward process. Chardy had not been with a woman for a long time. Among other anxieties he was frightened that he could not control his sudden appetite. But she understood and was helpful, guiding his hands, touching him when he was shy, pressing him where he was reluctant. Chardy felt himself passing through a great many landscapes, a great many colors. Was he in a museum? At some points he seemed to walk down a stately corridor at a stately pace; and at others he was racing upstairs or tipping dizzily down them, terrified of falling.

It seemed to last forever. When it finally finished, they were both sweaty and exhausted, worn in the pale light that suffused the room from the drawn shade. He could barely see her, she was only a form, a warmth in the darkness.

"It's been so long," he said.

She put her hand on his arm and they slept.

Around five, she roused him.

"Come on. Let's go to a restaurant. A really nice one. Let's spend some money. I haven't been out to dinner in years. You can wear your tie. I'll put on heels."

"Great," he said. "Can I get a shower?"

"Go ahead. It's through there."

He rose, walked absently to the bathroom.

"Paul?" Her voice had something in it, and as he turned he knew, and it astonished him that for a moment or two—or ten minutes or three hours or whatever—he'd actually forgotten, it had left his brain totally. Or maybe he'd willed himself to forget it so he could initiate her into his secret without shame.

"Paul," she said. "God, your back."

"Yes," Chardy said. His back: the living image of his weakness, written in flesh, a testament to his failure at the one important thing he'd ever tried to do.

"Oh, Jesus, Paul. My God."

Across Chardy's back were six clusters of scar tissue. Each identical to its five brothers: a central scar, a knot of curled piebald about the size of a half-dollar, a small, fiery sun, and around it a system of tinier agonies recorded in the flesh, smaller scars, streaks and comets and whorls of dead skin.

"Oh, Paul," she said.

She was staring at him.

"I sold you out, Johanna. I gave him you and Ulu Beg and the Kurds, I gave him the whole operation. I guess at the end I would have given him anything. But he didn't get it off me easily. It took him six days. Six sessions. I figured later he knew just how much my body could take. So he spaced it out. He took me as far as he could each day and then he quit and went to the officers' club. And I had to think about it that night."

"Oh, Jesus, Paul."

"He did it with a blowtorch. His name was Speshnev; he was the senior KGB officer in Iraq."

He looked at her.

"The fucker made me crazy. He scrambled my brain."

"Paul. They never told me. Nobody ever told me."

"Nobody ever knew. Nobody ever asked. You're the only person that knows. You and Speshnev."

"Paul—" She grabbed him, as though to hold him down, hold him in, control and comfort him, but he spun out of her grasp.

"Look at this, Johanna. You might as well see it all. Look carefully—they've healed up pretty good now." He showed her the scars on his wrists. "I cut 'em open on a flight to Moscow. But the Russians kept me alive."

"Please, Paul. Please, it'll be all right, it'll be fine," she said.

"No," he said. "No, it'll never be all right," he screamed. Then, with an effort, he controlled himself. "Look," he said, "I was raised by a crazy old Hungarian. He died in the nut house. He raised me to hate them. That old bastard—he used to whip it into me: 'Paulie, you must always fight them, you must never rest, you must always be a fighter.' Russians, Communists. But it was the way we lived, it was the way you lived in a city then. Fights every day, fights all the time, everywhere. Fights against everybody. You had to be tough or you were nothing. That's the first lesson, the one you never forgot. You're always showing them how tough you are. You had to do sports, do basketball, show them how tough you were out there. Listen, I was *king* in that world, that's how hard I pushed myself. Listen to me, Johanna, are you listening?"

He could not stop. He could not close himself down.

"Listen, Johanna, I never bugged out. I never did. I never let anybody down and I was in some tough scrapes. I was in Vietnam for seven years, Johanna. I was a company commander in the Marine Corps when I was twenty-three years old, I had two hundred teenagers depending on me. This was 'sixty-four, first year of the big battles in places nobody can even remember today. The gooks came out of nowhere in motorized regiments like panzer troops, with Chinese advisers calling the moves and coordinating artillery support. And all we had were dumb teenagers and a few tough old noncoms from Korea and pretend tough-guy lieutenants like me, and goddammit, Johanna, goddammit, if there was ever a right time to run, that was it''—he punched the wall behind her bed with a sudden, terrifying fury—''and we didn't move one fucking inch. That was some fight too, three days and nights without stop, and if you were going to run that was the time. Out of two hundred guys in that company, I had less than fifty left when the gooks finally quit.''

"Paul, you're hurting yourself. Your hand is bleeding—please, don't do tha—''

"No, *no!* You have to understand what he took from me. You have to see what this guy took from me. The motherfucker. The *motherfucker!''*

In his craziness he hit the wall again, crashing through the plaster. The blood ran down his arm.

"Paul, please, *please.''* She held him back, burying him in her warmth. "Jesus, you'll hurt yourself—you'll kill yourself,'' but he squirmed free.

"I had a hundred chances to split, to jerk off, to lie down. Johanna, the Agency put me in some jams, Frenchy and I *lived* for jams, we *loved* jams. We *specialized* in jams, we looked for them, we took some crazy, some stupid crazy reckless chances looking for jams, Johanna, I'm a lot of terrible, terrible things, but I was never a coward, never a *coward!''* He smashed at the wall.

"Paul, oh, God, you're hysterical, it's all right.''

But he could not stop sobbing.

"I fought him. I never fought anybody like I fought this guy but he wanted inside my head so bad, *so bad!* Why? Why was it so important to him to crack me? Did his life depend on it or something? Did he hate Ulu Beg that much? He wanted to split my head open and get in there forever. Oh, Jesus, why? Why, for Christ's sakes, *why?*''

Johanna suddenly realized what Chardy believed, and said as calmly as she could to the weeping, bleeding man in her bed, "Paul. He's not in there now. He's not."

"Yes, he is," Chardy said, furiously righteous in his conviction.

"You can drive him out. You can get rid of him."

"No. Never. He's in there."

"Please listen to me. Please, please—" She tried to push the tears from his face but was crying herself at the same time. "Paul, we'll get better. Jesus, what a pair. What a catch for the bin, you and I, Paul. God, we are so screwed up, God, what a freak show—the freak capital of America, this apartment." She was even laughing a little by now. "We'll get better, I swear to you—we'll beat them. We'll learn how to forgive ourselves, I swear we will."

"We'll help Ulu Beg. That will make us better."

"It will mend us. It will heal us."

She reached for his scars and touched them. Her finger traced the cruelest of contours, traced it around whorls, in an expanding universe, a spiral radiation outward and outward.

"Oh, Paul."

He heard her voice through the noise of his rage, his devouring self-loathing, and at last he let her reach him and calm him and they began to touch each other. Their mouths found each other and their bodies grew tense with physical hunger and he wanted her in the most piercing of ways but even as he held her, the first woman he had had in seven years, he thought he heard the Russian.

Dark had fallen. A buzzer rang in the apartment. Chardy could not identify the sound. She went to the wall and spoke into an intercom, asking who was there.

Chardy heard the name Lanahan.

"Paul," she called. "They want you."

"I heard," he said groggily. "Tell them I'm coming."

The wizard drove the van through the Cambridge traffic to a bridge over the Charles. The van reached a highway and turned toward the city and minutes later climbed the ramp to U.S. 93 toward Callahan tunnel, and finally Chardy said, "Where are we going?"

Lanahan sat up front, with the seat between himself and Chardy, and would not look back.

"You spend the day with her?"

"Where are we going?" Chardy repeated.

"I'm supposed to be able to tell them where you were all day. Were you with her?"

"I was doing my job, Miles. That's all you have to know. I don't report to you. All right?"

Lanahan considered.

Finally he said, "We're going to the airport."

"I thought Johanna was the point of this drill."

"You sure did your bit," Lanahan said.

"Don't poke me, Miles. I'll poke you right back."

"You guys are worse than a married couple," said the wizard.

"Just drive," said Lanahan. "We've got a plane to catch." He looked at his watch.

"You want to tell me what's going on, Miles?"

Lanahan held the silence dramatically, making some stupid point Chardy did not care much about, and finally said, "We think we know where Ulu Beg is going. And it isn't Boston."

Chardy almost smiled. He had just learned something—something that Miles maybe didn't want him to know. Now he saw it. Why was Miles so grumpy? He'd just gotten a big break. But Chardy knew why.

You bastards, he thought.

"You better tell me then, Miles," he said.

"Look"—Lanahan turned—"at what level was your political dialogue with him back during the operation? They're going to want to know back at Langley."

"It was pretty simple."

"Did you ever discuss the *origin* of the operation, its political context?"

"This was a few years ago. I don't remember."

"Well, you'd better try."

"Well, again I'd say, nothing fancy. He was curious. He had a great deal of admiration for America. He was passably acquainted with various American personalities—he listened to the BBC, just like everybody in the Mideast."

"And Johanna?"

"She talked with him. Of course. She speaks Kurdish, remember?"

"About?"

"Who knows? All kinds of things. She was there seven months."

Lanahan nodded.

"We just got a terrific break. One of our computer analysts—a real smart guy, they say—happened across a line of poetry Ulu Beg had written way back in 'fifty-eight. Did you know he was a poet?"

"They're all poets. Just like they're all revenge-crazy. It doesn't surprise me."

"And then he came across an anonymous political broadside, written years later, just after Saladin Two. It's from a radical Kurdish group calling itself HEZ. Do you know what that means?"

"Yes. 'Brigade.' The Pesh Merga was divided into ten *hez,* each composed of three to five battalions. Back in the mid-sixties Ulu Beg fought in big battles against the Iraqis around Rawāndūz and was a battalion commander in the Fourth *Hez.*"

"Well, HEZ is the name of a bitter group of veterans, violently anti-Western. Anyway, our analyst—he found an exact repetition of a phrase from Beg's poems in the broadside. *Exact.* It couldn't be coincidence. And the poem was too obscure for it to be quotation or allusion."

"He wrote the broadside then?" Chardy said.

"Yes. Do you know what it was about?"

"No."

"It was about a great and famous American villain, the mastermind behind the betrayal of the Kurds. It concluded with a sentence of death."

"The President?"

"No. Joseph Danzig."

Chardy smiled. "Old Joe," he said.

"Paul." Lanahan was furious. "Do you have any idea of the consequences if an Agency-trained and -sponsored Kurdish guerrilla with an Agency-provided automatic weapon were to put nine bullets into the head of one of the most famous men in America? You might somewhere, someplace find an obscure government document with a record of there once having been a Central Intelligence Agency, but you'd have to work awfully hard to find it."

But Chardy could see the logic to it. He could see the Kurd's fierce sense of justice. Joseph Danzig had pushed the CIA, which pushed Paul Chardy, who pushed Ulu Beg—into an abyss. Now the years have passed and here is Ulu Beg to push back: all the way to the top man. The same linkages, the same progression.

"Paul, you'd better stop smiling. They're very upset about this. They're *very* upset. Now they have to go to

Danzig, of course, and they don't like that. They've sent people to Nogales, to try and backtrack. They've—"

"I'll bet they're upset, Miles. Come on, Miles, tell me how upset they are?"

Lanahan said nothing.

The van had arrived by this time at Logan, but Chardy was not finished.

"You must have really thought I was stupid, Miles. You and Yost and—who? Sam? Is Sam in on it?"

"Chardy, I—"

"Shut up, Miles. Because didn't you think I'd notice we never spent much time on Ulu Beg's target possibilities in the first briefings? Did you think I'd miss that? Did you think I'd miss how important it was to keep me in sight—to follow me? Did you think I'd miss how upset you were when you couldn't find me this morning?"

Miles faced dead forward.

"You thought you knew who the target was. Your analysts told you so. The same boys who said he'd head for Johanna. You thought the target was *me*."

The van swooped into the cab lane and pulled to a halt at the Eastern terminal.

"You guys better hurry," said the wizard. "You can just make the six-thirty shuttle."

"Just a minute," Chardy said. "That was the real plan, wasn't it? Not to control Johanna at all, but to put me in the center ring and draw him to me."

"You don't know what you're talking about, Chardy," Miles said furiously. Then he said, "We had to use our assets the best way we could. You were covered the whole way."

"By you, Miles? I'd like to see you try to stop Ulu Beg from getting what he wanted."

"We did what was best. For everybody. Somebody has to make the hard decisions, Chardy. That's what—"

"There's a joke in this, Miles, though I doubt you'll find it funny. The joke is no man is safer from Ulu Beg in America than Paul Chardy."

Chardy choked on the bitter irony of it, and if he smiled now before these men, it was because he had trained himself not to show his pain. "In what the maps call Iraq but you and I know to be Kurdistan, Miles, in a battle in a foreign war, I saved the life of his oldest son, and Ulu Beg made me his brother."

14

His own capacity for adjustment sometimes amazed him; perhaps it was his real secret—and people were always asking him his "secret." In fifty-six years, for example, he had gotten used to being a Jew in Poland, then a Pole in the Bronx. He'd gotten used to Harvard, first as student, then as professor. Then he'd gotten used to government, to politics. And with politics, power. And with power, celebrity. And with celebrity—

Lights.

It seemed a journey from the darkness of ignorance to the lights of knowledge and in more than the metaphorical sense. Literally: Lights. He lived in them and sometimes felt as though his eyes would burn out from the strain of the flashbulbs, the glare of the TV minicams, as they were called (he knew the latest technical jargon), or, as now, the lights of a television studio.

This silly woman counted herself an expert on world affairs. She was a great toucher, as though her brains were in her fingertips. Even on the air she'd reach across and press them with gentle greed against his plump legs, and her eyes would radiate the warmth of love—or the warmth of enough barbiturates to flatten a dinosaur; it was difficult to say which—as she asked some astonishingly stupid question about the State of the World.

It was Danzig's habit—indeed, almost his trademark—that he consider gravely each nuance, each phrase, solemnly tensing his forehead, willing the light to drain from his eyes, before answering. He had studied himself on television—in fact, the administration in whose service he had labored as Security Advisor and Secretary of State (Oh, Glorious Days!) had paid a media consulting firm $50,000 to improve his televisability—and knew that his charm, so charismatic with one or two people, or small groups, or meetings, or parties, almost vanished on the airwaves, where he became an ominous, pedantic screwball. Thus he'd adopted (at the consultant's expensive counsel) the camouflage of the little professor. He even tended to overstate the slight Polish accent left in his syllables, on the ground that it forced reporters to listen more carefully, so they were less inclined to garble the quotes.

"And so, Dr. Danzig, in conclusion, would you say that we are again to enter a period of chill? Is the Cold War to begin again, or is there a thaw in sight?" She touched his knee again and looked at him warmly with those vacant, bagged-out eyes. You could have flown a plane through those pupils. More irritating, it was a question which proved conclusively that she had been paying not an iota's attention during the past several minutes. Still, this network paid him a handsome yearly retainer to fly up to New York once a week or so, and perform like a seal; and so he would.

But as Danzig took just an instant to formulate a response to the idiotic query, blinking against the fierce light, he was aware of several other aspects of his own circumstances.

He was aware that though this woman was stupid, and

vain, and frighteningly trivial, he'd like to make love to her just the same, even taking into account that as a rule television women were so punchy on barbs or their own faces, in bed they were rotten. Still, she was a star; and to have her was in a certain way to have America. Not to ignore the merely physical, however; of late he'd become conscious of his own long-sublimated libido, a buried secret self. In him, deep down, beneath the intellectual, beneath the political figure, beneath the celebrity, beneath even the old Jew: something prehistoric, primordial, a lecher, a rapist. He'd never needed sex before; now he thought of it all the time. He feared it would consume him; he half wanted it to.

But serious matters also consumed him: he was aware that the first volume of his memoirs—*Missions for the White House*—had just dropped two notches on the *Times* best-seller list, to Number 9, and that his paperback auction floor in Great Britain had been a meager £2,000, a great disappointment.

He was further aware that he was contractually obligated to deliver a second volume of *Missions for the White House,* the years 1973–1976, within two years; and that he did not want to. He faced *that* particular mission with an enormous reluctance, weariness even. There was, in fact, over half a ton of documents stored in his office in Washington and he had not even begun to examine them, and they would have to be absolutely mastered before he could ever begin to deliver up his vision of the past.

He was aware that the floor manager—more TV jargon—was standing just beside the bulky gray camera, circling his finger madly, signaling in the private language of television to speed it up, already.

And he was aware that standing a few feet behind the director, with a mild look on his calm face, a pinkish, healthy hue that set off his gray pinstripe suit, was an old friend and antagonist, Sam Melman of the Central Intelligence Agency.

"Karen," Danzig said, "these next years will be a test of our will, our nerve, our resolve as never before in human history. The Soviet Union must be put on notice that its raiding parties into the free world cannot and will not be tolerated. In this, I firmly support the President and the Secretary of State."

"Thank you, Dr. Joseph Danzig." She turned to the camera, smiled in brainless glee, and said, "And now to Terry, with this word."

"Cut to ad," somebody said. Onto a monitor a detergent commercial sprang to immediate life.

"Good, Kay, that was fine"—the godly voice from the booth. "You too, Doc, nicely done."

"You're a pro, Joe," said Kay—only the millions knew her as Karen. "You even read the camera cues, don't you?"

God, she was a beautiful woman.

"I *have* been on television a few other times," he said and she laughed. Beauty began with the teeth and hers were extraordinary. Her mouth. A shiver ran through him as he contemplated it. He ached for her. Now that the cameras were off them, she was not touching him. He wished she would. A beautiful, stylish woman. He ached for her. . . .

But she was up, unhooking her mike, and with a last nod raced back to the show's main set, which was surprisingly close by, just a few feet away, in fact.

The lights flashed off, leaving Danzig in darkness as he stood and demiked himself. He'd have to get the makeup off before he left—he looked like a Hamburg tart. He had a speech before the Council of Life Underwriters today at noon, for $7,500. As he unclipped the mike, his bodyguard—a shadow, but a shadow with a .357 magnum—

slipped discreetly into place a step back. Uckley today, the ex-marine—and a step behind came Sam Melman, with his bland, pleasant smile.

"Hello, Dr. Danzig," the intelligence executive said.

"Hello, Sam."

No hand was offered. Melman stood in his quiet suit—he must be here *alone,* Danzig realized in amazement, for he saw no entourage of earnest young men, no staff to open doors and call cabs and get coats, which surely a comer like Melman would have by this time earned—and waited patiently. He was a deputy director now, was he not? They'd been curiously friendly adversaries years back on the 40 Committee, when Danzig had been the White House adviser and Melman the slick Agency liaison.

"Has World War Three begun?" Danzig joked, for what else would bring a hotshot like Melman up from Langley to intercept him this early—not yet eight?

Melman smiled quietly—he had a deceptive easy warmth about him for such an ambitious man, a charm not unlike Danzig's own. A clever man, it was said, who if he played his cards right might one day be Director of Central Intelligence. Perhaps even now he had begun to fish for allies.

"Hello, Dr. Danzig. No, it hasn't, at least not the last time I checked. A certain matter has come up and I thought I might presume on our earlier relationship for a little chat." Sam was smooth; Sam was facile. His modest smile and warm eyes beckoned to Danzig.

"Of course."

"Preferably outside the precincts of a network show."

Danzig laughed. Yes, sensible.

"I'm free till noon, when I've got a seminar and a speech a few blocks away. Time enough?"

"More than enough, sir."

"Sam, let's dispense with the 'sir.' But I *would* appreciate it if you'd kneel and kiss my ring."

Sam laughed at this standard Danzig line.

A few minutes later they strode through the Rockefeller Plaza entrance of the RCA Building into the brisk, dirty New York morning. People swirled by, and Danzig coughed once, dryly, in the air.

"My limo? All right, Sam?"

"Would you be offended, Dr. Danzig, if I said I'd prefer one of our cars?"

Danzig, for the first time, began to see the urgency behind Sam's pleasant demeanor; the Agency didn't want anything on tape it didn't control.

The black Chevy drove aimlessly through the hectic Manhattan traffic, guided by a grim young man, next to whom sat Danzig's bodyguard. In back, Danzig listened while Melman talked. Danzig held—and occasionally looked down at—the Skorpion shell.

"And so I think you'll agree I'm somewhat understating the situation when I say we've both got problems," Melman was saying. "And for once your problem and our problem are the same problems."

Danzig looked at the shell. One penny's worth of metal from the farthest corners of the earth, and everything had changed. He looked up, out the window. Gray buildings lurched by as the car jerked uncertainly through the traffic. New York, always such a festival of sensation. Too much data, too many patterns, too many details, nothing coherent. Washington was a slower, saner city; here you never knew what you were going to get.

But it all dropped away; it meant nothing. A bullet in this world, in this most violent of all the decades in the most violent of all the centuries, was the ultimate reality, and Danzig was a collector of realities.

Of course there were always risks, especially in the Middle East, all those zealots, the whole thing so unstable, those fanatics, those bitter exiles. It had been rumored, for example, more than once that the PLO or various of its factions or units had put a mission out to eliminate him during one of his trips; but nothing had ever come of it. Or here, too, in America, there were always risks: cranks, nuts, screwballs, loonies with preposterous grudges; you could never guard against the crazy. But all that was generalized, distant, statistically improbable. That was then; this was now. Were those windows bulletproof? Perhaps. And how do you bulletproof glass, really bulletproof it? Can't the gunman simply get a bigger gun? And in these crowds of milling, insolent New Yorkers, angry and swarthy, could there really be this special man? Damn him, Melman had said a good man, a trained man. "We trained him ourselves, Dr. Danzig—that's the tough part. He's exceedingly competent. I'll show you the files."

No, Danzig had not wanted to see the files.

He looked again at the cartridge case and realized that while he had authorized airplanes to fly on missions in which so many tons of bombs were dropped on so many square miles in a certain North Vietnamese city, in full awareness of what statistically must ensue, he had never in his life held in his fingers this smallest common denominator of statecraft: the bullet.

He imagined one striking him, right now, through the glass, in the head. A blinding flash? A sense of surprise, of enveloping darkness? Or would the lights just blink off?

"It's not going to do *us* any good if he gets you; it's certainly not going to do *you*—"

"No, of course not."

"Well, I'd like to think we can work together on this thing."

Danzig didn't say anything. He stared gravely ahead.

"To begin with, we've got some suggestions."

Danzig remained silent.

"First, of course, your cooperation. That is, your silence. If the whistle is blown, if the media are brought in—God only knows what sort of a circus this thing could become. And it wouldn't make you any the safer. In fact, it might put you in more danger."

Danzig could see it: pools would be formed all across America, especially in the liberal areas, though also in the South and the Southwest, where he was also hated. When will the Kurd get Danzig? Money would be wagered. It would end up on the nightly news.

"Yes," he said.

"Good. Then, most importantly, we've got to cut down his access to you. If you stay still, you can be protected. If you don't, then you can't. You've got to cut down on your activities."

"I make my living that way. I'm booked for months. For years."

"Dr. Danzig, it's—"

"Yes, I know. Of course I'll cut down. I have to. But there are certain commitments that—*damn,* why did this have to happen?"

"Then, of course, beef up your security."

"Yes."

"And lastly—"

"Yes?"

"Well, we do have something of an advantage in this matter. We happen to have a man who knows this Kurd, who worked closely with him in fact. He even trained him. He was the Special Operations Division officer who went into Kurdistan in 'seventy-three."

"Yes?"

"His name is Chardy. He—"

"Chardy? My God, Chardy! I remember. He was captured, spent some time in a Soviet prison."

"Yes."

"Chardy," Danzig said again, turning the name over in his mind.

"The fact is, Chardy knows Ulu Beg, how he looks, how he thinks; that makes him immeasurably valuable. And he used to be a pretty good officer in a shooting situation."

"Well, I certainly hope this doesn't come to that. Is he going to run the effort to capture this Kurd?"

"Not exactly. He's no policeman. No, we had something else in mind for Chardy, something to take greater advantage of his knowledge."

"Yes?"

"We want to place him with you."

"Good God!" Danzig coughed. "With me? I just don't believe this is happening."

15

They discovered quickly that he was dead. Reynoldo Ramirez, killed by assailants in his own establishment in the prime of life, the newspaper said. What assailants? The newspaper was silent; so was the *Departamento de Policía*.

"They've been paid off," Speight said ominously.

Come on, thought Trewitt, but he didn't say anything. He had taken an almost instant dislike to Nogales—to Mexico. Blue and pink slum shacks hanging on the stony hillsides over a cheesy *turista* section of souvenir stalls, bars, dentists' offices and auto-trim shops. He hated it. A different quality to the air even, and the jabber of language that he could only partially follow did not ease his anxiety. Trewitt just wanted to get out of there.

But Old Bill sniffed something.

"I want to see Reynoldo Ramirez's *grave*," he said. "I want to *know* the man is dead."

Oh, God, thought Trewitt.

But they had hailed an Exclusivo cab and journeyed to the grave site. The place nauseated Trewitt. No clean Presbyterian deaths in Mexico: the cemetery was a kind of festival of the macabre, primitive and elemental. Crosses and sickly sweet flowers and hunched, praying Virgins painted in gaudy colors. And skulls.

Trewitt shuddered. He'd never seen the naked thing before, and here it was lying in the dust. Or rather, they: bones and heads everywhere, spilling out of vaults in the dusty hills, clattering out of niches and trenches. A wind knifed across the place, pushing before it a fine spray of sand that stung Trewitt's eyes and whipped his coat off his body like a flapping cape. He leaned into it, tasting grit.

"There it is," shouted Bill.

They stood by the elaborate marker, even now buried in dusty flowers. A weeping Virgin knelt over her fallen son amid the weeds. Trewitt was standing on a femur. He kicked it away. Looking out he could see scabby Nogales, hills encrusted with bright shacks, sheer walls over bendy little streets; and beyond that the fence of the border, like a DMZ line cutting through a combat zone; and beyond that, American Nogales, which was a neat and pretty town.

Trewitt looked back. In stone the marker read:

REYNOLDO RAMIREZ
MURIÓ EN
1982.

"There it is," he shouted. "Dead end."

Speight studied on the thing, looking it over.

"Wonder who brought the flowers?" he said.

Who cares, thought Trewitt. It would be dark soon; he wanted to get out of there. He looked across the boneyard to the Exclusivo cab awaiting them, its driver perched on the fender.

"Look, it's all over," said Trewitt. "He's gone. There's no link back to the night Ulu Beg came across. Let's get out of here."

But Speight stood rooted to the ground.

"Anybody could be down there. Or nobody," he finally said.

Trewitt didn't say anything.

"Maybe we ought to check out that joint of his," Speight finally said.

"Mr. Speight, we're not even supposed to *be* here. Now you want—"

But Speight did not seem to hear him.

"Yep," he said, "I think that's what we'll do." He started toward the cab, full of purpose.

Trewitt watched him go, and then realized he was standing alone in the cemetery and went racing after.

Several hours later he found himself undergoing a most peculiar torment: a deep self-consciousness, an acute embarrassment, a sense of being an imposter, all cut with a penetrating and secret sensation of delight.

The girl kept rubbing his thigh, the inside of it in fact, with her palm, dry and springy, knowing, educated in a certain way, and was simultaneously whispering of intriguing possibilities into his ear in Pidgin English.

"You got some nice money?"

"Ha, ha," laughed Trewitt uneasily, sipping gently at what was supposed to be a margarita but was most certainly warm fruit juice and ginger ale at eight bucks a crack, gringo rate. Other girls worked the floor of what was now called Oscar's. They were all tarts, but this one—Anita, just like in *West Side Story*—was all his, or he hers, as if by treaty or diplomatic agreement. No one impinged and he was trying to draw this out as long as possible, while Speight made inquiries. It occurred to him that maybe *he* ought to be asking the questions; after all, it was he who had unearthed this Ramirez, had unearthed this whole Mexican thing. He looked about uneasily, however, over fat Anita's shoulder, and saw in the darkness a sleazy room full of American students and Mexican businessmen. His loafers stuck to the floor; the odor of some kind of industrial-strength disinfectant lingered everywhere.

"You got some money. We go upstairs, baby?"

"Well, ahh—"

No, let Speight handle it. Speight was the old hand, Speight had been around, knew the ropes. And where was Speight? Trewitt had seen him talking to a big boy with a moustache. Had he disappeared?

"Come on, baby. Buy Anita a little drink. A little drink for Anita, okay, baby doll?"

"Uh, just a sec."

There. *There.* There was Speight, still with the moustache, talking animatedly at the back of the room. Give it to old Speight: he may have been peculiar in his ways, but he got things done. A pro.

"Come on, baby. Buy Anita some champagne."

Even Trewitt knew enough to nix the champagne—sure to be flat Canada Dry at $200 the jeroboam—and instead okayed something called a Mexican Hatdance: it looked like warm lemonade with a pale pink—did they use the same one over and over?—maraschino cherry in it, at only $12.50 a throw. At this rate he'd have to cash another traveler's check before long.

"Is okay?" asked the bartender.

"Fine, pal."

"Is Roberto." Roberto was a thin, handsome youth—he could not have been twenty yet—with a wispy moustache and soulful eyes.

"Glad to meetcha, Roberto," barked Trewitt, heartily *el turista estúpido* to the hilt, and commenced a little detective work of his own.

"Say," he said, "some fella was telling me you all had some excitement here coupla weeks back. A gunfight."

"Oh, sí," said the bartender eagerly. "A man, he was killed right here. Our boss Reynoldo. Bang-bang! Right almost where you are standing, señor."

"Shot down?"

"Just like the television. Real fast. Bang-bang."

"Wow."

"Roberto," said the girl in Spanish, "you stupid pig, keep your mouth shut, you don't know who this asshole is," then turned to Trewitt with a sweet Indian smile.

"What'd she say?" asked Trewitt.

"That you are the handsomest American she ever see."

"She's a fine-looking woman herself," Trewitt said, squeezing her flank.

Anita smiled at the compliment, revealing her remaining teeth. Yet Trewitt felt a strange attraction for her. She was so low. Somewhere deep inside his brain a tiny inflammation erupted; an image flashed before his eyes. He tried to banish it; it would not leave; in fact it became more exact, more perfect, more detailed. What drew him on was her offer of perfect freedom: for money you can do anything. It was simple and liberating. Anything. Against certain temptations he knew he was helpless. He could be pretty low himself. He was not a virgin and had twice been engaged; in each case he had made a goddess out of the young woman and fled in horror upon learning she was human. Yet here was a creature so human, so fleshy, so real, so authentic, she was driving him a little nuts. Here was freedom; here was escape. He thought of young nineteenth-century men who fled the hypocrisy of Victorian society and lost themselves in the privacy of the frontier, pursuing freedom and debauchery in the same impulse and, coincidentally, building an empire. American, British, Dodge City or Lucknow, it didn't matter; it was the same process. And here he was on the same sort of frontier, and here before him was a treasure of the frontier, his for the taking.

Trewitt shook his head. He could actually see her nipples beneath the clinging white top she wore. They were the size of fifty-cent pieces.

"Who did it, Bob? Gangsters?" Trewitt tried to get back on the track.

"Did what, señor?"

"The bang-bang. Poor old Reynoldo."

"Rest in peace," Roberto said. "Bad men. Evil men. Reynoldo has lots of enemies and even some of his friends—"

"Shut your mouth, stupid one," snapped Anita.

"What did she say?"

"She say she like you very much."

"Well, I like her too. A lot."

"Come on, baby," said Anita, running her open hand up the inside of Trewitt's leg, letting it linger warmly high up, "make Anita a happy girl."

Oh, Jesus, it felt good.

He swallowed, licked his lips.

"Anita make you real happy. There's a nice hole for you—take your choice."

Trewitt glanced about. Speight had vanished.

Trewitt thought, Well, if he needed me he would have gotten me, right? He just disappeared. What am I supposed to do now?

"Baby, we can do anything. Anything," she whispered. "I treat you real good. I make you real happy."

Oh, Jesus! Trewitt fought until he felt quite noble and then surrendered to his darker self meekly, without a whimper.

"Upstairs," he croaked.

"Anita must wash your thing. It's the rule," she said.

Maybe this wasn't such a good idea after all. *Thing,* she called it. He winced.

"Yeah," he said, his voice so quiet he had trouble hearing it himself. He tried to relax on the small cot but looked up to a Day-Glo Virgin on black velvet. It was only one of several religious gimcracks strewn and taped about the room: pictures, little painted statues, crucifixes. Was this some kind of shrine? His pants, meanwhile, were bunched around his knees, although he still wore his coat and tie and shirt; and a man with a coat and tie on whose balls are hanging out feels sublimely ridiculous. He gripped his wallet in his right hand.

Oh, this is a rotten idea. This is a really rotten idea. You ought to get out of here. You just ought to get the hell out of here. But he could not figure out how, and besides he'd already paid.

No door, of course. What did he expect, a Holiday Inn, complete with shower and Magic Fingers vibrator under the bed? Only a curtain sealed the dim little room off from the corridor and although the lights were low, the traffic in the hall was considerable. A regular rush hour. Now and then a peal of Mexican laughter would rise through the odor of disinfectant—it smelled like a *hospital* up here— and a man would swagger down the hall.

"I be back, baby," Anita said.

She dipped out the curtain and returned in a moment, holding a wash basin brimming with soapy water and a rough cloth.

"Rub-a-dub-dub," Trewitt joked bleakly.

She began to scrub him. She rubbed and wiped and grated without mercy to cleanse his tender equipment and though he had not been exactly fierce with desire in the preceding few moments, under this humbling assault he felt himself shrinking ever further.

"Be careful," he complained. Was she trying to *erase* it?

"It's nice, baby," she said. "It's not real big or nothing, but it's real good shaped, and clean. And gringos been trimmed."

Trewitt smiled tightly at this wonderful compliment.

She dried him roughly and then pulled back in triumph, flipping the towel into the hall, where it swirled to the floor.

She stood above him, an absurdly plump woman of nearly thirty-five, in a cheesy dress, all cleavage and density, an infinity of circles, globs, undulating horizons. She smiled hideously. Backing off, she reached down for her own hem, grabbed it and peeled upward, the dress constricting her flesh as it was yanked until she popped it off with a final tug and stood in cotton drawers, great gushy, floppy breasts with those enormous dark nipples wobbling across her front.

Now she'd step from those drawers next—panties was too modest a word for a garment of such magnitude—and a part of him was disgusted and debased, while at the same time another part, recovering, became entranced. She knelt to divest herself of the drawers, pivoting to deposit the huge filmy things on the table under the Day-Glo Virgin, and turned to face him, her bush a blot of darkness that seemed to separate her bulging belly from her thunderous thighs, without which the whole mass would collapse upon itself.

Yet the very peculiarity of the image—a huge Mexican prostitute standing above his pale gringo body, ribsy and stark—commandeered his imagination. The contrasts were vast and enticing: her hugeness, his frailty; his reluctance, her greed; her expertise, his clumsiness; his repression, her earthiness. His penis picked itself up in salute to the intensity of the moment.

"The mouth," he commanded hoarsely.

She knelt, obedient to his wishes.

Speight waited out back, beyond the sewer, in the yard of the shop called Argentina. He could smell the sewer, the suffocatingly dense odor of human waste, and hear water trickling through it. It was quiet here in the junky, walled yard but beyond, on the street, he could see whores prowling in the pools of light from the intermittent overhead lamps. The old fieldman in him looked for escape routes, just in case; but there were no escape routes, no real ones. Sure, he could hit the wall if things turned ugly, but at his age there was no way he'd scale ten feet of brick if somebody was shooting at him. So it was a simple, no-option proposition: he was lucky or he was not lucky.

He knew he should have briefed the boy—what was his name? It escaped him for just a moment: Trewitt, Trewitt. But Speight never knew what to say to such youngsters—there were so many of them these days, and he knew they thought him an old fart, long out of it, a relic, an antique. And what could the boy have done anyway? Covered him? With what? No, he would have complained and groused and second-guessed. Trewitt filled Speight with depression. If he was the future, the future was bleak. Speight didn't think Trewitt would work out.

He glanced at his watch. Oscar Meza had said fifteen minutes and twenty had passed. Speight coughed nervously, picked some scum off his lips, and wished they'd get there.

Five hundred dollars.

That's what it would cost for a chat with Reynoldo Ramirez, a chat with a dead man.

Oscar Meza, proprietor of Oscar's, formerly El Palacio, had wanted a thousand. Speight had thought more in terms of $300. Five hundred was all right, though he knew he'd have a tough time sailing it by Yost Ver Steeg if he didn't come up with something nice and solid. In the old days there was always enough money. You wanted it, you got it. No questions asked. In those days the outfit went full-out, first-class. Now, nickels and dimes and young smart kids who thought you belonged in a museum or a paperback novel. He knew he thought too frequently about the old days. Now—

The car swung into the yard. Speight crouched, watching. It was an old Chevy, a '58 or '59, rusted out badly. There must have been thousands of them in Nogales, rotting Mex cars, with broken windows and lead-painted fenders and doors from other vehicles.

Come on. Let's go, thought Speight.

The driver killed the engine. It died with a gasp and the car ticked hotly for several seconds. Speight could see the two men scanning the yard. They couldn't see him behind these crates. He could just sit there. It wasn't too late to forget it.

But he knew he couldn't forget the $500.

The $500 was now running the show.

Oh, hell, Speight thought.

He stood, stepped out.

"Over here, *amigos*," he called.

Now he was finished. He'd done it, or rather, had it done. He remembered similar moments from books— Rabbit Angstrom rising from the whore Ruth, Stingo from his Sophie—but they were no help at all. His experience was of a different denomination, with fat Anita on a dirty bed on a sticky floor in a room that smelled of Lysol, under the eye of a glowing Virgin. Yet he felt rather good. In fact he was astounded by his bliss. The actual moment, the actual ultimate instant, with the hulking woman down beneath him, working hard, his own hands gripping something, his muscles tense, his mind pinwheeling: yes, indeed. He smiled.

"Round the world, baby? Only feefty more dollar?"

"No. Oh, uh, no, I don't think so," Trewitt said dreamily.

"Come on, baby. We can have some more fun."

"Ah. I don't think so. I appreciate it, I really do. I just don't think so."

"Sure, baby. It's your money."

She retrieved her underpants and pulled the dress over her head and there she was, presto chango, the old Anita. It was as if nothing had happened, and he realized that for her nothing *had*.

He pulled up his pants, tucked in his shirt, and fastened his belt.

"Ten dollars, baby."

"Ten dollars! I already paid. Hey, I paid you a fair amount!"

"Rent, baby. You gotta rent the room. Is not free, nothing free. For the towel, the clean sheets"—yeah, fresh out of the dryer sometime in 1968—"It's for the big boss. He beat me up if I don't get it."

What was the difference? But this was costing a fortune. He was counting it out in ones when he heard the siren.

He raced down the steps two at a time, almost spilling out of control at the end as he lurched into the now-empty bar. The boy Roberto quietly polished glasses and nearby Oscar Meza sat at a table talking with a bulky policeman in a crisp tan uniform with a yellow tie—yes, yellow, canary yellow, screeching yellow—whose beefy shoulder was looped with a final ludicrous touch, a gold braid.

Trewitt tried to gain command of himself, but the cop looked over to fix him with a set of dead eyes.

Trewitt smiled casually, and tried to shuffle out.

He heard the word *gringo,* and the two men broke into laughter.

Trewitt reached the door and stepped into the night. He could see nothing except the railroad tracks beyond the street and beyond that, Oscar's competition, the Casa de Jason, another nightclub. Trewitt descended the steeply pitched parking lot to street level and turned. Five hundred yards ahead, beyond an arcade of canopied shops adjacent to the railroad tracks, lay the border; he could see it in lurid light, and the beggars and cabdrivers collecting there, a cruel, high fence, a traffic jam, booths, and a fortresslike bridge of offices overhead. He could see no flag; but, beyond the fence, he saw something perhaps more emblematic: the golden arches of McDonald's.

Then he saw the crowd. It had gathered just up the street at what seemed to be a bridge at the corner of Calle Buenos Aires and the Ruis Cortina. Indians, a few Americans, Mexican teenaged girls in tightly cut American jeans and blouses, but mostly policemen. Three or four gray pickups had been parked nearby and by their uniformity Trewitt realized they were official vehicles.

Warily, he walked into the crowd; he could hear, among other things, the trickle of water.

It smelled here. Something? What? The odor was overwhelmingly familiar. His nose picked it apart but could not identify it—too many other odors were woven into it. But it was disgusting.

The crowd had gathered at the bottom of the street. It was a cobbled, climbing street that traveled up the side of a hill, lit intermittently by overhead lamps. He could see signs of the shops that ran partway up the hill, before the road disappeared into darkness: a dental clinic, a TV and stereo shop, a small food shop on the other side of the street, and a few others. But Trewitt pushed his way through the crowd and came soon enough to the wall, where he stood by three policemen who were talking rapidly among themselves. Lights—there were lights back here. He could feel the warmth, the human warmth, of people all around. He was aware that the blank brick wall that stared back at him twenty feet away was the wall of Oscar's, of the whorehouse; the gurgle of water was very strong indeed, but he could not quite get to the edge, to look into the—the whatever it was that lay before him and had drawn all these people.

He gave a last, mighty shove, and broke through two men and came to the edge.

The scene, in fact, was a phenomenon of light. The Mexican faces, fat and slack, Indianesque in their unreadability, almost Asian, and the pencil moustaches; and the indifferently blazing headlamps from the police trucks, throwing beams that cut this way and that through the crowd, and a jumble of shadows on the wall beyond. And the Spanish, against it all, the Spanish in a thousand babbling tongues and incomprehensible dialects, jabbering, spiraling through the air. And the odor: he now recognized it for human waste, the stink of cesspool, of outhouse, of backed-up pipes, the smell of the toilet, the urinal, the smell of defecation. Miasmatic, it covered him like a fog, drilling through his sinuses; he winced at its power, feeling his eyes well with tears.

Bill Speight lay on his back in the sewer. Trewitt, at the edge, could just now make him out. Three or four different light beams pinned the old man against a cascade of stones and beer bottles and rusty pipes and assorted junk. The police were talking about *las botas,* Trewitt overheard as he stared at old Bill in the sewer.

Boots.

That was it: there was a delay until some high rubber waders could be found; no man would descend into the muck without them.

A flashbulb popped and in its brightness Trewitt could see that the old man had taken some kind of heavy-caliber or big-bore shell in the left side of the face. Shotgun, perhaps. The features had been peeled back off that side of his head; yet on the other, astonishingly, the old Bill prevailed. The vision so diverged from Trewitt's assumptions of human anatomy that he could make no sense of it.

Speight was soaked by the rushing water from a pipe. A shoe had come off and floated downstream, where it wedged against a rock. It was an old Wallaby.

They'd blown the side of his head in and thrown him into a sewer behind a whorehouse, Trewitt thought dumbly. He accepted and did not accept it. Only yesterday, as he sat throwing down rum-and-Cokes, old Speight had numbed him with an endless tale of the Korean War, an account that could have been in a foreign language, so full was it of obscure references, improbable characters, unlikely events. Halfway through, Trewitt realized he must have missed something important, for he had no idea what the man had been talking about. Now he was dead. In a sewer. Shot in the face.

Trewitt gripped the bricks before him for steadiness. Oh, Jesus, poor old bastard. He realized he was trembling, that he was cold. He looked again at Bill. Bill had been so alive just a few minutes ago. Trewitt thought he might be sick. He didn't know what to do. He could hear the police asking questions.

"Anybody know this old bird?"

"He was with another gringo in Oscar's. A young one."

"Where is he?"

"Still with his girl friend." There was some laughter.

"They get those boots yet?"

"Yes, they just arrived. Who's going down there?"

"Call Washington. Have them send a vice-president."
More laughter.

Then something occurred to Trewitt.

They—whoever *they* were—killed Speight for trying to find out about Ramirez.

He, Trewitt, had been with Speight.

He, Trewitt, had asked about Ramirez.

And then, and only then, did he panic.

16

On a Saturday night in Boston, in her high-ceilinged old room, Chardy lay beside her in the dark. Sleep had never come easily for him and it evaded him tonight. But that was fine; he would just listen to the breathing.

The night's lacework of shadows lay across the far end of the room, webs and links and flecks of brightness; moonlight threaded through the dark, gleaming cold. Chardy anchored himself against the coming of a bad minute or two by putting a hand against her arm. In Chicago there'd never been anything to touch.

Sometimes, then, over those years—frequently, if he was honest about it—he'd awaken weeping. A secret shame: big guys don't cry. Sometimes it was his back, which to this day became occasionally infected and could be quite painful. Or sometimes a sensation, a vision, would set it off: a twinge of pain, a picture of a hot blue flame. Or sometimes something even stupider: some police officer or fireman or boy scout's sudden heroism, as vicariously experienced through the newspaper; or an old pro basketball player, on the line looking at a one and one with a whole season's weight perched on his shoulder; or a young kid, a freshman, taking a jump shot in the last second of an NCAA game. It was the contrast that wrecked him each time: they'd passed their tests, he'd failed his.

Or he wept in confusion. There were so many things about it he didn't understand even now. Some aspects of it just didn't add up. He'd break it down and put it together again in a hundred different ways and it still never made sense. It was like one of those awful modern novels that everybody hated except three critics, full of fragments of plot, surrealistic moments of great vividness, odd discordant voices, textures achingly familiar but at the same time unknowable. He was not even certain what he did remember and what he did not; perhaps they'd used drugs on him. Whatever, it was all scrambled up; he could not get inside it.

Or he'd weep in rage. Punching walls was nothing new and once he'd broken his wrist. He dreamed of smashing heads: Speshnev's, Sam Melman's, his own. Them all: the Russians, for destroying him; his own side, for the cold, detached fury they'd directed at him; buddies like Frenchy Short for never coming by, whatever the rules—though of course Frenchy could not have come by, for even then he was dead; Johanna, for confirming his vision of himself. And, of course, last and most: himself. Sometimes he looked for fights. A cold need for pain would haunt him; he'd head for Rush Street and throw himself on somebody's girl, not caring for her at all; and the guy would have to challenge him and the guy would always have friends and Chardy would always wear a black eye for days, or lurch about with cracked ribs; he'd had three teeth knocked out—he wore an old man's bridge now— and a bad laceration on his chin, which the beard hid.

Nuts. Chardy, you are nuts.

Yet now, lying in the bed in the black New England night, it suddenly occurred to him with swift joy that he had a kind of chance. For with Johanna, all things were possible, a whole universe of things.

He felt he could save Ulu Beg from Ver Steeg and Lanahan. He could even save Joseph Danzig. He could save Sam Melman. All of them linked together by events of the past, chained and doomed, but he could break the chain; he felt the power. Ulu Beg, last reported at the border, moving probably toward them. He'd save him, and bind her to him forever. He'd make Beg in a crowd coming in on Danzig, and he'd nail him with a tackle and calm him down; then he'd talk to them; he'd get it all straightened out, somehow.

It's only been a week; there's plenty of time left.

Ulu Beg, I'll save you. He owed him, for not only had Ulu Beg brought him together with Johanna in the first place, seven years ago as now, he'd also, by allowing however accidentally his target to be known, virtually removed Johanna from the realm of interest of Miles Lanahan and Yost Ver Steeg and whatever other dark lords the two of them served. Chardy, whose importance seemed also to have diminished in the past several days, was for now free to travel on weekends and be with her, as he was now.

She moaned in her sleep, and shifted. He could not really see her, for the moonlight did not touch this corner of the room, yet he felt her: warmth, weight, sweetness of odor, a presence. Her arm warm and dry against his hand.

The telephone rang.

Chardy jumped at the noise, pulled himself up in the bed, and looked at his Rolex, which announced the hour of four.

Johanna stirred in the dark and seemed to swim for the telephone. He heard her speak briefly; then she turned.

"For you."

He took the phone.

Miles said, "Chardy? What the hell are you doing there?"

"It's the weekend, Miles. I can go anywhere."

"Not anymore you can't."

Chardy waited, and finally the young man said in a breathless, unpunctuated sentence, "Trewitt and Speight in Mexico and we lost Speight somebody blew his face off with a shotgun behind some whorehouse in Mexico where he wasn't supposed to be."

Chardy closed his eyes at the image. Behind a whorehouse. Old Bill, who was always around.

"Paul," Johanna said, "Paul, what is it?"

"Yost wants you down here. There's an early flight into National from Logan. We'll have somebody meet you."

Old Bill. In Mexico? Now why kill him? What had he come across? Who did it—the opposition, some jealous boyfriend, gangsters, a hunter whose shotgun wasn't on safe?

But there weren't any accidents in this sort of game.

"Paul. that flight. You'll be on it?"

"Yeah, sure," Chardy said, feeling suddenly that things had just changed and that the safety of the bedroom in which he lay hidden just seconds ago was forever gone. It frightened him a little. And then he had another thought.

"Look, Miles, you better get some people down there to bring that kid in. I could go myself. Without an old hand like Speight, that kid could get himself in a lot of trouble."

"Trewitt is missing," said Lanahan coldly.

"I see," said Chardy.

"He's dead too, you know," said Lanahan.

Chardy sighed. It was how these things worked.

"Yes," he said, "yes, I suppose he is."

17

Someone in the Dayton bus station had stolen his money.

Ulu Beg sat very still and tried not to panic. But without money he was dead. Any man in America without money is dead, but he would be deader than most, with no place to turn, no one to go to, and nothing but the Skorpion. He was still hundreds of miles from shelter.

They had given him a lot of money.

"By their standards you are a rich man. You could buy a Chevrolet car or a motorboat."

"I do not desire a Chevrolet car or a motorboat."

"Of course not. But remember, in America money is life. All things are possible for the man with money, all doors open, all women eager, all policemen friendly."

He sat in a plastic chair in a bright waiting room and tried to reconstruct the last seven or eight minutes. The bus from Louisville to Dayton was late, held up in traffic in Cincinnati. There had been a rush to get off. He had been mostly among black people, emotional, and at the arrival gate much hugging and squeezing had occurred as families reunited. He pushed through into this main room, all pale plastic, shiny and new. A few policemen and many more blacks stood about, also airmen in their blue uniforms.

And that is when he felt the lightness in his pocket.

Now seven or eight minutes had passed. He knew it had to have happened as he pushed through the blacks. So: a black person.

He examined them, wondering if the thief had fled instantly, and thought not. His eye searched out the blacks. An old man, invalid, in huge overcoat, talking crazily to himself. A beggar? Two tough boys with mounds of hair dancing to radios in a corner. A dapper businessman sitting three seats away, reading a magazine. Or a fat old woman in a flowered hat.

He didn't know what to do; he was helpless.

In the wallet, he had over $3,000. He could not go to the police. He ached at the loss of it.

He saw a third boy approach the two with the radios. They conferred quietly and then a ceremony began: one, then the other, slapped the outstretched hand, then clasped him by the wrist.

They were big young men in their late teens with unreadable faces and brown, blank eyes.

Ulu Beg stood, gathered his pack, and walked across the bus station to the three of them.

"You have a thing of mine. So give it back."

"Say what, Jack?" They looked at him suspiciously.

"You have a thing of mine. Give it back. Then, no trouble."

"What you talkin' 'bout, man?"

"A wallet. A wallet is missing."

"Don't know no motherfuckin' thing about no wallet."

"My wallet. I take it back now, please. Okay. No trouble."

"This dude lookin' for some trouble."

"You have my wallet," Ulu Beg said.

"Jack, take your face *outa* here."

"You have my wallet."

"Some kind of crazy motherfucker. Man, he tryin' for a trip to *Disneyland.*"

"Let's get outa here. Crazy motherfucker make me *nervous.*"

"Let's cut his ass up some."

"No, man. He motherfuckin' crazy."

"You have my wallet."

The three boys began to back away, confirming for Ulu Beg their guilt.

He followed them.

"Shit, man, you *nuts.*"

He followed them into the night.

They crossed a wide street under bright lights and headed toward a railway viaduct. They turned and walked up a small road that led up an incline.

"Hey, boy, we goin' up here, you come along and we bust yo' *face.*"

"My wallet," he called.

He could make out their dark forms standing at the end of the road on a kind of crest.

"Those boys hurt you bad, mister."

He had not seen the woman. She stood just a few feet away, under the bridge.

"They cut your face up. They make you walk with a limp for a long time. They even kill you."

"But my wallet. They have my wallet."

"Honey, 'less you got a million *dollars* in that wallet, you stay here. Don't be no crazy *fool.*"

He could no longer see them. Had they escaped? Urgently he began a kind of run, there was nothing here except mud and cinders as the road climbed up to track level. He reached into his pack and felt the Skorpion. But then he wondered what would happen if he shot them with it. There'd be a huge commotion, an extravaganza, a mess.

He reached the tracks. On either side the lights of this bleak Ohio city rolled away. He could see tall buildings, all lit up, a mile or so away.

"Boy, you some kind of motherfuckin' *dumb.*"

"Gonna cut yo' ass *bad,* motherfucker."

They were behind him. He turned. He saw a blade spring out.

"Cut his fuckin' ass. Go on, man, *cut* his fuckin' white ass."

The boy with the knife came at him. He was the bravest, the meanest. He led with his blade, feinted with it.

"Come on, motherfucker, come *on,*" he shouted.

He flicked the blade toward the Kurd's throat and Ulu Beg hit him with his open hand across the neck, crushing him to the ground. The blade clattered away. Something lashed into his head. One of the others had a strange fighting device of two stout sticks united by a short chain, and he'd just caught Ulu Beg above the right eye. He twirled it menacingly and Ulu Beg felt the swelling on his forehead.

"Gonna git you, motherfucker," the boy said and Ulu Beg leapt under the weapon and caught the hand that held it, then hit the boy an upward blow in the throat, knocking him back coughing and gagging. The third boy raced down the tracks.

Ulu Beg went and took the wallet from the boy he'd hit in the throat. It was not his. The boy lay on the ground, moaning.

"Somebody take from me, now I must take from you," he said.

He picked up his pack and went down the hill to the road.

"Baby, I didn't think you was comin' back."

She startled him again.

"I was about to call a cop."

"No. *No.* No police."

His sudden fierceness frightened her. She stepped back and he turned.

"Baby," she said, "you don't want no police botherin' you, you best not go walkin' nowhere lookin' like *that.*"

He felt blood running down his face from where the boy had struck him with the stick. He reached, wiped it away with the back of his hand. His hand was bloody. More blood came to his face.

"You banged up."

He looked at her. She was in her forties, a solid-looking woman. She wore a wig and smelled of perfume.

"Help me," he said.

"You get your wallet back?"

"No. Yes!" He pulled the boy's wallet out of his pocket. He opened it.

"There is no money here," he said.

"Where you get that?"

"From the boy."

"You done *took* them three?"

"I knock them down, yes."

"Honey, you best come home with me."

18

Chardy arrived bleary-eyed, his nerves edgy, ready for a fight. He had adrenaline coursing through his veins by the quart, he could feel his eyes dilated painfully, his breath shallow and tense. In the old days, when you lost somebody you'd go in and kick some ass. It was one of the oldest, the best rules, a rule that would have helped Bill Speight—or any agent—in his last moment or two. You always got back, you always went them one better; it was all personal. There were no truces. And maybe a part of him felt some joy, though he'd never admit it. For here at last was a prospect of action.

But when he crashed into the office, expecting men loading magazines into exotic automatics, others looking at maps, still others chatting bitterly in corners, he found only Miles, sipping coffee.

"Where is everybody?" Chardy barked, at first furious that they'd left without him.

"Relax, Paul. Jesus, you look half-crazy."

"You said it was an emergency, you said to get down here, you said—"

It occurred then to Chardy that he'd misread it all. Something in Lanahan's amused eyes, also the absence of stale, smoked-out air in the room, the absence of cigarette butts. Lanahan lounged at Yost's desk, as though trying it on for size and finding it fit nicely.

"Things have cooled. Considerably," Miles said, the half-smirk on his face.

"I don't—"

"Certain realities have set in. We got some news on Bill. We've doped it out. We've also got some orders from up above, declaring Mexico off-limits. And—"

"Where is he?"

"Where is who?"

"Come on, Miles. I smell Sam Melman in here. I smell Melman all over this place. Come on, Miles, where is he?"

"This is Yost's operation, Paul. This is Yost's office. You'd better get that straight."

"I smell Sam in this. Sam's a great one for cooling down, for taking it easy and slow, for not making any mistakes, for—"

"Paul, here are facts. Fact number one: the Mexicans have raised all kinds of hell. We have an informal agreement with them and part of it is that we don't run covert operations in their country without clearing it first with them."

"For Christ's sakes, this wasn't any operation. It was some old man and a kid—"

"We know that. But try to tell it to them. Look, it's a delicate working arrangement: they let us have all kinds of latitude in Mexico City around the Soviet Embassy, which is the hub of a lot of KGB activity. We have to protect that freedom. They're very kind to us; we make a lot of mileage off that kindness. All right?"

Chardy looked at him sullenly, unsure suddenly of a reply.

"Fact number two: oil. Oil talks in this world, loud and clear, and the Mexicans have tons of the stuff. So over and above anything on our level is that long-term issue. What they have and we need. We have to be very careful with them these days so that we can drive our Cadillacs around. Okay? We don't call them wetbacks or spics or greasers or zooters. We treat them *politely,* on all levels. So we're not going to bust in, shooting up some place when—"

"Kid, one—maybe two—of our people got clipped. Now in the old days—"

"It's the new days, Paul. Fact number three: we know who killed Speight."

Chardy looked at him.

"There's no Iron Curtain involvement, no Middle Eastern involvement. It doesn't have anything to do with Ulu Beg. There's no connection. It was plain, ugly, stupid luck."

"Who?"

"Poor Speight walked into a gang war. We have it he and Trewitt were very interested in coyote outfits—that was their brief, their only brief, to see what they could dig up on whoever smuggled Ulu Beg into this country. That, and only that. But they had to go a little further, and got themselves into the middle of a big fight in the Mexican mafia. It was something over a bar, the Palace, El Palacio, really a whorehouse. Stupid Bill walked into it. Asking questions like he was some kind of crime reporter. I don't know what got into him. It was a terrible, stupid accident."

"I don't believe it," said Chardy.

"You don't want to believe it. Anyway, it doesn't matter. Yost believes it."

"And where the hell is he?"

"Home."

Chardy picked up the phone.

"Give me the number."

"No, Paul. There's no point. He's had a long night, just like we—"

"Give me the number!"

"You're in no state to be talking on the phone. To anybody."

"Give me Melman's number, then. Goddammit, Miles—"

He made a move toward Miles, realizing he was dangerously near being out of control.

But Miles held firm.

"Just take it easy. Just settle down. Jesus, you old cowboys, you just can't wait to stir things up."

"He didn't have the guts himself to face me, did he, Miles? Yost." He thought of Yost—an unusual occurrence; he seldom thought of the man at all, but only of Sam Melman—and could not really conjure up a face. He remembered glasses and neatness and placidity and suits and that was all. "So he left you to do the dirty work. And you'll do it. You sort of enjoy doing it."

"Paul—"

"And now we kiss Mexican asses. *Mexican!* Jesus, the fucking Mexicans!"

"You better get used to the real world, Paul. You better get used to the eighties. This isn't 'Nam or Kurdistan or somebody's dirty little secret war. This is America. You do things certain ways here. All right?"

Chardy looked at him with great sadness. The world according to Lanahan was a dreadful place. In the old days, Special Ops always got its people out or at least back; and if it could only get the bodies, then it made certain someone on the other side had some burying to do too.

"Sometimes I wonder how things got so screwed up, Lanahan," Chardy said, wanting Johanna very much all of a sudden.

But Miles wasn't interested.

"They're bringing the body back. There's going to be a funeral. You'll be there, I assume."

Chardy nodded. He hated funerals but he'd go anyway. Old Bill. Frenchy. The business had turned so cold, and it was squeezing the old ones out so fast it wasn't funny.

He looked at Miles, an inheritor, and wondered how he could ever explain all this to him, but the kid glared at him and muttered something about how he'd better get himself cleaned up.

19

It was one of those curious events that briefly unite a dozen separate worlds, whose representatives, forced awkwardly to confront each other, stood around in stiff, silent groups. Several generations—contending generations, in fact—were there: the old warriors, ex-OSS types; and Chardy's bunch, Cold War and Vietnam hell-raisers; and the later, ascendant Melman crowd, drones, realists, the computer brigade. Speight had known and been known to them all. And outsiders, youngsters, presumably junior members of the administration of the moment, and maybe a staffer or two from House and Senate intelligence committees; and maybe some neighbors; and family.

Chardy, standing apart from the surprisingly large crowd ranged around the grave site and across the soft slopes of Arlington—Washington, falsely bright in the spring sun, gleamed across the river, through the dogwoods—saw with surprise that the family was young. Speight had married late then; or was it a second marriage? He didn't know. Speight had never said. At any rate, the widow in black, veiled and weeping, stood next to Yost Ver Steeg, and nearby were three little boys, Sunday-dressed, hurt or baffled.

Yost stood as though dead. The widow leaned on him,

but Chardy guessed the strength was cold, not warm. This wouldn't be a Yost Ver Steeg scene; he'd play it badly, although as Bill's last field supervisor, protocol mandated that play it he would. His dignity was not so much serene as merely placid; he radiated no calm into the chasm of grief. Bill's boys did not like him, Chardy could tell, and even as the ceremony demanded their attention, they shifted and fidgeted with repressed energy. Yost stood without rocking, knees locked, hands clasped dryly together. His crisp hair was short and perfect; a glare caught on the surface of those glasses again, blanking out the eyes. He looked like the lone executive at a miner's funeral.

Blue soldiers from a famous Army unit handled the ceremony, which was built around the folding of the flag until it resembled a tricornered, starred hat. It was presented to Yost, who presented it to the woman; she in turn gave it to the oldest boy, who'd seemed to figure out what was going on. Three crisp volleys rang out, echoing in the trees. A bugler issued taps.

Bill Speight, dead in a foreign sewer alongside a whorehouse. The Agency could or would say nothing about it, except in the form of an official presence at this ceremony and, Chardy hoped, an indication to the widow that Old Bill was on an op down there and not off whoring. Or would they even say that? Perhaps only silence was offered at this stage; you never knew how they figured these things on the upper floors.

Chardy looked around as the crowd broke. Wasn't that Miller, now a writer with two awful novels and a memoir to his credit; and that O'Brien, said to be drawing down half-a-mil on Wall Street? And he thought he recognized Schuster, the German, in this country so long now he'd almost lost his accent, recently an insurance salesman. Jesus, there were others, too: all these men, survivors of the hot '50s and '60s, of the Cold War in Europe and stations in sweltering deltas all across Asia. You could build a pretty good operation out of the talent just standing around here, Chardy thought. But of course nobody would.

"Poor Bill," he heard someone say. "Poor Old Bill." A thousand times he'd heard someone say it, two thousand. "Poor Bill," Bill, so much promise, such a comer once, such a bright hope; now this. "Poor Margaret, you mean," somebody else, a woman, said, "with those three boys."

Funerals unhinged Chardy, this one more than most. Though the sky was blue and the sun bright and the grass blinding spring-green, and the markers white, row on row of them like an image from a bitter Great War poem, he shuddered. Hated funerals, always had. So hushed, creepy. So Catholic, the faith he'd flown. Must be the Irish half of him, his mother's half: weepy at all the cheap theatrics, the tooting horns, the flappity-flap flags, the widows, the little boys. Chardy felt a black spell of brooding coming across him, enervating, ruining. Something bitter leaked into his blood; he'd be worthless for hours. A headache was due in shortly, and one of those awful sieges of self-loathing. All his sins and failures would come marching across his mind like these pretty blue soldier boys, Old Guardsmen, cadence perfect, bayonets gleaming in the sun. And just for a second the torrent of people before him parted and he saw a perfect tableau: the widow, head bent, weeping silently; beside her the three brave boys; and beside them all, holding her hand and seeming to encompass all their grief, Sam Melman.

Chardy had not seen him in almost seven years, since the hearings. Sam had aged well. Dressed in a dark suit, he was a man for helping widows and surviving sons over their grief, where poor Yost was not. It was a talent of his, the knack for the right word, for knowing how to handle unpleasant situations with dignity and aplomb. He was speaking to them all. Chardy could hear him in his mind: Just call me if you need anything. We'll be happy to help. We know how rough it is on you. We'll do our best. There'll be money.

Would the widow know that Bill and Sam were almost perfect contemporaries and way, way back were seen by many as potential long-term rivals for important jobs coming up in the future? No, she would not; Bill wasn't the type to take the office home with him.

Chardy turned away furiously. Melman had not seen him, but surely must have figured he'd be around. And just as surely wouldn't care. Chardy knew it would be no embarrassment to Melman to see him; there'd be no awkward look away, no shuffling of the feet. Sam would look him right in the eye, perhaps even smile. "Hello, Paul," he'd say, leaving awkwardnesses of the past far behind, "how are you? Are you doing all right? I hear you're on a contract now. Glad to have you back." And he'd mean it too, for in his own righteous way he'd have no doubts about his decisions in the hearings, and it would never occur to him that Chardy could bear him ill will. Perhaps he'd even have a little fondness for a maverick like Chardy, an old cowboy, a relic, like Bill, of a flamboyant past.

Chardy wished he had Johanna at that moment, something to cling to against the rage. With hands jammed deep into his pockets he began to climb through the shadows, away from the mob, thinking he would walk hard for half an hour, burn off some of his anger. He couldn't afford it, he had to be in top form, for tomorrow he met the Great Man himself.

"Paul? Paul, is that you?"

The voice was a woman's, familiar. He turned. She

was plumper now—had not aged as well, nearly, as Sam Melman. She seemed smaller too, certainly less attractive, for once she'd been a beauty.

It really was an afternoon for ghosts, for the dead. Am I that much older now too? he wondered.

"Marion," he said, trying to fabricate some spontaneity, knowing at the same time that if he'd seen her coming, he'd have changed direction immediately. "God, it's been so *long.*"

"Hasn't it? My God, nearly eight years."

"I'm sorry about Frenchy, Marion. I only found out a few weeks ago. I was sort of put into storage. I should have called or something." He felt terrible. He wanted to flee this failure. He owed Frenchy, he owed his widow, and he'd failed both of them.

"Paul, it's all right. You always took things so *seriously.*" She smiled her wrecked smile, too tight, and he felt as though he should touch her. "It was all so long ago. And I heard about your problems. Nobody is supposed to talk, but it always gets out. Walk with me, will you? Let's talk. I saw so many people today that I once knew. But I didn't want to talk to any of them. But then I saw you."

He fell into step beside her. They were on a path, under trees, on a hill. It was bright and he wanted to put on his sunglasses. Washington, like a white, phony, movie-set Rome, lay straddling the horizon. Chardy pinched the bridge of his nose because his head was beginning to hurt.

"It's terrible about Bill, isn't it?" Marion said.

"Poor Old Bill. But he lasted longer than most," Chardy said, and almost instantly regretted it: Bill lasted longer than Frenchy, floating in the Danube.

But she seemed not to have heard.

"What are you doing now?" he asked.

"I'm married again. My husband teaches English at a

branch of the University of Maryland, out near Baltimore.''

"Sounds great. A nice, calm life. I guess after the
Frenchman—'' He let it end, a wild memory of Frenchy
Short swirling in his head. Frenchy had cheated on her
horribly, every chance he got, but who could hold anything against the Frenchman? She'd probably known, and
forgiven him. Everybody forgave the Frenchman—it was
one of his great gifts. He was irrepressibly childish,
charming as black sin, without scruple, maliciously
clever, magnificently brave. He was one of those rare men
built for combat and his joyous ferocity, his sheer heat,
always left Chardy feeling pale in comparison. Frenchy
had taught Chardy everything and Chardy owed him a lot.
Frenchy also invented jams and wiggled out of them,
coming most vividly alive in the violent moments of extri-
cation.

"Even the Frenchman was slowing down," Marion
said. "Near the end."

"I can't imagine a slowed-down Frenchy," Chardy
said. He didn't really want to think about it. Though it was
true Frenchy also had a down phase, a real killer of a
crash, when he could hardly make himself leave his bed.

"I don't know, Paul. He'd mellowed, or burned out.
Maybe he was just tired of it all."

"Occupational hazard," Chardy said pointlessly. He
was trying to remember about kids. Frenchy never talked
about kids, he was always too self-involved. Were there
kids, little Frenchys, to feed and care about like the three
troopers Old Bill had left? Frenchy might have made a
good father—but Chardy suspected he might also have
been the kind of man best with other people's children,
for whom he can play hero and never have to change
diapers. But Chardy wasn't sure one way or the other—
and could think of nothing to say to poor Marion.

It is always hardest on the women, he thought. We chase around the world, playing cowboy on Agency expense accounts; they stay here and get leathery or brittle and try not to resent being sealed off so completely, until one day they realize they live in an entirely different world from their husbands'. Or maybe a call comes, with inadequate details, like the call Bill's wife had gotten or Marion. And then they get a folded flag from a stiff young Army sergeant, a few words with an oily grief merchant like Sam Melman, a little pension, and the door. This melancholy series of thoughts brought him to Johanna, for whom he still ached. He would never seal her off, he swore; finish this business, and that was it. No more secrets, no more operations. He was done with it.

Marion, meanwhile, was talking with considerable animation.

". . . and I'd never seen him so fascinated, not in years."

Now what the hell was she talking about?

"It meant some kind of security, too. Schlesinger was DCI then and he fired about two thousand people in six weeks and Frenchy was terrified he was on the next list. And he was so tired of the travel, the violence. So I think Frenchy was happiest then. I think it was his best time. He learned so fast; he was so good at it."

"Uh-huh," Chardy said dumbly, trying not to tip her off that he'd not been listening and had no idea what she was talking about.

"And then the Vienna thing came up. He just had to go—one last fling, I guess. But he loved those computers, he really did."

Computers? Frenchy Short, computers?

"The computers," Chardy said.

It didn't sound like Frenchy. Or maybe it did. Maybe Frenchy had taken a hard look at what was coming and realized the day of the cowboy was over. The future belonged to robots: to computers, to satellites, to microwave processors, to lasers. ELINT they called it in the trade, Electronic Intelligence, as opposed to HUMINT, Human Intelligence. So Frenchy had jumped to the side of the robots, the Melmans. Curious images floated around Chardy's head—he had no experience with computers and so to imagine Frenchy among them was difficult.

"I just can't see Frenchy with computers," Chardy said.

"It was the future, he said. He was tired of the past."

"He was thinking of you, Marion, I guess."

"It's nice of you to say that, Paul. We both know better. The Frenchman never thought of me."

"Marion—"

"No, it's all right. It doesn't matter. Don't apologize. But he was thinking of *you,* Paul. Before he left. You were in the Mideast or someplace. You two went back so far."

A jet filled the sky, a 727 roaring down the Potomac toward National Airport, its noise burying their words. The great silver craft banked as it sped by, close enough to be touched. Its landing gear locked down. They had climbed and now stood atop one of the hills across which the cemetery spread, and it all lay before them, the white markers spilling into the valleys and the clumps of dogwood, and beyond that a band of highways, a sluggish brown river, and finally a blazing white city. It looked even more like a movie Rome from here.

"I hate Washington," said Chardy. "I hate the people, the newspapers, the pretty women. It's no city for guys like Frenchy and me. I just hate it." His own sudden passion amazed him. But he did hate it.

"It's just a place," Marion said.

A cool wind whipped the leaves, chilling Chardy. He'd

left his overcoat in his car, from which he was now, in his wanderings with Marion, a mile distant.

"I'm sorry," he said. "I interrupted you. I'm not much company today, I'm afraid."

"Funerals depress everyone. Please don't worry about it, Paul."

"Thanks."

"I was telling you that Frenchy was thinking of you at the end."

"That's right."

"He had a message for you. He told me especially to tell you. But then he died and it was a difficult time and then I didn't see you and I started another life. The years went by. But now I remember. Seeing you, standing by yourself up on that hill with your new beard, I remembered."

"A message?" said Chardy, curious.

" 'Marion,' he said, 'Marion, when Paul gets back, tell him to fetch the shoe that fits. Got that? Fetch the shoe that fits? He'll know what I'm talking about.' "

Chardy couldn't keep a sudden cruel grin off his face.

"What does it mean, Paul?"

"Oh, Marion, it goes back so far, to another time. A terrible time. I hate to tell you."

"You can tell me, Paul. I'm a big girl."

"When we were running our missions into the North up around the DMZ with the Nung people, there was a Chinese opium merchant in the area named Hsu. H-S-U. Pronounced 'shoe.' Anyway, one of our patrols got bounced bad, and we just got out of there with our hides. It was a bad, bad time. And then somebody told us this Hsu was working for the North Vietnamese. He was their agent; he'd infiltrated our area to get a look at our operations. He was a very bad guy, it turned out. Well, we had our contacts too. We set him up. We let it be known that he'd done some work for *us*. His bosses didn't see the humor in it. The guy was found floating in the river in oil drums. Several of them. And Frenchy said—we were drunk at the time; you have to understand that—Frenchy said, 'Well, Paul, we proved the Hsu fits.' It seemed very funny at the time."

She didn't say a word.

"Marion, you're horrified. Look, we were in the middle of an ugly kind of business. People were getting greased left and right. It had come out that up north they'd put out a fifty-thousand-piaster bounty on our heads. You never knew which way was up and you went out on these long patrols with the Nungs and you never knew if you were coming back. It was a hard time, a difficult time, and nobody knows or cares about it anymore. And a lot of things seemed funny then that don't now." He was irritated that she seemed so offended. What did she think Frenchy's job was all those years?

"I had no idea it would be so *cruel.*"

"I'm sorry, Marion. I didn't mean to wreck your illusions."

"I can be an awful prig, can't I? It's not your fault. As you say, it was a different kind of time. But what about the 'fetch'?"

What about it?

"I just don't know what he was thinking about with that. I think he meant 'remember' or something. He was saying, 'Remember the times we had.' "

"Oh, it's such a strange world you and Frenchy had, Paul. I'm so glad to be out of it. Look, here's my car." They had reached a low brick wall that separated the cemetery from Fort Myer. Just beyond, in the Army parking lot, was a dirty yellow Toyota.

She smiled, her features briefly lighting. She'd really been a beautiful woman once, where Frenchy had always been especially ugly, and Chardy had always been impressed with his ability to earn the loyalty of such a lovely woman.

"It was so good to see you again, Paul. I'm so glad I came to this. It was nice to step into the past again. I really do miss him, Paul. I really do."

He thought she might cry, and said quickly, "Yes, I do too, Marion."

"Call me sometime, if you'd like. My husband's name is Brian Doelp." She spelled it. "We live out in the suburbs, a place called Columbia. Halfway between Baltimore and Washington. It's very nice."

"I will, Marion. It was nice seeing you too. It really was." He bent and kissed her on the cheek.

"Can I drop you somewhere?"

"No, my car's just over there," and he pointed vaguely in the direction of Maryland and the North Pole.

"Bye-bye then."

"Goodbye, Marion."

She climbed into the car, started it quickly, and disappeared into the traffic of Fort Myer.

Chardy walked back through the boneyard, a tall man, bearded, hunched against the wind, his hands in his pockets. He put on his sunglasses. The cemetery was empty now, except for a few tourists, and he walked among the American dead, thinking of his own losses.

20

Chardy sat in the back seat with Lanahan, while some Agency gofer—a kid, no introductions had been made—chauffeured them down Wisconsin Avenue through increasingly snarled traffic.

Lanahan droned: "And at four fifty-five the car takes you to National. You'll be covered the whole way, Paul, backup units, checkpoints, escort, the works."

"Just like I was in Boston, Miles?"

Miles plunged on. "By six you'll be on a Lear to Chicago. You land at Meigs, on the lake, not at O'Hare. From there it's just a hop to the Ritz-Carlton in Water Tower Place, where the conference is; there's a room for you there too."

"Miles, I don't think I'm going to make a very good bodyguard."

"Look, Paul, I thought Yost was clear on this. The last thing anybody needs is for this guy to wax Danzig. We're going to nail him. We're going to lay out such a net, there's no way he can get through. But if he does, Paul, if he should get through—you're there, you'll recognize him. Remember, nobody else knows what he looks like. You lived with him for over a year in the mountains. Have you got the piece?"

Chardy nodded. A Smith & Wesson Model 39 9-mm automatic hung upside down like a bat in a shoulder holster under his left arm.

"You've fired a nine-millimeter?"

"I've fired everything, Miles."

"Okay. Now let me brief you on Danzig." Lanahan at his most officious. His splotchy acne was particularly bad today, fiery red. The back of his neck hadn't seen a barber since the last ice age. Flecks of dandruff lay across the dark shoulders of his rumpled blue suit. His short warty fingers jabbed the air as he discussed Danzig, but his eyes were bright with their own special kind of intelligence. They were small, sharp Irish eyes, city eyes. Miles wouldn't miss much. He pushed ahead, lecturing Chardy.

"They say Danzig can be very charming. He likes to talk, he's got this way of grabbing hold of people, talking them into oblivion. So you have to watch yourself. He'll really rivet you if you don't."

Chardy thought of Joseph Danzig in all the hundred thousand pictures, on the TV shows, in the books: everywhere, like wallpaper. Of course, all that was a few years back, during his term in office and just afterward; still, the whiff of celebrity would cling to him. Yet Chardy knew he'd dislike him on principle, the way infantrymen dislike generals. For there'd been a time when if Danzig said go, a whole operation went: money, plans, papers, case officers, logistics people, on-site specialists. And somebody usually got burned and usually it was a Special Operations type — Chardy's type. Nicky Welch, greased in Laos. Tony Chin had caught it in Laos also, or maybe it was Cambodia, a sucking chest wound, slow death. Chardy couldn't remember. And hadn't Stan Morris taken some junk in Angola, the African op, and been turned into a basket case? Yes. And in every one of those scams, the outcome was the same. At the crucial moment, Danzig had pulled back. He'd seen the cost escalating and he'd pulled back, and Nicky and Tony and Stan and the others had bought nothing with their skins. As had Chardy bought nothing with Saladin II, a classic example. Once, down at the Special Warfare school in Panama, he and a bunch of other instructors, all old Special Operations vets, had tried to figure out how many had died on account of Danzig's way of doing things. The list had been long.

"Look, Paul, best thing around him is to play the robot. He'll try and provoke you; he loves to provoke people. Or he'll gossip with you; he loves to gossip. Or he'll try and get you to pimp for him. Lately they say he's really been chasing women. Any woman. At any rate, he'll want to dominate you, to own you. That's how he is. If he likes you, is drawn to you, he'll destroy you. Yost says the best thing is to just smile mildly at anything he says, no matter how outrageous. Don't try to top him, or get into it with him. He'll chew you up, okay?"

They had turned off the busy avenue and were crawling through a Georgetown back street under densely matted trees that blocked out the sun. It felt subterranean, the coolness, the shadow in the air. The brick houses, set primly back from the street, were red and narrow and shuttered and four stories tall and had small gardens alongside.

"Nice neighborhood," Chardy said.

"The guy's got dough. The guy's got more dough than you'd believe. He makes about a million a year lecturing and writing. He can knock off twenty G's a day giving these speeches." Lanahan spoke like the poor city boy he was, his resentment as tender and red as his acne. His face formed a snarl as he scanned the swanky Georgian facades. Chardy had seen the look a thousand times growing up; you saw it on playgrounds when a fancy car wheeled through the neighborhood, the hate, the envy.

But it was gone in an instant, and Miles turned back. "Look, Paul. Yost is parking you with a very touchy, egotistical guy who can do us a lot of harm, even now. It has to be you. Everybody wishes it could be somebody else, somebody not so controversial. Just don't blow it for us, okay? This is very fucking important."

Yost, nervous, handled the introductions. It was awkward: the Great Man, plumper and older, puffier, with human flaws normally invisible on television, such as a clump of hair in the crown of one nostril, a missed patch of whisker, a light spray of freckles—but still, totally and exactly and unavoidably Joseph Danzig, offering, as would any mortal, a hand. It turned out to be a weak one, smallish, with tapering fingers, and Chardy felt the delicacy of the thing and tried to avoid squashing it, though it seemed to collapse into bone fragments at his softest touch.

They sat in a downstairs study, a room that belonged in a department store window or an ad for the Book-of-the-Month Club. Chardy felt like a tourist among the shelved books, several of which must be by Danzig himself. He looked around at leather furniture, at polished wood, at muted damask curtains.

"It's a wonderful house," he said stupidly.

"The wages of sin, Mr. Chardy," said Joseph Danzig.

Nervous Yost kept making patter, small phony jokes at which neither principal in this peculiar blind date would laugh. Finally he said it was time to go and excused himself. In the confusion of his leaving, Chardy stole a glimpse at his watch and saw that he had forty minutes until the caravan left for the airport. He wondered how he'd kill them. He looked out a massive paned door—hate to have to clean the son of a bitch, all those tiny panes, hundreds of them—across a veranda to a backyard garden. Gardens in G-town were not large, but Danzig had more land than most, and his garden was consequently more than ample, reaching back to the brick wall that enclosed his yard. It had not quite sprung to blossom, though Chardy could make out its outlines, its plan: it was a place of severe order, of symmetry. It balanced, neat and crisp. The plots were cut squarely into the earth and low precise hedges ran geometrically through them. Four—not five, not three—four white wooden arbors stood to the rear, bulked with vines, two on each side of a simple fountain. When filled out, the garden would be a composition of immense order.

Chardy suddenly sensed a presence. Danzig, who'd last been heard from announcing he had to run upstairs to his office, was standing next to him, holding a sherry— Chardy had been offered one earlier and had refused.

"What do you think of that garden, Mr. Chardy?"

"It's very nice, sir," he said lamely. Nobody had ever asked him about gardens before. Then he added, "Do you garden?"

"Of course not," Danzig said tartly. "That is, I do not go out there with a hoe and a little set of clippers. But I designed it. The people who lived here before had a terrible Italian grotto fantasy. It looked like the sort of place where homosexuals go to meet each other. I made certain improvements. That fountain was a gift from the President of France. The trees along the left came from Israel. The trees along the right were imported from Saudi Arabia. Many of the plants and bushes come from other countries. It will never be beautiful, of course, but then, that is not its purpose. I do not care much for beauty, and having looked at your record I would say that you do not either. Perhaps on that basis we'll get along. But back to the garden: it expresses an idea, an idea I hold in extreme importance. It stands for perfect harmony, all components kept in check by other components. Do you understand?"

Chardy understood exactly, and the point was driven home by Danzig's sudden, wicked, facetious smile.

Just smile mildly, they'd told him; he'll eat you up otherwise.

But Danzig had been so vastly superior, so condescending, so celestially regal that Chardy's Hungarian blood began to steam and in his fury he came up with a rejoinder which surprised even him.

"I worked in a garden like that for a while," he said. "From the big house, far away, it looks great. But up close it's terrible work—sweaty, dangerous, grubby, disgusting. You might want to talk with your gardeners some hot July Saturday, Dr. Danzig. They might surprise you."

Behind their lenses, Danzig's eyes held him for a long moment, not quite in astonishment but at least in surprise. He considered a moment, then smiled again, wickedly.

"But, Mr. Chardy," he said, "to do it right—to make the right decisions, the long-term decisions—demands perspective, a cool intellect. You have to see the whole plan, the final limits. Gardening, after all, is not missionary work."

Danzig could not keep his eyes off him; the reflex surprised him and he found that charming, for there had been no surprises in his life lately.

The man kept to himself: big, somewhat sour, perhaps even shy. He was presumably under orders to keep his distance, and the beard helped, masking the features. But the eyes were lively, watchful.

You always wonder about them; all statesmen do. At the bottom of every policy, every necessary decision, there are people: infantrymen, bomber pilots, very junior consular personnel, intelligence operatives. And here was one of the last, the cutting edge of all the chatter in Washington offices, all the committee meetings, the working groups, the papers. Here was the man who had to make it happen.

Chardy had been good at it, the reports said, until his misfortune. Danzig had seen and studied the dossier, being not at all surprised at certain things—the military background, the athletics, the temper, the impatience—and stunned at others—the high IQ, for example. And of course he'd seen Sam Melman's final judgment: *unreliable under stress.*

Well, perhaps. Yet this Chardy seemed on first glance anything but unreliable. He seemed stolid, effective, prosaic even. The mind would be dull, although focused. He'd be the technical type, wholly uninterested in things beyond his arcane craft. It was hard to see him as one of the Agency glamour boys—a cowboy, they called them—most alive among far-off little people with grudges, in mountains or jungles, amid guns and equipment.

"I'm told, Mr. Chardy, that the most famous Kurd of all time was Salāh-al-Dn Yūsuf ibn-Ayyūb, Saladin of the Crusades, who fought against Richard Coeur de Lion and forced the Crusaders to abandon practically all of Palestine except for a few coastal forts. Perhaps giving crusades a bad name that we should have taken cognizance of in our own times, eh? Did you know that, Mr. Chardy?"

"You can't be around the Kurds without hearing of Saladin," said Chardy. "Like he was, they are superb soldiers." He paused. "When they've got the right gear."

"Are they a colorful people? I always expected Arabs to be colorful and they turned out to be simple boors. But what about the Kurds? Were you disappointed in them?"

Another leading question. What capacity would Chardy have to determine what was "colorful," what was not?

"They're obsessive. And obsessives are always color-ful. Unless it's you they're obsessed with."

Danzig smiled. Chardy insisted on surprising him. He admired the capacity to astonish, which was rare, as opposed to the capacity to *be* astonished, which was commonplace.

"You respect them, I take it?"

Chardy went blank and would not answer, as if he were holding something back. Danzig could guess what: his outrage, his contempt, his fury, his disappointment over his—Danzig's—"betrayal" of the Kurds. But Danzig could figure it out. The man had been among them, had known this Ulu Beg, had probably come to identify with them. The process was common. And when the operation had, of every urgent necessity, to be aborted, Chardy, and many others, would have taken great offense.

But Chardy did not express these sentiments directly. He said only, "Yeah, you have to," turning quickly moody. It was not difficult to calculate why either: Chardy would share with his hard-charging brethren the conviction that the Kurdish thing had been a No-Win situation from the start. Then why get involved, why spend the money, the lives, if you're not prepared to stick the course? the beef would run. Danzig had no doubt he could draw him out at great length: we needed more weapons, more ammo, SAMs, better commo and logistics, more sophisticated supply techniques, satellite assistance, naval support, germ warfare, psywar, defoliants, another front, tactical nukes. It would go on and on, no end in sight, a funnel down which could endlessly be poured gear and people and hopes and dreams.

"You do not approve of how it ended, I take it?"

The athlete in Chardy spoke. "I hate to lose," he said.

"Perhaps if you recall, at that precise moment in history certain events were taking place across the world."

Chardy nodded glumly. No, he wouldn't recall from living memory, since he'd been in his cell in Baghdad that week. But he would know by now: the Republic of South Vietnam was falling.

"A very complex and difficult time," Danzig pointed out.

"Yeah," was all Chardy could manage. His was not a particularly interesting mind. Still: Danzig was attracted. Not to the mind, but to the mind *and* the man, to the organic whole. Like an athlete who has nothing to say but is fascinating when he runs or shoots or dodges or whatever, that aspect—man-in-action, man-of-will, man-of-force—had a Nietzschean grandeur to it, a fascination, because it was in part how Danzig saw himself, although in a different realm: the man who makes things happen.

Not to declare Chardy a total original, of course. These crypto-military types had their limits, just as surely as they had their uses. Curiously, they almost always had a sports background; at the very heart of their vision of the world was an image of the Playing Field, on which there are certain teams and certain rules, and if A happens, then by all that's logical B must follow, mustn't it? and thus to the swift, the strong, the brave, go the spoils. A heavy, masculine, sentimental fascism ran through it all, a painful juvenile strain. It was best summed up by Kipling, the Imperial apologist and poet laureate of nineteenth-century British Steel, when he coined a brilliant term for it which caught at once the athletic component and the masculine component and the sentimental component: the Great Game. It was of course by now a useless, a worthless concept. Especially as the world progressed exponentially in its complexity, became more densely and dangerously packed with oddball nationalist groups, with sects and cults of personality, with zealots, with madly proliferating technology, up to and including nuclear weaponry.

Danzig took instead as his model a more recent metaphor, the second law of thermodynamics, the entropy law, which mandated that in closed systems, randomness, disorder, chaos tended to prevail over the long term. Centers would not hold; all systems disintegrated. A nation was a system; disintegration was its fate. But given this ultimate tendency, this spiral toward collapse (which even the most immense system, the universe itself, would some distant day undergo) small salvations were available within the process itself. It was possible for a clever man to make the law of entropy work for himself—or his nation.

As Clausius demonstrated in 1865, entropy grows out of all proportion to the energy expended in producing it. His famous example is the cue ball: dispatched into a formation of billiards, it transfers the energy of the cue into the formation of the balls; and while the energy of the system is thus transformed and momentarily increased, the entropy is increased *much more,* as demonstrated by the balls careening madly across the surface of the table. And that was only in two dimensions! Imagine this concept as applied in three: the complications are incredible, immeasurable!

The Soviets understood this principle instinctively, and built their own mischievous foreign policy around it. But Americans had some difficulty with it; they were not used to exalting disorder; it went against their mindset. But to Danzig it meant that his energy—the stroke of a cue— could drive a ball or a series of balls into various target billiards, and the results in entropy would be remarkable. This was the heart of what the news magazines termed "The Danzig Doctrine," in whose service the Chardys of this world labored. A series of small engagements could be fought in the Third World; at no one place would the full weight of the nation's will be committed, as had been done so foolishly in Vietnam; rather in an Angola, a Laos, a Bulgaria, a Yemen, a Kurdistan, a few special men, highly trained, superbly motivated, brave, resourceful— and expendable—would go in and raise a ruckus. The Soviets, like billiard balls driven into fury, would attempt to respond; they could eventually restore the local order, but the effort required resources of personnel, rubles, and effort drawn from other parts of their empire. And when they finally did prevail, a new battleground, in some other sector of the globe, would be found. The cost of these many small Third World battles was far less than any cataclysmic confrontation between the systems themselves, via strategic weaponry.

This was reality, geopolitical reality. Danzig orchestrated it; it was his legacy to the nation. He had the strength, the fierceness of will to do so. If it meant that he himself had to become ruthless and cynical, feeling the huge weight of having to betray so many times, then that was a part of the price too. In the long term he knew himself to be a moral man, perhaps the highest moralist, because he acted on behalf of the greatest number of people over the greatest length of time.

And if men like Chardy, like Ulu Beg, like the Agency's generation of cowboys had to be used up in the same process, then that too was a part of the price; they were not innocent victims and should not be mourned— suffering was their duty, their contribution. Their ignorance of the mechanisms that destroyed them in no way qualified them for pity or martyrdom. They took their wages and they died.

But damn them! Of course they didn't understand, or wouldn't; of course they'd take it all personally and insist on mad notions of honor and vengeance, and travel half the globe to strike back. And so here was Danzig's newest geopolitical reality—and his smallest: a big man with a beard and a cheap corduroy suit who moved like an athlete and had a boy's unformed rhythms of speech. And his counterpart, equally fascinating, a Kurd, born in the wrong century, now hunting him. It was a paradigm of the entropic absolute—fragmentation, randomness, strangeness, disorder, dissipation of energy, in a world too desperate to entertain such extravagances. The three of them locked crazily, linked by coincidences, odd twists, unreal developments, veering toward their strange fates. It was Kafkaesque, Nabokovian, Pynchonian, a ludicrous Master Plot from the crazed imagination of some Modern Novelist high on drugs and paranoia.

Yet Danzig, in all this, could not deny that it filled him with a certain excitement. There was that same rush, that dizzy, swooping, immensely satisfying sensation of being *at center* again.

"Would you shoot him to save my life?" Danzig asked. "I do have a right to ask."

"It'll never come to that," Chardy said laconically. "There'll always be people around: backup teams, men with rifles and scopes, with infrared gear, with dogs. The works. You have your own bodyguards too. Finally, after all that, there's me."

"Mr. Chardy, I have probably told more lies in good causes than any man on this planet. And so I recognize a lie in a good cause. And I have just encountered one." Danzig smiled, pushed ahead merrily. "It's not at all difficult to concoct a scenario in which he is raising his weapon and I am defenseless and you have—a pistol, I presume?"

"Yes."

"Are you any good with it?"

"Pistols are very hard to shoot with any accuracy."

"Very reassuring, Mr. Chardy. In any event, there you are. He's a man you've fought with, hunted with, trained, whose sons you knew. And I am a fat old Jewish professor with a bit of the heavy Polish about me and I show up on television a lot, was once upon a time an important man and to this day remain controversial. I am not remotely humble and can be numbingly unpleasant to be around for long periods of time. I once had a date with a movie starlet, I expect doors to be opened and other people to stop talking when I open my mouth. Those are your choices, Mr. Chardy. You have less than a second to decide.''

He watched Chardy turn the question over in his mind.

''I'd fire,'' said Chardy eventually.

''You have not convinced me. I believe I have a right to be convinced.''

''I'd shoot, that's all.''

''Even though to you he is the victim and I am the villain?''

''I never said that.''

''It's true, though; I can sense it. I have very good instincts in these matters.''

Chardy seemed to grow irritable.

''I said I'd shoot. It'll never come to that. I just know it won't.''

''Now that *is* reassuring,'' Danzig said. ''That is reassuring indeed.''

Yet, whatever Chardy's doubts, his interesting mesh of alliances and confusions, Danzig had to admit that in the capacity of bodyguard he functioned well. Chardy was at his side the whole time, a step ahead in crowds, though things had been set up in such a way as to minimize passage through public areas. The hotel, for example, was selected because it did not begin until the twelfth floor, being mounted atop a marble shopping center across from the Water Tower on Michigan Avenue. Where but America—and certain Arab countries—could such a gawky extravagance be conceived, much less executed? The wealth of the Midwest—the sheer, staggering accumulation of capital—always stunned Danzig, new to wealth himself, though he trained himself not to show his shock.

Chardy seemed equally unimpressed—or perhaps he was too busy. He looked at faces and stayed close, taking his leave only when security was tightest—closed rooms, Chicago cops, strange men with radio jacks in their cars, like Secret Service, but spiffier, and therefore probably a private service, rented at government expense for the weekend. Melman was really throwing the money around on this. God, it made Danzig happy to imagine Melman at an Agency budget committee meeting, bluffing his way through. But Chardy: Chardy was always there, in his one glum suit.

"Don't you ever get tired, Mr. Chardy?"

"I'm all right."

"I would think for a man of your special talents, your flamboyant background, this would be very boring."

Chardy was a robot today.

"No, sir."

"They warned you to keep your conversations with me to a minimum, didn't they?"

"No, sir."

"Mr. Chardy, you are a poor liar. You do not even *try* to disguise the falsehood."

Chardy's face began to show irritation. Danzig had heard the man had a furious temper. Hadn't he once beaten up some high Agency official? Chardy stewed in silence, however, disappointing Danzig.

"Chicago is your home, isn't it?"

Chardy looked around at the lush suite, the huge bed, the silks, the David Hicks wallpaper and carpet.

"Not this Chicago," he said.

———

Danzig gave his seminar on international relations to the American Management Association on Wednesday morning in a banquet room, and then was driven to the University of Chicago, where he addressed a hundred graduate students after a luncheon; and then back to the Ritz-Carlton for a cocktail party with the steering committee of the Association, where he was charming and gossipy and wicked and where Chardy stood around like a jerk, awkward but always close; and then on to the banquet for his formal address, a hell-raiser on Soviet domination; and then another hotel party, a more intimate one with the Management Association's board of directors; and then to his room to dictate into a recorder for an hour. An exhausting day, much photographed, talked at, pressed upon by the occasional autograph seeker, yet he remained by and large pleasant through it all, because of the adulation he'd received, which he loved, and because of the $30,000 he'd just earned.

"A busy Wednesday, Mr. Chardy."

"Extremely."

"We leave for the airport at ten."

"I know."

"No Kurds."

"Not this time."

"You've got that pistol?"

"I do."

"Good, Mr. Chardy."

Everywhere Danzig went it was the same. That's what TV did, Chardy guessed.

Everybody was drawn to Danzig. They tracked him, came to him, were mesmerized by him. And Danzig fed on it, he grew in it.

And these weren't teenagers either, but grown men from the world of business, who made decisions, hired other men, fired them. They inhabited a Chicago Chardy had never seen, and their confidence, their sense of rightful, silver-haired place, irritated him. Most had lovely younger wives too, girls who were beautiful and distant and did not see him except by accident.

"Who's he?"

"Some kind of bodyguard, I guess."

They poured in on Danzig, to touch him.

"It's like this everywhere," the other bodyguard, Uckley, said.

"Incredible," Chardy said. They stood next to the curtains at the banquet, in a huge room filled with blue smoke. Danzig—the top of his head, actually—was barely visible among a gang of executives and executive wives. In the far distance other lonely men held uncomfortable vigil: cops, Agency goons, private dicks, and somewhere Yost Ver Steeg must have clucked and fretted, and somewhere surely Lanahan would be lurking.

"How much longer will this last?" Chardy asked Uckley.

"Hours, sir," Uckley replied, eyes Marine-front, neck a steel lock, lips barely moving.

"You were in 'Nam, right, Sarge?"

"Yessir. First Marines. Two tours. Good people, good times. Better 'n this. Man's work."

No, this was not man's work. It was not any kind of work.

A discreet figure suddenly swam into the periphery of his vision, and he turned to meet it.

It was Miles.

"Yost wants to see you. He's in the hall," Miles said.

"Good, I want to see him."

Chardy unfroze, and walked through the hall, avoiding executives and tables. He found Ver Steeg outside, arms crossed, two new assistants close by.

"Hello, Paul. How's it going?"

"It stinks, Yost. I want out. You can find something better for me to do than stand around."

"Sorry, Paul. You stay."

"I can't play sentry. And I can't stand Danzig. And the most important thing is Ulu Beg."

"Sorry, Paul. I have to put my people where it counts. What good are you roaming around? You forget, you're the only man in America who's seen the Kurd."

"Ah," said Chardy.

"It won't be much longer. Something's broken."

He handed Chardy a twenty-dollar bill.

"A couple of nights ago, in Dayton, Ohio, the police picked up a drug dealer with a large wad of these. The Dayton people routinely ran the serial numbers through the Treasury. Thank God for those computers. It's part of the bundle Bill Speight had with him in 'seventy-three when you guys were setting up Saladin Two. Back in the days when a dollar still bought something in Iran."

Chardy nodded.

Ver Steeg continued. "It's not hard to design a scenario by which it would come into the hands of Ulu Beg, is it?"

"Where'd the dealer get it?"

"He said a pickpocket was distributing generous amounts of it in certain low spots about town."

"It looks like Ulu Beg got his money lifted in Dayton."

"Yes, it does. And without the money, he'll have a tough time getting anywhere."

"We ought to get right out there."

"People have left. I'm leaving myself tonight. Paul, I think this is it."

"I'll be packed in—"

"No, Paul. Not you. Sorry."

Chardy looked at him.

"Somebody's got to guard Danzig, Paul. Somebody."

21

Trewitt was down to $11.56 and some traveler's checks he didn't dare cash. And ten bucks bought exactly one night in his current quarters in scenic Nogales. The accommodations consisted of a straw bed in a hovel clinging precariously to the side of one of the hills. His roommates were chickens. At least the water ran—through the roof, into his face, and down into the straw, producing, in mixture with assorted animal droppings and liquid eliminations, an odor unlike anything he could describe. The view was breathtaking: across a chasm of reeking poverty to another dusty hill, on which sat—more hovels. But he was not without a beacon in this hopeless situation. At night, if he dared, he could creep halfway around the hill—being careful, for the drop was sheer on that side, one hundred feet down—and make out in a notch between the infested other slopes a wonderful symbol of the motherland: on a pedestal, high above the cruel barbed wire and metal mesh of the border, the golden arches of McDonald's.

Trewitt would have killed for a Big Mac—*el Grande,* they called them down here.

He would have killed for a shower too, a shave, a new shirt, clean fingernails. Had there been a mirror available he wouldn't have had the nerve to look into it, guessing what a week in a chicken coop will do to any man, turning him into a pitiful mock Orwell, down and out in Nogales, in a dirty costume of his own skin and rumpled summer suit. He'd lost his tie—when? Probably in the long running climb up Calle Buenos Aires. He had seemed to climb forever, up, up, still farther up, through chicken yards and goat pens (tripping once on the wire fence and sprawling into the dust). He was also sure he'd knocked down several people, but his memory wasn't terribly distinct. He remembered dodging in and out of big-finned cars, racing by small shops in which Mexicans lounged, drinking beer. Up one hill, down another. He ran aimlessly in the dark, in great heat, under a smear of moon in a foggy sky.

Near dawn he sought shelter in a structure whose purpose he could not quite divine. Its main recommendation was that it was deserted. He tried to get some sort of grip on himself. He was shivering miserably, almost sniveling (it was so *unfair,* it always had to happen to *him*) when a boy found him.

"Who are you?" the boy asked. He wore dirty jeans and black gym shoes and a dirty white T-shirt whose neck was all stretched out.

"A crazy gringo," Trewitt answered in Spanish. "Go away or I'll give you a smack."

The boy's scrawny chest showed in the exaggerated loop of the shirt's neck.

"This is my mama's."

"Where's your daddy?"

"Gone to America to be rich."

"You want to be rich?"

"Sure. In U.S. bucks."

"I need a place to stay. No trouble. Something quiet."

"Sure, mister. You kill some guy in a fight?"

"It's nothing like that."

"You can stay here."

Trewitt looked around without much enthusiasm. Bales of hay stood against one wall and shafts of sunlight fell through chinks in the roof. The place was built of corrugated metal. It smelt dusty and shitty all at once. Chickens wandered about, pecking at the ground.

"You got a bath in the house? A shower?"

"No, mister. This is Mexico, not Los Estados Unidos."

"I noticed. Look, it's a big secret, okay? Don't tell anybody. Big secret, you understand?"

The boy vanished quickly and returned with his mother, a huge, ugly woman with eyes of brass and a baby in her arms.

"I can pay," Trewitt said.

"Ten bucks, U.S."

"Ten's fine. Ten a week."

"Ten a night. Starting last night," she said, her brass eyes locking on to his. The baby began to squeal and she gave it a swat on the rump.

"Ah, Jesus," said Trewitt.

"And no cursing," she said.

Mamacita came with the meal—cold tripe in chili sauce. He fought the gag reflex; he could see the brown sauce crusting on the loops of gut. But it was better than yesterday's fish-head soup.

"Money," she said.

Trewitt forked over his last ten.

"How's my credit?" he asked.

"No credit," she said, handing him the plate. "Tomorrow you get some more money or you go."

He attacked the food ravenously, because he had not eaten since yesterday.

What now? Trewitt contemplated alternatives. Could

he find a way to make contact? Take a chance, ring up the people at headquarters? Maybe then somebody could bring him in—somebody good, somebody who'd been around, a Chardy? But he knew the waiting would kill him. It had already been two weeks since Bill got killed. So should he try the other alternative: take the risk, try and bust the border himself? It was a fairly simple proposition, a tollbooth plaza, like the George Washington Bridge. Just an easy stroll; head for the gate. It was wide open, no Berlin-style Checkpoint Charlies, no Cold War wall to cross like some existential husk of an agent out of Le Carré. For Christ's sake, you just walked up, following the sign. *Entrada en Los Estados Unidos.* What could be easier?

But then he remembered Bill Speight in the sewer. He remembered he was being hunted.

He rolled over and faced the scabby tin wall, waiting for inspiration. He had to do *something.* His mind was full of bubbles—a good deal of commotion and light and very little substance. He had a sudden blast of insane, giddy optimism. But it collapsed almost as quickly as it peaked and the downward trip was a crusher.

He heard a noise and turned.

"Oh," he said glumly, "it's only you."

The boy eyed him from the doorway, unimpressed. Trewitt had the terrible sensation of failing another test. Yet the boy liked him and in the two weeks Trewitt had spent in the barn, on most days the boy had visited him.

"You sure never kill no one in no fight," the boy said.

"No, I never did. I never said I did. Go away. Get out of here."

"Hey, I got some news for you."

"Just get out of here." It occurred to him to take a swat at his tormentor, but he didn't have the energy.

"No, listen, man. I tell the truth."

"Sure you do."

The truth, Trewitt knew, was bleak. He had failed utterly in his dream of unearthing information on Ulu Beg's journey through Mexico, in finding out whether the Kurd came alone—or with others. What he had succeeded in doing was inserting himself in the center of a Mexican mafia war.

Unless the one was part of the other.

Trewitt's mind stirred for just a second.

But he had to face reality. Reality was that he now had to turn himself in to the *Departamento de Policía*. The whole story would come out. CIA AGENT NABBED IN MEX, the headlines would say. Phone calls, official protests and denials, embarrassments, awkwardnesses of all kinds.

"I found him," said the boy.

Trewitt could see Yost Ver Steeg. He could imagine himself trying to explain.

See, we thought we found the guy who brought the Kurd across. We thought we could learn from him if—

Ver Steeg had no capacity for expressing emotion. The rage would be inward. Trewitt would sense it in constricted gestures, tightly held lips, a cool handshake.

You went *into* Mexico?

Uh, yes.

He could blame it on Old Bill.

See, Old Bill said that—

But Ver Steeg would have a hundred ways of letting him know he'd screwed up.

What were you doing there?

Well, uh—

Didn't you cover Speight?

No, I sort of lost track of him.

And Chardy would look and see a hopelessly incompetent kid. And Miles, that seedy little dwarf, would glow. Another rival x-ed off the list, another potential competitor screwed, shot down in flames. Miles would smile, showing those brackish teeth, and clap his tiny hands.

"You found who?" Trewitt said.

"The guy."

"What guy?"

"You know."

"I don't know a goddamn thing. Who, you little—" He lunged comically at the boy, missing. The boy laughed as he danced free.

"Him, man. *Him.* The bartender, Roberto."

"Roberto?"

"Roberto, the bartender. Who would not shut up. Remember?"

Sure, Trewitt remembered. What he couldn't remember was laying his sorry story on this kid here.

"I told you?"

"Sure. You come from the bar. Oscar's. Stay out of there, you say. A bad place. The bartender, a bad guy, an evil man."

Maybe Trewitt did have a vague memory of the conversation.

"So now you can go kill this guy Roberto. With a knife. Come on, I'll show you where he lives. Cut his belly. My brother done that to a guy once and is still in prison."

"You watch too much TV."

"Ain't got no TV, man. What you gonna do? Cut that cocksucker?"

"I don't know," said Trewitt.

The boy pointed in the dark.

"There. That's the one."

Trewitt traced the arc indicated by the small finger until he could see a certain house among a group of four of them, neither more nor less prosperous than its neighbors, a cinderblock shanty of flat roof and no windows.

"You're sure now?"

"Sure? Sure I'm sure."

The moon smiled above through a warm night. He and the boy were across a muddy lane in southern Nogales, miles from Trewitt's homey barn. They crouched in a gully, which Trewitt had come to believe contained sewage. But perhaps not; his imagination again?

"You better be right, *amigo.*"

"Sure I'm right. You have a nice tip for me, okay? For Miguel, a little money?"

"Right now I couldn't afford an enchilada," Trewitt said.

He checked his watch. Nearly five, sun coming up soon.

"And Roberto," said Miguel. "Soon Roberto. You'll see."

The light began to rise, revealing eventually a familiar landscape—the shacks on the muddy street, some shuffling chickens, sleeping dogs, puddles everywhere, pieces of junk strewn about. Into this still composition there at last came the figure of a man—a youth really—strolling along.

"He's late," said the boy. "You ought to kill him."

"I just want to talk to the guy."

"You should have seen what my brother did to this guy. He got him right in the guts. He—"

"Shhhh, goddammit."

The bartender approached, picking his way among the puddles. He looked familiar to Trewitt, though thinner, more delicate than the American remembered. His hair was pomaded back and he had the thinnest moustache over his upper lip. He wore a leather coat over his jet-black pants and white ruffled shirt. He looked to be about eighteen.

He walked, hands in pockets. Trewitt had studied judo, though he had never earned a belt, and when the boy paused at his gate, directly across from him, Trewitt lunged from the gully in two muscular bounds, got his arms on Roberto, and quickly and savagely broke him to the earth.

The youth squealed, but Trewitt gave him a squirt of pressure through his pinned arm which calmed him fast; then he shoved him into the gully and leaped after. He punched him twice, hard, in the ribs, and got him into a wristlock. Trewitt was far too brutal, for Roberto offered no resistance and only yelped as the blows landed, but Trewitt was working off weeks of rage and frustration. He sensed the wrist he was gripping give, and saw the fear bright in Roberto's eyes—and felt at once ashamed.

"I have no money, I have no money," wailed Roberto.

"I don't want money, goddammit," screamed Trewitt in English.

"Cut him," yelled the other kid, Miguel, watching from above with great, cruel joy.

"Shut up, you. *Silencio!*"

"Let me go, sir. I have only money for my sister and my mama and my two brothers and our dogs. Do not hurt me."

"Why was the old gringo killed? Come on, talk, god-dammit!"

He gave the wrist a quarter twist to the right.

"Ow! Oh! It hurts so. Ouch. No more. He went for the wrong woman."

Trewitt tightened up on the wrist.

"The real reason, dammit."

"You're hurting me."

"Of course I'm hurting you. Come on, goddammit, talk." He squeezed.

"Ahhhhhhhh!"

A cock crowed and Trewitt looked nervously about and saw no movement, though a goat in a pen down the way seemed to stir. He knew he'd better get on with it. In a few minutes this place'd be crawling with people.

"Why, why?" he bellowed in righteous fury.

"Ahhhh. Let me go, please. Don't hurt me no more."

Trewitt relaxed his grip a bit. "Next time I break it. Why'd they kill the old man? Why?"

"He ask after Ramirez."

"Okay. So?"

"The story they tell is that Oscar Meza set Ramirez up to take over his place. And here's this old gringo asking questions. And Oscar no like the gringos and he no like the questions."

"Oscar?" said Trewitt.

"Yes. Let me go. Oh, please, mister, it hurts so bad."

Trewitt almost did. He was exhausted and he was running low on energy and purpose. But his fury boiled up again darkly.

"No, goddammit, there's more." There had to be. He gave the Mexican another jolt.

"Ohhhh. No, I swear. On Jesus, on the Virgin. He kill me if he finds out."

If there wasn't any more, then Trewitt was in big trouble. Next step? He had no next step. This wasn't an intelligence operation, it was a gang war. He'd stumbled into the middle of it, and now the whole Mexican underworld was after him. Or was the youth lying?

He tried to think of what one of the old cowboys would do in his place. Chardy, a hero, a pro, an operator's operator. What would they do? Maybe the kid was lying; maybe he wasn't. There'd really only be one way to make certain,

and that would be to take him all the way. Put him on the
black edge of death and see what he said.

Trewitt knew in an instant that Chardy would be capable of a higher brutality here, for wasn't the other side of
bravery just the numb capacity to hurt and feel no guilt?
Suppose now, suppose a Chardy broke the kid's fingers,
both hands, then his kneecaps, then his nose, all his teeth,
then his wrists, and finally the kid broke. And this
Chardy-type then used the dope he got from the kid and
turned it into a real coup. Became a hero. A legend would
grow, a reputation; maybe a career would blossom. But
nobody, least of all Chardy, would remember the hurt
youth, humiliated, debased, raped almost, in a gully in a
scabby Mexican slum; the boy used, tossed away.

Weariness suffused Trewitt. His will vanished. "Ah,
Christ," he muttered, knowing he could hurt his victim no
more. He felt the youth slip away.

"Go on. Beat it. Scram," he said.

The young bartender fell back, rubbed his mouth and
then his aching wrist and crossed himself quickly for deliverance.

"You should not do this," said Miguel, perched on the
lip of the gully. "You should make him talk."

"Shut up. I cut your throat, little shit," said Roberto,
making a listless lunge that sent the younger boy scurry-
ing.

"Go on, get out of here. Both of you." For now Trewitt could not stand the sight of either of them.

Trewitt sat back in disgust and exhaustion. Next step?
Departamento de Policía. And damned quick, before
somebody from the mafia blew him away over the owner-
ship of Oscar's. Still, he dreaded it; it meant the coming
to an end of a phase of his life. For surely he was done at
the Agency; that much was clear—after a mess-up like
this, there'd be no future.

It was also clear to him that he *deserved* to be done at the Agency. He simply was no good at this sort of thing—he hadn't the hardness, the cunning, the fury. They never should have sent him; they should have sent somebody who knew what he was doing. He hadn't even taken the Clandestine Techniques course out at The Farm in Virginia, a basic intro to the dark side of the Agency.

He wondered where the nearest Federal Police station was. Enough adventure for one day, and it was not even 6:00 A.M. He treated himself to a last smile for his own dumb folly—it *was* kind of funny, except for poor Bill—and set off in search of saner possibilities.

"Hey, mister," somebody called—Roberto—"I tell you a lie."

Trewitt turned. The youth stood with a taut look of defiance on his face. What, did he now want to mock Trewitt, or even, out of some Mexican macho thing, to fight him?

The younger boy lurked close at hand, eyeing the two curious antagonists, still hoping for a little action.

"Hey, mister," said Roberto, "you got some money for Roberto?"

"Kid, I ought to—"

" 'Cause, mister, Roberto thinks Reynoldo Ramirez is still alive. And he thinks he knows where he is."

22

She wanted to walk.

"I just want to walk. Could we walk all weekend? I need the space—I don't know how to explain it."

"Sure," Chardy said.

"I just have to walk. Do you understand? I want to be with you but I want to walk too. All right?"

"No, it's fine. Show me this place. I want to see this place."

She took him down Mass Ave to MIT and back again. They went up Garden Street, and she showed him Radcliffe. They got lost in the little places along Brattle. Then they went onto the campus, and walked among the red brick Georgian buildings, under the vaults of the trees.

"How was your week, Paul? Your trip?"

"Terrible. I don't do anything. They won't let me do anything. I just hang around Danzig, except when they've got him locked up—like now. How was your week?"

"I didn't get much done. I didn't make any progress. It was depressing. I'm glad it's the weekend. I'm glad you're here."

The place was lousy with undergrads. They all dressed like hoboes in baggy, sexy rags, junk-shop clothes, insouciantly graceful. They seemed to Chardy like barbarians.

Frisbees sailed all over the place, skimming the ground, bouncing. Some rock group sang an amplified tune called "Dirty Deeds Done Dirt Cheap" from a speaker in a window.

"Look," he said, "let's sit down. Do you mind? You've really worn me out, all this trooping around."

They found a bench and sat quietly for a long time.

"This is quite a place," said Chardy lamely. "I always wondered what one of these places looked like. I went to college in a little town in Indiana. You could hear the grass grow. On Saturday night we used to hang out at—"

He stopped, because he could tell that she wasn't listening.

"What's wrong?" he said.

"Oh, I don't know," she said.

"Look, something is wrong, I can tell."

"I think what I like about this place," she said, "is the safety. Paul, there are people here who never come out. They are troglodytes. They live totally interior lives. They spend forty years studying a certain molecule in an amino acid or a certain sixteenth-century Italian poet. It's very safe. Nothing intrudes."

Safe? Chardy looked out on the crowd scene before them.

"Johanna—"

"Paul," she went on, "I get so scared sometimes. I lie there and I think of all the things that could happen. I think of him, of Ulu Beg. I think of the Kurds, a lost people. And I think of us, and how we're so responsible for it all, how we tie it all together, and how we haven't really done anything. Sometimes my mind gets going so fast I can't get it settled down. I don't sleep. I don't eat. Paul, I can get very crazy. You have no idea how crazy. I can act very strange."

He turned to touch her but saw she was not agitated. In fact, he'd never seen her so calm.

"Paul," she said suddenly, "teach me something. Will you? Help me."

"Anything."

"Teach me bravery. Your kind of bravery, a man's kind of bravery. War bravery, battle bravery. There must be a trick. You were so brave. Whatever else, for so long you were so brave. That attracted me from the first. I fell so in love with it. Teach it to me. I'm sick of being scared."

"I don't know much about it anymore. It used to be so important to me. A guy I thought was the bravest man in the world—the guy that taught me everything—ended up floating in the Danube. He left me a message, and it had an eerie ring to it. He told me to fetch the shoe that fits. The shoe fits? It was a joke, I thought. But now I don't know. Frenchy was trying to tell me something. About all this. He was scared too, because he was going in solo and Frenchy hated to work solo."

"He was a hero?"

"In our line of work, he was the best. Yes, I suppose he was a hero. Yet even the Frenchman came unglued at the end. His wife—his widow—told me about it. He grew up, he burned out, he got tired."

"Still, he died for something. Scared and tired and old, he died for it. That's really it. That's the lesson I want to learn. This Frenchman—he went ahead. He pressed on."

"Yes. You'd have to give him that."

"He died for something he believed in?"

"The joke is, when you think you're dying, the last thing you think about is what you believe. You think about crazy things. I thought about basketball." *I thought about you,* he thought.

"Still, it's the act that counts, not the motive. That's a shoe that fits."

"I suppose it does."

"Paul, I want to go back to the apartment now. Can we go back and make love?"

He looked at her in the hard light. It was noon, the sun harsh, the breeze stirring old limbs in this leafy place. Slivers of light cutting through the overhead canopy lay about them on the ground, on the walk. She was without color, a severe profile, almost stylized in her beauty.

"Of course we can. Sure. Let's go. Let's run back."

She laughed.

"Johanna, I hardly recognize you."

"No, I'm fine. It's you, Paul. I really do draw from you."

"Johanna, I—"

"Please, Paul. I want to go back. Let's go. The shoe fits."

He had always thought beautiful women a breed apart, and maybe they were, some mutant species, made crazy by all the hits on them, or made cynical, contemptuous of the twerps kissing their asses so desperately, or, the worst, made devious, unable to respond until they had figured out just what they stood to gain or lose. But not Johanna: she seemed to him none of these things except achingly, innocently beautiful as she sat before the mirror working on her hair, an abundant woman, flawless in the late afternoon light, after their lovemaking.

"Jesus, are you fun to watch," he called from the bed.

She smiled, but did not look over.

The telephone rang. Chardy rolled over to look at the ceiling.

Johanna said, "It's for you. A woman."

He took the phone.

"Hello?"

"Paul?"

The tone, queerly familiar, seemed to arrive from another universe.

"Yes, who is this?"

"Paul, it's Sister Sharon."

"Sister Sharon! How are you? How in the world did you find me?"

The nun taught at Resurrection, back in his other life. She had the third-graders, and was a funny, quiet, plain girl, so young, who'd always liked him.

"Paul, it wasn't easy. You left an address with the diocese to forward your last check; one of the secretaries gave it to me. It was a government office in Rosslyn, Virginia. I went to the library and got out the Northern Virginia phone book and looked up the government offices. I finally found one with the same address. It took an hour. I called the number. I got a young man named Lanahan. I told him who I was and he was very helpful."

Lanahan. Sure, he'd break his Catholic neck to help a nun.

"Finally he gave me this number. Am I disturbing anything?"

"No, uh-uh. What's up?"

"There's a telegram for you. It came to the school. They were just going to send it along but I thought it might be important."

Who would send him a telegram?

"I had to open it to see if it was an emergency."

"What's it say?"

"It's from your nephew. He wants money."

Chardy, an only child, had no nephew.

"Read it to me."

" 'Uncle Paul,' it says, 'onto something, need dough. I beg you. Nephew Jim.' "

Trewitt.

"Paul?" Sister Sharon said.

"It's fine, it's fine," he said, but he was calculating. Trewitt had found a soft route back in, trusting no one except his hero, and reaching him through his whole other life. Trewitt, you surprise me. Where'd you get the smarts—from some book?

"Is there any kind of address?"

"Just Western Union, Nogales, Sonora, Mexico. Is it all right?"

"It's fine. A college kid, a little wild. Always in trouble, always after me to bail him out."

"I'm glad it's not serious. Paul, we all miss you. The boys especially. Even Sister Miriam."

"Give 'em my love. Even Sister Miriam. And, Sister Sharon, don't tell anybody about this. It won't do the kid any good. He's probably in some jam with a girl and he doesn't want his folks to know about it."

"Of course, Paul. Goodbye."

She hung up.

"Johanna, I have to go out. Is there a Western Union office around here? Come with me."

"Paul. You look ecstatic."

And Chardy realized he was.

23

For the moment, the Kurd could wait, Chardy could wait, it could all wait. Other things occupied Joseph Danzig.

He was astonished. What little rabbits they were. He had lived most of his life in a kind of sexual sleep; then, at forty-seven, catapulted into an absurd celebrity, made preposterously powerful, imprinted upon the collective imagination, he was also granted, almost as a fringe benefit, an astonishing freedom with women. Not that they were attracted to his body—it was a wreck, a blimpish shamble of wrinkles, almost toneless muscles, a wilderness of wattles and fissures, a great, white dead thing—nor even his power (for they could not partake of that) nor his mind (they never talked about *anything*). They sought him not for cocktail party conversation or to get jobs with the State Department or for exclusive interviews to advance their careers in journalism or to punish their husbands or lovers.

Why then?

He asked one once, a lissome Georgetowner, thirty-four, ash-blonde, Radcliffe, old Washington/Virginia connections. They were at the time both naked and had just consummated the act with passion though not a great deal of skill—in this field, Danzig was well aware that he was merely an adequate technician. With prim efficiency Susan, for such was her name, was preparing to dress, arranging her Pappagallos, her Ralph Lauren double-pleated slacks, her cashmere turtleneck (from Bloomingdale's, he guessed; it's where they all dressed these days), her subtly checked tweed sport coat that re-created almost hue for hue the Scottish heather.

"Susan," he said suddenly, "why? I mean, really: Why? Be honest."

"Well, Joe," she said, matter-of-factly—and paused. He knew she was the mother of two girls, three and five, and that her husband was a Harvard law grad in the midst of a flourishing career with the FCC. "Well, Joe"—naked she was small and fine, with tiny shapely breasts and delicate wrists. She was slender enough to show ribs and had creamy, mellow skin. She had tawny hair, expensively taken care of, and had been a champion golfer and an excellent doubles tennis player. "I guess you could say I was curious."

Curious!

He had shaken his head then. He shook it now; he was with a twenty-six-year-old congressional aide, a bright Smith girl he had met casually at an embassy cocktail party. They had just accomplished an exchange of favors intense and satisfying and wholly meaningless. They were on the top floor of the Georgetown house in what had been a previous owner's music room—a wide space that drew in light from the brightness outdoors and splashed it abundantly around. Meanwhile, birds sang and bees buzzed and the flowers and bushes in his garden grew under the skillful nurture of a Philippine gardener.

The girl—by coincidence her name was Susan too, which was perhaps why the first Susan had so recently been in his mind—was dressing quickly and without, it seemed to him, regret. The room stank of sex, a peculiar odor, of which he could never get enough when aroused but which disgusted him afterward. He was, in fact, a little nauseated with himself. He had come, of late, to enjoy certain deviations from the standard male-female menu, certain varieties of dish or sauce. It was always the same: what had seemed exotic, astonishingly inviting, fascinating, erotically *creative* almost, seemed now merely unwholesome, to say nothing of unhygienic. He wanted badly to brush his teeth and use mouthwash, but was unsure of the etiquette: would such a gesture seem impolite? She had not brushed her teeth and she had used her mouth quite as industriously as he had used his (and simultaneously). He felt gross, an ogre. Yet it was not his fault. These girls these days! A nod, a nudge, a gentle suggestion as oblique and encoded as a secret cipher, and off they went like Bangkok tarts after treasures their mothers could not have conceived of, would not have even had the vocabulary to describe. And they expected—demanded—he reciprocate.

Such odd creatures. Their minds, really, were different from men's. For one, they were more grown-up, less romantic (as a rule, no matter that it defied the popular stereotype), more organized. Their brains were full of little compartments. This Susan, the other Susan, too, *all* the Susans, could fellate him like tigresses, smile, get dressed and return uncontaminated to their other lives. They'd go back to husband or lover, having entirely separated their adventure of the afternoon from their reality of the evening. Meanwhile, he or any man would brood and fret and remember, feel tainted and unworthy, clinched with guilt. Astonishing!

So now he stood wrapped in his robe at the broad window, peering down at the mazelike garden beneath him.

"It's quite attractive, don't you think? This new one works awfully hard, although I don't think he understands me. I certainly don't understand him."

"Huh?" Susan said, getting her haunches (she was not quite as slim as the first Susan) into her pantyhose with a final pump of the pelvis.

"The garden. I was talking about my garden and the new gardener."

"Yeah," she said, self-absorbedly.

"It has such order. It is a very pleasing design."

"Joe," she said, "I'm going now."

"Huh?"

She laughed. "I can see how much this all meant to you."

"I'm sorry. Do I seem preoccupied? I do apologize. Forgive me, won't you?"

"I just said I was going."

"I'll see you out, of course."

"No. That's fine." She worked quickly on her makeup. Seeing her sitting before the mirror, one fine leg stockinged and crossed over the other (Danzig loved their legs), in her sensible plum wool suit, mundanely studying her own face and making improvements in it, he stirred.

With a moan of lust singing between his ears, he walked to her almost uncontrollably and reached to touch her breast, inserting his hand quickly between her buttons and the elastic of the bra, feeling the weight, the heaviness of it.

"Joe! God, you frightened me!"

"Don't go."

"Oh, *Joe!*"

He had his whole hand inside her cup now and the nipple was between his third and fourth fingers and he was squeezing it with what he took to be finesse.

"Please, I do have to *go.*"

"Don't. Please." He was startled at the urgency of his need.

"Joe, really—"

"It's still early. Please. Please."

He could feel the nipple tighten.

"Oh, God," she muttered.

He bent and began to lick her earlobe, another trick he thought especially stylish; they all loved it. He reached and touched the inside of her leg and ran his finger up it and rubbed her, feeling the contours, the definitions, the fleshy rolling mounds of her cunt through her pantyhose. He kissed her on the mouth, their tongues groping.

For a second time they were finished and Susan rose to dress.

"Please," she laughed. "I'll get fired if I don't get back. You're a maniac."

He smiled, seeing it as a compliment. He had not had sex twice the same day before in his life, much less in the same hour. He was astounded at his power. What was reaching him?

He looked and she was at the mirror working on her face again, dispassionately. He watched her sadly. Women were leaving him all the time; it had never bothered him before.

"I'm going," she said, "*this* time." She laughed; she was a friendly girl, good-hearted.

"I'll call you."

"Sure," she said.

"No, I will."

"It's all right, Dr. Danzig."

"Call me Joe."

"It's all right, Joe, I do have to go. 'Bye."

"Goodbye, Susan."

And she really did leave. He could hear her steps receding in the hall until she reached the stairwell and descended. A minute later he heard a quiet thud as the door closed. He wondered if the agents down below were polite to her. He hoped so. Damn, they'd better have been; if they weren't, he'd have them reassigned faster than the coming of night. He told himself to check on it later.

Now he stood again at the window. He felt vulnerable, unprotected. Could this odd state of affairs be traced to the presence of this phantom Kurd assassin, who everybody is so confident will be shortly apprehended wandering desperately in the greater Columbus-Dayton-Cincinnati triangle? Perhaps. But he felt, rather, another presence, a brooding thing that pressed at him from beyond the wall.

For beyond the wall was another room, almost the twin of this one. It was high-ceilinged and immensely bright. Potted plants stood green and smart against cream-white walls, and muslin curtains softened the blaze of the sun. It afforded a view almost the duplicate of the one he now enjoyed, the downward vantage to the mazelike perfection of the garden. That room, like this, was neat and orderly; that room, like this, had a red-hued Persian on the floor; that room, like this, had a desk, a mahogany worktable, a sofa bed. But unlike this room, that room had: one Xerox 2300 tabletop-size copier, four cans each of Xerox 6R189 toner and Xerox 8R79 fuser oil, three IBM Selectric typewriters, one DCX Level III Dictaphone, six Tensor steel-jointed lights, several dozen pounds of Xerox 4024 dual-purpose paper, to say nothing of carbons, erasers, Bic fine-line pens, Eagle No. 3 pencils, a Panasonic Point-O-Matic electric pencil sharpener, a blotter. And against one wall, tightly locked and as yet unopened, his files, his logs, his documents, his reports, his minutes, his clippings, his borrowings—his past.

That was the room of the book, and it terrified him.

In that room, in one thirteen-month period of intense effort, he, three research assistants, two exceedingly patient secretaries, and two editors down from an august publishing firm on Madison Avenue, had written a book. It was a book largely of triumph.

But soon another book was due from that room and there was, as Danzig saw it, no sadder thing in this world than a room in which a book must be written if you do not want to write the book.

Danzig did not want to write the book.

He preferred to ad-lib speeches and doodle in television and avoid his wife and pursue the limelight and make love to an endless procession of curiously pliant young or youngish women. But not the book: the book would take him back to the season of catastrophes, the year 1975, when Vietnam came tumbling down, take him back to sad, groping days with a new and short-lived President. It would be a book of defeat.

He secretly feared he'd lost his edge, his ambition. Poof! Here one day, gone the next. His reputation was that of a fiercely ambitious man, a ruthlessly ambitious man; and perhaps once it had been true. But another Danzig, a softer, a lonelier man, a man more anxious to explore the realms not of power but of the senses was beginning to emerge from under the shell of the old Danzig. He hoped it was a process of transformation or transfiguration. But he was terrified that he'd reached the age of entropy.

He thought he'd call another girl, because he did not think he could be alone in this room, next to that room, another second.

24

It occurred to Chardy that he would not tell them—not Lanahan here, not Yost, expecially not the man whose presence he thought he felt in it all, Sam Melman—about Trewitt, about Mexico.

"Paul, I guess you'll just have to get back to Danzig," Lanahan said. "Ver Steeg"—Lanahan said it bitterly, for he was turning out to be no fan of Yost's—"says he'll have it wrapped up in a day or so."

They sat in the Rosslyn office, a ghost office, full of echoes and silence and stale air, on the Monday morning following the news from Trewitt.

Miles was bitter—he was not on the Dayton team. He had been shelved, it seemed, in favor of men Yost either trusted more or feared less.

"Relax, Miles. You'll get a shot at Ulu Beg. Yost won't get him in Dayton."

"They've got Dayton *sealed*. They've got it *nailed*. It's only a matter of time," said Lanahan bleakly. He was sweating. Drops of pure ambition ran from his hairline.

It occurred to Chardy that Lanahan flatly, coldly did not want Yost to take the Kurd. Not without having a hand in it himself.

"No, Miles. Yost doesn't really *know* this guy. He

thinks he's some gun-happy Third World terrorist. Just a brainless shooter, a man with a gun and a screwball cause. He doesn't realize: Ulu Beg's got *it*.''

It? What?

But Lanahan didn't ask, merely stared angrily at Chardy. "Little rats like Yost don't catch hero-types like Ulu Beg," he finally said.

"Something like that.''

"Chardy, it's all nonsense. That's a silly notion, a schoolboy notion. It's full of romance, myth. It's full of bullshit. Ulu Beg is being hunted by men armed with computers, sophisticated electronics and optics. And *man-power*. Carte blanche. All they want. Bodies and more bodies. A whole agency full of bodies. You make him sound like Geronimo. He can only be caught by the righteous. It's out of the last century, which, in case you hadn't noticed, ended some time ago.''

"Okay, Miles. Don't say I didn't tell you. I almost like you, Miles. You want into the big time so bad.''

"Just leave it alone, Paul.''

"You want in. You want buddy-buddy with the Harvard boys.''

"Just forget it, Paul. I have to tell Yost where you are. You better get where you're supposed to be.''

No, Chardy would not tell Miles about Trewitt. Because Trewitt had no brief for Mexico, because there would be all sorts of problems if Trewitt was suddenly operating in Mexico, which Yost had specifically forbidden.

And it also meant one other thing, which may have pleased Chardy the most and explained his decision the best: for the first time he knew something *they*—all of them—didn't.

Let Trewitt have some time, some space. Maybe he could come up with something. But what, or who?

Chardy smiled.

I just put some money on Trewitt, he thought. Dreamy Trewitt, preppy kid, all eagerness and sloppy puppy love, full of insane, ludicrous notions of adventure. Weighted with legends, inflated with heroes—a fan really, as far from shrewd, grim, pushy little Miles as you could get.

Chardy thought of the good men he'd backed and who'd backed him in his time, heroes from Frenchy Short on down; and here he was with his chips on Trewitt.

"What's so funny, Paul?"

"I don't know. It all is, Miles. You, me, all of it."

But Miles wasn't smiling.

"You better get going, Paul. The great man is waiting. And you better get ready to move this weekend. There's a job coming off."

Chardy turned, stung.

"I thought he was staying put—" He'd had plans for the weekend.

"It just came up. But maybe Yost will get lucky before then."

"He won't."

"Don't worry, though. You're going to Boston."

25

Her name was Leah; she never asked him his. After the first day she began to call him *Jim*. He never questioned it.

She was a tall, strong woman with furious wide eyes and a flat nose and long fingers that were miraculously pink inside. Her hair was cut short as a boy's and she had three wonderful wigs —red, yellow and jet black—which she wore depending on her mood. Her skin was brown, almost yellow, and she was a proud woman with a grave and solemn air until she had a few glasses of wine, which she did every night, when she laughed and giggled like a loose-limbed girl. She worked in the basement of a place called Rike's and he never understood what Rike's was, except that it had to do with clothes because she brought him some: a suit like an American businessman's, a rain-coat, a dapper hat.

"They for you, baby," she said.

He looked at the clothes. He could not have clothes, a wardrobe, because he had to move quickly. He could have no luggage, no luxuries. Wealth was of no interest to him. He turned to look at the black woman, whose face was eager.

"They are beautiful, Leah. But I cannot wear them."

"But why, baby? I want you to look *good*. You a *fine-*

looking man, tall and strong.'' She'd had several glasses of wine.

"Leah," he said. "I cannot stay much longer. I have to go on."

"Why you in such a *hurry,* Jim?"

"Ah." He was evasive. He almost thought he could trust her but he knew he'd never be able to explain. It would take so long and go back so far. "I have a special place to go. Someone special to see."

"You up to something," she said, and laughed explosively. "You up to something *sly.* I seen that look before. I been seeing that look for years and years and years. Somebody 'bout to *take* something from some other body. Just you don't git caught, hear?"

That was Leah: she would not judge. He fit into her life as smoothly as if she'd practiced all this, as though she'd taken bleeding men home time and time before. She asked nothing except his company, and if he never went out, if he had no past and would not speak of the future except in the most guarded and general terms, then she would accept that.

"Why, Leah? Why you help me? I can give you nothing."

"Baby, you remind me of somebody. 'Dey take my wallet' ''—she imitated his voice—''and up that hill you go, like to get yourself killed dead. And one minute later you comes down. Never seen nothing like it since my brother whipped Sheriff Gutherie's boy Charlie back in nineteen fifty-eight in West Virginia. Everybody says, 'Bobby, he's going *smack* you, boy.' Bobby, he just say, 'He took my *money,*' and Bobby go on up to the house and he kick that boy bad and he get every last cent back. Nobody seen nothing like that 'round there in years and years.'' She laughed again at the distant memory.

Bobby sounded like another Jardi.

"A brave man. A soldier, this brother Bobby?"

"Oh, Bobby, he was somethin'. He won the West Virginia High School four-forty-yard dash in 'fifty-seven. My baby brother, oh, he was somethin'. White people say he robbed them. He got sent to prison, up in Morgantown. Somebody stick a knife in him. He wasn't in that place no more than three weeks when they killed him."

"A terrible thing," said Ulu Beg. He had been in a prison in Baghdad for a long time, and knew what things happened in prison. "God have mercy on him."

"Mamma died after that and I came to Dayton and here I been ever since. I been at Rike's twenty years now. It ain't the life I wanted, but it sure is the life I got."

"You must be strong. You must make them pay."

"Make *who* pay, Jim? Can't make *nobody* pay nothin'." She took some more wine.

The apartment was small and dark, in an old building with garbage and the smell of urine in the halls. The lights had all been punched out and people had written all over the bricks. Ulu Beg had recognized the English word for freedom scrawled in huge white letters. Everybody who lived there was black; when he looked out the window he could only see black people, except occasionally in the police cars that prowled cautiously down the street.

"Don't worry none about them, baby," she had said. "They ain't comin' in *here.*"

"Say, Jim," she said now, "just who are you? You white? You *look* white, you *walk* white, you *talk* funny white. But you ain't white. I can tell."

"Sure, white." He laughed now himself. "Born white, die white."

"But you ain't no American."

"Many peoples come to America. For a new life. That's me—I look for the new life."

"Not with no *gun,* Jim. I looked in your bag."

He paused a second. "Leah, you shouldn't have."

"You on the run? Running *to* or running *from,* Jim? It don't matter none to me. Have some wine. You going to waste somebody's ass? It don't matter none to me. Just don't get caught, you hear, because they put you away in a bad place forever and ever, Jim. You the strangest white man I ever did see."

He stayed a long week. He made love to her every night. He felt full of power and freedom with the black woman in her small apartment in a ramshackle city in the fabulous country of America. He rode her for hours. He lost himself in the frenzy of it, sleeping all day while she worked, then taking her when she returned. He had her once in her kitchen.

"You a crazy man. I'm pushing the damn broom 'round Old Man Rike's store all day thinkin' 'bout crazy Jim."

"You're a fine lady, Leah. American ladies are fine. They are the best thing about America."

"You know another?"

"A long time ago," he said. "A real fighter, like you, Leah."

"A white girl?"

"White, yes."

"No white girl know nothin' 'bout no fighting."

"Oh, this one did. Johanna was very special. You and Johanna would be friends, I think." An odd vision came to him—he and Leah and Jardi and Johanna and Memed and Apo. They'd be at a meadow, high in the mountains. Thistles were everywhere, and the hills were blue-green. Amir Tawfiq was there too; they were all there. His whole family was there; everybody was there. His father, also Ulu Beg, hanged in Mahābād on a lamppost in 1947, he was there too. There were partridges in the trees, and deer too. The hunting was wonderful. The men hunted in the day and at night the women made wonderful feasts. Then everybody sat around in the biggest, richest tent he had ever seen and told wonderful stories. Jardi talked about his own crazy father, the Hungarian doctor. Johanna told of her sister Miriam. Leah told of her brother Bobby, and even as these people were mentioned they came into the tent also and had some food and told some stories and raised a great cheer. *Kurdistan ya naman,* they cheered, *Kurdistan ya naman.*

"Jim? Jim?"

"Ah?"

"Where you been? It sure wasn't Dayton."

"It's nothing. Tomorrow I will go. I have to go. I stay too long; I must move on."

She looked at him, her eyes furious and dark.

"You go off someplace with that gun, they kill you. No lie, they kill you, like my brother Bobby."

"Not Jim," he said.

"Baby, don't go. Stay with Leah. It's nice here. It's so nice."

"I have to go on. To meet a man."

"To the bus station? Cops catch you sure."

"No cops catch Jim."

"Sure they do. Where you going?"

"Big city."

"Big-city cops catch you in a bus station sure. I know they will."

"I have to go."

"*Jim,*" she said suddenly, "take my car. Go on, take it. It just sit there."

An awkward moment for him.

"I cannot drive an automobile," he said.

She threw back her head in laughter, sudden and light and musical.

"You some dude, baby, you some old dude." She laughed again. "Hon," she said, "you the strangest white man I ever heard of. You so strange you almost ain't white."

And so she said she'd drive him.

26

To Trewitt the world seemed considerably more attractive with a full meal in his belly, a shower, a night in a decent place—the Hotel Fray Marcos de Ninza, not exactly Howard Johnson's, but it had TV and running water, hot if you waited long enough. And locks on the door. So a little confidence had returned to Señor Trewitt with the arrival of Chardy's money; not that a sudden shadow, the report of a car backfire, a hard set of Mexican eyes flashing his way didn't still wreck him, but he was at least done with cowering in a barn.

Look at me. Look at me! So pleased he thought he might burst, in love with this new image, for he was a clandestine operator now; he was an agent. He felt he'd finally joined a fraternity that had been blackballing him these many years.

Look at me. Look at me! And he did, too. He could not keep his eyes off himself in shopwindows, in the mirror of his room—lean young man, quiet, willful. The eyes deep and quick. The hand never far from his weapon.

For Trewitt was now an armed man.

He'd sent the boy out with $50 of Chardy's money and specific instructions.

"An automatic. Not some ancient Colt or Remington

or Pancho Villa special. An automatic, short-barreled if possible, but I'd settle for one of those Spanish nine-millimeter Stars or even a Llama from Spain if it's big enough, nine mil at the least. Can you do it?''

''Sure I can.''

''Don't screw me now.''

''I'm no screw you.''

''Just don't.''

The boy returned with a worn yellow box, its faded label displaying a pale square of print. In, of all unlikely things, Italian.

''Italian?'' wondered Trewitt, much concerned, and ripped the box open greedily. ''Jesus, a Beretta,'' he said in wonder. ''Must be fifty years old.''

The small blue pistol glinted up at him, antiquated and stubby. It had an odd prong flaring off the butt-stock to give it an Art Deco look. Ten oily rounds stood upright in a tray along the box's edge.

''That's all you could get for fifty American?''

''Inflation,'' the boy explained.

But Trewitt was secretly delighted with the small automatic. He fired one of the precious 7.65-millimeter rounds that night into a gully wall. The pistol was accurate to maybe seven feet, something out of an old Hemingway novel, fresh from the retreat from Caporetto, but it was his, his alone. Its weight in his waistband pleased him, and he carried it with a round in the chamber, but at half cock, pushed around on his hip. He tried his draw too, in private moments, groping quickly for the weapon. He needed to improve, and vowed to spend half an hour a day in practice.

Look at me! For the pistol was only the beginning. The shop-windows and the mirror also threw back the vision of a dashing young gangster in a yellow leisure suit, a double-knit polyester thing only recently arrived from

Taiwan, and a white-on-white imitation-silk shirt (also Taiwanese) with a huge flappy collar and no buttons above the sternum. He looked like a pimp, an assassin, a failed movie star in the getup, a zoot suit, a blast of sheer arrogant yellow that would have burned the retinas of his friends. The bad taste of it was awe-inspiring and of his old self only his Bass Weejuns, tassel loafers in a muted oxblood, remained, because the Mexican shoes all ran to three-inch heels and seemed to be made of plastic.

And Trewitt had one more treasure of considerable significance to him: he had a new recruit, No. 2 in his network. The bartender Roberto had signed on. He had been sacked by Oscar Meza for stealing and like many another Latin male, unjustly dismissed only for playing by what he understood the rules to be—they had been Reynoldo Ramirez's rules, after all—was insane with a desire for vengeance, *la venganza,* and dreams of glory. He too had an image problem: he wanted to be a tough guy, a knife fighter, the kind of man whom all the women wanted.

Roberto's story: One of his less pleasing jobs in the brothel involved the sorting of laundry, going through the towels. "The whores use a lot of towels," he explained, and Trewitt kept his face blank, remembering the job done on his privates by Anita with just such a towel.

"And guess what I find, three weeks running, every Tuesday?"

Trewitt could not, or would not.

"Bandages with pus. Yards of adhesive tape with hair in the sticky part. Bloody linen."

"Maybe somebody got rough with the girls."

"Not that rough," said Roberto.

"So where's it from?"

"I try to keep my eyes open. Where, I wonder, where does the Madonna go on Tuesday afternoon?"

"Who's this Madonna?"

"The upstairs lady. The pecker-checker. Fat and ugly. Eeeeeiiii. She been a nurse or worked in the hospital or something, I don't know. She takes care of the girls."

Trewitt nodded, thinking about it. Where *did* the Madonna go?

Now it was Tuesday, and behind cheap sunglasses, in his yellow outfit, Trewitt lounged on a bench in the hot shade of a mimosa tree. He was among Indians, country peasants, shoeshine boys, hungry scabby dogs, an occasional cop, a more than occasional gaggle of Exclusivo cabdriver pimps, in a small park at the corner of Pesquirica and Ochoa streets. Beyond him were railway tracks glittery with broken glass; beyond them another hundred yards, the Casa de Jason; beyond it, the Ruis Cortina and on the other side of the Ruis Cortina, tucked into the rising bulk of a sandstone bluff otherwise bristling with shacks, Oscar's. Weeds fluttered in the gritty breeze; skinny dogs and kids fled this way and that; banged-up Mexican cars roamed up and down the streets, jammed full. The sky was blue; the sun was hot.

But Trewitt just sat, one leg tossed over the other, and kept his eyes pinned on a small figure beyond the tracks, just down the block from the nightclub. The boy Miguel. Somewhere closer yet lurked the other boy, Roberto. The three had been so arranged for some time—since ten, and it was nearly one. The heat and the boredom were beginning to get to Trewitt. Not long ago he'd bought a chicken tortilla and a Carta Blanca from a street vendor, downing them both quickly, and was now just a little logy. He had not yet adjusted to Mexican time, in which nothing happens quickly, and was stifling a yawn when the boy leaped.

The boy leaped, then Trewitt. He was up in a shot, panic huge and bounding through his brain.

The car, goddammit, the car!

He sprinted up the street where, among the '53 De Sotos and the '59 Edsels and the '63 Falcons, there was wedged an '80 Mexican Chevette, rented that very morning from Hertz at the hotel under his real name, a big chance. Trewitt reached it, unlocked it, jumped in.

It was maybe 300 degrees inside—the car had been baking for about three hours in the sun. Still, Trewitt got the key into the slot, started it, cranked the wheel and pumped the pedal. The car accelerated rapidly to almost ten miles an hour and seemed to have some trouble getting into second gear, and just then the younger boy, having threaded his bold way across the tracks and through the traffic, reached him and climbed aboard.

"Go, mister, go."

"Where? Where?"

"Down there, down there!" the boy screamed.

Trewitt rammed the car across two lanes, took a hard left just beyond the Casa de Jason, and skyrocketed over the tracks on a dirt crossing. Where the hell was the other kid? But Trewitt saw him running hard, his hair flying, his face dark and angry. He had seemed to appear from nowhere—a trick these Mexican kids had—and slid into the back.

"Okay, man, turn right fast," he commanded.

Trewitt turned and sped into downtown Nogales, for just a few seconds under the bluffs of shacks and then into a flatter part of the city.

"She's in a green Chevy. Just ahead. Hurry, man."

But Trewitt could not hurry; he was suddenly in traffic up to his eyeballs.

"A Mexican freeway," shouted Miguel, laughing.

"Goddammit," shouted Trewitt.

"Hurry. Hurry."

"How the hell can I *hurry?*" Trewitt complained. All

of Mexico out for a drive that afternoon. The traffic lights all fouled up, strange directional signals giving him orders he couldn't understand. Somebody honked and cursed. The sidewalks were dense with people who roamed in and out of the small stores and spilled aimlessly into the streets. An ice-cream wagon was parked in the middle of an intersection. Kids fled in and out.

"Wow. You almost hit that cocksucker," said Miguel.

They moved at a stately pace. Trewitt searched ahead through the jumble of automobiles and people. He couldn't see a goddamned—

"There! There, I see her," yelled Roberto, who'd been craning crazily out the window.

"Watch it, kid," Trewitt warned, but joy flooded him.

In Le Carré, this would have been handled differently, Trewitt told himself as he bombed and bobbed and lurched sweatily in and out of the traffic, guiding the sluggish yellow Chevette among the dented '50s hulks that dominated the streets. Goddamn this woman—she had the only *fast* car in the country.

In Le Carré, it would have been bleak, icy professionals, drab men with sinus problems and wretched home-lives, following one another through an Eastern European drizzle. Every brick, every nuance of thought or action accounted for, every alleyway diagrammed, every bitter irony underscored; here, instead, dusty crowded streets, ice-cream wagons, fruit wagons, kids in plastic shoes, hills set with powder-blue shacks, a hot sun, a dry, dusty wind, streets whose names he'd never learn, two Mexican boys shouting into his ear.

"She turned."

"No, she didn't."

"Which is it?"

"She turned."

"No, she didn't."

"I can't see her."

In Le Carré tail jobs were handled by teams working in units of four, with silhouette changes, a control van with something childish scrawled in the dust high up where no child could reach. In Czecho or one of the old territories, or on Hampstead Heath, but with Moscow Rules. Le Carré knew the nuts and bolts, the trade craft, knew it cold.

"She turned."

"No she didn't."

"Aw, shit," he bellowed in exasperation, braking the car to one side of the road in a shower of dust. A scrawny chicken hoppity-flipped in front of it from a hole in some-body's coop and wandered off the shoulder onto the road-way, where it was immediately smashed by a huge Mercedes Pepsi-Cola truck, knocked up into the air as if in a cartoon to spiral down leaking feathers and drum-sticks, and land with a thud in the dust.

"Jesus Mary, did you see that?" Miguel asked.

Trewitt had seen it and began to wonder if anywhere in the works of John Le Carré, chickens got creamed by Pepsi trucks and if so, what that decent, weary, brilliant old professional, that traveler in the shadowy labyrinths of espionage, George Smiley, would have made of such a thing; but at that moment, blocks ahead, he saw the green Chevy.

From the avenue they climbed another hill, then down, then up again. Perched all about in no order save that of first claim were tarpaper shacks, corrugated tin roofs, wire fences, pink or blue one-roomers; Trewitt was beginning to believe there was but one street in Mexico and that he'd been down it a thousand times.

He could read the dust floating in the air, however, which told him the Madonna's car had screeched through moments before, and now and then he could see the vehicle, disappearing on a crest above or careening wildly beneath him as he hurtled down the same hill.

"Where are we?" he asked his guides.

"People from the desert or the mountains end up here," said Roberto. "The poorest of the poor. Reynoldo, he comes from this place."

"It's a very bad place," said the younger boy.

The car ahead vanished. Trewitt slewed to a panic stop, skidding. But beyond him there was no dust.

"Oh, goddamn," he said.

"She must have turned off."

"Dammit."

He looked back, forward. It was the same, the muddy little streets twisting up and down, the sheds, the wire coops, the TV aerials.

"Back up. Slow."

He began to back. He could have used one of Le Carré's four-man teams about now.

"There. There, I see it." It was Miguel.

"Yeah, yeah," said Trewitt, for he saw it too, pulled off at a funny angle halfway up a nearby hill.

He pulled ahead slowly, turning a corner, and parked near a small store, the Abarrotes Gardenia.

"Okay," he said, breathing hard, "Miguel, you go on back to that house. You're least likely to attract attention. Play it cool, huh? Nothing stupid. Just see what you can see, okay? Roberto, you drop on back to that little store. See what the guy behind the counter says. Don't force it, just see—"

"Okay, is okay," said Roberto, sliding out.

Trewitt waited. He slouched behind the wheel of the car, his cheap sunglasses slipping down his nose. He felt preposterous, a costumed clown playing games. It was hard to accept any of this. But he could accept Bill

Speight, in the sewer: that was real. He wondered if any of the others ever had this sort of problem, ever felt themselves playing absurd parts among unlikely characters. He doubted it; they were trained men, and would think always in terms of their training, look for expediencies, for angles, for escape routes. They'd be so occupied, so *busy,* they'd have no time for the longer view. Trewitt had only the longer view. He'd never been trained in the clandestine arts; he was an analyst, a historian. Nobody had ever thought about dumping him into an op. Yet here he was.

The boy Miguel returned first.

Trewitt jumped as the boy slipped in. Damn, he'd been silent.

"I couldn't get too close. There wasn't much cover. I didn't want to wreck the whole thing."

"That was probably smart."

"But I got into the garbage. Here." His trophy: a crusty strip of gauze, pink-brown and stiff.

"That's blood, all right," Trewitt said, stomach queasy all of a sudden at the elemental essence of the artifact. "And lots of it."

"Sí," said the boy.

"Now if only Roberto would get here."

But Roberto did not get there. A long time seemed to pass. They sat in the car in the alley. Maybe the youth had decided to forget *la venganza* for the time being and had skipped out. Or maybe—

But Trewitt knew smart field operators didn't sit around chasing maybes in their brains. No percentage, nothing but grief in it. Still, he couldn't stop his mind running off. Maybe he'd run into a gang. Maybe he'd—

But the youth arrived suddenly.

"Where the hell have you been?"

"In the Abarrotes Gardenia."

"You were in there an *hour.*"

"I had some trouble."

"What kind of trouble?" Trewitt had to know.

"Suspicious old men in there. They watch me close. Who am I, what do I want? So I tell them I was from down south, I was going to go to *el otro lado* tonight. The wire."

"They buy it?"

"Maybe yes, maybe no. But I did not think I ought to run out. So I had a Pepsi-Cola."

"So you were drinking a—"

"But then two others showed up."

"Americans?"

"No. Latins. Tough ones too, gangsters."

Trewitt nodded grimly. He didn't like the sound of this.

"They hurt him pretty bad, the owner. Hit him with a gun, a pistol."

Trewitt turned, the boy leaned into the light, and Trewitt saw an ugly red swelling above his eye.

"Jesus, Roberto—"

"Hit me too, the cocksuckers. Tough boys, real evil ones."

"What did they want?"

"They wanted to know about a wounded man. They'd heard there was a wounded man in the neighborhood."

"Did he tell them? This old man?"

"It was that or die. He told them."

"Dammit," Trewitt said. He reached with a pale hand and touched the automatic in his belt.

"They must be there by now," said Roberto.

"Fireworks," said Miguel gleefully. "Fireworks."

27

"Goodbye, Leah," he said. "God will be kind to you."

"Baby," she said, "you be careful. Don't you do nothing *stupid*. Don't let no cop bust your head. Stay away from cops, you hear?"

"I do," he said.

The city was huge. It was no Baghdad, nor even any of the other American cities he'd seen, but something, more America than he'd seen in one place, America piled high, America all over the place, America crazy, bewildering, America spinning itself out. There was no rhythm to this place. It was all one speed, which was fast, and one tone, which was loud.

"Don't let no big-city boys take you to town," she said. Behind, a cab honked. The traffic fled by. The air was gray and cold and dirty and smelled of exhaustion. He looked down a canyon of buildings and the details were too multitudinous to be absorbed. His head sang in pain; sullen men on the sidewalk looked at him.

"Jim," she said, "honey, ain't nothing here for you. Come on back. Come on back to Dayton."

"I can't."

"You got that same look as the time you went up them

tracks. You got Bobby's look. You come back to me. You hear? You come back to Leah. You promise me that.''

"I will, Leah. By my eyes, I will.''

"Don't know nothing 'bout no eyes, Jim. I just want you back.''

"I'll come,'' he said, and stepped to the curb and she drove away.

He was near the bus station and he found another small, dirty hotel. She had given him $100 and he paid the clerk $15 for the night. He stayed in the room for a long time, two days. The next part of the trip would be the most difficult.

It took him a long time to find the right place. He knew the name, the address even—from the telephone book— and one night, late, he found a black man.

"I want to find a place. This place.'' He showed him the page ripped from a phone book.

"Jack, you talkin' to the wrong man.''

"Tell me how to get there.''

"Man, you gotta take a *bus*. Make a *transfer*. Take another *bus*. Jack, that's enemy territory. Ain't no way I'm going *there*.''

"What bus? Tell me of this bus.''

"Jack, back way down. Take a *cab*, rent a Hertz *car*, ride the train or the subway. Man, stay away from me.''

"You must help.''

"No way, Jack.''

Ulu Beg shoved some money at him. "Here. Show me. Show me.''

"Jesus, Jack, you must be *hungry*.''

It was a small place, tucked away in an obscure old section of the city. He memorized the route, returned late the next night. The neighborhood was quiet then. He waited across the street, watching in the shadows until he was sure the place was empty. Then, at last convinced, he ran across the street and hid in the back another ten minutes. Occasionally a car rolled by, and once a police vehicle crept down the alley, but he lay still until it passed. He stood finally and tested the door, which did not give to his effort. He'd expected nothing else. He moved to the window and examined it carefully.

"Bars you'll see right away. But look especially for wire. Everybody in America has wires connecting them to the police or to alarm bells, because in America everybody steals from everybody all the time." He was beginning to see that they were very cynical about America; they hated it. But their vision of it was usually correct and their counsel well taken; he always obeyed. "In the window, along the edge of the glass, the wires. It's a small place in a poor part and they probably can't afford anything fancy. But in America, who knows? A salesman may have come along and sold them something fancy. It happens all the time in America. There may also be a dog. If so, it must be killed immediately."

He looked again at the window: no wires, nothing.

He reached into his pack and pulled out a short-bladed knife. He leaned forward and—expertly, as he had been taught—inserted the blade in the slot between upper and lower windows. It was so easy. He worked the blade to the lock quickly and nudged the point against the lever of the lock. Twisting and shoving the blade, he got the lock to move—it fought him for just a second, and then popped free. He withdrew the blade and quickly lifted the window.

He listened for the yapping of a dog. Only silence. He looked each way in the alley; it was empty. From the open window a current of warm air rushed toward him, carrying a familiar range of odors with it. But he could not pause to admire them; he tossed in his pack, and followed.

He lay on the floor, letting his eyes adjust in the dark. A splash of light from the street cut across the floor. It was a simple room, with a few tables encased in cloths, their chairs stacked atop them. Ulu Beg moved swiftly across the floor to a door on the other side and came into the kitchen. It smelled largely of strong industrial soap, but even under this blinding American smell he could pick out the familiar: scents of lamb and chicken, of falafel and grape leaves, of honey cake, spinach and cabbage, kibbe cakes, mint, other spices. It all felt good in his nose and the temptation came to tear open the cupboard, but he didn't; first, because the longer he stayed, the more danger he was in, and second, because to yield would be to admit how he missed what he'd left, how the grief at losing it cut so very deep.

He moved swiftly. He opened his pack and there, under the wrapped Skorpion, removed a tin.

They had explained it to him very carefully.

"Americans, who live in vast houses, aspire to more primitive things. They cook over coals, like hill people, and think this makes them rugged and vital. You may buy the fluid by which they light their coals anywhere for a dollar without suspicion. It's less volatile than gasoline and less pungent; it is, quite simply, perfect."

He opened the linen cupboard and squirted the fluid into it. He moved through the kitchen, squirting rapidly. He could smell the fumes filling the air in the dining room; he doused the curtains and sprayed patterns on the walls.

Then, with a match, he ignited the curtain. The flames spurted in one hot instant, billowing up with a crackling hiss, filling the room with light. He winced in the power of the blaze, watching it go from one puddle to another, in each unleashing a pool of flame that splashed through the room.

He stood for just a second by the window; he could see half a dozen fires in the room, each feeding and leaping. Two joined to become a single larger one; then a third joined in. Through the door of the kitchen he saw bright flames.

He hoisted himself through the window, feeling the air cool and sweet in his lungs. It seemed to him that once in a battle against the Iraqis he'd been trapped in a burning building. A memory of encircling flame came to him, but he could not remember how or when. He only remembered the same joyous feeling as the cool air hit him.

Gripping the pack tightly, he cut down two alleys and was on a far street when he first heard sirens. A police car rushed by, light flashing.

Another thought came to Ulu Beg and he rationed himself one more bitter smile: for had not Jardi once made a prophecy? Some day, Jardi had promised, you'll burn Baghdad. You'll burn it to the ground.

As before, Jardi was right.

Ulu Beg turned and walked more quickly into the night.

28

They could see a Ford parked outside the shack.

"That's it," cried Roberto. "That's their car."

Trewitt grunted uncomfortably.

"Now go shoot those guys," said Miguel.

"Just a minute," said Trewitt. He looked about in the twilight and saw nothing, no *policía,* no other humans. It was the quiet hour in this slum. Usually there were chickens about and goats and children and old ladies and tough young men. But up and down the crooked little lane he could see nothing.

"Use that gun," coached the younster. "You got a fifty-dollar gun. Go up there and shoot those cocksuckers."

This kid was really beginning to get on Trewitt's nerves. Sure, use the gun. Who do you think I am, kid, G. Gordon Liddy? An immense bitterness settled over Trewitt. His options were so bleak. It was not fair.

"Sure," the older boy now, "go on, shoot those shitheads."

"You just don't go shooting people," Trewitt instructed. But his thoughts were beginning to focus on the pistol, for there seemed no other place to focus them. He sure wasn't going up there *without* it. A crappy little Beretta, probably fifty years old, older than he was, a veteran of the Abyssinian campaign, where he was a veteran of nothing beyond several libraries.

"You better do something fast, mister."

"I know, I know," said Trewitt, who did not want to do anything at all, much less anything fast. "Maybe we ought to wait," he said, through a sudden accumulation of phlegm in his throat.

Both boys looked at him. How did he ever get stuck in this anyhow, with an ancient pistol and two kids?

"Okay, okay," he said.

The sun, a huge orange ball, a grapefruit, rotting and opulent, descended behind a line of sleazy blue and gray hovels.

"You better do something, mister," Roberto said.

A scream rose from the house. They could just barely hear it.

Trewitt reached for the pistol, and found that it had worked its way around until it was almost in the small of his back. He plucked it out of his pants with two fingers. He looked dumbly at the thing, oily and ugly and squat. He couldn't remember if it were cocked or not. His mind was empty.

"I think somebody just got killed," said Roberto.

Trewitt finally remembered the principle of the automatic pistol and threw the slide with an oily *klack,* ramming back the hammer. A perfectly fine cartridge spun out of the breach. Goddamn, it *had* been cocked. Roberto handed him the bullet.

Trewitt popped the magazine out of the handle and reinserted the slug. He slid the mag back up until it locked. He got out of the car and stood for a second on shaky legs, trying to devise a plan. Yet the more he thought, the more nervous he became and in the end he simply ran up toward the shack, keeping exactly in line with the corner, out of view therefore of the windows. He ran low, as he'd seen it done in the movies, and his Weejuns kept slipping in the mud. He made it to the house and paused for a second at the door. He heard muffled sounds of agony. Somebody was getting punched around pretty bad. Yet he could not move, was frozen to the earth, his tasseled loafers sinking into the very planet itself. The two boys had left the car also and were watching him.

At last Trewitt tested the door with his shoulder. It would not budge. He leaned again, harder—nothing. He heard somebody hitting somebody.

Oh, fuck it all, he thought.

These words seemed to liberate him. They filled him with violence and courage. He leaned back on one leg and with the other leg drove his Weejun against the door, blasting it open.

There were two of them, as Roberto had said. It did not occur to Trewitt that he had fired his pistol—he had no sensation of recoil, heard no report—but indeed he must have, for one sat down with a sudden terrified oafishness, mouth open, eyes open, hands flying to midsection. The second man recovered swiftly from the shock of the flying yellow apparition that was Trewitt and struggled to free a pistol from his own belt. But Trewitt had the small automatic pointed at him from a range of about four feet and was shouting *"Stick 'em up"* insanely, his eyes bulging, his veins swelling, and something of his abject horror must have communicated itself to the man, for he threw his hands up.

"Don't move. *Don't you move,"* Trewitt commanded. But the man moved. He smiled and waved his hands to show that they were empty and walked over to his friend.

"Don't you move. *Freeze, goddammit,"* Trewitt shouted. "I mean it, I'll shoot." Trewitt could imagine the bullet plunking into the man's neck.

The man smiled, still waving his hands to prove his harmlessness and bent to pry his dyspeptic partner from the floor.

"Kill him," somebody yelled.

"Don't move. *Goddammit,* don't move," Trewitt shouted.

The two began edging toward the door.

"Kill them. Shoot them!"

Trewitt could see the white face just above the dark blur of his pistol. The range was less than five feet. The man wore a white shirt inside a dirty seersucker coat. He needed a shave. He had veins in his throat. One of his teeth was brown.

"Kill him. Kill them," came the command. "Shoot!"

"Freeze," Trewitt ordered. "Goddammit, I'll—"

He fired—into the ceiling—to show he meant business.

The unwounded man just looked at him numbly—he was terrified too, Trewitt could see, pupils dilated like dimes, his lips smiling a lunatic's grin—but he just kept shoving his friend toward the door. Until he reached it.

Trewitt aimed at the fleeing figures as they ambled down the hill and off into an alley. He still had not decided *not* to shoot. It still occurred to him that shooting was a possibility. Yet he could not fire. They disappeared.

"Yeeeeeeee-*Owwwwwww,*" howled a fat, mad Mexican, corkscrewing from a chair even though his hands and feet were bound and hopping about like a toad. "You should have killed them, Mother of Jesus, you had them, you should have shot them *bang* right in the face."

"I did shoot *one,*" Trewitt protested.

"You should have killed those cocksuckers," Miguel said.

"Well," Trewitt began to explain. But his eyes hooked on the woman.

The pool of blood—blackish and thick—in which she

lay had almost soaked her clothes strawberry. So much? He was astonished. She lay like a doll, terribly, totally dead, deader than he could ever imagine anyone being, if only because a woman, if only because innocent of this whole business and slain for random cruelty, if only because defiled by the pints of her own blood soaking her, its vaguely menstrual associations troubling his brain. Her face lay in it, tilted, one nostril half under the surface of the pool. Her eyes were mercifully closed. The wound in her throat had drained and was clean. Her mouth was partially open and he could see teeth and tongue. Her dress had collected around her waist and her thighs were bubbly with cellulite—Trewitt, the Beretta still in his hand, was mesmerized by these details—and her calves and shins badly needed a shave.

"Mother of Jesus," the fat man was saying in Spanish, "you hear her scream? She wake the dead." Somebody had untied him. His face was swollen from the beating he had so recently absorbed and he was rubbing his sore wrists. He gave a little chuckle of astonishment. "She sure was loud," he said again. "Old Madonna, squawking till the end. Old ugly lady. Mother of Jesus. Jesus." He laughed again. "Hey, mister, how come you didn't shoot those two bastards? This could be big trouble. I don't think you did much damage with that little gun. You have given that one a stomachache, but they'll be back. If you have an advantage in these things, you should always use it. It's a hard lesson, but you've got to be strong if you want people to respect you."

Trewitt puked chicken tortilla and Carta Blanca all over himself, all over his yellow polyester suit, his tassels, his Beretta. He went to his knees, broken and helpless by the rebellion of his gastrointestinal system, and felt it all come up, all over everything.

"Hey, what's with him?" asked Ramirez.

"Patrón, I don't know," said Roberto. "Maybe the food don't sit good in his belly."

"That's a very bad mess, mister. It's going to smell something terrible."

"Oh, God," Trewitt moaned. Would no one comfort him? No. He took off his jacket and wiped his face and hands with an unsoiled section of sleeve, then chucked it into the corner.

"We better get out of here, *patrón,*" Roberto said.

"Who is this crazy American anyhow?"

"He just showed up one night. Asking questions. His friend got killed. At your place. Oscar's place, now. He fired me. He fired all your old people. He's a big man."

"I'll throw him in the sewer one day, you'll see."

"Can't you shut up? I mean," Trewitt bellowed in moral outrage, *"just shut up!"* in English.

Ramirez looked over at the trembling American, then at Miguel.

"Who's this kid?" he asked.

"Just some little snotnose with the American."

"We better get out of here," said Miguel.

"At least he's making some sense," said Ramirez. "You got a car, Roberto?"

"Yes, *patrón.* The gringo's. How do you feel?"

"Those whoresons hit my face pretty hard. And my chest is on fire. But I don't feel as bad as the Madonna. Jesus," he called to the corpse, "Ugly Woman, you saved my life." He turned back to Roberto. "I never seen such an ugly woman. Ohhhh! Ugly!"

Roberto led Trewitt to the car. Trewitt sat in back, groggily. He still held the pistol in his hand.

"Somebody better take that pistol," Ramirez said, "before the American shoots somebody else."

The gun was pried from Trewitt's fingers.

They all got in and Roberto began to drive down the

twisting hilly road. Twice he hit garbage cans and he killed a chicken and just missed some kids.

"Where to?" Roberto asked.

"Ask the American *patrón* here, the American boss," said Ramirez.

"Oh, Christ," said Trewitt, whose mind was too fogged to bother with the Spanish, "don't ask me."

29

Yost Ver Steeg would catch Ulu Beg in Dayton and be the hero. Yost! So hard for Miles to see him in a heroic light—or in any light.

Miles nursed his grudge bitterly, and under careful tending it became a fearsome thing, providing him huge amounts of energy. He hated them all: Yost and his chum Sam, Harvard buddies, watching out for and helping each other, without regard for him; and on the other side, Chardy, from another tribe altogether, jock, all heat and rage and power, who wouldn't even see the slight Miles, he was so busy gazing into the mirror admiring his own heroism.

Miles hated them, but this turn of events had its curious benefits. First, he was amazed at how totally Yost had committed to Dayton. A slipup could spell massive disaster; then bye-bye Yost, and there'd be nothing Sam could do to help. But, secondly, Yost's absence had a positive side: it gave Miles a taste of responsibility. Back in Rosslyn, people now reported to him. Sullen Chardy, though that was worthless. But others too, though they clearly didn't enjoy it. Miles didn't care what they enjoyed.

The wizard, for one, who'd come down from Boston for the day with reports on the surveillance of Johanna, and was astonished to find Ver Steeg gone. He sat in the office now, eyeing Miles uncomfortably, as Miles paged through the transcripts.

"I've marked the potentially significant ones," the wizard said.

"Fine," Lanahan said abstractedly. The exchanges were so boring, so banal. He tried to act them out in his head.

C: I miss you.
J: Oh, Paul, why can't you be here?

But he could not bring them to life. They lay beyond his capacity to imagine, his realm of interest.

"She's not cheating on him, shaking up on the side, anything like that?"

"Uh-uh," the wizard said. "Or if she is, the phone transcripts don't show it. Look at May twenty-sixth."

Lanahan found it.

"Who is this guy?"

"A boyfriend. An ex-boyfriend."

Lanahan read:

Someone told me they saw you with a guy. Twice. In two places, on two weekends.

Yes. An old friend.

You were holding hands.

Yes.

Johanna, are you in love with this guy?

I suppose.

Is he that guy you'd never tell me about? The guy you met overseas, when you were in Iran? The spook?

David, I have to go.

Johanna, I just want to make sure you're happy. Are you happy?

I am, David.

Good. Then I'm happy too. It really makes me happy that this guy has brought you out of your funk.

Thank you, David.

If you ever want to talk, to chat, just shoot the breeze, or if you're ever lonely or need somebody to see a movie with, you know where I am. Okay?

Okay.

I just want you to be happy. That's what I want.

Thank you, David.

Okay. Goodbye.

Lanahan smiled. This David wanted Chardy out of the picture and himself into her bed, that's what he wanted. "I just want you to be happy." Lanahan shook his head again.

At twenty-eight, he was as cynical as a Roman whore. In all human behavior he recognized but two motives: What's in it for *me?* And, what can I keep *you* from getting?

"So she's clean? She's okay?"

The wizard backed off immediately. He was an older man, plateaued out, stuck in Technical Services. He'd go nowhere, he'd been nowhere. He swallowed, a little uncomfortable on Lanahan's spot.

"I just record it," he said. "I don't judge it. That's for the analysts."

"But you're an old pro, Phil," he said. He thought the name was Phil. "You've been around. Off the record. She's clean. Come on. For me."

The wizard tried a joke. "You're not recording *me,* are you?"

Lanahan laughed. But yes, in a sense, he *was* recording him, if only in his head for possible future use.

"Of course not, Phil."

"It's Jay, Miles. But she's clean. Or she's got an operation going that's so deep cover even *she* don't know about it."

He offered another smile, but Lanahan didn't respond, noting the grammatical error under stress, figuring the man's true origins had just shown. Working class, just like me. Only he stayed there; I transcended.

"How about visual surveillance?"

"It's way off. He cut us way back. Mr. Ver Steeg."

"He wanted people to take to Dayton with him," said Lanahan.

"I stop by the house every third or fourth night and pick up the tapes. Then I have a girl transcribe it."

"But there could be up to a three- or four-day lag?"

"That's right, Miles. It's the way he wanted it."

"He smells the Kurd in Dayton," said Lanahan. "He smells a deputy directorship."

He scanned routinely through the transcript, seeing nothing beyond the mundane.

"Okay, well—" he halted.

He looked again, more closely.

Goddamn! he thought.

"You see this?"

"Huh?" The wizard rushed over, transfixed in the terror of having made a big mistake.

"Oh, *that,*" he said with relief, "sure, I *saw* it"—he had to make that point—"but I didn't see anything in it." He laughed. "So Chardy's nephew in Mexico needs a few bucks? It didn't seem to me—"

"No, you're right." Lanahan had always known how to lie smoothly. "Look, give me a few more minutes with this stuff, okay?"

"Sure, Miles," he said, and left.

Lanahan leaned back in the immensity of his victory. A great excitement raced through his limbs.

What was his next step?

Tell Ver Steeg?

No, the hell with Ver Steeg. Tell Melman? Go straight to Melman, secret lord in all this? Should he go straight to Sam, who already liked him? His imagination inflamed suddenly. Here was a ticket up another step. Up, *up!* Briefly he saw himself on the deputy director level by thirty. *Thirty!* Youngest in history by seven years (he'd once checked) and the only Catholic to have risen that high. The image pleased him. He toyed with it, turned it in his mind, savoring its hues. He was not given to daydreams except on the topic of his own career, whose secret rhythm and contour he loved. He saw himself with power, prestige, respect.

He picked up the safe phone to call Melman.

"Operations."

"DD's office, please."

"One second."

"DD's office."

"This is Miles Lanahan. His Eminence available?"

"He's on another line. Can you hold?"

"Yes, I can," remembering her vaguely as a severe single woman.

In the dead silence of hold, he turned it over in his mind.

Trewitt alive in Mexico. Chardy was running him.

What the hell did it mean? First, he was amazed. Chardy that devious? Chardy, sour, touchy jock, cowboy, sap for women? What could he be up to? What game is this?

Lanahan turned it over and over.

Was Chardy working on his own? Did he have secret communications, connections, links? Or could the whole thing be innocent?

Nothing was innocent. Ever.

Could Trewitt have set Speight up?

Could Chardy be working for the Russians?

This idea did not disgust him at all; in fact, it thrilled him. It filled him with wonder and amazement, almost awe. God, could he go to town on that! Jesus, he could build an empire off that. The guy who had nailed Philby had eaten free lunches off it for years.

Miles considered it more carefully. The Russians had had the guy for a week, worked him over bad. In fact, had cracked him wide open, had turned him inside out, the clear implication of the Melman report. Then the Agency had tossed him out.

And maybe in his seven long years of exile he'd hardened and bittered. Perhaps he'd come to hate those who let him languish in that cell in Baghdad, while the Russians worked him over. What did he expect, an airborne assault to free just one man? Chardy just wasn't being realistic, a common flaw among cowboy types. But in his exile, his bitterness, he'd come to hate his own people. Lanahan could understand the psychology of it: he was another outsider, with the stink of dark churches and novenas and holy mumbling about him, and was short and splotchy and damp and unlovable, and the patricians who ran the agency would always look upon him with distaste. Lanahan could imagine Chardy, among those kids, at that bleak school, surrounded by crucifixes of the faith that had failed him in the clinch, turning blacker and blacker by degrees until the only conceivable course would be betrayal, treachery. . . .

And in a flash Lanahan saw the end game: the Russians would set up the Kurd for Chardy, who'd blow him away. He'd be a hero again, the resurrected man, would be readmitted to the inner circle, on the way up again. Giving the Russians what they'd always wanted, what they'd never been able to get, a man up high on the inside.

Lanahan's heart thumped.

"Melman."

"Ah. Oh, Sam."

"Yes, what is it, Miles?" Melman's voice was crisp and driving and its suddenness scattered Lanahan's thoughts.

"Ah," he fumbled, "did those reports of the security setups for Boston reach you, Sam?"

"Yes, they did. Just this morning."

"I was just checking. I wasn't sure if Yost had sent them on before he left."

"Yes, it's here, it looks good."

"Is there anything from Dayton yet?"

"They have several reported sightings. The reports I get are optimistic. He's got the bus stations, the railway stations, all of it closed up."

"Good."

"Incidentally, how's Chardy doing?"

Tell him, he thought.

"Complains a lot. Wanted to go to Dayton."

"That sounds like Chardy."

"He sits around over there at Danzig's just like you wanted."

"Good. That's where he's needed."

"I'll see that he stays there."

"You're running things in Boston?"

"Yessir. It's only a weekend thing. Up Friday night, back Sunday morning. No sweat. I've got Boston PD cooperation, I've hired some private people. Everybody involved is cooperating."

"It sounds good, Miles. I'm sure you'll do well."

"Thank you, Sam," Lanahan said. Tell him. *Tell him.*

"Was there anything else?"

". . . No."

The line clicked dead.

Now why hadn't he said a thing?

I didn't have enough dope. But in subtle issues like these there's never enough dope.

Because even now I can't believe such deviousness in Chardy?

Perhaps.

Because something was wrong? Somewhere, deep inside, Lanahan was puzzled. Something was wrong and he didn't know what to do about it.

30

Chardy knew it was a bad idea but he couldn't help himself. He was so close and Danzig was in his room safely, snoozing away on creamy Ritz sheets, and he told her he'd try to make it and the cabby smiled when he said Cambridge and now here he was, $8 the poorer, heading up the walk of the hulking old house. He buzzed in the foyer and she let him in and he bounded up the dark stairs with energy that seemed to arrive in greater amounts the nearer he got. He plunged down the old house's hall, not caring that he thundered along like a fullback, and saw her door open.

"You made it," she called.

"Even Danzig sleeps. He's got a busy day tomorrow. He checked in early."

He embraced her; they kissed in the doorway.

"I'm so glad."

"Jesus, I'm beat, Johanna, I'm so *old*. Look at me, an old man; I can't take this running around."

He went inside. He could see that she'd been working on her book at the typewriter, where books and manuscript pages were collected. He went to the refrigerator and pulled out a beer can and popped the top. He swilled half of it down, then paused long enough to shed his jacket and fling it to the couch.

"A pistol?"

"They want me to carry it. Johanna, how are you? You've been working, I see. Did you get a lot done on the book? I want to read it. I bet it's good. I bet it wins prizes. Let's just sit and talk like we've been married for fifteen years and bore each other to death. Come on, tell me everything. Tell me everything you've stored up. It's—"

"Paul, that gun really bothers me."

He realized suddenly she was upset. It hadn't occurred to him; he'd been full of his own joy at seeing her.

"I'm sorry. I didn't realize they bothered you. Let me dump it someplace."

"Paul, not the gun itself, gun as object. Guns don't scare me. Paul, *that* gun. It's for shooting him."

"Johanna, it's a sidearm issued for an Agency security operation. They want me to wear it; they expect me to wear it. It's that simple. Nothing has changed."

"Paul. You were going to help. You said your first allegiance—"

"I'm on a security detail. They expect me to carry a gun. They expect me to protect him from Ulu Beg. If they feel I'm not willing to do that, then they have no more use for me. They'd get rid of me and I couldn't do anything."

"I hate it. Take it off—hide it. I don't want to look at it."

"Okay, sure." He peeled off the complicated holster, a harness of elastics and leathers and snaps, a mesh of engineering surrounding and supporting the automatic, and tucked the whole ungainly thing under his coat.

"Better?"

"Yes."

"But it's not. I can see."

"No, it's not."

"I'm sorry. What's wrong?"

"It's really hopeless, isn't it? We're just pretending? It's gone too far; there's nothing we—"

"No." He went to her and took her shoulders in his hands. "No, we can bring it off. We just need that first break. I have to be able to *get* to him. If I can talk to him, reason with him, explain things, then I can go to them. I can get them to help me set up a deal. I'll go to god-damned Sam Melman; I'll crawl to him, if that's what it takes."

"We haven't brought anything off. We're just *sitting* here."

"They think he's in the Midwest. Somebody stole his money, they think. I've been trying for a week to get them to send me out there."

"So they're closing in, and here we sit. Talking."

"I'll make something happen, I swear it. I'll go to Sam on Monday, soon as we get back. I'll tell him the whole story. I—I just can't offer more than that, Johanna. I don't have anything more than that."

"Somehow it's just not working out. They're closing in, you're spending your time with Joseph Danzig a thousand miles away, I sit around working on a book that I can't finish, that I can't make good, and—and we're just not in control. It just isn't working."

"Johanna, please don't say that. It's working perfectly. I'm getting them to like me; I'm getting some influence. You just watch. And they're not going to catch Ulu Beg in Dayton. He's too smart. For Christ's sake, I trained him. He'll be all right. Johanna, I think he'll be out here within the month. I know he'll get in contact with you. Or with somebody who knows you. He'll have thought it all out; he'll be very careful. Johanna, we'll bring it off, I swear we will."

"I'm sorry, Paul. I went for a walk down by the river

today. A helicopter, one of those traffic things, came screaming over the trees. It spooked me—it really did. I told you I was a little nuts. Oh, God, Paul, I get so scared sometimes.''

"Okay, okay, I understand. I understand.''

But she had started to cry.

"You've never seen me like this, Paul. But I can just crash for days, sometimes.''

"Johanna, please. Please.'' He tried to comfort her.

"We're just not doing anything,'' she said. "We're just sitting here. The whole thing is falling apart. It's just no good.''

"Please don't say that. It *is* good. We *will* get it done.''

"Oh, Paul. Since I got back, I've just become a basket case. I have a terrible darkness inside me.''

"Johanna, please.''

It terrified him that he could not reach her, that she was sealed off.

"Look,'' he said, "would this help? I think I could get by, late tomorrow. Danzig's got some kind of party not five blocks from here, on Hawthorne. It's with old colleagues, faculty people. It's not on any itinerary. I know I can skip out, about eleven o'clock. Would that help? And then Monday I'll go to Sam. Shit, I'll go all the way to the DCI. I'll get the whole thing changed around, all right? I'll get all the guns put away. We'll work a deal of some kind, I swear it.''

"Oh, Paul.'' She was still crying.

"Is that some kind of help?''

She nodded.

"Here,'' he said. "Just let me hold you for a while. All right? Just let me hold you. We'll get through this. I swear we will.''

He felt her warmth and thought he loved her so much he'd die of it.

She was not sure when he left finally; she drifted off and he had not awakened her. When she finally did awake it was around five; and he had covered her.

The television was still on, and she recognized the movie, *White Christmas,* with Bing Crosby and Danny Kaye. The scene involved a reunion among some ex-GIs at some hotel in Vermont that a general owned. It seemed a ridiculous movie to run in Boston in the spring.

But she did not have the energy to turn it off. She felt almost ill, feverish at the very least. She did not feel like doing a single thing and wondered again about her strength, her sanity. She tried to lock her mind up in *White Christmas:* idiotic Danny Kaye raced around; Bing just stood there and sang. Who were the women? Rosemary Clooney—whatever happened to Rosemary Clooney? Vera-Ellen. Did Vera-Ellen have a last name? Was it Ellen? Ms. Ellen? Johanna had seen the movie years ago on a giant screen; she remembered it now. The theater had been air-conditioned. The movie was Technicolor. She saw it with her big sister, Miriam, who was killed in a car crash, and her brother, Tim, who was now a lawyer in St. Louis. All this had been years ago, epochs ago, in the Jurassic of the '50s. She remembered it with brutal clarity and had no urge to fabricate it, to make myths out of it. Miriam had been very pretty and bright, but she'd left them, Johanna and Tim, all alone, because she'd snuck off with her boyfriend, whom Mommy and Daddy didn't want her to see anymore. Miriam was bad. She was fast. There was no controlling her. She had the hots. She had lots of boyfriends and worried Mommy sick. She was always in trouble. She was beautiful and bright and wicked and when she'd died her freshman year at Vassar in a car crash with a Yale football player (who survived) nobody was surprised. Johanna remembered that somebody whispered that Miriam got what she deserved. She was a bad girl. She deserved it.

Johanna started to cry again. She cried for Miriam, of whom she'd not consciously thought in years. Poor Mir. She was so bright and pretty and not until Johanna was in her twenties did she know what she should have said to anybody who said Miriam deserved it. She should have said, Fuck you. Miriam deserved the world. She was bright and pretty and good. Miriam was good. She was so good.

I am bad, thought Johanna. I'm the bad one.

She shifted her position slightly, with great weariness. Paul had sat there. And he was the man she loved. She would give herself to him. She would do anything for him, anything he wanted. She loved that chalky, locker-room body, that Catholic's body, with its slight coating of fat under which there was great strength. It was a big, loose-limbed, hairy body (Paul had hair everywhere; he left a trail of hair), a scarred and hurt body. But she loved it. He was not brilliant and she loved that too. She'd known brilliant men her whole life and now she hated them. Clever, wicked, tricky, cunning bastards. Intellectuals, geniuses, artists. Great scholars, predatory lawyers, egomaniacal doctors. She was tired of brilliant, interesting men without guts. All the trouble in the world came from brilliant, interesting men without guts who loved to hear themselves talk. They were all babies. They were the real killers of this world.

She reached and touched the rumpled fabric where he had sat. It was not at all warm. He must have been gone for a long time. Her fingers lingered against the material; she sat up, shook her head, and reached across the coffee table to where a rumpled issue of the *Globe* lay. Chardy's feet had even touched it. She picked it up again—as she had a thousand times before—and opened to the metro page.

FIRE GUTS MIDEASTERN RESTAURANT

A three-column headline over a ten-inch story explained in the mundane voice of daily journalism how arson was suspected in a blaze on Shawmut Avenue in which a restaurant called The Baghdad had burned down.

Noon of the second day after the fire, you will pick him up across from the restaurant, they had told her. The technical term for this kind of arrangement was a blind link, and it was the most secure, the most sure method: no phone contact, no dead-letter boxes, nothing by mail, nothing at all. It's for operating in an enemy country.

Tomorrow, noon tomorrow. She would pick up Ulu Beg. Here, in Boston, ten thousand miles from the mountains. And Joseph Danzig would be that same night only five blocks away, unguarded.

She'd gotten Chardy out of there now. She'd done half the incredible. If she could get Ulu Beg in, she'd have done the other half.

She was not as he remembered; she'd been a hard, youthful figure then, boyish and strong and active; a part of Jardi and very much not a part.

Now, in the automobile, she was nervous and plump and dry-lipped and pale.

"Your trip. Hazardous?" she asked.

"Somebody stole my money."

"Yet you got here so much faster."

"A fine lady drove me. A fine black woman."

"There was trouble at the border."

"What? Oh, yes."

"They know you're here. They've guessed what you're here for."

They drove in bright sunlight through sparkly Boston streets. Everything here was made of wood. There was so much wood, wood in abundance. Wood and automobiles: America.

"How?" he said finally.

"The bullets from your gun. They traced them to nineteen seventy-five."

He nodded. Of course.

"You should have brought a different gun."

Yes, he should have. But they had insisted, hadn't they? It had to be this gun. They had given him this gun. This would be his gun.

"It doesn't matter," she said. "They're convinced you're in Ohio still. That's where they're looking for you. We have an incredible chance. The best chance we'll ever have. You would say it's all written above."

She told him about Danzig and the party that night, that very night. She told him how relaxed they'd be, since the party was a private thing, among old friends. She told him she had gotten the university faculty guide and found the address of the one member of Danzig's old department that lived on Hawthorne. She could take him there late tonight and point him. She told him that the only man who could recognize him would not be there.

"Who?"

"Chardy."

His face did not change. In many ways it was a remarkable face; the nose was oversize, like a prow, and the cheekbones high and sharp. The eyes were gaudy blue, small and intense. In the mountains he'd worn a moustache, huge and droopy, but now he was clean-shaven. He looked almost American. He did look American. She was astonished at how American he'd become, in blue jeans, with a pack, a tall, strong man who could have been a graduate student of athletic bent, an adventurer, an outdoorsman, any vigorous thirty-five-year-old American, and the streets were full of them, fit, lean joggers, backpackers, professional vacationers.

"You are his woman again?"

"It seems so."

"He is with us, then?"

"No. He doesn't know. He came back into my life because of all this. I realized at once that I had to become close to him again. I could learn things from him, and through him I could convince important people that I was harmless."

"But you are his?"

"It's not important."

"But you are?"

"Yes. He's a different man too. They were very hard on him. His own people. And the Russians tortured him horribly. They burned his back with a torch. He's a very bitter man, a hurt man. He's not the same Chardy at all."

"He works for them again?"

"He does."

"I will never understand Americans."

"Neither will I."

"You will betray him?"

"Yes. I have thought about it. I will betray him. The political is more important than the personal. But I ask a condition. It's very important to me."

"Say it."

"There will be other people there. People from the university. They are innocent. You must swear not to hurt them. To kill Danzig is justice. To kill these others would be murder. I can't commit murder. I saw too much of it committed myself."

"You Americans," Ulu Beg said. "You make war, but

you don't want there to be any bodies. Or if there are bodies, you don't want to see them or know about them.''

''Please. Swear it. Swear it as a great Kurdish fighter would swear it.''

''I can only swear what I can. But what is written, is written.''

''Still. Swear it. Or I can't help. You'll be on your own. And we've both figured out long ago that on your own you have almost no chance.''

He looked at her. Was she insane? He saw it now: she was crazy; she had terrible things in her head. Who could keep promises with bullets flying?

''Swear it. Please.''

''On my eyes,'' he said.

''All right.''

They pulled into a parking lot a few minutes later.

''Here.'' She handed him a key. ''It's a motel. I've rented you a room at the far end. Go there; stay inside. Clean up. There're some clothes in the room, American clothes. I hope they fit. I'll pick you up at ten. He said he'd come to my place at eleven. We'll wait outside until we see him leave. Then I'll help. I'll help you get inside. I'll help with the other business too.''

She fumbled with her purse.

It was a small, cheap revolver.

''I bought it in the city.''

''I have a weapon. I don't want you there with a gun.''

He turned to leave, but she reached for his arm.

''I'm glad you came. I'm glad it's nearly finished.''

''Kurdistan ya naman,'' he said.

31

Only Chardy and Uckley, the security man, remained. They stood discreetly in one corner of the living room in their lumpy suits. Lanahan was off somewhere playing Napoleon, and the private detectives engaged by the Agency had not accompanied Danzig from the television studio.

Dramatic people swirled about, bright and glittery, and in the center of it all sat Joe Danzig. In point of fact, at no time in their brief association had Chardy seen him quite like this: a sheen of perspiration stood out on his forehead and upper lip and he held a half-empty scotch glass almost like a scepter. He knew everybody here—or most of them—and he had taken his coat off and loosened his tie and collar, an absurd costume, since he still wore his vest. They came to him, the younger ones with some respect, the older ones out of camaraderie. Chardy was surprised to see so many kids. He thought kids hated Danzig, architect of bombing in Vietnam; but no, they did not, or *these* kids did not. Danzig listened earnestly and awarded the brightest with a smile or a nod which pleased them immensely. And the women: the women especially were drawn to his preposterous, rumpled figure. They crowded around him, touching and jostling. Even in these clever precincts? Chardy had no idea what being on television meant, what celebrity meant.

"They love him, don't they?" he said to Uckley.

"They sure do, sir," said Uckley.

The room had jammed up and become bright and hot with people. It was not so much furnished as equipped, largely with spacey-looking hi-fi components, a jungle of plants and books. Somebody loved books, for they were ceiling to floor on three of the walls and the other was bare brick. There were little steel spotlights mounted on racks on the ceiling, throwing vivid circles of light on Japanese prints and twisted modern paintings. It was like some kind of museum; somebody had spent a lot of money turning this living room into a museum. Chardy was catching a headache and all the noise and smoke pitched it higher. It looked like Danzig would be here for hours—until the dawn, among the horde of intellectuals.

Not all, but most, *most* had the same look: the high, pale foreheads, the glasses covering wasted eyes, the delicate wrists. They all had weak hands and looked sick. Funny, after the Marines, Chardy knew a uniform when he saw it, and here were uniforms: suede shoes, baggy chinos and plaid shirts, and an occasional little off-color tie. Everybody was drinking wine; everybody was talking, gesturing with unfiltered cigarettes. A woman drifted by in leotard and tights, smoking a cigar. She had a slightly crazed expression on her face and was made up like an Egyptian goddess.

Chardy checked his watch. It was 11:20.

"Have you seen Lanahan, Sarge?"

"No, sir," said Uckley.

Chardy hunted through the mass of bodies and at last spotted Miles sitting by himself in a corner. He turned back to Uckley.

"Look, do you think you can handle this?"

"There's nothing to handle, sir."

"I'll stay if you'd prefer."

"No, sir."

"I may be back in a little while."

"Take your time."

Chardy shook himself free of the wall and edged through the crowd. Lanahan sat disconsolately by himself.

"Not your crowd, Miles?"

Lanahan looked up, but did not smile. "I don't have a crowd," he said.

"Look, would it be a big deal if I slipped out a little early?"

"It would be a very big deal."

"Well, I'm going to do it anyway. Why don't you talk to somebody, have a good time? Meet some people. You look like the village priest at the great lord's manor for the first time."

Lanahan looked at him through narrow dark eyes in a field of skin eruptions. Flecks of dandruff littered his small shoulders.

"You shouldn't joke about priests, Paul."

"Miles, I'm going. All right?"

Lanahan didn't say anything.

"Come on, Miles, cheer up."

"Just go, Paul. You don't have any responsibility; you can sneak off. I'll stay. I'm expecting a call from Yost anyway."

"Be back shortly," said Chardy. He fought to the hall, squeezed down it to the door, where an older woman stood talking to several others in the overflow.

"Leaving so early? Did you have a coat?"

"No, I'm all right."

"Glad you could come."

"I had a wonderful time," he said.

He stepped out the door, went down three steps, and followed the short walk to Hawthorne Street.

"There he is," she said.

They watched Chardy pick his way down the steps, pause at the sidewalk for just a second, and then head down the street. They watched in silence until he disappeared.

"Just Danzig. Nobody else. Please, you swore."

He turned and looked at her with a cold glare.

"Please," she said. "You promised. You swore."

"I go now."

"I'll come too."

"No," he said. "I can go alone. Many people, no guards. People come and go. America is open, they told me."

"Please. I—"

"No."

"I'll be here then. To drive you away."

"No," he said. "It doesn't matter if I get away. Get away yourself, now. Cross that border now, Dada Johanna."

He climbed from the car and strode across the street, a tall, forceful figure.

She watched him move. A pain began to rub inside, between her eyes. She sat back. She could not face the future, the explanations, excuses, attention. It all seemed to weigh so much. She thought of it as weight, mass, as substance, a physical thing, pressing her down. She fought for breath. She thought of facing Chardy in the morning. She thought of the pain her parents would feel. She could not imagine it.

She watched. Ulu Beg knocked on the door. She could not see his gun; he'd hidden it, probably under the tweed sport coat.

The door opened. She could see them talking. What would he say? She wanted to cry. She was so scared.

Chardy knocked on Johanna's door.
There was no answer.
"Johanna?" he called into the wood. "Johanna?"
Now what the hell was going on?

32

Trewitt's fever rose and rose and rose, pulling him through an absolute kaleidoscope of discomforts, each spangling and fanning into something more unbearable, and since his imagination—the basic stuff of this journey through the fever zone—was prodigious to begin with, the trip was incredible. His fantasies were built of gore and sex and they centered on the body of the woman lying in her own blood. But soon they began to lessen in intensity. Gradually, by the second night, his head began to clear somewhat. It was very cold. The air hurt to breathe. He pulled something about him, a thin blanket that offered no protection.

On the third day he awoke to find himself in a stone shack with no glass in the windows, a stove that burned only junk wood, and a dirt floor across which there scampered a flock of chickens herded by a couple of listless mutts. He felt as though he'd come to in the middle of a movie and looked about for stock figures. But no: only the titanic figure whom he now understood to be Ramirez, in his (Trewitt's) yellow pants with his (Trewitt's) Beretta in the waistband, reading a photo-novel whose Spanish title translated into "A Smart-Alecky Young Miss Gets Her Comeuppance," while munching on a greasy drumstick from El Coronel (Sanders, of Kentucky; Trewitt could see the striped barrel on a shelf), his cowboy boots up on the table.

Trewitt hauled himself up, wobbling the whole way.

"You want a wing? We got a wing left," was Ramirez's welcome-back to the man who'd saved his life.

"I feel like shit," said Trewitt groggily, in English.

"You look like shit," said Ramirez, also in English.

Trewitt moaned. Somebody had looped a metal band around his forehead and was tightening it with great strength and dedication.

"Where are we?" he finally asked, shivering and noticing that his breath soared out from his lips in a great billowing cloud.

"Hah!" howled Ramirez in great delight. "Jesus Mary, they really give it to this girl!" He looked at the comic with warmth and enthusiasm. "She's a real stuck-up princess. They give her a smack on the bottom with a great big paddle. You're in the mountains, my friend. Way up high. A long way from the city."

Trewitt twisted so he could see out the window. In the distance, glittering in the sun, stood a ragged line of peaks. The haphazard up-and-down of the composition could have been a graph of his fortunes these last several days.

"Reynoldo was born down there," Ramirez said, "in the village, before electricity. He used to come here to hunt." He smiled, exposing two gold teeth which Trewitt had not noticed before. Gold teeth? This *was* getting to be like a movie.

"Who were those men? The killers," Trewitt asked in his Spanish.

"Who knows? It's a big mystery. Mexico is full of mysteries. It's a land of mysteries." Ramirez laughed.

"Gangsters? Pimps? Dope runners?"

Ramirez finished the drumstick and threw the bare bone across the room into a corner, where a dog scuffled after it, and wiped his hand on his pants. Trewitt was beginning to feel as if he'd awakened in the cave of the Cyclops.

"They make pretty good chicken," said Ramirez. "That Colonel. I bet he's a rich man."

He yawned, then looked over at Trewitt. "Mister, I'll tell you something. A man has to piss, somebody gets wet. Do you understand?"

"Ahh—"

"Oscar Meza, he get wet. The Huerras of Mexico City, anybody. It could go back years and years."

Shakily Trewitt stood, discovering as he unlimbered from the skimpy blanket that he was now in cheap cotton trousers, the trousers of a rural peasant. He went to the doorway. Outside he saw a goat pen, a trash heap, a dirt road falling away rapidly, and a brown surge—scabby, scaly, dusty, stony-cold, and silent—of peaks.

"Where the hell are we?"

Below he could see a flash of trees and valley, and some cultivated land. But this was wild country, raw and high and scruffy.

"Near El Plomo. In the Sierra del Carrizai. Due west of Nogales. About sixty miles."

"Where are the others?"

"Down below. In El Plomo. This is a big adventure. The little one, he cry for mama last night. But now he's okay."

Trewitt nodded, hurt. Poor little guy. Why the hell hadn't they let him go? Now he was God knows where, involved in *this*.

"They'll be here soon. But, hey, mister. Who are *you?*" The Mexican watched him carefully.

"Just some guy who got mixed up in some stuff," was

Trewitt's lame response. "I was looking for adventures too."

"Crazy people want adventures. Reynoldo wants to die in a nice bed somewhere. With a bottle of beer and a nice soft fat woman who don't give you no trouble."

Trewitt, leaning in the rough doorway, looked down the little road for the yellow rented car. Boy, was he going to have a bill!

"At least," he said, "we're safe. This is a good place to lie low."

"Yes, it's real safe up here," Ramirez laughed. "Yes, it's real safe." The grin radiated blazing humor.

"What's going on? What's so funny?"

"The answer is I called my good friend Oscar Meza from El Plomo. I told him all about this wonderful, safe place."

Trewitt stared at him. At first he thought he'd discovered an unusually perverse sense of humor in a surprising locality. Only when the man's fiery, crazed grin did not break into something softer and wittier did Trewitt acknowledge what had been laid before him, and its force struck him with a physical blow.

Finding next a sudden rush of strength, he began to shout: "You did what? you what? you what? that was really stupid, you *told* him?"

Trewitt looked down the road. At any second it could yield a carload of Mexican hoods. And they had a Beretta. With four rounds left.

"Hey, mister, come look at this," Ramirez called.

The Mexican led him to a corner, pulled aside a dusty rag to reveal the lid of some kind of cabinet or chest buried in the earth. Kneeling, he unlocked and opened it. He pulled out a rifle with a telescopic sight.

"We do some hunting up here," he said. The grin did not diminish, yet to Trewitt it had turned savage.

There was a sudden sound, and Trewitt thought he'd die.

But it was the yellow car returning.

33

When he reached the door he had no idea what to say, no plan.

He knocked on the door, wondering what God willed for the next few minutes.

The door opened and he found himself face to face with a woman of advanced years who wore a look of great, eager American friendliness and who said only, "Hello."

"Yes, hello, how are you?" he replied.

Something he did—he'd never know what—must have perplexed her.

"Yes? Are you here for the party?"

He had no idea what to say. Beyond the door lay a dim corridor and at its end a brightly lit room choked with smoke and people. He could sense them crowded in there; the noise was intense and laughter bellowed heavily in the air.

"Yes?" she repeated. She wanted to help him. He could tell.

"It's all right," he said.

"Oh," she said, "you must be Dr. Abdul."

"Yes. Dr. Abdul."

"It was so nice of you to come. Joe admires your work

intensely, even if he doesn't quite agree on Egyptian hegemony.''

"I look forward to talk."

"Come in, of course. Let's not stand here. Oh, you're so tall, I had no idea."

"Yes. It is a gift from God."

"Yes, I suppose so. How long will you be with the department? Do you return to Cairo at the end of the term or in the winter?"

"Term."

"Oh, I hate those short appointments. Jack and I were in Munich, but the grant only lasted eight months. You can't get a real sense of a culture in less than two years. How do you like America?"

"Ah. I love it."

"Good. Go on in. Jack is over by the wall at the bar. He'll get you a drink. And if you can fight your way to Joe, say hello to him for me. I haven't said two words to him since he arrived."

"Ah. Thanks."

He stepped by her and walked down the hall to the noise. A few couples talked privately, lovers perhaps, in the darkness. He edged by them and stood in the room, at the edge of the crowd.

Danzig knew she was his. She was beautiful too, and very young, exotic. She may have been mulatto even, or a Eurasian, or some odd mix of Filipino and Russian. She had not yet spoken to him but she was staring at him. He knew it was a preposterous idea and that the technical problems—how to get her back to the hotel, how to get her back *from* the hotel—were immense. Yet he wanted her!

She'd come with a man probably. But who? That tall dramatic one staring furiously from the doorway? Perhaps, but Danzig, who was by this time quite exhausted with conversation, and not a little drunk, decided to risk it anyway.

"Ah, miss?"

"Yes?" Faint accent.

"Ah, I couldn't help wondering. Are you a student at the university?"

"No, Dr. Danzig. My husband is an associate professor in the physics department."

"Oh, how pleasant. I'm sure I couldn't begin to understand the first thing about his work. He must be very brilliant. Is he here?"

"No. I came with my lover." She said it quite matter-of-factly, but clearly to shock him, to see something register on the famous face. "You spoke with him earlier. He's that brash younger man in political science. Jeremy Goldman."

Danzig vaguely remembered somebody who might fit that description, but the details were hazy.

"Yes, yes, he made a number of interesting points. A very interesting man, as I recall. I don't think he cares for me."

"Oh, he loathes you. He loathes everybody. But he's fascinated."

"May I ask . . . pardon me if I seem forward, I really mean no harm and am an extremely harmless man"—the famous Danzig self-deprecation, charming and cruelly vain—"but do I fascinate *you?*"

"Well," she said, pausing. Her face was beautiful, witty: very thin, with high, fiercely chiseled model's cheekbones, the eyes vaguely Oriental, the lips full as plums. "I would say—a little. Yes. A little."

"Well, what an excellent compliment. How nice you are to an old and rather vain man. May I ask further—

again, I don't mean to be forward and please stop me if in any way I am intimidating you—"

"Oh, I'm not intimidated."

"Well, may I ask then, is he around? And do you plan to leave with him? I'm sure you do; I don't mean to *press* you."

She made a cool pretense of looking around the room.

Chardy! Danzig realized suddenly that Chardy could drive them back to the hotel and then take her on to her place. But would he mind?

Of course not. He'd better not mind. He looked too, but for Chardy.

Ulu Beg could see him now. He looked thicker than in pictures, the hair flecked with gray, the eyes beady behind the thick glasses, the stomach plump and straining in the vest. He leaned over a bit, his ungainly body slightly atilt, talking earnestly to a woman. Twice, in fact, he'd looked at Ulu Beg directly, freezing him. But the eyes quickly returned to the woman; he spoke in a low insistent voice.

Ulu Beg edged through the crowd. He bumped somebody.

"Excuse me," somebody said.

"Well, I—"

"Who's the—"

"Well, sorry, I seem to—"

"Oh, are you trying to get—"

At last he was sixteen feet away. He reached back under his coat and felt the Skorpion. He cautioned himself to draw it slowly and steadily and to fire with both hands. His fingers touched its hardness, its metal.

Yet he hesitated.

A fat man talking to a pretty girl in the middle of his civilization.

He'd killed a hundred men, but all were soldiers and

would have killed him. He tried to think of his sons, one dead, one so hideously wounded that he himself had done the final act out of mercy and love. The memory flooded over Ulu Beg and the stench of burning fuel seemed to come alive in his nostrils and he could feel the dust heavy in the air from the rotor blades and the bullet strikes.

Someone jostled him.

"Sorry, old man," said a man in a sweater and a pipe.

Ulu Beg turned. The woman was laughing at something Danzig had just said, and the man himself was smiling, chatting confidently.

"Drink?" somebody asked Ulu Beg. He turned to look at him in astonishment. He had no sensation of removing the weapon.

"He's got a gun," somebody was screaming. *"Oh, God, he's got a gun!"*

Ulu Beg pivoted, raising the weapon with both hands until the fat man on the sofa filled the sights.

The noise rose, a light fell, shadows reeled in the room.

Danzig stood in stupefied terror and raised his hands.

Ulu Beg fired.

Glass everywhere. Chips of wood, pieces of table, ruined books. Danzig lay on the floor. He could see the carpet. Somebody was still shooting.

Make it go away.

Oh, God: *Make it go away.*

The girl was crying, "Oh, Jesus, oh, Jesus, Jerry, oh, Jerry, Jesus," and bled badly, all down her front. She was on the sofa. He could not—would not—move to help.

Danzig lay still. Uckley had fired at least twice before the tall man had killed him.

"Where is he? Where is he?" The boy Lanahan, the Agency man, a pistol in his hand, danced in fury and terror.

"Oh, Christ," someone shouted, "oh, Jesus Christ, he had a gun, a *gun.*"

Sirens.

Sirens: somebody had called the police.

Danzig would not look up. The tall man. Had he left? God save him from the tall man.

He lay on his stomach curled up behind the couch. Three times he'd been hit, maybe a fourth, knocking him backward. Where was the doctor? Please let there be a doctor. He thought his heart would explode. He needed a pill.

Danzig began to cry. He wept uncontrollably. His chest hurt awfully. He had wet himself in fear and didn't even care. A great, furious self-pity welled through him. He had figured out that he would not die. The vest—the material was called Kevlar, very expensive, spun steel and high-density nylon, developed for his trips to the Middle East—would stop the bullets. But what if it hadn't? Why did his chest hurt so? He could not stop crying or shaking.

"My God," somebody was still shrieking, "he had a fucking *gun.*"

Chardy heard the sirens. He started to run down the hall. By the time he got outside at least three squad cars had sped by. Chardy ran after them. Across from the house he found her, in the car. The muzzle blast had blackened the side of her face and her eyes were closed. The pistol was still in her hand. Across the street, police cars and ambulances with their flashers all squirting red and blue light into the night had gathered, but Chardy didn't even look. He opened the door, laid her gently on the other seat, and got in, turned the key, and drove away.

34

"*Nada*," the boy said. "Nothing."

"You're sure?" Trewitt demanded.

"Sí. I said, *nada*. Nothing."

Trewitt, stung, exploded. "Goddamn," he said bitterly. "*God*damn. What's wrong with him?" The fury cut through him. "Goddammit. You're *sure?*"

"He said, didn't he? Mother of Jesus," said El Stupido, as Trewitt had begun to think of Ramirez, a great fat greasy farting boorish creep.

"All right," said Trewitt.

But it was not all right. It was another day. How many now, five, six, a week? Trewitt could discover in himself no talent for waiting. He would have made a lousy sub skipper, bomber pilot, sniper. This sitting around, playing one of Peter Pan's lost boys in the Never-Never-Land of this mountainside, yet with real guns and a pig like this El Stupido for companionship—he glanced over and saw his antagonist reading the same goddamn book! "A Smart-Alecky Young Lady Gets Her Comeuppance"! Ramirez could read it over and over and over, his lips forming the words in the balloons over the photographs of the actors, and still chuckle in deep and profoundly satisfying amusement when the little maid got swacked on the butt with a two-by-four at the end.

"Aiiieee!" He looked up happily. "Hey, come look at this one, Señor Gringo. They really give it to her. Right on the back bumper!"

"And no others? No visitors, no questions?" asked Roberto, fourth member of this hilltop Utopia.

"Nada. Not in El Plomo," said the boy. "What's for supper?"

"I can't figure out why he hasn't gotten back to me. What the hell is going on back there?" Trewitt said self-righteously. But he had deep suspicions. The El Plomo postman—he was also the mayor, the sanitary commissioner, the general store owner, the traffic cop—had been recruited, for a substantial fee, of course, to drive fifteen miles to the nearest town of consequence and dispatch another telegram via Our Lady of Resurrection to Trewitt's own particular saint, Saint Paul.

"UNC," the telegram had read, "FOUND BIG TACO BUT MUCHO OTHERS WANT RECIPE SPICY GOING SEND HELP EL PLOMO SIERRA DEL CARRIZAI

NEPHEW JIM"

But what if the public official had taken the money and said screw the gringo and his telegram and headed for the nearest whorehouse?

Trewitt shook his head. His rage, which was mostly self-pity, was inflating exponentially. Who the fuck knew what was going on back there anyway? Maybe Chardy had gotten the can. Maybe he should have sent his first message to somebody sensible like Yost Ver Steeg. Forget the cowboy; go for the corporate executive.

Trewitt began to pine, to mourn, for lost opportunities. Maybe it wasn't too late, sure, even now, send an open wire to Yost, care of Langley, Va., dear Yost, it may surprise you to know that . . .

But—

But it was true Bill Speight had been murdered. It was true there were men trying to murder Reynoldo Ramirez. It was true all this began almost immediately after the Kurd, Ulu Beg, had come across the American border in a blaze of gunfire, assisted by Reynoldo Ramirez. And it was true that at any second an odd squad of gunmen might arrive. The linkages were not definite but they were certainly suggestive. Somehow it all fit together, though try as he might he could not exactly imagine how or why.

Who was pursuing them?

There's your key, Trewitt. Mexican gunmen, trying to rub out El Stupido for his nightclub, or for a past betrayal, or for . . . ? Or some other force?

Trewitt shivered.

Behind the scabby line of mountains the sun collapsed into a great hemorrhage of purple swirls. Beneath, the valley was quiet and dark. Down there on those gentle slopes grew maybe fifty million bucks' worth of marijuana. It was a wild country, bandit country, gun country. Around here everybody carried guns. It was a violent place.

Trewitt advised himself to deal with the reality of the situation, and forget the overview for the time being. Forget also his desperate prayers for Resurrection. He was going to have to get out of this one by himself.

He took the rifle off his shoulder, a Remington Model 700 in 7-mm magnum, with a 6X scope. Ramirez had two, for desert sheep, which once or twice a year the old Ramirez—prosperous vice lord and whoremonger—came up to stalk.

"Hey, some food is here," called Roberto.

Trewitt reslung the rifle. Food meant more beans and

rice, which meant farting all night, and he knew he had the two-to-six shift when the farting would be at its worst.

Jesus Christ, *that* was something Le Carré never wrote about.

35

This was his third day; by now he had established his talents and been nominally accepted, though no one had ever asked his name or inquired where he came from. They knew more important things about him: that he could hit from twenty-five feet out if given the shot, that he would dive for a free ball, that he set picks that would knock your teeth loose, that he was a furious rebounder, and finally, that he was honest.

"You do the pros, old man?" the tallest, the star, said to be a postman in real life, put to him sullenly.

"I had a week in the old Chicago Packers camp. But I couldn't stick it."

"Say, Jack: you think *I* could make it in the pros?"

Chardy paused a fraction of a second. He was, after all, a vulnerable figure, the only white man on the playground, even if the dome of the United States Capitol could be seen in the distance, across the river, an immaculate joke for the thousands of black teenagers who threw balls through hoops here.

"No," he finally said. "No way. Sorry. You're just not good enough."

Chardy thought the postman might hit him. He was maybe twenty-two, six five, and had some great moves.

He'd probably had a year or two of college ball before flunking out, or quitting.

But the postman thought it over and seemed to back off. Perhaps he was too elegant for a punch-out, or too smart; or perhaps he secretly knew the truth of Chardy's judgment; or perhaps he sensed that Chardy didn't give a shit about much of anything and would have fought him to the last bloody blow.

"Then let's play, old man," said the postman.

"Let's do it," Chardy replied, and they began again.

Chardy had by this time worked his way up to the best court, where the most talented players went five-on-five full distance. At first the blacks had let their rage show: they'd crowded and roughed him, and he'd been knocked to the asphalt more than a few times. But he fought back with elbow and hip, and his shots were falling. He was still the jump-shooter. You never forgot. It never left, that gift. He went for net, not rim or backboard, although these skirts were woven of chain, which clanked medievally when the ball fell through them. It was as though a kind of enchantment had fallen over Chardy. He played to lose himself forever, to hide, to vanish in the game, the glorious game. He knew only that he had to play or die. His limbs had ached for the sport.

He'd left Boston and driven straight from National into D.C., stopping only at a sporting-goods shop in a suburban mall to buy a luxurious pair of shoes—Nike hightops, leather, the pro model—and a good Seamco outdoor ball, and headed deep into the city until he saw a playground, a good one, a big one, across a bridge in a meadow between a highway and a slow river. The place was called, after the river, Anacostia. He knew the best ballplayers would go there.

He felt he could play forever. At thirty-eight, he felt sixteen. If there was a heaven on this earth, he had at last found it: a playground, two hoops, and a shot that was falling.

Jesus, was it falling.

"Fill it."

"Drop it."

"Put it *down,* man."

"Jam it."

"Damn, you hot."

He hit four in a row, then five, then six before missing. He fired rainbows that fell like messages from God, dead center, without mercy. He tried tap-ins and finger rolls and fallaway jumpers and drives off either hand. He fought to the baseline to receive a pass and curled backward through two defenders for a reverse lay-up. The ball felt like a rose, it was so light and smelled so sweet. In a trance he shot a wish from forty feet, only to watch it drop without a rattle. Even the postman gave him a tap on the butt after that one.

But eventually, in the hazy hour of twilight of the third day, when the moths had begun to gather in the cones of the fluorescent lights that would illuminate the hoops until midnight, into this athlete's Eden there came a snake. Chardy pretended not to notice; but how could he miss the only other white face among so many black ones, even if it was far away, behind the windshield of a nondescript car.

Whoever was stalking him had patience. He waited like a grim statue in his car through several more games, even allowing Chardy to drink a can of cold beer that someone offered from a six-pack.

Finally, almost into full dark, as Chardy was firing from the baseline—a rare miss, too—the door popped and a short figure emerged.

Lanahan. They'd sent Lanahan.

Chardy missed the next two shots, and the man he was theoretically guarding put in two buckets.

Lanahan, in his disheveled suit, wandered over shyly, paused, and finally found a seat in some bleachers adjacent to the court.

Chardy missed another shot. All of a sudden he could not buy a basket. A terrible weariness suffused his limbs.

"Come *on,* Jack," the postman ordered.

The ball came to him on the perimeter. Inside, a man on his team slipped open and Chardy should have hit him at the low post with a bounce pass; greedily he merely faked it. Chardy dribbled back and forth, the ball rising to meet his eager hands. He searched for an opening. Another teammate slipped out to set a pick and Chardy drove suddenly to it, losing his defender in the process.

He set himself for half an instant, and felt the ball rise and almost of itself decide to flee the thrust of his two hands as he leaned from behind the pick. The ball, obediently, disappeared through the basket.

Chardy got two quick baskets after that, and the postman finished the run with a ringing slam-dunk. Chardy raised his hand, announcing the desire to sit one out, and a high-school boy of great repute but few words jogged in emotionlessly to take his place.

"Nice stuff, man," the kid said.

Chardy plucked a towel off the grass and circled the court to the bleachers. He flopped down a row behind Miles, stretching his legs out before him and working over his face with a towel. One of his knees was bloody. He couldn't even remember a fall.

"You're good," said Miles, watching the new game before him, the cuffs and shouts and bounces now reaching them through the heavy summer air. "I had no idea how good."

"I seemed to be on tonight," said Chardy.

"We had a lot of trouble finding you."

"I just had to play some basketball."

"Sure."

Chardy watched for a while. Before him, in the glow of the overhead fluorescents, the postman and the new kid went after each other.

"That tall guy is pretty good," Lanahan said. "Not the kid, the other guy. He could play in the pros."

"No, he couldn't," said Chardy. "Who gets the ax? I saw the papers. We got out of it pretty good. I didn't see any mention of the Agency or any mention of the Kurds. Thank Christ, Danzig didn't kick off anyway on a heart attack with all the excitement."

"Two people did die, Paul."

"Three. Johanna."

"Well, I meant in the shooting."

"Johanna was shot," Chardy said stubbornly.

"Paul, it's really not possible for us to see her as a victim."

"No, I suppose it isn't."

"In any event, nobody ever connected her with Danzig. We didn't ourselves until yesterday. Somebody must have moved her if she was close to the shooting."

"She was across the street."

"So it was you?"

"Yeah."

"That was smart, Paul. It was real smart. It could have gotten so complicated, so lurid if the papers had tied it all together. Can you imagine *Time?*"

"I wasn't thinking about the papers, Miles."

"It doesn't matter what you were thinking about, Paul. It only matters what you *did.*"

"You still haven't told me who got the ax. But I can guess. Not you, or you wouldn't be here. Not me, not with

Ulu Beg still around with his machine pistol. I'm still an asset. That leaves—''

"He didn't do very well. He deserves what he's getting. He authorized the cutback on the surveillance of Johanna. He overcommitted to the Midwest. Sam called it a dreadful performance.''

"Ver Steeg is out?''

"Way out. They bumped him over to a staff job in Scientific Intelligence. Something to do with satellites. He's one of the old guys; he goes way back with Sam, so they didn't fire him. Imagine what they'd have done to one of us, Paul?''

"So Sam's running things. They've moved it to Operations? He's calling the shots?''

"Well—'' Miles smiled. His fiery skin seemed neon in the fluorescent light. His teeth were still bad.

"You, Miles?''

"I was lucky. I didn't catch the flak. And they needed someone who was all read-in. So I'm field supervisor.''

"But under Sam?''

"Sam's a smart guy, Paul. He's had his eye on me for some time. We work well together. But I'm not here about Sam. I'm here about you.''

"Suppose I say no? Suppose I say I'm tired of it, it's only going to end in more senseless killing?''

"Well, you can't say no. You signed a contract. We could make it pretty sticky. Your name's on the dotted line. You can't just back out. But Paul, consider. Danzig really wants you. He believes in you.''

"The jerk,'' Chardy said.

"Paul, look at it this way. Danzig wants you, Danzig's got clout. That means Melman wants you. Melman's going places, Paul. He'll get the top job one of these days. He's one of the inside boys. Paul, you and me, we've always been on the outside and we'll always be on the outside unless we have an insider really pulling for us. Somebody who's old Agency, Harvard, WASP, upper-management. That's Sam, Paul. He can really help guys like us, Paul, two Irish-Catholic Chicago street kids. He wants to start over with you, Paul. Clean slate. No 'seventy-five hearings, no recommendation for termination. It all disappears. Paul, you could have your career back. You could have it all. If Sam owes you, Paul, you're in extremely good shape when he lands on the top floor. He could take you with him.''

Playing the seducer in the Anacostia night didn't suit Miles. His features were too squirrely, his acne too fierce. As he spoke his tiny dark eyes lit with conviction and he jabbed and gestured with his small hands. He pressed, crowded, yipped. A good case officer—Chardy had known a few in his time—could charm you into selling your mother, but Miles had no talent for it. It was a question of timing, of rhythm; he came to the point too fast.

Melman must be on the desperate side to have resorted to a clumsy operator like Lanahan. It was a curiosity: Why couldn't Melman have come up with somebody smoother? No, he was recycling the people he'd started with, simply shuffling them around. For some reason he wanted to keep the operation contained, keep the number of players down.

Chardy looked across the river. The unlovely city gleamed cool and glossy on the far shore. The Capitol, arc-lit and melodramatic, loomed frozen against the night. Near it, also lit for drama, rose the shaft of the Washington Monument—cathedrals in the Vatican of government, a faith which just now Chardy saw as desperately hollow, as much a hoax as the Catholicism in which he'd been raised.

But did he have a choice? Of course not. Which perhaps was Melman's real message in sending this awful kid.

He thought of Johanna and his promise to her. Was it invalidated by her treason? Or Ulu Beg? What did Chardy owe the Kurd, who had made him a brother? He wondered about all sorts of things too: why was Melman so desperate to have him back? Why had Melman been so driven to destroy him seven years ago? Who really was running Ulu Beg? And what about pitiful Trewitt, stuck out on his secret limb in Mexico?

He knew that whatever the answers were, they would not be found on a playground.

"Let's go, then, Miles," he said.

36

Danzig sat in his bathrobe out back, by the garden. There were at least seven men around, three of them with radios. And beyond, in the thickets, still more men. Government cars orbited the block too: nondescript Chevys with two men in suits and Israeli submachine guns. And helicopters? Perhaps even helicopters.

"You certainly appreciate *scale*," he said to the man next to him.

Sam Melman laughed.

"With all the taxes you pay, you deserve something a little special," he said. "How's the chest?"

Danzig winced. The Kelvar vest had stopped all three slugs and diffused the impact; still, they'd cracked two ribs and left him nearly immobile, with bluish bruises running from inside his arm across his chest to his stomach. He'd been kept sedated much of the past few days, the pain had been so acute, and he remembered it only vaguely. His wife had appeared heroically at his bedside and gone on television shows with communiqués; she seemed to enjoy the process and it gave her something to *do*. Meanwhile an ocean of telegrams poured in, sweet words from men who loathed him, mostly composed under the impression he would soon die (the early reports had been confused).

"My chest is splendid," said Danzig. "It's wonderful."

"I saw the medical reports. I bet it hurts like hell."

"It hurts terribly," Danzig said. "Please spare me any witticisms. Laughter would kill me." He looked off glumly into the garden, a full green universe by this time. "I suppose if it took you three days to find Chardy, your own man, who was not even hiding from you but was playing basketball in a public park not three miles from here, you haven't had much luck with the Kurd."

"No. But the troops are out now. We are optimistic. It's wide open now, so perhaps it all worked out for the best. Now we'll get him. It's really all over."

"It certainly didn't work out for that poor girl." Danzig could remember watching her die. He could place the exact moment: a certain sloppy repose slid through her limbs and her head fell back spastically. A beautiful woman held herself with a certain discipline and pride; it was a universal. And when he saw that go, he knew she was finished. There was blood on her everywhere. Later he found out a ricochet had torn through her aorta. Curious and frightening, the ways of this world: from fifteen feet a man had fired a sophisticated modern weapon at him and, because of a trick of technology, failed to harm him seriously; this poor woman, whose only crime was to be present, had paid with her life, falling victim to a missed bullet that had deflected off of something. Their parallel fates were an accumulation of statistical improbabilities that were astonishing.

"It's tragic, yes," said Melman. "Tragic and pointless. But we didn't bring the Kurd. The Kurd came himself."

"Still, you can't be pleased with the Agency's performance."

"Of course not. But steps have been taken to prevent a recurrence."

Danzig nodded, but what had really happened was that the system had broken down. Entropy again, the factor of disorder and randomness. They'd had him in a net tight as a drumskin for weeks, but gradually it had worn down of its own volition, and the Kurd had slipped through. And no amount of precaution could prevent it from happening again.

"Here, Dr. Danzig." Melman handed him something. It was a mashed piece of copper. "That one would have killed you. That's the one. Thank God for the vest."

Danzig preferred to thank the Secret Service and the U.S. Army whose Natick Research and Development Laboratory had developed Kevlar for his early trips to the Middle East.

"I'm not sentimentally attached to little souvenirs," he said. "Is it of any significance?"

"No. We've a dozen more."

Danzig stood and awkwardly threw the bullet into the lawn; the pain came in a sudden wave, but watching the thing disappear into the grass gave him a kind of pleasure he felt even as he doubled over, wincing and grunting. He wished he could make all the bullets in the world disappear.

"All right, Sam," he said, turning, "tell me. Who's trying to kill me?"

Melman studied him with some detachment. A cool customer, this Melman. No wonder he was doing so well now. A faint smile crossed Melman's well-bred face.

"A Kurd. They're a violent people. They don't appreciate the subtleties of your strategic thought."

"Please. I'm not a stupid man. Don't address me as one."

"Dr. Danzig, we have no information, not the tiniest scrap, to suggest anything other than—"

"Who recruited the woman, the Harvard instructor? The one who so conveniently has committed suicide and is therefore beyond our questions?"

"She was with Ulu Beg in the mountains for over seven months. They endured the collapse of the Kurdish revolution together. Perhaps they made an agreement then. He simply got to her and—"

"You were watching her."

"Intermittently. She'd been investigated and declared clear. The officer in charge made a grave error. He made several grave errors. He has been removed to other duties."

"Yet this Kurd and this girl had enough know-how to outwit your professionals."

"They were also exceedingly lucky. Don't forget that. They had Chardy in their pocket. They had you in Boston. And still they failed."

"They got a good deal farther than luck can explain."

"Dr. Danzig. I say again, we have no information to suggest that this is anything more than it seems. A conspiracy of two people."

"Somebody's pulling the strings. No matter what your information says or doesn't say. Somebody's . . . and I want to know who."

But Melman said nothing, until after several seconds.

"Dr. Danzig, I think you've been reading too many thrillers."

Not long after, Chardy returned to Danzig's life, in a new suit. If Danzig expected contrition he did not receive it. Contrition is bullshit, Danzig's most important employer had once observed, and the man Chardy exemplified this principle to the utmost. He looked a little thinner in his new clothes. All that exercise? But he had that same shambling reserve, a quiet, athletic containment. Yet he had recently lost a lover, who had in turn betrayed him and, most cruelly, made a fool of him, had he not? He should have been destroyed, fired at the least. A failure of judgment, calculation, sheer common sense, of the highest order. Danzig had seen the reports and was aware, where Chardy was not, of the considerable emotion of an anti-Chardy faction among senior Agency personnel. How headquarters people loved to see a former glamour boy brought low! Danzig had observed this principle where it applied to himself; he was not surprised to see it at play in the issue of Chardy. The man Ver Steeg was behind some of it; before his reassignment he had attempted desperately to place all blame on Chardy. He had lobbied feverishly, calling in old favors, bending the ears of old acquaintances. His rage found willing ears; ripples of discontent spread through the Agency and the larger government of which it was ostensibly a part. The story of Chardy's cuckolding by the idea of murder for vengeance against Joe Danzig spread and spread; even the President might have heard of it. At the end of his string, the desperate Ver Steeg, on whom full blame was decreed to fall for his commitment of resources in the Dayton area, had even said Chardy was a part of it: the three of them, working together, Chardy, the girl, the Kurd.

But it had been Danzig himself who demanded that Chardy not pay Yost Ver Steeg's price.

Danzig wondered about his own motives. A curious question for him: why this thing for Chardy? Was it that he felt a kinship with Chardy, casting himself in the ex-champion's role that so many seemed to reserve for Chardy? Or perhaps also it was that Chardy had a simplicity to him that Danzig had not encountered among the sophists of his many circles. And certainly another part of it was Chardy's aloneness, which by itself recommended him to Danzig, who in an untoward moment of self-acuity admitted to a ferocious Italian interviewer that he enjoyed acting alone and knew that Americans were drawn to the spectacle of the lone fellow performing great deeds. Cowboys. So in this way, as a pure reflection of certain of his own aspects, was Danzig attracted to Chardy. There was also the fellow's lip; he was a great and furious retorter, a man of fierce pride, a real fighter, which engaged Danzig.

Chardy also had no grief; he was a mighty represser, goal-oriented, who hammered his feelings deep inside himself and would admit no weakness. Danzig knew this to be dangerous—indeed, almost self-destructive—but also the only way really to accomplish things. Chardy had exiled his feelings from his body; his face was blank and a trifle dull, as usual. If the dead woman had been and still was, by some sadomasochistic twist in personality, dear to him, he would not show it. It was quickly and smoothly business as usual. The events, bloody and horrible, of the week past, seemed not to have happened at all for Chardy.

"You said he'd never get close, Mr. Chardy. He got to within fifteen feet while you yourself were off in pursuit of dubious pleasures."

Chardy nodded.

"I was no good guessing the future. Poor Uckley had to pay for it."

"Uckley was a professional. He knew the risks. A sizable sum was settled on his family. It is exceedingly dispiriting to be shot at. Tell me—you are said to have some expertise in this matter—does one ever *adjust?*"

"Never," Chardy said.

"But we seem to have survived again, haven't we?"

"Thanks to the vest."

"Do you know, I've been wearing it so long I'd forgotten about it? Forgotten absolutely. I thought he had me. It

must have been ten seconds—which can be an eternity—
before it occurred to me I would not die.''

Chardy had no response.

''Is there news?''

''No, sir. Nothing.''

''I'm not leaving this house until they catch him.''

''That makes sense.''

''Will they catch him?''

''They say they will.''

''I know what they say. They say it loudly and often.
Yet I sense a certain softness in their position. Their performance so seldom lives up to their promise. What do
you say?''

Chardy thought for a second. Then he said, ''No. Not
for a time. What they keep forgetting is that *I* trained
him.''

''An ego, Mr. Chardy? How pleasant. That makes two
of us.''

37

Lanahan's rise was sudden and wondrous: he reported directly to Melman. He called Melman "Sam." There was no Yost between them; it was as if a generation had been sliced out of the hierarchy. That is, Yost, the bishop, was gone; Lanahan reported directly to Sam, the cardinal. He had responsibility, control, power. He had people. He had nice little perks—a driver, a girl, a coffee cup that miraculously never seemed to empty.

"And they seemed to be getting along?" Sam asked in his mildly interested way, referring to Chardy and Danzig.

"Yes, Sam." Miles rubbed his chin, where a pimple had burst that morning. "For some reason Danzig *likes* Paul. My people can't figure it out."

Melman sat back. "There's an attraction to Paul, without a doubt."

"Yes."

"He has a certain World War Two glamour. Some of the older men, the old OSS types, had it too. And a few of the Special Operations people too. But only Paul, these days. It can be very exciting stuff."

"Well"—not that Lanahan would disagree with Sam on anything of consequence; still, he'd throw out an occasional inoffensive counterpunch so as not to be thought the total yesman—"to a certain juvenile turn of mind, yes. Poor Trewitt loved Chardy, and look what it got him. It surprises me," he blasted ahead confidently, "that a realist like Danzig could fall for a bullshit artist, a cowboy, like Chardy."

"He's scared, Miles. That's the psychology of it."

"I suppose."

"You're monitoring them? I mean, without being overly obvious about it?"

"Yes, Sam. Of course."

"Anything else?"

Ah. This looked to be a good moment to lay on Sam the story of Trewitt in Mexico and the secret link to Chardy via Resurrection, which Lanahan had been storing away for just the right moment. He took a quick look about Sam's bright office, and leaned forward as if to begin to speak.

"Now there is one thing, Miles." Sam cut him off. "I've been meaning to speak to you about this. I foresee one potential problem. I've already run into traces of it in Danzig."

Was this a test?

Miles said nothing. He still felt as though he'd blundered into an audience with the cardinal.

"Miles, both these men—Danzig and Chardy—have tendencies toward paranoia. Well-documented, wouldn't you agree?"

"Yes."

"What bothers me is that if their bond becomes too close, there's no guessing what they might concoct. And certain ideas can be very dangerous to our line of work. Remember the great double-agent scare of the mid-seventies? No, of course not, you were just starting. And you don't remember the fifties either, when *I* was just starting.

At any rate, this sort of thing can wreck a division, a whole directorate. The whole shop. Do you follow?''

Sam peered at Miles intensely. He had pale, shallow eyes. Sam was a handsome man. Smooth, brilliant Sam. Everybody wanted a little of Sam's famous calm charm.

"Yes, sir," said Miles.

"Let's declare a first operating principle. A bedrock, a foundation. And that's that this is first of all a security job. A matter of protection. Perhaps even protecting Danzig from himself. As long as you see it in those terms, and remember that the enemy is Ulu Beg and Danzig's own paranoia, you'll be able to keep your bearings.''

What was Sam warning him against?

"Miles, you're doing well. You've managed, early on, to get into a crucial position on an important operation. You realize there are men around here who've tried for *years* to get where you are, and have never made it?''

Melman smiled, showing white, even teeth. His charm, remote from public view, was well known in the Agency. It was not a pushy charm, or flamboyant; rather it was a warm thing, enveloping. He had a way of including you in a pact against the world: you, he, united, would stand in tight circumference against the outsiders.

While yielding fully to it, Lanahan at the same time acknowledged it for what it was: a treatment, a technique of manipulation. But he had an immense urge to give Melman something for the privilege of being included. He felt in the presence of a charismatic priest, a great priest, and wished he had a sin to offer up so this man could forgive him.

Trewitt in Mexico.

"Sam—''

"Wait, Miles. Let me finish.''

He fixed Miles in his calm gaze, seeming to draw him in, to make him absolutely his. "Paul hates us. You have to understand, though I wonder if you're old enough, the kind of man he is. The kind of grudge he's capable of manufacturing. A certain kind of mentality can tighten, can fix, on a situation and turn it inside out. And come to believe—genuinely *believe*—his own version of it. It's a lesson in the human capacity for self-deceit, the power of will over reality. Chardy has this talent; it's a characteristic of the fanatic and it's what makes them such potent, such powerful, such astonishing men. In a way I admire it, and wish I had a little of this power for myself. For these men, to admit any but their own vision is to doom themselves. Their strength is their will, their absolutism; their weakness is their inflexibility.

"Miles"—he looked especially hard into Miles's dark, small eyes, nailing him back against the chair—"you've seen his file. The Russians turned him; they broke him in two. He gave them the Kurds, and the woman he loved, driving her from him forever, turning her against him in the cruelest of ways. And make no mistake, love is a very powerful, an almost magical force for a man like Chardy. You've no idea how a man like him needs it. So God knows what kind of construction he's put on his own betrayal; and God knows what her death has now done to him."

Miles nodded. He felt curiously full of faith; in his own Church, in the Agency, and in Sam. Some of Sam's wisdom entered his soul, as if Sam had willed it there.

"Miles, there'll come a time when he'll test you. He'll demand you make a choice. A choice between himself and us. And I warn you, he can be very attractive. He has that rough grace that commands. In a crisis he radiates energy and purpose. You'll see it in his eyes. I'm convinced that the reason Speight was killed and Trewitt is missing is that they exceeded their instructions from Ver

Steeg and were off on some crazy mandate from Paul. You saw what it brought them.''

Tell him, thought Miles. Tell the priest. Confess. He was in a dark booth and could only feel the power of the man's love, his warmth, his infinite wisdom through the screen. He ached to tell. Tell him: Trewitt's alive. He's still on the case. You're right, Sam, Chardy the treacherous is working something.

''Miles, Chardy is not stupid. He seems stupid, he can play dumb better than any man I've ever seen. If you read through the transcripts on the Saladin Two inquiry, you'll think you're seeing a stupid man, a man so shocked and addled and fatigued that he is unable to defend himself. But I never laid a glove on him. It was a brilliant performance. I never got inside him. There's something in that head of his, something he never even let us see. And now he's got Danzig; he's made some sort of pact with Danzig. The whole thing troubles me immensely. Yet I can't get rid of him, as I'd want to. He bungled it terribly in Boston, walking out like that. I'd love to ship him to the North Pole, and I would too; but I can't, because of Danzig. So Miles, only this warning: Watch Chardy, watch him carefully. All right? He's much more than the man he's letting you see.''

Miles nodded reverently. Yet he was befuddled by the passion in Sam. He felt he'd missed something somewhere; he was a little frightened. He realized now that Melman hated Chardy. Hated him, feared him: weren't they the same?

Tell him, Miles thought. You have it in your power to please the cardinal, to bind him to you forever and ever. He will give you the Church; he will make the Church yours. You will move through its halls, through its hushed and purple rooms, to its most privileged sanctums.

Miles wished he could genuflect.

Yet he saw also there was a secret and dangerous game between Melman and Chardy—a game whose stakes were so high neither man would speak of them directly.

"Sam," he heard himself saying, "you can count on me."

38

When would the boy return?

"He should have been back hours ago," Trewitt said irritably.

"He probably stopped to steal a chicken," Roberto said. "The little snotnose." Roberto had taken over the Beretta, his proudest possession. He sat under a scrub oak polishing as obsessively as he'd once polished the glasses behind the bar at Reynoldo's. He had already fired three of the remaining seven bullets for practice.

Trewitt shifted uncomfortably beside him. As he moved he bumped into his own armament, which had been propped against a log in front of him. He'd had some practice too; with the scope, it was like shooting at the star of a drive-in movie.

"No," he said, "he's had plenty of time. They left yesterday—in the postman's Jeep they could have been back by one. It's almost five now."

"Forget it. What does a little snotnose know? He don't know nothing."

"He knows enough to get back in time. Dumb kid." The kid was important because he was a kid and Trewitt liked him, but also because he carried another telegram for Chardy, care of the Resurrection. If this try didn't work, Trewitt had resolved to go out in the open, the hell with the risk. He was done with waiting.

"Don't wet your pants. He'll be back. Little snot-nose."

Trewitt picked up the rifle, slid it back against his shoulder. They were two hundred yards upslope from the stone shack. The move had been Trewitt's idea, arguing that if they were at any moment apt to be jumped they couldn't just be caught in the shack; they had to have a *plan*.

Ramirez looked upon this strategic innovation with great curiosity, and then went back to his smart-alecky maid and her comeuppance.

But Trewitt insisted, and ultimately prevailed. Still, some plan. The *plan* was to blow the brains out of any-body who poked around.

And what if Chardy showed up? Well, Chardy wouldn't show up. There'd been some kind of screw-up.

But Trewitt was determined. He'd get this Ramirez back somehow, whether he wanted to or not, back to Chardy. There, Chardy, what do you think of that? You decide, Chardy. Trewitt had no other chart to work by. His head was still packed with confusion. All espionage tends to end in farce, Malcolm Muggeridge had said, and boy, he sure had this one figured out. Trewitt was not certain whether he'd decided on this course of action or whether it had been decided for him. Things just happened, and here he was, halfway up a dusty mountain in a hot sun on a clear day with a sniper's rifle in his hands.

Above, a hawk pirouetted, slid on a thermal, high, re-mote, coldly beautiful. Trewitt watched the bird with idle envy: the grace, the power, the freedom, the dignity com-mandeered his imagination. The lovely thing skidded back and forth brainlessly on the currents, wheeling into the valley, then soaring upward again.

Trewitt wiped a drop of sweat off the end of his nose and studied its dampness on the end of his finger, and did not see the car.

But when he looked up, there it was, a Mercedes 450 SL, gunmetal gray, sitting before the shack.

Roberto was squirming into cover next to him.

"Jesus Mary, now we going to see some stuff."

Oscar Meza got out from the passenger's side, held his hands wide to show that he was unarmed.

"Reynoldo," he called to the mountain, "can you hear me? These people here want to talk to you. That's all, a little talk. They sent me ahead. Come, have a little talk, and we will let the little one go. Don't be no fool, Reynoldo, it's just a little talk."

There was silence.

"Reynoldo, think it over. Take your time. You got fifteen—"

The shot rang out crisp and clear. Oscar Meza sat back on his expensive fender, holding his middle. He breathed deeply. His sunglasses fell off. His knees cracked and he pitched forward on them. Then he fell the rest of the way.

"Goddammit," bellowed Trewitt, "he shouldn't have—"

"Right in the guts! Reynoldo sure can shoot a gun."

Trewitt stared stupidly at the dead man by the car. For a long moment nothing happened. Then the car began to gently back up, leaving its fallen passenger. It moved as though it were pulling out of any suburban garage into any sane, pleasant street, turning as its driver swung its nose to bear in the right direction. Then, slowly, it began to descend the dirt road.

"Shoot! Shoot the whoreson. I cannot see him," commanded Ramirez from his cover.

"What?" Trewitt said.

"Shoot him! Mother of God, shoot!"

Without thinking, Trewitt brought the rifle to his shoulder, throwing the bolt. He felt the press of the stock against his shoulder, the weight of the rifle in his hands. His eye went naturally to the scope and after a moment of blurred dazzle in which nothing made sense, he caught a glimpse of the gray car as it plummeted toward safety. Against the cross hairs, through the rear window, there now appeared, almost magically—a head. A man's head, held low as he hunched in terror behind the wheel, holding the car in a straight line for the turnoff, gathering speed.

Trewitt readied himself.

"Shoot! Shoot!" Roberto commanded.

Only seconds remained until the car reached the turnoff and would be gone. Trewitt took a whole breath, released half. The head lay in the foreshortened reality of the scope, just beyond the muzzle. He felt he could touch it.

Shoot, Trewitt told himself. The 7-millimeter would burn into the skull, exiting, hugely, through the face, taking features and bones and eyes and brains with it, spraying them indiscriminately against the windshield. Trewitt felt a split-second's nausea at what he was about to do. He took the slack out of the trigger—

"Shoot!" Roberto hooted.

The car swirled around the turnoff in a great roostertail of dust, and was gone.

"What is wrong with you? Are you sick, man?" asked Roberto.

"I—I didn't have a very good shot," Trewitt said. "I couldn't see wasting a bullet."

"You should have shot anyway."

"Well, I didn't want to throw a bullet away."

The youth looked at him suspiciously.

Trewitt sat back.

"I don't know why he shot that guy," he said to nobody. "I don't see what that accomplishes." Oscar Meza lay a hundred or so yards down the slope on his stomach. Trewitt could now see that he was wearing an expensive suit and fine boots. He was a curiously formal figure in the litter of the yard.

"That son of a bitch kick me out of my job," said Roberto.

But Trewitt now had to think about the boy. What about the boy?

"They'll kill him now," he said.

"Kill who?" Roberto asked.

Trewitt's desolation was total. It became rage. He wished he'd shot the man in the car, blown his fucking head to pieces. "The little boy. Miguel."

"He should have stayed with his mama," said Roberto.

Trewitt sat back against the tree, the rifle next to him. Around him the bleak mountains lay in dusty splendor. He looked for the hawk but it had vanished. He looked about: he seemed to be on the face of the moon.

"Hey, *patrón,*" Roberto called to Ramirez, who ambled toward them, "the *norteamericano* wants to go down the hill for the little snotnose kid."

"You just get killed, mister. Hey, how come you didn't shoot? You should have shot him."

"I couldn't see him very well," mumbled Trewitt.

"That's a fine telescope on that gun. You should have been able to see him real good. Maybe you weren't working it right."

"He's just a kid!" Trewitt screamed, leaping to his feet. "Come on, we can't stay here. Let's get going. Maybe it's not too late." He began to stride manfully down the slope. He turned when they did not move and fixed them in a steely glare.

"Let's get going," he commanded icily.

"You must be a real crazyhead," said Ramirez. "Go down there? They just kill you. They're going to kill you anyway, but why rush it?" He laughed. "I'm hungry. Let's get some food. They'll be back pretty soon."

"WE'VE GOT TO SAVE THAT KID!" boomed Trewitt again.

"He *is* a crazyhead, *patrón,*" said Roberto. Wonder filled his eyes.

The two Mexicans, laughing between themselves, walked past him to the shack.

Trewitt stood alone, the rifle tucked against his hip. He watched the fat man and the youth. They stepped over the body of Oscar Meza and ducked inside.

Then Trewitt started down the hill to the shack for some tortillas too.

39

Chardy was made uneasy by the approach of night. He had a history of unpleasant evenings, for during them, late, when he was alone, the things that he could not control by sheer will crawled out to harry him. And when he had found Johanna in her car, across from the blinking police lights, the rushing officers and medics, the gathering crowd, he was aware that in some strange way a trap had been sprung in his mind. He had stared at her, knowing exactly what had happened, and why, and how: he saw it now. A pain came and took his breath away and almost knocked him to the sidewalk.

He had thought he heard somebody tell him to be reasonable.

The memory would not die; it had increased the next several days, all through his time as athlete, among the postman and his friends.

Be reasonable, somebody was telling him.

The voice was sane and calm; it was almost compassionate.

"Paul. Be reasonable."

Chardy was alone in his little Silver Spring apartment, on the night after he returned from Danzig's. A baseball game was over on the tube, it was that late. He'd had a few beers. He'd laid out his new suit, a clean shirt, and his shoes for tomorrow. He felt like another beer, but realized he was now out and wondered if it made sense to dress again and drive around until he found an all-night liquor store or a bar with package goods.

Be reasonable, he told himself.

But the voice was not his. It was affable, pleasant, colloquial, American. It was the voice of a pudgy man, about fifty, with merry, alert eyes and thinning blond hair, almost white. He wore a Soviet major's uniform, army, with artillery boards and insignia, but he was KGB all the way. The uniform made this point explicitly: no Soviet military careerist would be seen in a Third World country in such a disgraceful uniform, rumpled, spotted, humorously unpressed. An orthodox man could not wear such a uniform under pain of instant censure and discipline; thus the wearer was not an orthodox man. He enjoyed special privileges. He was permitted his eccentricities.

"Paul," he had said, "come on. Let's be reasonable, shall we?"

Chardy's Arabian Nights, which were not 1001 in number but only six, were beginning to reassemble in his mind this night in his little apartment.

"It's so difficult, this business," said Speshnev. "I'd much prefer to be your friend. I really would. Will you please talk to me? Please, Paul."

But Chardy would not talk. He remembered instructing himself: don't give them anything. If you start, you will not stop. Don't give them anything. The first surrender is the only surrender; it is total, it is complete. Time. Play for time.

He studied the cell. Down here, the walls sweated. The air was moist, almost dense. This room had probably been cut from living stone a thousand years ago, by slaves.

Who knew what pains it had witnessed? Had it always been a torture chamber?

"Paul, let me explain how it works. I'm going to have them burn a hole in your back. The pain will be—well, it will be indescribable. But I think you can get through it. You are a very brave man. I think you can get through it. Then tomorrow, Paul, tomorrow, I'm going to have them burn another hole in your back. You'll have all this evening to think about the hole they're going to burn. You'll know exactly what it's going to feel like. There will be no surprises. Paul, the day after that, I will burn another hole. You'll have a night to think about that one too. And on and on, Paul. On and on and on. If we run out of back, then we'll move to the chest. Do you understand? That is the future, Paul. That's all the future there is."

You can do it, he told himself. You can stand it, he told himself.

Oh, it's going to hurt so. Oh, Christ, it's going to hurt.

You can do it, you're Chardy, you're so tough. You've been begging for this one your whole life. To see how tough you are.

They burned the first hole in his back.

"Paul, it's so absurd," Speshnev told him on the second day. "What do you gain by resisting? We win in the end, of course. But think further: *What* do we win? Frankly, not much. We win a momentary advantage, a half a point's shift in momentum. Perhaps I win a promotion, or at least advance a few inches closer to promotion. And what of it? Is the world really changed? Is one system that much better off than the other? Of course not. Let's face facts: our two nations face each other on a thousand different battlefields, a thousand different contests each second. Some we win, some you win. But nothing really changes. The process of change is implacably slow and no human endeavor may be seen to affect it. So what sense does it make to resist us? None at all. It's thoroughly ridiculous, an exercise in playground heroics. Now, in this cellar, you are being a hero, an authentic American hero, fighting the pain, the psychological pressure, fighting alone without help, without hope, standing against everything we can do to you. It's incredible; it's quite moving. You have my respect. I couldn't have done nearly so well. I'd have cracked in the first session. I'd certainly have cracked by now. You are a champion. Paul, must I have them burn another hole in you? Must I? Will you force me?''

Chardy's wrists were tied before him; he could see old stone and smell his own sour perspiration. He'd spent the night thinking about his back.

"Paul, please. Help me on this. We can work together.''

They burned the second hole in his back.

"How was your evening, Paul? The guards say you screamed all night. They say you woke several times with nightmares. I would imagine the psychological pressure is immense. I know this business weighs heavily on me as well. I hope we can finish it today and that you're able to cooperate. What do you say, Paul? Do you think you'll be able to help me?''

Chardy was silent; in his peripheral vision he could see Speshnev standing behind and beside him in his rumpled uniform.

"Paul, now let's think about this. At this very moment an American from the IBM Corporation is selling a Russian from the Committee on Scientific Research highly sophisticated computer software whose intricacies are a thousand times more complex than you or I could ever understand. A traitor? No, it's done in the open! Business-

men! With the support and endorsement of both governments. It's simply trade. Also being sold are licenses for
the bottling of Pepsi-Cola and the manufacture of Ford
Pintos. In exchange we fork over tons of our desperately
needed minerals, crude ore, and so on. So against this
panorama of exchange, this Technicolor extravaganza of
commercial greed, of ideological co-option, what can you
expect to accomplish? Paul, be reasonable. You prevent
one man, me, from becoming a full colonel. It's really
quite humorous, Paul. I wish you'd work with me on
this."

They burned the third hole in his back.

"Paul, they tell me you had a terrible evening. The
guard says he thinks you did not sleep at all. And you do
look feverish, Paul. Frankly, you look awful. You look
terrible. I think yesterday I let them go too far. That
wound is terrible. Paul, if you could see it you would be
disgusted. And the flies. The flies must drive you insane.
Paul! How much longer can you let this go on. You are
destroying yourself!"

Chardy had given up, by this time, any idea of heroism.
Courage had no meaning in a cellar among men with
blowtorches. He'd quit caring for the Kurds; they could
have the Kurds, they could have Ulu Beg and his band of
lunatics. And the Agency—what good was it? They'd let
him hang on ropes for three days now, in his own filth, in
a cell with rats, a medieval place full of damp straw where
other men screamed in the night, and his nightmares were
huge and terrible and he could think of nothing but the
torch.

"It's not as if anybody cares," Speshnev said. "Do
you really think all those Ivy Leaguers care? I mean, think
about it, Paul: have you been really satisfied with your
treatment from them? Haven't they always regarded you

with contempt as some sort of working-class adventurer, just a shade above a mercenary? Do they even bother to conceal their superiority? Tell me if I'm not right: they all wear pinstripe suits and black shoes, don't they? I'm right; I know I'm right. They seem to pad along. They wear those pink-rimmed glasses, plastic things. They all know each other, and each other's fathers, and all went to the same schools. They play squash. They send their children to the same schools. They all live in the pleasanter Washington suburbs. McLean or Chevy Chase. They drink wine and know about French food. They speak a different language. And you terrify them. You scare the pants off them because you are one of those rare men with talent. How ordinary people hate talent! They despise it! It terrifies them! You have a talent for action, a will, a courage. They envy it fiercely and they hate you for it. Think about it, Paul. Be reasonable. Are those men worth suffering these torments for? Think about what I'm saying, Paul. They'll leave you here to the next century. They have no capacity to imagine what you are undergoing. Paul. It would be so easy to tell me.''

And it would. Speshnev wanted the frequencies, the times of transmission, the code system of the radio linkup with the Kurds. It was so simple. The frequency was 119.6 MhK, nothing fancy at all, but the Kurdish receivers and the Agency transmitter in Rezā'iyeh were calibrated exceedingly fine so there was very little band waver going in or out. Radios were an Agency specialty. You had to be parked right in the groove to intercept and if Speshnev didn't get the frequency he had no chance. The codes were easy too: Fred to Tom on the odd days, Tom to Fred on the even ones. It was so simple it was primitive, straight out of a World War II OSS handbook. He could tell Speshnev in ten seconds. He could be off the hook in ten seconds.

"Please don't hurt me again. Please," he said.

"You'll cooperate?"

Chardy twisted on his ropes until he made eye contact with the Russian. He begged forgiveness with his eyes and the Russian responded.

"Don't you understand?" Chardy said hoarsely, whispering. "I—I—just can't."

Johanna was among the Kurds. He'd have to give them Johanna and he would not.

They burned the fourth hole in his back.

By the fifth day Speshnev was growing desperate. Chardy could hear him pacing in the cell, hear his boots scrunching on the straw.

Chardy tried to think of Johanna.

"The early burns are festering badly, Paul. There are maggots in them, and flies. The infection looks gruesome. The pus is something terrible, Paul. I'd like to get a doctor in here. I don't know how you can stand the pain. The pain must be intense."

He had never seen her naked. He never would see her naked. It had always been in a sleeping bag. He tried to imagine her naked. He tried to put her nakedness between himself and this room.

"Those flies can lay eggs, Paul, that get into your bloodstream. Your blood distributes them throughout your body. They hatch in odd places, Paul. They hatch in your lungs, in your toes, in your genitals, in your heart, in your brain. Paul, all those little insects in you, eating you up. All that corruption and filth spreading through your body, devouring you, absorbing you."

Her breasts. He tried to imagine their heft and weight, the size of the nipples. He concentrated desperately.

"Paul, a little antibiotic and the problem is instantly taken care of. It's just a pill, a shot, and modern medicine takes over, vanquishing the invaders. Or they eat and grow fat on your flesh, grow corpulent on your organs, Paul. And out there, eating you from this side, Paul, is the torch. Always the torch, Paul. The torch is here. Tell me, Paul, are you ready for the torch again? Paul, you are making it so hard on me. But you force me to do my duty. Help me, Paul. Let me save you from the torch and the insects, Paul. Help me.''

But Chardy was thinking of nothing else in this world except Johanna and could not help him. They burned the fifth hole in his back.

The Russian was desperate on the sixth day.

''Damn you, Paul! Damn you, Chardy, the codes! The codes, damn you. The frequencies.''

Chardy hung on the rope. Before him, the wall. He could hear the wheel of the cart as they brought the heavy acetylene torch in. He had never seen it, but he'd heard it bang against the walls, heard the squeak as its metal wheels rolled across the stone floor. He had no idea who was working the torch, who actually applied it, but for certain, whatever happened, happened at Speshnev's direction.

He could hear them now adjusting the nozzle, could hear the soft turning of valves as the gas and oxygen mixed. He smelt the gas, as he always did, and he began to gag reflexively, to choke and twist on his ropes, to retch up food that wasn't there.

''It's here, Paul. The torch. It is once again the hour of the torch. Are you ready, Paul? The torch is here; he's got it lit. Its flame is blue, Paul. Its pain is indescribable. He's going to wait a second, adjust the flame.''

Chardy's head lolled idiotlike on his chest. Drool played across his chin. Very little was real to him except the torch, whose approach he could feel all the way to his inmost cells. The rope cut into his hands. His fingers looked like blue sausages. Blood ran down his arms. He hung in his own waste.

"Paul, don't make me debase you again! Don't!"

Chardy fought them with his last weapon. It was his game. He tried to think of basketball. He tried to keep the game at the front of his brain. He tried to remember what he loved most about it: the pebbly feel of the ball as it came up to his hand on the dribble; the exultation that fired through his veins when a long one went in, especially late in the last period in a close game; the sheer fury, the physical ferocity of the struggle under the boards. He saw himself in a vast dark gym. He could not tell if there were fans in the seats or not, for he could not see. He could not make out the people he was playing against either: they seemed to be shadows, swatting at him, throwing their bodies at him. But he could see the hoop, the only spot of light in this great arena, an orange circle, crisp and perfect, its white net hanging beneath it. And he could not miss. He kept putting it in. He kept firing that ball up there and it kept going through. He could smell his own foul sweat, and exhaustion clouded his vision. His legs didn't work and fatigue blurred the precision of his moves. He could get it in, though. He thought he could get it in.

"Paul, it's working now. The torch is working now. We are ready. They tell me you screamed all night, Paul. You're feverish, you're in great pain. You've fought so hard. But you're not going to make it. You are not going to make it, Paul. I've won. You knew I would. Paul, it's a matter of time. It's only a matter of time. The torch is ready."

Chardy could hear two grunting men shove the thing over, hear the squeak of the wheels.

"Paul?"

"Please," Chardy said. "Please don't."

"Are you ready, Paul?"

"Please. Help me. Don't hurt me. I'm begging, oh, Jesus, I'm begging you. Don't hurt me. Please. Don't hurt me. Don't hurt me."

"Burn him."

"No. *No!* PLEASE, OH, JESUS, PLEASE DON'T HURT ME! PLEASE! I'M BEGGING! OH, SHIT, I CAN'T TAKE IT! PLEASE!"

"You'll talk then?"

Chardy hung on his ropes. He tried to pray. Dear God, spare me. Spare me, please, dear God. I pray to you, dear God, help me. Please, help me.

"Paul. Your answer?"

Chardy whispered.

"What? Louder, Paul. Louder."

Chardy tried to find the words. His tongue caught in his throat. He could hardly see. He was so scared. He could feel his heart thumping.

"Yes, Paul? Yes?"

Chardy croaked, "I said, fuck you, cocksucker."

They burned the sixth hole in his back.

Chardy lay in the ropes. How much time had passed? Pain-time or real time? Pain-time is different: longer. In pain-time, years, decades. In real time, maybe three hours. It was just night. He stared at the crumbling stone. He heard rats in the darker corners of the cell. He knew that tomorrow he would crack. It would be tomorrow. He was not even sure he could last the night.

He heard the cell door open. Off schedule. Were they going to give him his seventh day's dosage now, and cheat him of the pleasures of brooding upon it? But he couldn't turn to see. His neck barely worked.

Rough hands cut him down. He fell limbless to the straw. He was dragged toward light. They lifted him up.

"Ahhhhhhh!"

"His back, watch his back, you fool."

"Yes, *Agha.*"

He seemed to sit.

"Get him some water."

It was presented in an earthenware cup, held for him because his gray hands would not work. He felt the rough texture of the vessel with lips and tongue as the water sweetly entered him.

"Enough."

The water was taken away.

"Paul? Can you hear me?"

Chardy could not focus. He squinted and recognized the voice. He could almost see the face and then it swam into clarity. The Russian peered at him intently.

Chardy smiled stupidly, feeling the skin of his lips crack and split. A tooth fell out. His head lolled forward; he raised it again. He shook his head.

"Paul, listen to me. We've captured another Kurd from Ulu Beg's group. A deserter. We broke him with the torch just minutes ago."

Chardy thought about it. He almost passed out. More water was poured into his mouth, until he almost choked.

"I—I—I'm the only one who knows the fre—fre—*fre—*"

"Frequency, Paul. Frequency."

"Frequency."

"Paul, he didn't have to tell us about the frequency or the codes. He told us enough. He told us about the woman."

Chardy stared groggily at the man. His back fired off on him, curling him in a spasm of pain.

"Jo—Jo—Jo—?" he began weakly.

"Yes. Listen carefully. Here it is, a one-time-only offer. I'm not going to give you much time. You've got about thirty seconds. Paul, either give us the information or I swear to you, I'll bring you her head. If you talk, maybe we can get her out. We can try, at any rate. She's beyond anybody else's help. The Agency can't help her. The Iranians can't. She's with his group and we're closing in and we'll have them in a matter of days, a week at the most. Only one man can help her, Paul. You, Paul. You decide, Paul. Does the woman live or die? You tell me, Paul, or I swear that within the week, in this very chamber, I will hand you her head. I'll take it from her myself.''

Chary had begun to cry. He found the strength to lift his hands to his eyes to shield his shame. Fat tears fell onto his filthy body and ran into the straw. He choked on them.

''Paul. Ten seconds.''

Speshnev stood.

Chardy fought for his strength as he watched the Russian go toward the light. He felt himself slipping into the straw. He watched the others join Speshnev at the door and begin to file out. Speshnev pulled the heavy door closed behind him.

''No,'' screamed Chardy. ''No. God help me. God help them all. God forgive me. No. No. No.''

''There, there, Paul,'' he heard the Russian crooning, as he lifted Chardy's head gently from the straw. ''It's going to be all right. You're being reasonable at last.''

They cleaned him quickly after he told them, and shot him full of pain-killer. The rest he remembered poorly. They took him up several floors to some kind of operations center. He sat at a Soviet artillery radio, an older model. It had evidently already been adjusted to proper frequency. Several technicians hovered about and he could tell that his condition shocked them. He almost passed out twice. The radio crackled.

"What do you want me to say?"

Speshnev told him about the helicopters, and Chardy told Ulu Beg, and then they gave him some more pain-killer and he went to sleep.

He awoke in a hospital room, on his stomach, in the presence of two Soviet Marines with AK-47s. He was much improved, though groggy. Bright sunlight flooded in through the window, and beyond he could make out the city. They brought him a glass with some high-protein concoction in it, mostly egg and wheat, and he sucked it down.

The door flew open and the Russian came in.

"How are you, Paul? How are you?"

Chardy had no answer and looked at him stupidly. He could only think that he had just begun a day where there would be no torch.

"We broke it, Paul. Yes, we did it. *I* did it, Paul. Broke it, broke the revolt. We broke the Kurds, Paul. All American advisers have been ordered back to Rezā'iyeh. The mission there will be closed down. The Shah has arrested the Kurdish emissaries in Tehran, and closed the border. It's all over."

He looked carefully at Chardy.

Chardy had trouble concentrating. Even now his memories were beginning to jangle on him, to mix and twist and fabricate themselves. His back felt numb. He'd been jacked up to his eyeballs on narcotics. He could hardly remember his own name.

He looked away. Stupidly, he lurched from the bed. One of the Soviet Marines grabbed him, but he pulled away and stumbled to the window. He looked across Baghdad from a fifth or sixth story and saw a filthy sprawl of stone slums and crappy modern buildings spilling to the horizon. A sluggish bluebottle struggled against the dirty glass. The sun was shining, though a hump of clouds gathered in the distance, over the mountains far to the north.

"A wonderful city, eh, Paul? Beautiful Baghdad, storied Baghdad, city of princes and miracles. Beautiful, isn't it, Paul?"

Chardy said nothing. He sensed the Russian beside him.

"Ah, Baghdad! Do you know in my last post I had a fine view. I could see a river, a giant old Ferris wheel, white baroque buildings. Europe. Civilization. Perhaps now I will be going back there."

"The girl," Chardy said. "Johanna. Please?"

"Well, Paul, the news is optimistic. We believe she got out. We have examined the bodies and hers is not among them. Unless she was killed earlier, of course, in which case of course I can take no responsibility. But—"

"Bodies?" Chardy said.

"Yes, Paul. We killed them. We killed them all."

Chardy fell to his knees. He began to weep. He could not stop himself. He sobbed and gagged. He tried to hide his face from the Russian towering above him.

"You are truly a broken man, aren't you, Paul? I wonder if you'll ever be any good again? At anything? I hope when you get back you can find this woman and get her to marry you. You've certainly paid a dowry. Perhaps the highest in the world. You can marry her and live in the suburbs and work for an advertising agency. Tell me, Paul. Was it worth it?"

That night, on the flight to Moscow, Chardy managed to open both his wrists with a broken glass. He bled considerably, but they caught him and would not let him die.

———

Chardy blinked awake in his apartment, alone in the cold night.

Be reasonable, he told himself.

He rolled from the bed, went to the refrigerator. There was no beer; he had not gotten any. Was it too late? He badly needed something to drink. He looked at his Rolex and discovered it was the hour of four. He stared out the window above his sink. A sprawl of streetlights lay beyond the filthy glass.

Chardy stood barefoot in the kitchenette. He got himself a lukewarm glass of water in a plastic glass and was too spooked to chase down ice. He thought of Johanna, who was dead, and Ulu Beg who soon would be. He thought of Speshnev too, and even thought he heard the Russian's voice now, lucid, full of reason and conviction. Speshnev said, and Chardy heard it as if the man were here, now, in this room: "In my last post I had a fine view. I could see a river, a giant old Ferris wheel, white baroque buildings."

Chardy could see nothing. This was the suburbs; there was nothing to see. Chardy thought of the Russian looking at his white baroque buildings, and marveled that in the man's mind there was room enough for pleasant views and baroque architecture and the theory and practice of the torch.

He shook his head, took another sip of his water. He looked at his watch, to discover that only a minute had passed since he'd last checked. He knew he'd never get back to sleep. He looked again into the darkness and at that instant, that exact instant, it hit him with such force as almost to drive him through the linoleum that in only one city in the world could there be such a congruence of rivers, Ferris wheels, and white baroque buildings. He'd been there himself.

The city was Vienna, where Frenchy Short had been found in the Danube after a solo job.

40

The strange patterns of fortune that swirled through it all disturbed him, made him deeply suspicious: things were always baffling, always astonishing, constructed as if with an Arab's cunning. The curious passage by which, as Chardy left the arena, Ulu Beg entered—as if it were written above that their meeting be postponed for a different day. Then again, the Kurd reflected, the play of whatever force had kept the fat Danzig alive. From fifteen feet he'd fired, seen the clothes fly as the bullets hit, seen the man knocked down. He'd seen it, with his own eyes. Then by what magic did Danzig survive?

DANZIG SHOT AT CAMBRIDGE PARTY
2 KILLED IN GUNBATTLE
FORMER SEC'Y IN 'STABLE CONDITION'

Was it some American trick, whose subtle purpose no mind could divine? Or had he in fact failed?

He had read the newspaper until he came to an explanation.

A vest to stop bullets! A vest!

And then, when he thought he was done with surprises, he'd turned a last page and found still another, a familiar face gazing at him from under another disturbing headline:

> *Harvard staffer*
> *found dead*
> *in Roxbury*

She was dead. Two strangers also. Two ex-brothers, one hunter, one hunted, pass in the night. And after it all, this Danzig still lived.

Ulu Beg sat back wearily and rubbed his hand across the stubble of his beard. He was tired, his eyes raw. He'd been on the move now a week since it happened and he was running low on money. He needed a shave, to wash, to rest.

He looked about him. The train station was crowded, even at this late hour. Outside it was raining. America was supposed to be full of miracles, and yet this train station smelled of the toilet and was dirty and hot. It was also full of peculiar people: madmen, old ladies, mothers with wild children, sullen soldiers, rich dandies; in all, a much stranger range of passengers than the buses. Or maybe it was his desperate mood or his fatigue, and the knowledge that his chances were growing more slender each day; he would never reach Danzig; he would be caught.

He had nowhere to go, nowhere to hide. Nobody would guide him. He'd made a terrible mistake a few minutes ago, confusing a quarter and a fifty-cent piece and there'd been a scene at a little coffee bar and a policeman had wandered by to straighten things out. Even now the officer was watching him from behind a pillar.

The Kurd looked at the clock. In a few minutes—unless the train was late and they were always late—there would come a train that would take him to Washington. In Washington, he would find Danzig's house. He had a picture of it still from a newspaper he'd read weeks ago in Arkansas. Somehow he'd find it. And this time he'd get close enough to place the muzzle against the head before he fired.

He sat back, looking up at old metal girders. His head ached. The rain beat a tattoo against the roof. The smell of the toilet reached his nose. He felt himself begin to tremble. He wished he could sleep but knew he must not. He thought he might have a fever.

He wished he had some help. He wished he knew where he was going. He wished he knew what was written above. He wished he knew what surprise would come next.

A man sat next to him and after a few seconds turned and said, "Do you care for a cigarette?"

It was Colonel Speshnev.

41

Now Roberto was gone too. Trewitt had seen him die, shot in the lungs at long range.

"May Jesus take his soul," said Ramirez, crossing himself, "and may He take the soul of that abortion out there with a rifle and telescope and wipe His holy ass with it."

Trewitt was wedged behind some stunted cripple of what passed for a tree in the higher altitudes of the Sierra del Carrizai. He shivered at the memory of Roberto's sudden passing, which was—when, yesterday? the day before? And he shivered also for the cold, which was intense, and thought briefly of all the coats he'd owned in his life, nice, solid, American coats, parkas and jackets and tweeds and windbreakers, a whole life written in coats, and now, now when he *really* needed one, he didn't have it, didn't have a goddamned thing.

"Mother of God, this is one fine mess," said Ramirez. "Jesus, Mr. Gringo, I wish you'd hit that fart in the car."

Trewitt wished he'd hit him too. He also wished Ramirez hadn't shot Meza and maybe had talked to "them"— whoever *they* were. He also wished he wasn't on this mountain.

A shower of pebbles now descended on him, and he

turned to watch the big Mexican slither off. Wearily, Trewitt knew he had to join him. The trick was to keep moving, keep crawling and sliding and hopping from rock to rock and gulch to gulch and knob to knob. They were being stalked by—how many now? Who knew? But bullets came their way often, kicking up vivid little blasts where they hit. Scary as hell. You never knew when it was coming.

At the same time Trewitt was almost beyond caring about moving on. His terror had eaten most of his energy, and his exhaustion had claimed what was left. He bled in a hundred places from assorted cuts, bruises, and nicks. He was rankly filthy and his own odor revolted him. A terrible depression, a sensation of worthlessness, a sense of having once again fulfilled his own lowest expectations of himself haunted him.

You really are no good, Trewitt. You really are a fuck-up. You always were; you always will be.

He watched the Mexican slithering through the rocks like a wily lizard. Something else troubled Trewitt about all this: there was only one way to go, and that was up, but what happened when they got all the way to the top and ran out of mountain?

"We make a stand. Big heroes," Ramirez said.

"Maybe we ought to try and talk to these guys."

"Okay. You go talk. Go ahead, be my guest, you go talk."

"Who are they? How many are there? Is this Kafka?"

Ramirez had no opinion on Kafka. He had no opinion on the identity of his pursuers either. But he thought there were at least five.

This Ramirez was something: totally incurious, totally indifferent to all things beyond himself. Trewitt knew he himself only existed to Ramirez as a kind of pointless but exotic addendum to reality, a kind of minor character good for a page or two in the Cervantes-scale epic of the Mexican's own thunderous life. A *norteamericano*—Ramirez despised Americans, but it was nothing personal, for he despised Mexicans as well. He despised everybody, everything: it was a mark of greatness, a symbol of the kind of huge, greedy will that in more primitive times might have made of Ramirez some kind of legend, a Pancho Villa, an Aztec chieftain, a dictator. Or was this Trewitt's imagination rollercoasting all over the place once again? For on the other hand, the more prosaic hand, Ramirez was just a large, stupid peasant with a peasant's slyness and hard practical streak.

Yet he was important.

Somehow he fit into a pattern Trewitt could not understand.

He was important enough to kill, which made him important enough to save.

"Hey, Mister Gangster Man. You coming?" the Mexican called in his border English.

Trewitt rolled over and began to squirm up the mountain. At least where he was going there was a view.

42

Chardy awoke with a headful of ideas, but before he could begin to decide how to pursue them, the telephone rang.

"Chardy."

"Chardy, it's Miles. Listen, you better get over here. We've got a bad situation on our hands. Danzig."

"What's wrong?"

"He wants you. And only you. He doesn't want us. At all."

"Miles, I—"

"Chardy, you have to get over here. The guy is acting crazy. *Get over here,* goddammit."

Chardy dressed and arrived within an hour and found Miles pacing the library, pasty under his acne, surrounded by other somber agents who would look at nothing.

"Take him up," Miles directed coldly.

Chardy turned to leave with a younger man. But Miles grabbed him.

"Paul. Just calm him down. All right? Just take it easy with him. Don't stir him up. Okay? Don't let me down on this, all right?"

"Sure, Miles," said Chardy.

Chardy rose through the levels of the house with the other agent, coming at last to the top floor.

"It's down there," the man said. "Third door. His office."

"He's really flipped?"

"He called Miles a Russian dupe. *Miles.* The little priest. He said we were all KGB. He said he was being held against his wishes. He tried to call Sam Melman. Miles almost died. He said he knew reporters all over town, he was going to have a news conference. He was going to tell them the Agency was trying to kill him—the whole thing was an Agency plot. He ordered Miles out of his house. He told him to go hide at the cathedral. He told him he could have the DCI over here in fifteen minutes. He told him he was looking for a gardener, would Miles like the job? All the time he was in his bathrobe, with his cock hanging out. He smells like a wino. All in all, it was quite a morning. And before nine. Jesus, Chardy, I want off this one. A bad op can stink up your records for years. I want to go back to South America, where it's safe."

Chardy thanked him and went to the door. He knocked.

"Chardy?" The whisper was ominous.

"Yes."

"Are you alone?"

"Yes."

Locks clicked and tumbled; the door cracked open.

"Quick."

Chardy slipped into the twilight. The shades drawn, all lights off. In this darkness Chardy stood, momentarily paralyzed. Behind him the door clicked shut.

His eyes adjusted. The room, large, was cased in books. Files lay all around, sheets of paper, index cards, clipped articles, photocopies. Two card tables stood inundated in paper. Two desks against a far wall bore heavy loads as well.

"Sit down. Over there."

Chardy walked, slipping once on a pencil. Cups, glasses with a few stale ounces of liquid in them, were everywhere. He sat gingerly on a folding chair.

"What time is it?"

Chardy smelled something sour as he turned his wrist to see his Rolex. "Nine," he said. "In the morning."

Danzig, unshaven, sat across from him in a bathrobe. His hair swirled about his head, unwashed. The odor was from him.

"They say this room isn't wired," Danzig said.

"I don't think we wired anything," Chardy said.

"Where have you been?"

"I had to go home. I was only gone a night."

"You look tired."

"I haven't been sleeping well."

But Danzig wasn't interested in Chardy's sleep. Now, with an almost comically exaggerated look of conspiracy, he seemed to swoop in on Chardy, his features enormous, rabbinical, his eyes quite mad. His odor was overpowering.

"It's all a setup, isn't it? It's completely phony—it's a scheme, isn't it? Or are you part of it? They tried to ruin you, you know. When you came back from prison. Then just weeks ago after the shooting. *I* saved you. I intervened. Chardy, they want you dead. They hate you too. They hate me. For something I did, something I know. And it's all part of—"

He stopped suddenly and began to weep.

Chardy was embarrassed for him. He watched silently.

"Chardy. Help me," Danzig said. "Don't let them kill me."

"If you stay here, you'll be all right. Just stay here—you have nothing to fear from these men downstairs."

A sudden spurt of energy jerked through Danzig; he

lurched up, twisting away, staggering through stacked books and sheets of paper and files, slipping, knocking them aside.

"You and I are natural allies in this thing. We are. We're the same man, really. Yours the physical component, mine the intellectual. Help me, Chardy. You've got to promise; you've got to help me. They're trying to get rid of *both* of us, don't you see? You and I, we're linked. Somehow."

Chardy watched him stagger through the room.

"Do you swear to me, Chardy? You'll help me?"

"I—"

"The Kurd is a triggerman. Don't you see? Perhaps *he* doesn't even know the real reason behind all this. The woman was another pawn. Perhaps you are still a third. It's a plan, a plot, a design only *they* know. Why? I have to know. Why?"

Chardy said, "They tell me only that it's as straightforward as it seems. That Ulu Beg is here for vengeance, because he feels we—you—betrayed his people and let the Russians kill them."

"Do you believe that? Chardy, look at me. Do you believe that? Really, deeply, do you believe that?"

"I don't know," said Chardy. "I just don't know."

"It's phony. And I'll prove it."

"How?"

"The answer is here. In this room."

Chardy looked around the dishevelment. Yes, somebody had been looking.

"Do you know what I've got here? I've got a duplicate set of the Agency operational reports for the years during which I was Secretary of State; I've got the records; I've got the secrets; I've got all the analyses, the—"

"How the fuck did you—"

"I've had it for years. I had my friends in the Agency

too, you know. For some time there was a considerable Danzig faction. I used a lot of the material for my first book. It's in here, in these records. I'll find it. But I need time. And they *know* I need time."

"I just—"

"Chardy! Listen!"

Danzig had closed in on him and stood inches away. His eyes gleamed, he seemed on the verge of a seizure. He touched Chardy.

"Chardy. This man is a foreigner. He's six feet two inches tall and probably doesn't know the difference between a nickel and a dime. He doesn't know what a hamburger is. Tell me this: Why hasn't he been caught? They said it would be days. It's been weeks. They've got him somewhere. They're manipulating him into place."

"Just stay here. Stay in this room. Don't leave this room unless I tell you to. You'll be all right. You have nothing to fear."

"You'll get me my time?"

"You've *got* your time. Trust me."

Trust Chardy? Trust him? That was the core of the problem: trust whom? Trust Sam? Trust this dreadful altar boy Lanahan? Trust the renegade Chardy?

Danzig sat back. He was into the second week of a headache. His chest still hurt. Chardy had gone.

"I won't be around today," he'd said. "I'll be back tonight."

"Where are you going?"

"You check your files, I'll check mine," Chardy had said.

Danzig sat back in the chair. He was afraid he might start hyperventilating again. He tried to escape his memory of the Kurd and his weapon and that terrifying moment when the molecules seemed to freeze and the man stood there fifteen feet away, about to fire, and Danzig knew he would die. He remembered the eyes, blazing, set. Something vivid and graceful about him, strong. The terrifying thing about it all was that it fascinated him. That's the Jew in me, he thought. I can talk it out, think about it, compare it to a thousand books and essays, examine its themes and motifs, its subtextual patterns, make epigrammatic witticisms about it, and yet I cannot do one thing to survive it.

He considered himself by way of contrast and the contrast was bleak. For fifty-six years he had not paid the slightest attention to his body. He abhorred exercise. He looked down at his belly, a slack mass protruding from his robe. Too much weight, too weak, too slow. He imagined himself scrambling up a hill or down an alley, the Kurd after him. He would slip and scrabble. The Kurd would come on in huge athletic strides. Danzig had nothing, nothing to fight him with. All his brains, his glory, his power: nothing.

What would he do? He knew the answer. He would die.

His headache leaked down his spine and into his back. A Jew in an attic, hiding. The same old pattern, ceaseless. Centuries of attics. It came down to this, finally, didn't it, this game they play when they are bored. The game is Kill the Jew. Kill the stinking kike, boys, kick him in the stinking teeth, kick his stinking ass. Kill the Jew, boys, kill him.

He shook his head. Madness stalked him—he knew it. History haunted him. It had been said of a dreadful king once that he was at his best when things were easiest, and Danzig had always loathed him for it. Other images came before him: Jews marching into ovens, slaves politely assisting their traffickers, Christian martyrs smiling in the flames or animal pits. The weak perished: another law, as binding as that of entropy and, in a certain way, related.

All right, he told himself: to work.

He rattled through the papers before him, various drafts of ideas, theories of conspiracy, lists of men and organizations that could benefit by his death. The list was impressive.

Maybe you *are* the fool, he thought, and issued a joyless laugh at the absurdity of his own predicament. Maybe you are just another crazy Jew; go on, go to Miami Beach, relax.

But a step creaked and he knew it was an Agency security man with an Israeli submachine gun and an earplug and he went back to work.

The promotion sat like an anvil on Lanahan, bending him to the earth. His small eyes were even shiftier than normal and he was breathing raggedly and too hard. He would not let Chardy alone, had followed him through four rooms now.

"What did he say, Paul? Did he say anything about me? Did you calm him down? You know he said *I* was working for the Russians, he really did. Paul, he's crazy. Paul, is he settling down? He said he was going to call reporters. Oh, *Christ,* can you imagine if—"

Chardy had seen it before: the brilliant underling who knows 3 percent more than any man who ever gave him an order finally gets the chance to give a few himself and is destroyed by it. He who talked so loud behind the backs of others is now devoured by imaginary conversations behind his own; he trusts no one, wants to know everything.

"I think he's calmer now. He had a bad night."

"I always did think he was a little manic-depressive; you could see it even when he was in his prime. What's his beef?"

"The standard. Conspiracies, secret plots, that kind of stuff. Nothing you haven't heard before. He's finally realized he might catch one in the back of the neck. It's tearing him apart.''

''Okay. I want you around. In case he throws another one of those horror shows.''

''He's all right now. He just wants to go through his files.''

''Still, you stay here. It's what Sam wants; it's what I want. Just in case. You can reach him. Nobody else can. It's that—''

''I've got something to do, Miles.''

''Chardy—''

''Sorry.''

''Chardy.''

''Fire me, Miles. See how that goes over with Danzig. See what he does then. See if you make archbishop then, Miles.'' Chardy smiled. ''Be good, Miles. Don't forget late mass.''

He turned and stepped out the door into the bright Georgetown morning.

Chardy made the Chevy in the traffic of Colesville Road, out near the Beltway. It was green, with a high aerial. Nothing ever changes, does it? You'd think they'd get new cars, but they were always dark Chevys. He slowed, it slowed. He sped up, it sped up. He pulled into a station, it pulled to the side of the road.

He filled the tank and paid the kid.

''Isn't there a town called Columbia around here?''

''It's out further. Straight out. About ten more miles.''

''Thanks.''

He pulled back into the lane of traffic and the Chevy moved to join it too. Chardy lagged a little, and cars started to honk behind him, then swing by him. Several people cursed as they wheeled past. He was going about twenty in a thirty-five zone, and stopping occasionally with indecision. Suddenly there were no more cars behind him except the green Chevy, which could not pass. In his rearview mirror he could see two grim young faces staring fixedly ahead. He stopped for a light.

When the light changed, Chardy dropped into reverse and hit the accelerator. The two cars met with a huge smash that whipped Chardy back against his seat. He shook his head clear for just a second, came up to first, and fired out of there. As he drove away, he could see the smashed grille of the car behind him, and a pool spreading under the engine block. One of the agents was out, screaming.

"Chardy, you motherfucker!"

Chardy sped down Colesville.

He paused. So unlike D.C. or any eastern or midwestern city. Perhaps something of California or an easterner's dream of California. Chic wood houses, fading fashionably from brown to gray; windows full of ferns; sensible cars like Volvos and Rabbits; loopy, winding streets that led nowhere except back to their own beginnings. He'd wandered in the rolling, hilly utopia for an hour now, searching out a fanciful address: 10013 Barefoot Boy Garth. Could there really be 10,000 houses with 10,000 Volvos and 10,000 ferns on this garth? And what the hell was a garth, anyway? But at last he'd connected. He'd found the garth—it was just a street—and come to a grouping of mock-Normandy farmhouses whose numbers were of the proper dimension. He tracked as he traveled, until he saw it, on a circle linked to the main road, a solid place. He pulled in, noting a child's plastic trike on its side, bright orange and slung low. So maybe there were kids. Or maybe the guy she'd married had them. He got out, stepped over the trike, and headed up a short walk.

He knocked. Suppose she wasn't there and he'd wasted

this long drive? He should have called first. But suppose she didn't want to see him? You could never tell; perhaps in the aftermath she'd thought the better of stirring up the old memories.

A muffled voice came from behind the wood.

"Who's there, please?" A little fear? Did people worry out here in paradise too?

"Marion, it's Paul Chardy."

The door shot open.

"Paul, my God!"

"Marion, hi. I should have called. Something brought me out here and I thought, what the hell?"

"How did you find me? Nobody can find *anything* in Columbia the first time."

"Lucky," he said, sparing her the tale of his lost hours.

"Come in."

He stepped into a hall and she took him down a step into the living room, which was cream-colored, filled with plants and light and spare, clean furniture.

"It's very nice."

"Sorry about the mess. My husband's kids are with us this month."

"Don't worry about it. You ought to see *my* place."

"Sit down, Paul. Can I get you some coffee?"

"Thanks. I'd appreciate it."

She went to the kitchen as he sat down on the sofa.

"Paul," she called, "it's so nice to see you."

She came back with two cups.

"I remember that you drank it black."

"I haven't changed. Remember that night in Hong Kong? Frenchy and I were just in from Vietnam. You met us at the airport. 'Sixty-six or 'sixty-seven?"

"Nineteen sixty-six."

" 'Sixty-six, yeah. And how we celebrated that night?

We went to that place out in Happy Valley. The Golden Window, I think it was. Right next to the furniture plant, and you could smell the lacquer and hear the buzz saw next door. Remember that place had all those fish, six tanks of them? They glowed? Jesus, and we got drunk. Frenchy and I did anyway. And we were supposed to check in with Cy Brasher the next day at oh-eight-thirty. And you had that taxi driver find a place that was open at about five. And you ordered coffee and made us drink it. Black coffee. And wouldn't let us go back to the hotel. You really saved our tails that night, Marion. Do you remember?"

"Yes, I do, Paul."

Chardy sat back, took a drink of his coffee. "That was some night."

"And wasn't there a girl who wouldn't leave you alone? At the Golden Window. And then you disappeared on us for three days after you got through the thing with Cy Brasher."

"Oh, yeah," Chardy said.

"And of course we knew where you'd been."

"Oh, yeah," said Chardy, leering as if he remembered the tart. And then he did, a Eurasian girl. She lived in a crappy little apartment in the city with three children. She'd given him a dose, too. And Frenchy had her, but that was on another trip, when Marion wasn't around.

"Marion, I just can't get it out of my head. We really had some times in those old days."

"I used to think about it too, Paul."

"But you quit? God, how? I'm still stuck back in the sixties."

"You were very young then. That was your youth. You always remember your youth. And for me I suppose it had to do with starting a new life. A new family. New friends. You just have a different circle."

"But you must miss him. The Frenchman. I miss him terribly."

"I do, Paul. Of course. Frenchy was one in a million. I miss him all the time."

"Old Frenchy. He taught me so much. Oh, he taught me a lot."

"But Paul, it can be dangerous back there. I never told you this—or anybody this. But after Frenchy died, I had a very rough time. I had to go into a place for a while. And they made me see how he was killing me. And I had to let him go. I had to let it all go, and move ahead."

"I wish I could."

"You can. Frenchy always said you were the strongest."

"Ah, Frenchy. The old bastard. Marion, where did they put him? I'd love to go see him. Just once, for old times' sake."

"He's in Cleveland, Paul. A very nice place. He was cremated, and he's in a vault in a nice cemetery outside Cleveland."

"Maybe I'll go there sometime," Chardy said.

"Paul, have you been drinking?"

"Not enough," he said, laughing loudly.

She nodded, disturbed. She was still a pretty woman; or rather he could still see her prettiness underneath her age, her thickness. She'd seemed to turn to leather. She was so tan she glowed. Her legs were still slim and beautiful. She'd been a stewardess, he seemed to remember. Yes, Frenchy always had a gift for stewardesses; they responded to him somehow.

"I'm just so mad he was dead all that time and I didn't even know. The bastards could have told me that, at least."

"I never liked the secrecy. I hated all that."

"Ah, they don't know what they're doing." He dismissed them with a contemptuous and exaggerated wave of his hand. He laughed loudly, threw down some more coffee. "Christ, the bastards," he said.

Marion watched him. "You *have* been drinking."

"A bad habit. Nothing serious. I drink, I shoot my mouth off. I make enemies, I take afternoons off. I get sentimental, look up old friends." He laughed again. "Look at me now. Chasing ghosts."

"Paul, you need help."

"No, no, Paul's fine. Old Paul, the strong one. He's the strong one. Frenchy really said that?"

"He did."

"I loved him. Marion, I have to know. What did they do to him?"

She seemed to take a large breath. She stood at the window. She looked out upon other Normandy-style mock farmhouses.

"It's such a pretty neighborhood, Paul. It's so leafy and bright. It's a wonderful place to raise children. They have pools all over the place and playgrounds they call 'tot lots.' They have little shopping malls they call 'village centers.' It's a wonderful place. I'm so happy here."

"Marion. Please tell me. I have to know."

"Paul, I don't want to go back there. I had so much trouble. You don't know how much trouble I had. I think it would be better if you left. This just isn't working. I can't go back there. Do you know how hard I had to work to get to this place, Paul? To have this life? This is the life I wanted, Paul, I always wanted."

"Help me, Marion. Please help me. I need your help."

"You're not here for the old times, Paul. You're not here out of love or loyalty. You're still in it. I can smell it on you, Paul."

She stood by the window.

"It's so important, Marion."

"It really was awful, wasn't it, Paul? All the things you and Frenchy did. You thought you were such heroes, such big men, flying all over the world. Your duty, you called it. You were fighting for freedom. You were fighting for America. But you were just thugs. Gangsters. Killers. Weren't you? Maybe that's the shoe that fits."

"I don't know, Marion. I don't know what we were."

"Frenchy told me, years later he told me, that in Vietnam accidents happened all the time. The wrong people always died. And in South America the soldiers you worked with were brutal men, who hated everybody. There was just too much violence sometimes, it couldn't be controlled. It just slopped all over the place."

"Terrible things happened. That's what it was about."

" 'Hairy.' Isn't that the word? That was Frenchy's favorite word. 'Very hairy, babe,' he'd say when he came back, just before he drank himself insensible. What it means, though, is that a lot of people had just gotten killed in some terrible and arbitrary way, for no reason. Isn't that what it means?"

"Sometimes."

"Do you know, Paul, that Frenchy didn't make love to me for the last five years of his life? Tried, tried hard. He just couldn't do it. The war was eating him up. It was destroying the great Frenchy Short. He was trying to get out before it killed him and he knew he wouldn't make it. He knew. That last trip, he *knew.*"

"He knew?"

"Here they come, Paul. Look."

Beyond the yard, beyond the fence, two boys and a girl in bathing suits and sneakers were running down the street, the smaller boy way ahead, running crazily, chugging like a cylinder, the second boy too cool to notice, the girl taking up the rear, laughing.

"They're good kids, Paul. So good. I only have them a month and five or six weekends a year, and they didn't come out of my body but, Jesus, I love them, Paul. Oh, Jesus, I love them."

She turned; he could see she was crying.

"Paul, you'd better go. I really don't have the energy to make introductions. All right? Just go; just get out of here."

"Marion. Please help me. How did Frenchy die? Go back, just one time. It's so important. You have no idea how important it is."

She started to sob. He went quickly to her, but when he touched her she recoiled.

"I'm all right," she said fiercely. "I'm fine." Her face had swollen; her eyes were red and wet.

"Did he drown?"

"That's what the Austrian death certificate said. But—"

"Yes?"

"Paul, when they were getting him ready for cremation, I got a call at the hotel. This was in Cleveland. It was the mortician. He asked me to come by. I drove over in the rain in a rented car. He was an old man, the only one there. He said he was sorry to bother me, he didn't want to make any trouble. The instructions said closed casket. But somehow something had happened in the mortuary. The box had been opened by mistake. He wanted to know if I wanted to make any kind of inquiry. Something was wrong; I should know about it. He was just trying to protect himself, he said. So I said, what is it, what is wrong?

"Paul, he took me back and he showed me. I had to look at it, Paul."

She paused.

"How did Frenchy die, Marion?"

"They killed him with a blowtorch, Paul. My beautiful, beautiful Frenchy. They burned him to death, slowly. They burned his face off."

43

At last there was peace.

Ulu Beg slept a great while, arising to cleanse himself and to pray. He slept, he ate. He lay in the bed, staring at the ceiling. Hours passed, days perhaps.

"We will simply have to go again," Speshnev said in his crisp English, their common language.

"Okay," said Ulu Beg.

"A vest," said Speshnev. "A vest that can stop a Skorpion from close range. What a fine American invention."

"The head. Next time the head."

"Of course."

"But when?"

"Soon, my friend. But for now, relax. Enjoy this place."

"Where are we?"

"In the State of Maryland, on a peninsula. This old estate was built by a man who made millions of dollars manufacturing——cars? airplanes? washing machines? No. Mustard! For sausages. Ten thousand acres, gardens, pools, tennis courts, a nineteen-bedroom house, two guest houses, a collection of exquisite paintings, Chippendale furniture, rare old books. From mustard! And now the taxes are so high, only the Union of Soviet Socialist Republics can afford them!''

The fat Russian smiled with great appreciation of his own humor; he had spoken with such precision that Ulu Beg was certain it was a treasured speech, delivered a thousand times before. He saw from the Russian's expectant eyes that he was presumed to see the wit in it too, and he smiled politely, although he didn't know what this ''mustard'' was.

Rewarded, the Russian sat back. They were in an opulent bedroom of a guest cottage down a path from the main house. Outside, a pond in which swans glided gave way to a marsh. And from the front one could look and see three distinct zones: a meadow, a marsh, and a sparkling body of water, flat and calm. This world was green and blue—*kesk o sheen* in the Kurdish—and quiet. A gentle breeze frequently moved across it; it was a vision he took great sustenance from.

''I am still overcome with what you managed to accomplish,'' the Russian said. ''You traveled across a foreign country to strike your blow. Then, having done so, you fled through an extensive manhunt. And when we finally made contact, you were planning your new attack. You are an extraordinary fellow.''

The Russian's technique was to flatter excessively. Ulu Beg had grown used to it; still, he wondered how much steel was beneath all this flab. The Russian had gray eyes—kind eyes, really—and blondish hair that in some lights was almost white. He wore rumpled suits and moved comically, yet this excess weight seemed also to conceal great strength. The Palestinians who had helped train Ulu Beg at the Raz Hilal Camp near Tokra, in Libya, called him, for reasons Ulu Beg never understood, Allahab, meaning, literally, The Flame. Ulu Beg took this to refer to the purity of his passion, his strength.

"Do you need anything? A woman? A boy? We can arrange anything."

"I am content," said the Kurd. He was somewhat offended; he was no buggering Arab. "Some rest. Freedom from pretending. Then another chance. This time I will not fail."

"Of course. The secret of my success—which is considerable, I might add—is simple. They ask me in Moscow, 'Speshnev, how do you do it?' 'It's easy,' I tell them. 'Quality people.' I use them here. I use them in Mexico. I—"

Ulu Beg blinked.

"The *best* people," Speshnev amplified.

"Oh." A compliment. The man would go to any length. "You are most kind."

"It's only true," Speshnev said.

Ulu Beg nodded modestly. When would this fellow leave? The Russian's warmth and nearness were overpowering. Ulu Beg felt suffocated in love. The Russian reached and touched his shoulder.

"You are an inspirational man. Your story, your deeds, your heroism will last for centuries. Your people will make a great hero of you. They will sing songs."

But even as this ornate thought was expressed, it seemed to evaporate. The Russian rose gloomily, went to the window. He stared out of it painfully, not seeing the marsh and the sky and the bay. Russians were said to be a moody people. How quickly they changed.

"It is the contrast," he said. "I cannot stand it. It hurts me. It physically hurts me. The contrast between you and the other."

He brooded on the placid landscape. In the radiant light, his hair became almost pink, the color of his jowly face.

"The other?" said Ulu Beg.

"Yes," said Speshnev. "The man who troubles my dreams."

"A man troubles mine too," said Ulu Beg.

"But not the same man. You think of the larger betrayal, the historical betrayal, the political betrayal. Of your people, as an act of state by the Americans to advance their own cause. You think of Danzig and the justice denied you, the justice deferred. You think of cold-blooded calculations made thousands of miles away by men in suits looking at maps. I think of something hotter, more immediately personal."

Ulu Beg followed nothing of these Russian ravings, moody wanderings through a gloomy landscape. The intensity was surprising, for in his normal life the man was the jovial type.

"I think of a man with a talent, a great genius. The talent is for evil. He is an artist, inspired, a poet."

Ulu Beg looked at him uncomprehendingly. Yet the Russian seemed not to notice and plunged madly on.

"You know, in this business it is not uncommon to get to know your opponent. Most often he is a chap such as yourself—decent, hardworking, a man you can respect, a man whom you could befriend were it not for the obvious politics. Yet once in a career one encounters what can only be called this talent for evil. It is not cold; it is hot. It is a kind of lust or need or obsession. A fervor. An absolutism that has nothing whatsoever to do with cause. It has no motive other than selfhood. It is the highest human vanity. I speak of a man who would sell his brother or torture someone helpless, not for politics or adventure but purely for the sensation of ego triumphant."

The short man gestured violently. Ulu Beg watched him, befuddled and unsure. Where was all this taking them? What significance had it? He had a terrible feeling of increasing complexity—what had been so simple must now take on another dimension.

"I speak," said the Russian, "of the man you call Jardi."

"But, Colonel—"

"Stop. If you thought you knew this man, you do not. You know only a part of him, a part he allowed you to see. You know the soldier. But let me tell you another story."

Ulu Beg nodded.

"After we captured him, I girded myself for the struggle, knowing full well how tough he'd be. He was, after all, an operative, a professional, for the American intelligence service. But such was not the case; in fact, exactly the opposite happened. He saw immediately how tight a bind he was in, where his best interests lay. And thus he did more than cooperate or collaborate. He gave us your group, for his own skin, but also, I tell you truly, for his own pleasure, his own pride. I confess I was shaken by this, perhaps even intimidated. I knew I should kill him, take him off the surface of the earth. Yet I hesitated; who could kill a helpless man? That indecision cost me dearly. He quickly insinuated his way into the favor of the Iraqis. I couldn't touch him. In fact, the last twist, the helicopter deceit: that was his idea. I argued against it—we had won, after all, by then. But no, he insisted on a gesture. Think of the future, he told the Iraqis; here is a chance to make a gesture of such contempt, no Kurd would face the light for a thousand years. After all, he maintained, Ulu Beg is famous; let his end become famous as well.

"I tried to convince them, to dissuade them, to make them see reason. Be reasonable, I pleaded. But he had won them over.

"Do you know no Russian pilot would fly that mission? No, our boys would have no part of it. The Iraqis flew it themselves. And Chardy went along!

"Naturally, I lodged a formal protest. But then I was arrested. He had me arrested! He had convinced the Iraqis that my opposition to the mission proved I was a traitor to their cause.

"They took me to a cellar, Ulu Beg, in that same prison where I found you years later. And Chardy interrogated me. Ulu Beg, can you imagine what he used on me? He used a blowtorch. He burned six holes in my body. I fought him for six days; I fought with all my might and will, Ulu Beg. And finally, when I was nearly dead, he brought me to the point of confession. I would have signed anything at that point. But somehow I found the will to resist one last hour. I lasted six and a half days, Ulu Beg, under the cruelest of torments. Insects picked at my wounds. He mocked my beliefs; he used the name of the woman I loved against me. It was a profane performance. I was only saved at the desperate intervention of my own people, who at last located me. Chardy disappeared soon thereafter. I never saw him after the cell."

He looked at Ulu Beg. He was perspiring quite heavily now, in the memory of his ordeal.

"You see how our quests are united, Ulu Beg. You will kill Joseph Danzig. And I will kill Paul Chardy."

44

The postman was in a cruel mood that evening. He took somebody out with an elbow and people started staying away from him. After a while it got a little ridiculous and Chardy said, "Hey, listen, you're playing way out of control, man. Just calm it down. You haven't—" and the postman hit him in the mouth.

"Watch yo' face, motherfuckin' white trashman. Watch yo' fuckin' mouth."

Chardy picked himself up from the asphalt. A black circle formed around him.

"All right," he said. "No problem. Didn't mean anything."

Then he dropped the postman with a shot to the cheekbone.

He was never sure who called the ambulance. It seemed to get there awfully fast. There was a great deal of confusion and he was explaining everything to a young cop.

"You better stay off this playground," the cop said. "You want to play basketball, you go to the suburbs. Go out to the University of Maryland. Go to the Y. But don't come here, and then when they shove you around, don't punch anybody. We find bodies out here all the time, mister. I don't want to have to find yours."

"You better let us check it out," the medic said. "Your pupils look a little dilated. You might have a concussion and they can be tricky. You might need some stitches to close that cut. You got Blue Cross?"

"Sure."

"Then let us check you out, man. Just to be safe."

"My car's here. I'm not going to any hospital."

"In the wagon, man. Let me look at that eye in the wagon."

"All right. Christ."

He climbed into the back of the ambulance and the medic opened his black bag and took out a .357 magnum and said, "Now just relax, Mr. Chardy."

They took him to a small Catholic hospital in Southeast Washington, Saint Teresa's, and led him in, handcuffed, through a loading dock, up an old freight elevator, and down a quiet hall to what at one time must have been an operating theater but was now just a high-ceilinged room with tables and a few blackboards about, where a single man waited.

"Unlock him. Sorry. You like to do these things neatly. You're being watched, of course."

"Who the hell are you? What's going on?" Chardy asked angrily.

"Just sit down and relax. They say you've got a temper, but try to control it. Just for once, okay? Here, this'll help." He opened his wallet and showed off the card, which sported a photo of a square, blocky face next to an announcement of the presence, in official capacity, of Leo Bennis, Special Agent of the Federal Bureau of Investigation. Chardy looked from the plastic-covered image to the real Leo Bennis, softer in life and a little older, and smiling mildly.

"Howdy," Bennis said. "You're a hard man to track down."

"Feds. What the hell do you want?"

"Let's say we've become fascinated recently with a certain situation."

"Make an appointment with Mr. Lanahan. He's the boss now. He's a very busy man. He can probably see you sometime next spring."

"Paul, you're so hostile. You're seething with hostilities and resentments. Just calm down. Be nice."

"This is your party. You set it up; you brought it off. Get to the point."

"We always get this when we deal with the Agency. You people are such prima donnas. You think you're such gods."

"I think I'd like to go. Is this official? Are you making an arrest? No? Then I think I'd like to go."

"Paul, I saw a movie last night. Let me tell you about it. It was a western."

"Bennis, just what the fu —"

"It was about an old gunfighter, a cowboy. Off teaching school. Suddenly his old outfit asks him to buckle his guns on again. Sure, he says, why not? Anything for the old outfit. But my, my, some strange things begin happening. To name just one, he goes out to see the widow of an old chum. All of a sudden, bingo, in the middle of the day, off he goes. And when two of his pals tag along, he ditches them very neatly. He knows what he's doing, this old cowboy. Of course he doesn't ditch *us*. Because *we* know what we're doing too."

"Where were you?"

"Overhead. Chopper. We had six cars. Nobody was with you for more than a mile, and the chopper coordinated it all. I was in the chopper, Paul. We've got quite a unit going on this thing." He smiled.

Chardy looked at him. "Okay, so it's a big deal to you. So what?"

"Back to the movie, Paul. Why'd the cowboy go to the widow? Did the cowboy smoke out some kind of link that might put the pieces together for everybody?"

"Maybe he's just a sentimentalist."

"Won't wash. Then why bother to drop the Agency tail? Why doesn't he want the Agency to know he's a sentimentalist? In fact, there's all kinds of things he hasn't told the Agency. He hasn't told them about his nephew in Mexico. He sends the nephew money, his own money, from his own pocket. Everybody else thinks the nephew is dead. Now isn't that curious? What do you suppose is going on in the western, Paul?"

"I never go to movies."

"I don't either. Hate 'em, in fact. But I'm kind of worried about this old coot. He's playing an awfully funny game. And we're only beginning to catch on to how funny this game is. What's the Agency trying to pull, Paul? How come they sent losers like Trewitt and Speight down to Nogales under Alcohol, Tobacco, and Firearms cover? How far out is Ver Steeg? How far in is little Lanahan? How come the Agency requested us to program our computer to kick out any dope on seven-six-five Czech auto pistol ammo? And, on the other hand, never requested assistance in looking for Ulu Beg? Our people are good, Paul. They could have helped. Except they would have had to ask a lot of questions, Paul. And maybe somebody doesn't want a lot of questions asked."

"They must hire you guys for your imagination. You ought to write books. Are you done? Can I go?"

"Oh, I wish you'd be my friend, Paul. I really do."

"It's getting late."

"Just remember what happens to the solo artists, Paul. Give it some thought. This business eats up the solo artists. Frenchy tried to go solo, and he got waxed, didn't he? And Old Bill, in the sewer. Teamwork, backup units, technical support, infrared surveillance, computerized files—that's the ticket now."

"Go back to the movies, Leo. There's nothing anywhere that says I have to help feds poking around."

Bennis smiled. He had a bland government-issue face, an office face, baked in twenty years of fluorescent light. He was pudgy, in his forties, with sandy hair.

"Paul, I know you think I'm just a cop. Right? A cop here to horn in on a wobbly Agency operation, a redhunter, a security goon hungry for a bust. That's what you think."

"I don't know what your game is. I just don't want fifty guys crashing in on me. I have to work this thing out on my own. I really do. You want to recruit me? Sorry. I'm working strictly for myself."

"Let me ask you, Paul, you think that kid can hack it down there? That's bandit country. A cowboy like you, maybe. But that kid? That's some first string you're running. A beat-up old cowboy and a kid four years out of college, held together by a nun in Illinois, and up against you don't even know what, except that you know people keep getting dropped, and nobody can get a line on Ulu Beg. You're the one with the imagination if you think you're going to get anything out of it except what Speight got. Here, let me show you something. Take a look at this."

He handed Chardy a typescript with several lines underscored in red.

Chardy read it.

"Where the hell did this come from?"

"Came into Johanna's apartment long-distance, the

day after she died. We've managed to track down the guy that answered; he's a Boston cop who was there as part of the civil investigation. He didn't know anything about you or Ulu Beg or the Agency. He said he'd take the message in case he ran into you. But he never did. He must have forgotten. Cops—you can't trust 'em.''

It was a wiretap transcript of Sister Sharon trying to reach Chardy with a message from Trewitt.

"He sounds like he's onto something. And he's in trouble," Chardy said.

"We got it two days ago from one of your Technical Services people up in Boston who was closing down the tap on her phone. And our next step was to put an intercept on any Western Union messages that came through to you care of your old school. This just came through and it's why we decided to bring you in tonight."

Chardy read:

UNC WHERE YOU? HAVE JEWELS NEED HELP BAD BANDITOS ABOUT EL PLOMO MEX NEPHEW JIM

"El Plomo's a town in the Carrizai mountains, west of Nogales, just over the border. The message was sent Tuesday by a Mexican national. It looks like Nephew Jim's out on a very dangerous limb. Now we could go to the Agency about this, go to Miles Lanahan and—"

"No," Chardy said.

"No, of course not. So what we're going to do, Paul, is we're going to go down there, yes we are; we're putting together a little party tonight just for that. You see, Paul, we do like you. We want you to come along."

"Then let's go," said Chardy.

45

Dawn was coming.

Trewitt forced his tongue across his dry lips, scanning the rocky slope before him. He could see nothing except scrawny grass, the spill of boulders, the crumbling mountainside itself.

"Hey? You okay?" Ramirez called.

"Okay, I guess," Trewitt said.

But he was not. The wound no longer hurt and the bunched shirt pressed hastily into it had at last stanched the bleeding. But he felt like he was going to fall out of his head. He'd vomited twice during the night too, whether before or after he was hit he was not sure. But at least with the sun would come some heat and perhaps he could stop shivering.

"They coming pretty soon now, Jesus Mary. Hey, you got any bullets left?"

Trewitt thought he did. Somewhere. In a pocket. He thought he'd look for them in a little while. What was the rush?

"Kid, hey, kid. *Kid!* You all right?"

"Fine. I'm fine."

" 'Cause, goddamn, it look like I almost lose you there, and Ramirez don't want to be on this mountaintop alone." He laughed. He seemed to see something funny, insanely humorous, in all this.

Trewitt tried to concentrate on what was swimming out of the night before him: the slope and, three hundred feet down, a line of crippled oaks and pines.

And behind him? Nothing but blue space and miles of worthless beauty. They had run out of mountain. They were at its top, backed to the edge of a sheer drop-off. Hundreds of feet of raw space lay just beyond the crest.

Trewitt became aware of a warm, wet sensation near his loins. He thought he was bleeding again. No, it was his bladder, emptying itself unaccountably. He was surprised he had anything left to piss and disgusted and ashamed for having lost control until he realized the bullet had probably wrecked the plumbing, the valves and tubes down there—it had hit him in the back, just above the waist, and not come out.

"You gonna die, kid?"

Trewitt thought, probably.

He rubbed his hand across his face and felt his matted beard. He sure wished he had a drink of water. He could smell himself—and he'd always been so *clean*. He wished he could get warm. He wished he didn't feel so doped up. He mourned the child. Why did they have to hurt the child? It was terrible about the child. Trewitt began to cry. A tear wobbled down his nose; it was so close to his eye it seemed huge and luminous, a great light-filled blur refracting the world into dazzle. But it fell off. The scrawny grass, the rocky slope, the dusty mountains all returned, lightening in the rising sun, under a mile of gray-going-silver sky. The sun rose like an abundant orange flare to the east.

A shot rang out, kicking up a puff of dust nearby.

"Wasn't even close," said Ramirez. "Come on,

whores," he screamed in his richest Spanish, "you can do better than that."

Through his cracked lips, Trewitt again offered his one question:

"Who are they?"

"Who cares?" Ramirez answered. "Evil men. Bandits. Gunmen, gangsters. Mother of Jesus, I'd like to kill me one. Mother of Jesus, send Reynoldo a present so that he will not die with a curse for you on his lips." He threw the rifle suddenly to his shoulder, and fired.

"Missed. Virgin, you disappoint me. He drew back. Son of a whore." He recocked, the spent shell popping out and rolling down to Trewitt, who hid beneath him in a gathering of rocks.

"I think maybe they're going to rush us now. Why not? It's light; they won't shoot each other up. I'll introduce you to them in a few seconds, Mr. Norteamericano. I'll introduce you to Señor Machinegun and his friend Señor Other Machinegun, and his friend Señor Still Another Machinegun. And there's Señor Telescope Rifle. I want them to meet my good friend over here, Señor Gringo Crazy Fool Who Wanted Adventures—Hey, what is your name? You must have a name?"

"Trewitt. It's Trewitt," Trewitt said, anxious to get the information into Ramirez's brain for some reason.

"Mr. Crazy Gringo Trewitt Who Wants Adventures. Well, he sure got himself a hell of a one, didn't he? In Old Mexico. Hey, Mr. Crazy Gringo Trewitt, I think they going to come any second now, oh, yes, any Mother-of-Jesus moment, and then we'll see who the whores are, *Hey you whores, come on, get it over with, whores,* ha, they ain't gonna stick their heads up, no sir."

He carried on like that crazily for a while, imploring them to come at him, begging them, blaspheming their mothers and their fathers and their children and their pets. He finally seemed to run out of energy.

"Oh, Jesus," moaned Trewitt.

"He won't help you now, Mr. Crazy Gringo, no He won't I don't see no Jesus around. I don't see no Virgin, I don't see no priests, no sister, no nothing. No church up here, no Holy Mother. I'd like to get me that black whore's abortion with the telescope rifle. Oh, Holy Mother, give him to your sinning child, Reynoldo, just give him to me so I may shoot his balls off, please, I'll go to mass every day for the rest of— *Hey!*"

"Huh? Oh, I must have dozed off."

"A fine time for a nap, Chico. Hey, mister, I don't think you gonna get off this mountain. I don't think Reynoldo Ramirez gonna make it off either."

Another shot struck the ground.

"Close, he sure was close on that. Jesus, I never thought I'd end up on a mountain with no place to go. I figured I'd get it from some crazy woman. Women, they're all whores, crazy as monkeys. They cut your kidneys out to eat, you let 'em. I figured one'd get me good. Never figured on no mountain with no gringo, no sir. Madonna, *Give me more time,* damn you, She's such a holy bitch, that woman, She wants you to light Her candles, but then when you need a miracle She ain't around. GIVE ME MORE TIME, VIRGIN. Oh, yes, sí, here he comes, one of our friends, yes, I think I have him"—he lifted the rifle—"yes, yes, so nice"—and fired—*"missed,* you whore, you son of a black whore, he just ducked back. I just miss him by a hair—"

"Oh, Jesus, I think I'm dying," said Trewitt.

"I think you are too. I think I am too."

Trewitt tried to bring himself to a sitting position. He was tired of lying down on the rough stones. But he couldn't. His rifle skidded out of his grip. He coughed once and was amazed to notice a strand of pink saliva bridging the gap from his lips to the rifle, a scarlet gossamer, delicate and tense. Finally it snapped and disappeared.

"Oh, Mother. Mother. Mom. Jesus, I'm so scared."

He tried to grab on to something.

"Hold it down, okay? Your mama ain't around," said Ramirez.

"Help me. Help me, please."

"Sorry, Chico. I got worries of my own."

Shock, golden and beautiful, spread through Trewitt's body, calming him. It was a great smooth laziness flooding through him.

From the side came a sudden burst of automatic fire. It chewed across the rocks in which they hid, and Trewitt felt the spray of fragments as the bullets exploded against the stones and knew enough to shrink back. He heard the Mexican scream. Then Ramirez fired his rifle, threw the bolt furiously, fired again, screaming, "Black dark whores, flower of pus, human filth." He paused.

"I think I got him." He was breathing laboriously. "But he got me too. Oh, Virgin, forgive me. I want a priest. Virgin, forgive your sinning child."

Trewitt heard the rifle land on the ground and begin to slide down the rocks.

The man with the automatic weapon sent another burst through the stones, kicking up dust and splinters. Trewitt shrank back.

"Hey," shouted Ramirez, "come and kill us, *abortions.*"

"Mother. MOTHER!" shouted Trewitt, trying to jackknife up.

Another burst ripped across the crest.

"I'm dying, oh fuck, I think I'm dying."

"Here they come," said Ramirez. "Here come our

wonderful friends.'' He was holding one bleeding arm awkwardly. He bled also from the scalp. ''Oh, look at the whores. Whores. I spit on the whores. Soldiers. Look, Virgin, soldiers.''

They were quite brazen by this time. Six, it turned out. Six men, most with AK-47s and one with a Soviet Dragunov sniper's rifle, coming up the slope. They wore tiger suits, baggy camouflage denim, and red berets. Professionals. Real commandos. Trewitt lay and watched them come.

''Hey, we fought them abortions pretty good, Mr. Crazy Gringo. Hey, I give you one hell of an adventure, one crazy hell of an adventure. We made 'em bleed some, we did. The whores. We took some whores with us. They had to bring in a fucking army to come take us away.''

The men were half up the slope, their assault rifles at the high port. They were not merry with triumph at all, but moved with vivid economy of line and gesture, impassive and implacable, hard-core military, in a hurry to be done with it.

''Whores,'' Ramirez was saying. He was weeping too, and had fallen to his hands and knees but kept trying to stand. There was blood all over him. He kept trying to get a leg under himself but it would not work and he pitched forward. ''They had to get an Army to get us. You *whores!* You bags of pus and shit. Virgin, I ask your forgiveness, for I have sinned. I seek to make a contrition. Accept your child Ramirez. You *whores!* Come ahead, whores, and be done. Ramirez is not frightned. I am so frightened. Lord Jesus, I am frightened. YOU BAGS OF SHIT!''

But his imprecations could not speed them—they came at the same grim pace, picking their way through the rocks.

Trewitt sat upright in a sudden spasm. He had the feeling of being in several worlds at once. His wound had opened and he bled profusely. He sat in a puddle and felt dirty. He wanted his mother. He mourned Miguel. A big bird flew overhead, its dark shadow skipping across him. It roared, a big flapping bird, huge as anything he'd ever seen in his life.

"Mother, OH, MOTHER, PLEASE!" he shouted.

The black bird hovered above him; it was a helicopter and it caught the assault team in the open. It had come from nowhere—from below the peak, hurtling up the sheer wall behind Trewitt and Ramirez. A Huey, painted black, no insignia, its roar like a bottle fly's, slow-moving, insistent. Trewitt's vision blurred and he could not track the details in the sudden commotion of dust and gunfire, but he saw a long burst cutting across the slope after the scattering commandos. Tracer bullets pursued the running men and took them down. The chopper swung after two who escaped the kill zone, pausing atop each to blow him away. The last man—he had the Dragunov—threw his weapon far and raised his hands. Above him the bird circled, then hung. The commando stood in an oval of whirring dust thirty feet beneath the stationary machine. Suddenly the helicopter shot skyward. It rose free of gravity, as though escaping the soldier beneath. The man detonated in a startling clap and flash.

"Jesus, Mary, he had a bomb," Ramirez said.

The helicopter was above them now and then had settled a hundred feet away. Trewitt could not hear a thing but he twisted to watch as, out of it, sprang three men in blue uniforms and baseball caps with M-16s.

Trewitt raised his hand to greet his rescuers and recognized the first of them as Paul Chardy, who was pausing only to jam another banana clip into his weapon before racing to him.

Trewitt died somewhere in the air during the hop to the other side of the border. Chardy did not see the exact moment; perhaps there was no exact moment. Trewitt had never been fully conscious after the rescue. He lay blood-spattered and filthy on the floor—deck, in the patois—of the Huey. Chardy had been here before, a thousand times; in Vietnam in the '60s, in Peru, and always it was the same: the huge roar, the wash of bright light and turbulent air from the open port, the vibrations, the stench of fuel, the stink of powder from recently fired weapons—and the dead man on the deck.

They'd thrown a sheet across his face and tried to tuck his limbs neatly, but an arm fell free in the airborne pounding and twisted the hand into delicate frieze. Trew-itt: he sure didn't look like the dreamy young man Chardy had seen in Rosslyn, in a suit, in an office, in the middle of a civilized afternoon. He looked like any grunt, a soldier, dirty and tired and dead. It occurred to Chardy that he knew so little about him.

And there was nobody to ask, for Trewitt had no friends among them—besides Chardy the two FBI special agents sitting across from him in the gloomy space, with impassive faces, really just police beef. And then that other curious treasure, a Mexican, huge and wounded and sullen, eyes insane, who said *Jesus Mary, Jesus Mary* over and over. Who could he be?

Chardy looked at him. The man's arm was stiff in a U.S. government-issue gauze bandage and he leaned groggily against the quilting of the forward bulkhead.

Who are you? What's in that stupid head of yours? What secrets, you pig?

With a suddenness the pitch of the engine dropped and Chardy felt the craft descending. A cascade of white light rushed in upon them as the bird finally settled dustily into the reflection of the sun off the desert floor, and seconds later, with a jolt, they had landed and the engine died.

Blearily, they got out. Men rushed over, numerous FBI special agents and Border Patrol officers. Chardy stood alone in the great heat as the activity swirled around him, men who knew what to do. He fished about in his pockets, came up with his sunglasses, and hooked them on to drive off the glare of the penetrating radiance of this latitude. They were at a Border Patrol installation astride the Camino del Diablo, the devil's road, in southeastern Arizona, a freeway for illegal immigrants and dope traffickers, whose ease of transit this new installation had been built to impede. An American flag hung limp against a bright blue sky. Away from the Quonsets and cinderblock sprang brown sandy hills, a little spiny greenery, and rocks. Chardy had been here before too, a thousand times: a little jerry-built outpost where men occasionally died.

He looked back to Trewitt, now a form under a blanket on a stretcher beside the quiet helicopter.

"Coffee, Paul?" asked Leo Bennis. "Or iced tea? We've got some iced tea."

"No."

"Jesus, I don't know how he lasted so long with a bullet through him there."

"I guess he was a tough kid," Chardy said.

"He did okay. He did fine."

"Hey, mister?"

It was the Mexican.

"Hey, you cannot do this. Take me from my country. You must take me back."

Chardy didn't say anything to the man. Shouldn't somebody be looking after him?

"You'll be taken care of," said Leo. "Don't worry."

"It's going to cost plenty, I tell you that now. Plenty, huh?" He smiled. Then he said, "Hey, that boy, crazy boy, he don't know nothing. You got to wipe his nose for him. I thought all gringos was big men. Ain't you got no better guy than this?''

He smiled, showing his bright teeth.

Chardy smiled back, then hit him in the nose, feeling it smash as the man went heavily down into the dust. He would have killed him too, except that Bennis and ultimately several others held him back.

46

Lanahan's moment of terror was approaching fast now. He ran a raspy tongue across leather lips; he looked at his watch, the water glass before him, then at Sam Melman's water glass across the table. His mouth and throat begged his brain for water, but he had sworn to himself to yield nothing to the men in this room—all of them older by at least ten and more likely fifteen years, none particularly friendly, the Operations Directorate elect at the weekly division-head meeting at Langley—and so he would not take any more water than his mentor over there. But Melman had a notoriously high discomfort threshold and could do without water for hours. He had not touched his, not at all. The guy next to him must have blown a couple of networks to the Russians that very morning, because he'd already tossed away a glass and a half. And there had to be bad news due from Soviet Bloc too, because that man was really sucking the fluid down while looking about with a kind of abstracted horror seen only in meetings—a wash of pallor and a mad flittiness of the eyes, a radiant and all-encompassing fear.

But Sam, across the table, sat in calm splendor. He reached across the polished wood, showing a quarter-inch of cream-colored French cuff, and idly caressed the glass.

Lanahan watched his fine fingers on the cool vessel, then diverted his gaze to his own glass, just a few inches from his fingers. It stood under a rectangular fluorescent light whose glow made the glass seem impossibly vivid.

Water, water, everywhere and not a drop to drink. The line rattled around in his skull idiotically, something remembered from parochial school; it would not go away. He concentrated to drive it out.

At the other end of the table a studious fellow off the European desk was detailing at tedious length a recently completed transaction with a Soviet naval attaché in Nice. It was a pointless and self-serving narrative, full of allusions to people and events Lanahan had no knowledge of. Hearing classified stuff like this had long ago lost its titillating charm and the speaker's loquacity was agonizing; for Lanahan knew that after Europe stood down, it was Far East's turn; and then came Special Projects. And Melman, among so many other things, was Special Projects. He looked again at the agenda in pale, blurred mimeograph before him as if to make certain and saw, yes, yes, under the Special Projects rubric, it was still there:

Danzig Update (Lanahan sup'v.)

He reached and touched the glass. He touched it with one stumpy finger, felt its smoothness. He knew mystically, out of a private bargain with himself, that if he gave in to the temptation and drank the water, catastrophe would follow inevitably. It was foreordained; it was certain. Yet, suicidally, that only made the water more attractive. His throat ached for it. He looked at his watch. Thirty seconds had passed.

Lanahan was in a real jam. He could not find Chardy. Chardy had disappeared on him. He'd shaken his two babysitters and not been seen since early the previous afternoon. He had not been at his apartment. And Miles had been under special instructions to keep watch on Chardy. And he knew Melman would ask about Chardy. And that if he tried to lie, he'd blow it. And that if he told Melman that Chardy had something going with Trewitt in Mexico, he was in deep trouble. And he knew that if Chardy had gone to the Russians, he was in desperate trouble.

Miles's tiny hands formed fists. Why had those guys let Chardy get away! How could he be expected to run things with third-raters like those two! It wasn't fair. He shouldn't have been responsible for both Chardy *and* Danzig. It was too much, especially with Danzig acting up too.

Far East had the floor. A rear admiral—though he'd worked in the Agency for years now, he still wore his uniform, his vanity—he spoke in austere, oblique phrases, reading through half-lenses from a typewritten page before him on a topic so obscure Lanahan had no chance of comprehending. Yet almost as he began, he finished, and sat back blankly.

"Discussion?"

"Walt, on the Hong Kong apparatus? Are those the same people Jerry Kenny used back in 'fifty-nine?"

"Some. Old Li, of course—he's been around since the war. But the real energy is from the younger people, the post-Chiang generation."

Who the fuck is Jerry Kenny? Lanahan wondered.

"Okay. Just wanted clarification. I don't think Jerry was terribly fond of Li."

"Li has his uses."

"I suppose."

"More?"

Oh, Lord, Lanahan thought; and then he thought,

Chardy, you motherfucker—and was astonished at himself for uttering, even in his own mind, such a filthy word.

"Sam. Aren't you next?"

Melman was talking. He had them, Lanahan could tell. He had them, was lulling them, rolling them this way and that: the operation in synopsis, high points, low points, fates of some long-gone participants, status of the survivors, constant flattering references to his Number 1 right-hand man and field supervisor, Miles Lanahan, at which Miles could only nod and smile tightly.

He's setting me up, Miles thought. He knows I've screwed up—he must have his sources; he's just setting me up.

Miles patrolled tongue along lips again. Oh, Christ, it was hot. He hoped the perspiration hadn't beaded up on his forehead; he wished he could get to the john; he was dying for a sip of water.

Where was Chardy?

Why didn't I give him to Melman earlier. I had a scoop, good stuff. I had to play it too fine, push it too hard, shoot for an even bigger . . .

He could still hand over Chardy. It wasn't too late. He owed Chardy nothing. He remembered guys like Chardy from high school and college: jocks, heroes, they thought they owned the world; they thought they deserved more space. The priests loved Chardys; they'd barely nod to a bright but tiny boy like Miles. Chardy carried the glory of the faith; Miles only did his job.

Where was Chardy?

He'd had a team there all night. Nothing. He now had people at police stations, at hospitals. They could reach him still, in seconds, even though he had only seconds remaining until he was up, only seconds—

The hell with it, thought Lanahan.

He took a swallow of water, and another; it was gone. He'd finished it in one shot. He could feel horrified eyes on him; had he made some gross gulping noise? Had a tradition been shattered, his career ruined? It turned on such small things, after all: not on who your dad was or where you went to school, but how much water you drank and whether your socks were right and did you know when to laugh and what to laugh *at?*

He rubbed his nose, where a blemish throbbed.

"Miles?"

"Ah!"

Not listening.

"Your status?" Sam looked at him with great kindness and expectation.

"Well"—his voice a pitch too high; he brought it down—"well, Sam and gentlemen"—the wrong note, didn't mean to seem obsequious; the trick here was *presence*—"it's currently a holding situation. Dr. Danzig is to some degree cooperating with us by staying put, and we've got that house sealed up."

"Miles, what kind of liaison are you working with the FBI?"

"Extremely low-level. One of their supervisors offered me a blank check but I thanked him and backed off. I didn't see any point in involving them any more than necessary. They wanted to ship over bodies, but you never know who is reporting to whom."

"What about Secret Service?"

"I consulted with them on setting up my perimeters; they were quite helpful. But they didn't offer people and I didn't ask for people. We've got our own men in the house and grounds; in addition, we've got vehicular patrols orbiting the house, as well as an emergency CP in a house down the block. It's very tight. They almost arrested *me.*"

"They *did* arrest me," said a well-known acquaintance of Joseph Danzig's, to much laughter.

Miles began to hope that—

"And what's Danzig's status?"

"Ah. He's under great strain. It's a very difficult time for him, and for us. He's bearing up, although not without his little outbursts."

"How are your people doing?"

"I've no problems to report. They seem to be doing well. They're professionals; they know what's expected."

"Anything else, Miles?" asked Sam.

"That's it. Nothing more to say."

"Well, unless there's any discussion—"

"Isn't Chardy on this one?"

"Yes," said Miles.

"Now, Paul was a fieldman. Talk about pros. One of the real cowboys." The voice was warm with nostalgia, with dewy memories for what some of the men in this room must have thought of still as the Good Old Days.

And fuck him. Fuck him to hell. Out of nowhere, out of a sweet weakness for a dreadful past, had Chardy's ugly name come up and onto the table. Miles looked quickly to the far end of the room but could not identify the speaker. They all looked the same anyway: gray, pleasant, bland men in suits, vaguely aloof, prim smiles, calm eyes.

"Danzig likes him, I've heard," somebody else said curiously.

"He seems to have conceived an affection for Chardy. The strain, I suppose," said Miles. "I don't think it's—"

"Didn't Chardy do some time in a Soviet prison? Miles, do you think it wise, considering—"

But Melman cut in swiftly:

"David, we're all aware of Paul's flamboyant—and checkered—past. It was my decision to bring him into this, because he was linked to Ulu Beg. In all frankness, one of our first thoughts was that *he* would be the Kurd's target; we wanted to make him more visible, in that case. It didn't work out. Now he's important because—''

"I know he's important. Is he reliable?" The voice was ugly.

"It's a risk I think we should be willing to run. We are monitoring him carefully."

"I say any man who beat up Cy Brasher deserves a *medal,*" somebody new said, again to a great chorus of laughter.

"I'm not shedding any tears for Cy Brasher, Sam, but that's exactly the kind of wild-eyed, out-of-control behavior that this Agency can no longer afford. That's why I ask if he's reliable. And that's why—''

"So far, Paul has done his work diligently," said Sam.

"Except for Boston," said David, whoever David was. "If I read those reports right, if he'd stayed on station, the whole mess—''

"Or again, it might have been worse. And if he had panicked, and not thought to move that suicidal woman's body away from the scene, a minor catastrophe might have exploded into a major scandal. Paul cuts both ways. He can help you in a way nobody else can, and he can hurt you to just the same extent. So you've got to keep him on a very short chain. Miles wouldn't have the job he's got if I weren't satisfied he's a good man with a chain. Miles, what have you got him doing now? Is he still at the house?''

Sam certainly had mastered the techniques of blandness. This was the question that would destroy Miles right now, before all these division heads, and it had been asked in the softest, the most reasonable tone Miles had ever heard. Sam sounded again like a cardinal.

"Well, he's—" Miles began, wondering where he

would end, at the same time enchanted, fascinated, by the catastrophe of the moment. But exactly as his mind purged clean of words, some factotum—Miles hadn't ever seen him enter—leaned and placed before him a message, which Miles proceeded to read in a confident voice as though he'd known it all along, despite the fact that he was as amazed as any of them to discover that late last night Chardy had been playing basketball with some inner-city kids on a lit playground in Anacostia and some rough words had been exchanged and poor Paul had been beaten rather severely.

"He's in Saint Teresa's, in Southeast."

He smiled at Sam.

"Is there any more water?"

47

Now they had him in a far city and a secret place. He had been tended and cleaned and cared for. He had expected a trial to begin soon and knew that he was guilty. It didn't matter the crime, he'd committed so many. Jail held no terror—he'd been there and knew he'd flourish if his health held—but he missed his dry heat and his beer and his girls and his food. He missed the Madonna even, old ugly cow. At least he'd escaped the Huerras. It would be nice to head back to Mexico City when this was all over and cut the old man's throat. He'd flop like a fish when he bled. But Ramirez knew he'd never get close enough. Still, in this cool, dull American room it was a pleasant thought to fill his head until the trial. He wondered if they'd give him a lawyer; they'd already given him a doctor to fix his three gunshot wounds and his broken nose. He never knew it worked like this. He thought maybe they'd broken a law too, but he also realized that in this world, if you were strong and bold and well equipped, there were no laws.

But there was no trial. And the Americans were not interested in his crimes. They didn't care for the drug-smuggling, the illegal-running, the whoremongering. They cared for only one thing: pictures.

"Pictures? You bring me all this way to look at pictures? Pretty strange."

"We have." His interrogator spoke Spanish. Tape recorders whirred, the lights were bright, some kind of apparatus had been strapped around his chest and arm, and tense men huddled about his bed. Whatever he knew must be pretty important.

"Show me pictures, then. What the hell? I want you to be happy."

"Look carefully at this one, Señor Ramirez."

He squinted through his swollen eyes.

"Jesus Mary. He didn't have no beard," Ramirez said in his border English. "And he was dressed regular, like some kind of *norteamericano*. I thought he was. But that face."

"You brought him across the border?"

"Sí."

"And there was shooting."

"I shoot no one. That one done the shooting. I swear it. I shoot no one. I didn't even have no gun. He took my gun before. He's a very smart *hombre*, I'll tell you. He came to me in my place and say, 'Hey, mister, you take me to Los Estados, I pay you good.' And I tell him—"

"All right, Mr. Ramirez. We're very short on time. Here, look through these. I have here over two hundred photographs of men. I want you to look at them closely. You tell me if you've seen any recently."

The faces flicked past. A dreary group—out of focus, blurry. Men in uniforms of strange countries, men photographed at long distance, men in cars or the rain. Most had hard features, the sharpness, the seediness of Europeans; only a few were Latino.

A familiar set of features suddenly were before him. He studied hard.

"Leo," somebody said, "the needle just jumped through the roof."

"That one, Mr. Ramirez?" Now he knew why he was here.

"Never seen him."

"Leo, the needle's still climbing. It's going into *orbit.*"

"Mr. Ramirez, our machine tells us you're lying. You have seen this man before."

Ramirez settled his vision in the far distance. Wire mesh ran through the windows—so he was in a prison then, was he? They really had him.

"Mr. Ramirez, we're not here to prosecute you. You are not part of any legal proceedings. Nothing you say will be held against you. In point of fact, officially this is not happening. We need your cooperation."

Ramirez sat and stared placidly ahead.

"Mr. Ramirez. Look on it as a debt of honor. The United States, your friendly northern neighbor, sent a young man to save you from your enemies. Then a helicopter. Your life was saved twice. It seems to me you owe us. It's a debt of honor. I know how important your honor is."

"Is no debt," said the Mexican. "The debt was made no good when the man with the dark beard hit me in the nose. I want some money. Is no honor here. Your people, they have no honor."

"Now that's a mentality we can deal with," somebody said.

"Okay, Sal, cut the smart stuff," the one called Leo said. "All right, Mr. Ramirez, how much?"

"I want," said Ramirez, "two hundred dollars."

"Two hundred dollars?"

"Two hundred, U.S. In cash."

"I think we can afford that," said Leo.

"Now," said Ramirez.

Leo reached into his wallet, counted out some bills. "I have only twenty-three dollars on me now. And some change."

"How much change?"

Leo searched his pockets. "Sixty-three cents."

"I take it all. You get the rest later."

"Twenty-three dollars and sixty-three cents, here you are," Leo said. "Haggerty, make a note of that, okay?"

"Sure, Leo. We won't stiff you." There was some laughter.

Ramirez began to speak.

"He wore a cream suit. He try to kill me. He get me *here,*" and he pulled open his robe to show them the recent wound. "He and another little pig, a fat pig who didn't say much and needed a shave."

"Probably Sixto. They worked as a team in Nicaragua."

"What happened, Mr. Ramirez? This is a very dangerous individual."

"I shot him in the guts and his friend twice—in the head. With a little Colt I used to keep at the register."

Nobody said anything for a long moment.

"Jesus Christ," somebody finally said. "Did you hear that?"

"Is he lying?"

"Leo, we get no increase in respiration."

"He got 'em both? Jesus, Leo, can you believe that?"

"I know," said Leo. "They didn't even bother to hire anybody. They went after him themselves, with their best people, right from the start."

"That would make those guys Chardy wasted on the mountain part of that crack *Cinco de Julio* commando brigade that raised so much hell in Angola."

"They really went after him with the cream, Leo. They wanted him greased something bad."

"Christ," said Leo, "wait till Chardy hears his friend Mr. Ramirez took down a full colonel and a major in Cuban Military Intelligence."

48

The nun smiled and said that yes, Mr. Chardy could have visitors, at least until four, when the hospital would be cleared. There were visiting hours again at six, until eight.

"Thank you, Sister," Lanahan said—at his most charming. "And how are you?"

"I'm fine, young man," she said.

"I'm so glad to see you're still in the habit, Sister. You don't see it so much anymore. I don't care for these new uniforms. Some don't even wear uniforms, which is quite a bit too far out for my taste. The habit communicates such seriousness, such dignity."

"That's the way we feel, young man."

"Goodbye."

Miles, warmed by the conversation, rode the elevator up four stories and turned down one hall and then another, tracking room numbers. His soles clicked crisply on the linoleum. He walked through doors and along corridors, surprised that the place was so huge. Crucifixes adorned every wall, and pictures of Jesus and Mary. He smiled at the nuns. It had been—how long since he'd been in an exclusively Catholic institution? So long. Too long. He thought of asking where the chapel was, and stopping for a moment. The warmth and love of the place embraced him. And pleased him; Chardy, in a place like this? It would be good for him.

At last he found the wing.

NEUROLOGICAL, the sign said. It figured. Chardy, the nut-case, in the loony department. He stepped through double doors. No nuns or priests here, not even a doctor in this bleak green corridor. He paused, counting the room numbers.

CHARDY PAUL, read the typed card framed next to the doorjamb.

He paused again. The door was closed. What crawled on his spine? A feeling of things wrong, dead wrong, all about him. His profession, however, inclined him to paranoia, and one succeeded in it by virtue of controlling these devouring sensations. Yet still he felt sucked in. Gray light came through the window just down the way at the end of the hall, displaying a slice of the panorama of the city, though one without monuments.

Lanahan's attack at last quelled itself, and he felt okay again, ready to check in on Chardy, to see him with his own eyes, to *know* that everything was all right; and then to have it out with him, the whole thing, who was boss, the cavalier attitude, his whole rotten *bad* attitude that had poisoned things since the very beginning; and then finally to the business of Trewitt, which he meant to pop on him by surprise to break him down with; and then to call Sam, make a fresh start. And therefore spare himself any further rites of terror such as the one he'd undergone at the Ops meeting yesterday.

He knocked.

"Yeah?"

It *was* Chardy.

"Paul, it's Miles," he called, and sailed in. "Paul, I—"

When Miles came at last to reorient himself, he was astounded to discover that through some Alice in Wonderland trickery or illogic, *he* had become the patient. He had a terrible, a profound sense of a fundamental change in the fabric of his reality, as if in stepping through the door he'd exchanged one universe for another, fallen down the rabbit hole.

Several men stood around him, and were not friendly, among them Paul Chardy, dressed, sporting no trophies of a beating. If anything, Chardy had *done* some beating recently, for the knuckles of his right hand wore a blazing white gauze strip.

"Paul, what the—"

"Just relax, Miles."

"Paul, this—"

"Miles, be quiet." Chardy's teacher voice, Chardy's teacher look, authoritative, unarguable. What Chardy was this? A Chardy in command? What the hell gave Chardy the right?

But Miles shut up. He'd been deposited firmly into a straight-back chair, trussed not by bonds but by the weighty presence, the will, of others. Who were they? What kind of hospital was this, anyway?

"Miles," Chardy said, "we start with one question. One important question."

"He's not wired yet," somebody said.

"It doesn't matter," said Chardy.

"Hey, Paul, this—"

"Shh now, Miles. Shhh. Trust me."

Chardy solicitous? What kind of new Chardy was this?

For yes, this was a new Chardy. Had he found his religion, or lost it? He'd never seen a calmer Chardy, a less hostile Chardy. Where had Chardy's chip gone, the one that weighed a ton that he carried around on his shoulder? Where was that ex-jock's snarl, that willingness to punch out, fuck the consequences? It was as though he'd had a face-lift or a brain-lift or something.

"Look," Chardy began, almost pleasantly, "one little question. Help us, okay? We know you were monitoring me; we know you had guys on me; we know that guy in Boston who was recording Johanna was reporting to you. So you saw the wiretap transcripts. Right?"

Lanahan looked sullenly at Chardy.

"Sure you did, Miles. You wouldn't have missed a chance like that. Now here's the big question. A call came to me. From Illinois, from Resurrection. From a nun. You may remember helping her find me. Anyway, she read me a telegram. Okay?"

"Okay, Paul."

"Did you see it?"

A moment of triumph. Lanahan could not help the little smirk.

"Yes," he finally said.

"I knew you would. Didn't I say so, Leo? Miles is very, very smart. Here's the tough one. Let's take it another step, and we need the truth on this, Miles. I'll have them blast you full of sodium p if I have to."

Somebody looped a strap across Lanahan's chest and drew it tight. Another man leaned over him, pushed his sleeve up, and bound onto his arm an elastic band.

"Hey, you have to have my permission to polygraph me," he said.

"Now, now, Mr. Lanahan, let's just be patient. He's all set. Let me get a control reading here. Is your name Miles Lanahan?"

"Miles?"

Lanahan was silent.

"Come on, Miles, play the game. Answer the man."

Miles looked at the ceiling, at the men in the room, so many of them.

"Who are these guys, Paul? Just what the hell—"

"I'm Leo Bennis of the Federal Bureau of Investigation, Mr. Lanahan. These people are on my staff. They're all professionals, and they all have high-level security clearances. All right?"

But Lanahan shot a look of horror at Chardy.

"Feds! Jesus Christ, you went to the feds. Oh, Paul, I'm so disappointed in you. Oh, Jesus, Paul, Sam is going to *screw* you, he's going to—oh, Paul, that's just the worst—"

"They've been on this thing for a little while, Miles. And they listened. You guys wouldn't. Nobody else would. So I had to go play with them. It's their ball. Come on, Miles, let's get going. Give the man your name so we can get the game started."

"Paul, you—"

"Miles, this wouldn't be going on if we didn't think it absolutely fucking had to. *Had to*. Come on, Miles. Come on."

Miles looked around again. It was said that Chardy had been worked with blowtorches before he finally cracked. But that had been different, a kind of war. He'd had time to get ready; he'd been trained. Miles looked around the room, then back to Chardy, whose glare leaned in to him. He broke away from it, looked elsewhere. But there was no mercy for him anywhere in this room.

"My name is Miles Lanahan."

"Where do you reside?"

Miles gave the address.

"What's your mother's name?"

Miles answered.

"Okay," the technician said. "It would be better if he

wasn't so excited, but I guess that can't be helped. I've run them on jumpier guys. Go ahead, Chardy."

"Okay, Miles. What did you make of the telegram?"

Miles took a deep breath. Here was a test he was going to pass.

"You're running Trewitt. In Mexico. Trewitt's alive."

"See, Leo, I told you he had a nose for this stuff. He's sharp; he can do an awful lot with very little dope. Okay, Miles. Here's the last big one. Who did you tell?"

"Paul, these guys are just using you. They don't give a shit; they're just conning you. They love to scramble the Agency. Paul, you're going to get in so much trouble. Paul, this isn't—"

"Shoot him up, Leo. Miles, I have to know. It's very important."

"Don't stick me, goddammit. Keep that thing away."

He looked around the room, finding it surprisingly big. He saw that once upon a time it had been an operating room: high ceiling, bright yellow walls ribbed with pipes. Now it was—what? HQ for some weird fed operation, Judas Chardy up there rubbing asses with G-men.

Sam's words came to him, delivered only days ago, clear and penetrating: He will make you choose. He will tempt you, test you. He's clever, smart. You've never seen the man he really is.

"Miles, let's go. It's confession time. Who'd you tell?"

"Nobody."

"What kind of reading you get?"

"Respiration's flat. No jump. Unless he's stoned on downers or a real pro at riding these things, which he might be."

"I was never on one of these things in my life," Lanahan said irritably, offended at the notion.

"Why, Miles? Why didn't you tell Sam? It was a big scoop. It was your ticket to the top."

"Because I couldn't read it. I played it over two hundred ways and I still couldn't read it. I wanted to develop it, or hold it in reserve, and pull it out when it really counted, or when it took me someplace."

"You played it just right, Miles. We're very lucky nobody in that outfit is quite as bright as you."

"Good old Miles," Leo said.

Miles saw that the tension in the room was considerably released. Now what the hell?

"Trewitt got a guy out of Mexico—yeah, Trewitt, Dreamer Trewitt—that a lot of people want dead. But somehow Trewitt did it. It only cost his life. A Mexican smuggler and vice lord who brought Ulu Beg across the border back in March. He's in the room next door, under my name, right now."

"I don't—"

"This fat slob had one secret and one secret only. Not that Ulu Beg was in America—we knew that. But that the Cubans were running interference for him, backtracking to wipe out his tracks."

"Jesus, Paul, what would the Cubans—"

"Come on, Miles. The Cubans are acting for the Russians. This means Ulu Beg isn't here on his own, but as the final part of a Soviet Intelligence operation."

"They should know that at the Agency. We should tell them that at the Agency."

"No. Because if they know that at the Agency, the Russians will very quietly put a bullet in Ulu Beg's skull and back off. We've got to let them push it the last step, so that we can flip it over on them."

Miles said nothing.

"All right, Miles," said Chardy. "Now I'm going to

tell you how you're going to stop them. Stop Ulu Beg and a Russian named Speshnev, who's running their op, who thought it up. Miles, you're going to be a cowboy. A computer cowboy.''

49

Danzig sat in his office, amid the litter, the empty cups, the craziness. The room seemed full of black bats, broken glass, the stage props of melodramatic insanity; on the other hand, it also seemed just a dirty room, a room in which once a book had been written but which was now a mess. He sat inertly. He could hear, *hear* the slow drain of time slipping away: most peculiar. The world is made of atoms, as we know, and even smaller particles; what can this thing we call *time* be, except the passing of one particle, then another, as they transform themselves into another dimension?

Crackpot stuff, of course. Yet lately he'd been taking refuge in the crackpot, the harebrained, the addled, the twisted, the hopelessly banal *stupid* ideas of this world. The Bermuda Triangle, for one, held a great fascination for him, as did this notion of Chariots of the Gods. Can Aliens in pre-Biblical times really be responsible for this lurid thing we call civilization? Can an Alien influence, a Martian shadow, be divined in his current predicament, rich as it is in literary irony? Are moonmen behind it all?

Or again: Bigfoot? Fascinating creature, the missing link; they even had it on film. It looked strangely like a man in a monkey suit—but no matter! It was a system of belief, a way of organizing data coherently. Which Danzig at this point in time lacked, and he was not willing to sit in judgment on any other man's techniques for doing so. There were others too: saucers, phrenology, Rosicrucianism, Mormonism, Scientology, nudism. All systems of belief, perfectly logical, askew in only one tiny detail which, like one degree's misaim in a compass reading, took them further and further into the ether the farther out they got, yanking them off into the realms of the purely crazy. Yet comforting! Full of abiding love! Offering safety!

I have no safety, Danzig thought.

What I mean is . . . What do I mean?

He looked about. Files spilled into files everywhere.

He needed a way to organize it. No matter how insane, how Rosicrucian, how bizarre, he needed a single theory by which the thing could be looked at, tested, then, if false, disregarded.

He needed science.

What he had was madness.

The room terrified him. It was the entropy principle, once again: randomness, disorder, the release of pure energy to no meaningful purpose other than disaster.

There lay the file on BANGLADESH, in one terrible isolated corner, starvation and treachery reeking from the jumble of typed pages (he remembered the photos of the Paki intellectuals bayoneted to death by teenagers for the benefit of the Western cameramen). And over there, huge one, most of it blurred papers, that thin stuff from State with a mad mix of CIA documents thrown in for good measure, CHINA, carbons, wads of it (he remembered Chou in the great hall: curious, a pinnacle moment in Western and Eastern civilization, the two cultures meeting as equals for the first time in two million years of humanhood, and all he could remember about it now, having talked and written about it extensively for almost a decade, were the terrible Chinese toilets, pissholes, sinks, shitdrains of primordial infection); and over there, tidier, a much smaller pile, indicative of how history had really passed her brave, pretty buildings and picturesque mountains by, W. EUROPE; then AFRICA, undeveloped, a few niggardly papers; and a huge and messy pile for SE ASIA, where history had paused for seven long and bitter years; and finally—he hadn't the nerve to face it—MIDEAST, all the little countries, the passionate, violent, rich, desperate little lands, a horror of exile and betrayal and steel will, profligacy. Who could make sense of it? No man. Not even a man of outstanding intellect and ambition, a Danzig.

He spun (barefoot in tattered terry-cloth robe, his flat veined feet and yellowed toes before him) to face it: MIDEAST. It covered half a room. He'd begun, one time or other in his hibernation here, to divide the huge archive into smaller piles, IRAN and IRAQ and SAUDI ARABIA and the terrible, terrible little PALESTINE and a huge ISRAEL. It looked like a fleet, a formation, stacks and stacks of paper: working papers, reports, indexes, trade tables, economic profiles, intelligence reports, satellite photos, computer printouts, abstracts, memo drafts, think-tank bulletins—the gunk, the stuff, the actual plasm of history. And all this was A-level documents, the cream of the cream. In the basement there lurked still another ton and a half of ungraded documents; and in a warehouse in Kensington still more, press clippings, embassy invitations, routing slips. No man could master it all, the complexities, the strange subtleties. And in it somewhere, in one file or in a hundred, lay the ANSWER: who was trying to kill him. And why. No wonder he was going insane. Who wouldn't? It's a miracle I haven't gone crazy before. No wonder I seek solace in crazy ideas, fascinated at the bizarre halls through which human minds can drag the hulking bodies that surround them.

He stared at the piles, aware finally of his own sour odor. He felt like a character in a Borges story lost in a paper labyrinth, time having been decreed to stand still. Truly: he was in a situation that could only have been designed by a blind Argentinian librarian-genius. Yet there was no other place to be. He could not leave. They would kill him if he left the labyrinth.

He pinched the bridge of his nose. Now, suddenly, the bridge of his nose hurt. It had supported glasses for all his adult life; yet now, in an hour of maximum stress, it too revolted. His body ached; he was disgustingly flatulent; his head ached, always, always, *always*. All systems were breaking down; he could not concentrate for more than a few minutes (he kept whirligigging off on wild tangents). Each time he set out to do something, he thought instantly of something else equally urgent, and veered to it immediately. Consequently, nothing even *neared* completion. He was becoming Howard Hughes, walled genius, brilliant lunatic, out of touch with any reality except the lurid one between his ears.

I am out of control. I am an exile in my own house, my own brain.

He stood suddenly, but in the effort lost contact with the reason for standing. By the time he was fully up he could claim no reason for the move. He sat down again, just as suddenly, and began to weep.

How long did he weep? It must have been hours. His self-pity took on Homeric weight and gravity. He wept forever. Night was falling. He was growing weary. Twice men had crept down the hall to listen. He was trying to control himself, but he could hear them listening.

Oh, help me, please. Somebody. Please.

Who would help him? His wife? She was worthless.

They had not fucked in years. When he spoke he saw her eyes wander to the ceiling; she had the attention span of a grasshopper. Sam Melman? Help me, Sam, please help me. But Sam was too greedy, too smooth, too ambitious.

Help me, oh, please help me.

Lanahan? The little priest, whose adolescent acne still erupted on his bitter young face, so bent, so determined to succeed. Yet Lanahan was more insane than he was, even.

Help me, help me, oh, help me.

Help me, Chardy, help me.

He wished Chardy were here. Yet he hated Chardy also. Not Chardy; Chardy was another disappointment. Chardy had disappointed him too. Chardy had looked at him dumbly. He'd sat there stolidly, eyes dull, radiating aimless violence. Chardy was another fool.

Danzig stared into dim space, working himself into rage over Chardy's stupidity. Chardy didn't know a thing. Chardy was entirely a figment of Danzig's imagination; he was an invention, a contrivance, an assemblage. He was a simple soldier, man of violence, narrow of mind and imagination. Danzig had foolishly built him into something he was not. It was where his illness had begun, this business of Chardy. It was the first sign of his weakness. Hadn't Chardy almost gotten him killed in his carelessness with the Harvard woman? Hadn't Chardy allowed the Kurd to get within killing distance? Chardy was no good. He was ordinary in the worst sense.

He hated Chardy. It occurred to him to call Sam Melman this second and demand that Chardy be fired, be let go. No, more: that he be punished, disgraced, imprisoned. Chardy was no good. You could not depend on Chardy. Once Chardy had come aboard, the whole thing had begun to fall apart.

His rage mounted. He saw Chardy arrested, interro-

gated, humiliated. He saw Chardy in prison among lunatics and blacks and hillbillies. Chardy violated, Chardy
abused. Chardy ruined. Danzig absorbed a great satisfac-
tion from the scenario. He drew warmth and pleasure
from it and at one point actually had the phone in his hand
(miracle that he could even find it in the rubble) and had
dialed the first two numbers.

But then he froze.

Perhaps they *wanted* him to hate Chardy. Perhaps they
had driven a wedge between him and Chardy, knowing
them to be natural allies, fearing the potency of any allegiance between them. Maybe, therefore, it would be better
to . . .

Once again, he sat back.

My mind is going nowhere. I'm agitated at nothing.
They are taking my mind away from me—this Kurd,
whomever he works for.

His bowels began to tense. The scalding need to defecate came over him. He thought he would mess himself,
foul his own nest, the ultimate degradation.

My own systems betray me also. They are in revolt.

He passed a terrible burst of gas. Its odor nauseated
him. He ran into the adjacent bathroom and sat on the
toilet. He sat there for a long time, even after he had
ceased to defecate, making certain the attack was over.

I can still do one thing, he thought.

I can still shit.

He reached for the toilet paper and unreeled a long
train of sheets, gathering them in his hand. Yet as he
pulled loose the last of them, separating it at its perfora-
tions with a smart tug, something fell away to the floor. In
the dark he could not see. He leaned over, his fingers on
the tile. He felt a piece of paper. He brought it quickly to
his eyes.

Metternich, it said.

Danzig cleaned himself, rose, and went swiftly back to his office and to the shelves.

He picked up *Metternich, Architect of Order,* by Joseph Danzig, Harvard University Press, 1964, and began to page through it.

A piece of paper fell out.

You must flee, it said.

They will kill you, it said.

It told him where to go, and when.

It was signed *Chardy.*

50

"All right, Miles. Now we're going to talk computers."

"So talk," said Miles. He would just sit back and be pleasant. He would not get anybody mad. It would all work out and then he'd go to Sam so fast—

"No, Miles. You're the one who has to talk."

Miles said, "I can't tell you anything about computers. All that stuff is highly classified."

Leo said, "I can still shoot him up."

"No," Chardy said, "we need him sober."

He turned back to Miles.

"Miles, we're very close to something very big. And it's come to pass that you've got the key."

Miles just looked at him blankly.

"The files. All on computer discs, right?" Chardy asked.

Miles answered with silence. But his eyes must have signaled yes, for the conversation continued. But he wasn't sure where this computer angle had come from all of a sudden. It seemed to come from nowhere. Or maybe it had been there all along, and he just didn't know.

"Harris got the contract, didn't they?" asked a new

voice. "The fifteen-hundred line of terminals in the pit. They bump 'em up to seventeen-fifties yet?"

An expert. They had an expert.

He said nothing.

"Mr. Lanahan, if you want I can show you photocopies of the contract. We're on pretty solid ground."

"Paul, why are you doing this to me?"

For the first time Chardy showed his temper.

"Look, nobody's done a thing to you. People are dead on account of this business, have died horribly, pointlessly. People were ruined, people were destroyed—"

"Paul—" Leo was trying to hold him back.

"That's the way it's played, that's how rough a game it can be. And you still don't have a clue. Nobody's ever even breathed hard on you. So don't tell me you're having troubles, Miles, because I just don't have time to listen."

He'll make you choose, Sam had said. Sam had known. Sam must have had his suspicions all along, had it doped out, tried to warn him, give him some strength. Sam had known it would fall this way: Sam and Paul locked in it for Miles's young soul.

"It doesn't really matter," said the expert. "If you can fly the fifteen-hundred you can fly the seventeen-fifty. It's keyboarded up the same, has the same command vocabulary. It's just bigger, more flexible, and has a much faster response time, which can be important if you're in a rush."

"I'm not sure the seventeen-fifties have gone on-line," Miles finally said. "They were slated to go in earlier this year, but that stuff is always behind. I've never worked at a seventeen-fifty. In my time in the pit, we were fifteen-hundred all the way. If you know so much, then how come—"

"Okay, Miles, fair question. Here's the answer. We

think there's a piece of information buried in the Langley computer memory. And we—"

But Lanahan, computer genius himself, instantly saw the flaw in the supposition and could not hold himself back.

"That's crazy," he said in utter indignation. "That's the largest, the most carefully tended, the *best* system in the world. It's limited access all the way; it goes off of generators on-site. There're no lines into it, no lines out of it. You couldn't possibly tap into it, or tuck something into it."

"The guy who buried this item buried it a long time ago, back in the first days, when the system was being set up. He worked there for a little while. And he buried it very carefully."

"Tell him," Lanahan petitioned the expert, "tell him that the capacity of the Langley computer is two billion bits. You can't imagine a number that big. That's all the libraries in the world; that's a trillion words. And it's all broken down into individual units or entries called slugs and the slugs are in directories. And there are directories inside of directories. You fetch a directory by its code. It's got ten thousand coded entries. One, just one of those, gets you another directory. Same thing again. You've got codes inside of codes, combinations. It's the biggest combination safe in the universe. First"—he looked around desperately—"first you've got to have access to a terminal in the pit. I mean, physically you have to get into the goddamned building, past all the checkpoints, ride the elevator down, and get a terminal, and the terminals are always busy, every morning, every night, every afternoon, every second of the day."

He took a deep breath and saw that he was not impressing them.

"Then," he went on, *"then* you've got to have the

right code, or code sequence. I mean there's no dial-information to help you. You've got to know it, know it cold. And it can be anything—the different directorates have their different styles. It can be letters; it can be numbers; it can be a sequence of both, a combination; it can be—''

He paused again. Damn them, when would they be impressed?

''The whole thing is built so that only a guy who knows exactly where he's going has a chance. It's built to keep people from stumbling into things. You have to know. You've got to go from directory to directory, from slug to slug. It's not the sort of system you can browse through. It's a labyrinth. Paul, forget it. I worked in that room for two years. I was a champion down there. It can't be done. We used to try and figure out just as a joke how you could crack the system, but it can't be done. Paul, I know. That was my war. I never lost.''

He looked beseechingly over at the expert.

''Tell him,'' Miles said.

''We need that information,'' was all the man said.

A moment of silence came to the room. Somebody snorted; somebody coughed. Miles had a feeling of loss, of hopelessness. He was so alone. He felt like a martyr, trussed for a chestful of pagan arrows.

He now saw what they expected.

''Forget it,'' he said. ''Paul, just get it out of your head. Do you think I'm *crazy?*''

He stopped, breathing hard.

But Chardy was just looking calmly at him.

''It's academic, Paul. Even if I got in, even if I got 'em to plug in the right disc, even if I got a terminal—even if I got all that, I still wouldn't have a thing without that code. You can't even—''

''Miles—''

''You can't even begin to *think* about it without that

code. It would be like walking into the biggest library in the world and randomly pulling volumes off the miles of shelves—"

"Miles—"

"—in search of an index card somebody once taped to a page. It's—"

He ran out of words.

"Miles," said Chardy, "we've got the code."

Lanahan was suddenly cold. He shivered. When had he gotten so cold? He rubbed his dry lips. How could all this be happening so fast? Father, help me. Father, tell me what to do. Father—

"Give me a break," said Miles.

"I can't give you a break, Miles. You're *our* break."

Miles said nothing.

"The thing we're looking for was put in place by a guy named Frenchy Short, an old Special Operations Division cowboy who spent six months in Computer Services, right when Harris got the contract and the new system was installed. Frenchy left me a message right before he went off on a solo job to Vienna, where he got killed in a bad, bad way. It's the sort of thing an old agent would do, and Frenchy at one time was one of the best. Frenchy left me a message with his wife; she was supposed to tell me if he got killed. But things happened, and I didn't get to see her for six years. Finally, a month or two ago, I got that message. Fetch the shoe that fits, Frenchy told Marion to tell me, Miles. *Fetch,* these FBI geniuses say, is the key. It's a computer command; it's how you order the computer to bring something up out of its guts so you can look at it. The code is the shoe that fits, Miles. It's H-S-U. That's pronounced *shoe* in Chinese. So it's H-S-U or S-H-U or something like that. A smart operator, they say, with just that much, could probably dig it out."

Miles looked at him. He was so damned *cold*.

"What's down there? What are you fishing for? What's the shoe that fits?"

"The reason why poor Frenchy sold me—sold Saladin Two, sold the Kurds—to the Russians. To a KGB officer named Speshnev. The reason why he blew us. And the man for whom he did it."

"Paul, I—"

"Miles, haven't you caught on yet? To what this is all about? You're a smart guy. I'm surprised you're so slow."

"Paul—"

"Shhh, Miles. Let old Paul tell you why. Miles, the Russians are going to a great deal of trouble to eliminate Joe Danzig, because when he gets to a certain section of his second volume of memoirs he'll be the first man in history to look carefully at the operation we called Saladin Two, the operation in which we channeled arms and ammo to Kurdish insurgents in northern Iraq from nineteen seventy-three to nineteen seventy-five. You see, somebody in the Agency, one of Danzig's fans, has slipped him, among a lot of other stuff, the operation files. And when he looks at it carefully, analytically, as he's sure to, because a lot of his reputation depends on how he justifies it, he'll see that according to our own files, the Soviet helicopter ambush was sprung in the middle of the afternoon of the sixth day after I'd been captured. But the Russians didn't crack me until the *evening* of the sixth day."

"They had it set up," said Miles.

"That's right. They had it beat from the start. They knew it all—the codes, the frequencies, everything. They got it from Frenchy Short, in Vienna. But what they needed to hide the fact they'd gotten it from Frenchy was somebody to take the blame. That's why it was so important to Speshnev to crack me open. He already had the script. He had a voice expert do me reading the phony stuff to Ulu Beg—that's how well set up it was. Then that night, I read the same words into a dead mike.''

''Paul—'' Miles wanted to stop the terrible onrush of information.

But Chardy wouldn't let him off: ''Frenchy sold us out on orders, Miles. Somebody didn't like the way it was going in Kurdistan, and what it would do for the careers of the people involved, especially Bill Speight's. So he sent Frenchy to blow the operation and clear out fast. But Speshnev was too smart; he caught Frenchy and took him into a cellar and broke him down with the torch. And he found out who'd sent him, and why. And then he owned that man, Miles. He owned him.''

''Paul—''

''Miles, don't you see it? Don't you see what this is all about?''

''Yes, I do,'' said Miles. ''The Russians have a man inside.''

51

Ulu Beg sat by the pond watching the swans. They were curious creatures, elegant, savage, evidently brainless. He watched the necks, so sleek and graceful, and the quick thrust of the head, a snapping, biting strike, when a bigger one would drive a smaller one squawking from his mate.

There was an old Kurdish proverb: The male is born for slaughter. Its grimness seemed confirmed in the ugly drama on the placid pool.

He lay back, depressed. Beyond the marsh he could see a boat on the bay; behind him was the great house. And he knew that nearby, like discreet shadows, the two security men sat. Their patience, their willingness to endure excessive idleness, seemed to him a particularly Russian trait. Russians could watch ice melt, flowers grow, clouds pass.

But he did not really care about Russians. Dreamless days evolved into dreamless nights to become dreamless days again. The weather held fair; the bay, the blue of the sky, the dun of the marsh, the birds—these were the constants of his life now. He had not thought of Chardy, of any of it, for a week now, ten days. A gull fluted in the air, spiraling down, then lunging up. The sky against which it performed had epic space to it, vast and oceanic, with a few clouds near the horizon to give it scale. He would sleep, he thought. He had not prayed in days. There seemed no point. He thought of Leah occasionally.

Yet at that lazy, drifting moment a man approached from the trees. He looked beyond Ulu Beg, up the lawn, and the Kurd turned to follow his gaze. He could see the figure—white, he wore some kind of white suit—of Speshnev coming down the lawn from the house, leading a retinue of aides.

"How are you?" asked the Russian.

"I am fine."

"All rested now? They tell me you pass peaceful days, nurturing your strength."

"Yes. I feel good."

"Strong? Strong as a horse?"

"Yes, strong."

"You were watching the swans?"

"It's a pleasant spot."

"Well, I've got news. Excellent news. Come on, let's walk."

They walked along the edge of the pond.

"First. From Mexico. I'm anticipating certain developments. A troublesome loose end has finally been dealt with. Your old friend, the fat Mexican. Remember him?"

"Yes."

"They have him cornered on the mountain. He cannot hurt us. When he dies, all record of your connection to us dies."

"Good."

"Necessary. Awkward and risky, but necessary. But there's more."

"Yes."

"Real news. We've been at rest for so long because our quarry was at rest. The man Danzig, under great strain

in Boston, had retired to his house. He was beyond our—
your—reach.''

''And this has changed?''

''Yes. Information has reached us that he's left his
house. Not officially either. He's escaped his own bodyguards, fearing them because of his mental imbalance.
He's out in the world, on his own.''

''And Chardy?''

''Chardy's in the hospital. Badly beaten during a
child's game. An excessively violent man, Chardy. Always in some kind of trouble or other. His own people
distrust and detest him.''

''But what good can this do us? The Americans can
organize a huge hunt for this man Danzig as soon as they
see he's gone. They'll catch him soon: a fat old man,
trying to evade his own police. He's no trained man. We
cannot hope to rival them in this search.''

''Ulu Beg,'' said Colonel Speshnev, ''we have an extreme advantage over the Americans in this matter. We
know where Danzig is going. We sent him his instructions.''

52

Thank God for baseball.

Danzig could hear the volume of the television set rising through the back stairwell. The agents talked animatedly among themselves. The system was breaking down: its vitality was spent; its energy had leaked away.

Suppose Ulu Beg had come here? What would these men have done? Where was their commander, the altar boy whom nobody liked, the dreadful little Lanahan. He certainly could not be here, for whatever his flaws, his individual failures of taste, he ran a taut ship; but now the agents clustered in the study, gathered around the game on television. Orioles against Yankees. Baltimore and hated New York. The provinces against the imperial city; of course. A natural, rich in drama.

Danzig paused in the littered kitchen. His housekeeper had left for the night. The agents had disturbed her by turning the kitchen into a sty. Empty Coke cans, sacks of cheese snacks, pretzels, crackers, everywhere. It was like a fraternity house.

Hoots rose from the study. Something important must have happened, but Danzig slipped into his backyard. Shouldn't there be a man back here? It terrified him that his escape from his supposedly impregnable house was progressing so smoothly. It occurred to him that the mandate of these men had been to keep others out, however, and not him in; thus their defense would be calibrated for the perimeter, not the interior. He walked into the cover of the grape arbor and disappeared in the complexities of his garden. Yet he knew the way. He found the gate and paused, waiting for a challenge. Down the way in the dark alley he could see the glow of an orange cigarette tip.

So there was a man.

Then he heard a voice.

"Tango Bum, this is Foxcroft. Tango Bum, do you copy?"

A pause.

"Hey, Charlie, Yanks score? I heard you guys shouting. Twice? Off Palmer? Christ, that showboat. Okay, thanks."

The cigarette arched out and bounced in the gravel of the alley. He could barely make out the shape of the man, visible against the lights out on the street, who walked to the cigarette butt and disgustedly ground it out.

Danzig stepped out and walked in the opposite direction, staying close to the wall. He passed swiftly to his neighbor's backyard, where huge bushes overhung a low fence, and against them he felt safe. He walked swiftly on. He had escaped.

One alley led to another until he reached Thirty-second Street, which he followed to Wisconsin Avenue, there disappearing in the crowd that had begun to gather in the warm spring night. He stopped at a drugstore to buy a pair of $5 sunglasses—they cost him $10, of course—with which he hoped in some way at least to stall the recognition process, if not actually halt it. They were vulgar things—gold, swoopy, a Phantom pilot's glasses that mocked the shape of angel wings or teardrops; the surface of the lenses was a mirror also, very much the style. If the clerk noticed him, he did not give it away; perhaps he was jaded by important government types slipping into the store at all hours to make degrading purchases—the Supreme Court justice who loads up on laxative, the famous hostess who buys a strawberry douche, the senator who purchases a salve for his hemorrhoids—or perhaps he simply did not recognize the former Secretary. It puzzled Danzig, who was used to being recognized, who expected it. Yet as he moved out of the store and into the crowd, sporting the ludicrous goggles, a feeling of curious invisibility began to seep through him. He had wondered, as he engineered his getaway, how he would handle what he expected to be the most difficult of all problems, the gawkers, the tourists, the autograph hunters, the flesh-pressers, all of whom, he supposed, would be drawn to his famous face, sunglasses or no. Yet he now slid through the crowd, down the jammed avenue, past the smart shops, virtually unnoticed.

It occurred to him that celebrity was largely trappings; that is, in a limousine, at a dinner party, at a meeting, a press conference, a seminar, people were prepped for him, expecting him, ready to genuflect to the heat of fame. Out here in the spontaneous world, it was every man for himself in a battle for sidewalk territory, for space near the windows full of fabulous swanky goods. His famous face on a magazine cover demanded respect; on a plump body clothed in nondescript polyester sport clothes, animated by a frantic awkwardness, among the many, it received only indifference. Though once or twice police cruisers prowled by, leaving him uneasy. Yet, he counseled himself, they had not in all likelihood discovered his absence; perhaps they would during a seventh-inning stretch. And again, what crime had he committed? None. What law had he broken? None. And therefore, what recourse had they?

The answer was the same: none. Yet he knew legal nice-ties would not stop them; in his (or their) best interest they would snatch him from any public thoroughfare.

As he moved through the streets, wary in the crowd, eyes down, moving tentatively on his stubby legs, pausing now and then for a furtive glance about, a sense of *déjà vu* flooded through him. He had lived this moment before. But when, where? A dream? It had the quality of dream to it: the details, the seething streets, the young flesh all about, carnival rhythms, glossy goods on display. He as-sociated it all with music, and could almost hear the tune. It played in his skull. South American? Asian? No, no, it had a Teutonic ring to it: it was the "Horst Wessel Song," sung by valiant hordes of young athletes strutting through the streets on a glorious and torchlit spring night in the year 1934 in the city of Danzig. He was eight, with his father. He was a Pole then, but also a Jew, in a Polish city that was also a German city. Very much the same feeling then as now. So much animal strength about. So much color and muscle. Perhaps it was these odd lamps strung through Washington which had about them the earthy quality of torchlight. He could see no banners and remem-bered from those days the gammadion cross festooning everything, hanging everywhere. It had no evil association then to his young eyes; he found it a curiosity. He asked his dark father, who watched the parade bleakly.

"It's a German thing," his father had said. "Pay it no heed." It was the first time his father had drawn a distinc-tion between himself and others. It filled the young boy with unease. The man the boy became remembered in crisp detail that moment: the sense of unease overcoming innocence. A signal moment in a young life, perhaps the first moment he realized his future would not be Euro-pean. And he remembered his father, who got them out in '37, giving up a career in the university.

Danzig stood in the street, and felt in a totalitarian shadow once again. He glanced at his watch—a Patek Philippe, beautifully elegant, gold—and saw that he had three hours before meeting Chardy. He looked about nervously for sanctuary and located it at once—a movie theater down M Street. He walked swiftly to it and was pleased to find it uncrowded. He paid his admission—at last he thought somebody recognized him, because the girl gave him the oddest look—and ducked inside. Only then did he realize where he'd come.

No man sat next to another in here, in the darkness no man would look at another. On the screen, in blinding lucidity, so big and tangled that he could make almost no sense of it, a giant mouth sucked a giant penis, riding the shaft up and down. He could not tell if the lips were male or female; he wondered if it mattered. Moans and cheesy music issued from the screen. Danzig sat down, terribly embarrassed.

Yet at once he began to feel safe; in here, certainly, nobody would pay any attention to *him*.

53

*M*iles, Chardy had said, *it has to be you. You have to go in and fish it out.*

Now he was by the first checkpoint, Badge Control, had traveled the length of the D Corridor and reached the elevator. He passed several sets of guards patrolling the halls even now, after hours; they'd smile politely and look straight to the ID he wore around his neck on a chain. He waited until the elevator arrived, stepped in it. He descended in silence, feeling the subtle suction of gravity. He could see the green light flicking through the floors. Finally he touched bottom and the doors opened to deposit him in another green hall where guards waited.

"Hi," he said, overplaying the breeziness, and they looked at him with barely concealed uninterest. "Lanahan, Operations. Headed to the pit."

Their eyes locked on the image of himself annealed into the plastic of his badge, then to the letters around the edge which designated his rights of passage, then up to the living face, then back to the picture.

"You've got to sign, Mr. Lanahan."

"Sign? You didn't used to—"

"They changed it last month, sir," the younger guard said evenly.

"They're always changing things, aren't they?" Miles said, scrawling his name on a card.

"Just a second," said the guard. He took the card, inserted it into a device that drew it up by roller and spat it back just a second later.

"The machine says you're all right. Here—" With some ceremony the guard reached into a drawer and removed a new necklace, whose centerpiece was a blank plastic card. He handed it over. "It's coated with alloy. If you wander into the wrong section, the sensors will pick you up and off go the alarms."

The prospect of alarms did not fill Miles with joy. He smiled weakly as he dipped to accept the new jewelry and turned to face a double set of doors, which opened with a lazy pneumatic gush to reveal another long corridor down which he now propelled himself. The walls were blank; he knew he walked the tunnel adjacent to the pit. Then at last he came to the entrance, which had not changed since his years there: desks at which sat the Computer Control officer and his staff flanking the door itself, a revolving affair, by which one was transported from this world to that.

This late no supergrade would be around; indeed, the man calling the shots was Miles's age, or younger, who'd drawn his turn at night duty. He looked vaguely familiar and when he saw Miles approaching, he stood with a smile.

"Mr. Lanahan!"

It occurred to Miles that he must be some kind of a hero to the people in the pit; first, because he'd done so well down there, with his Hun-like mind especially suited to working with green symbols in electraglow, in a great cool space in which no wind would ever stir; and secondly because he'd done the impossible: he'd got out, joined the mainstream. He was already case officer on a big operation too!

"Hi," he said.

"Bluestein. Michael Bluestein. I was just breaking in your last couple of months."

"Oh, yeah. Thought I recognized you."

Next to Miles, Bluestein was a giant, a blondish freckled giant. Miles had never seen a Jew who looked so Protestant—to the blue eyes, in fact, and the large bony hands and wrists. Bluestein grabbed Miles's hand, pumping it, at the same time swallowing it.

"I was here the night you blew the whistle on that Israeli tunnel. Do you remember?"

Lanahan remembered.

"You proved the Israelis had built a listening tunnel up close to the Soviet cipher room in the Berne embassy. You tracked down the actual building permits they'd used in their cover project, if I remember correctly."

"I *predicted,* based on the data, where the permits could be found," Lanahan, stickler for accuracy, corrected. But Bluestein was right. Because with Lanahan's break, American operatives in subsequent weeks had been able to tap into the Israeli land lines, helping themselves to anything the Israelis got. It was a great source for six months, free of charge. And when the Israelis, said to be so good in the trade, tried to sell them the same dope, they could never understand why the Americans said no. And all because Lanahan, sitting at a terminal ten thousand miles away, had happened to come across a low-graded report from an English free-lancer claiming he'd observed in a Berne cafe an Israeli national with whom he'd been at Oxford years ago when the chap had taken a first in mine engineering.

Lanahan nodded, remembering the evening of glory two years ago. He hadn't had much glory since.

"I was very lucky that night."

"I had a lucky night—a lucky Sunday actually—a few months back. I—"

"Of course you really make your own luck. The better you are, the luckier you get. Right?"

Bluestein smiled.

"Yes," he said. "Yes, it's really true."

This was going to be easy. Lanahan puffed with confidence.

"I'm on a funny one for some upstairs people. I wanted to run a 'seventy-four disc, see what I can shake out of it."

"We're slow tonight. I can get somebody to do it for you."

"No, don't bother. It won't take long. And maybe I just miss the keys a little too."

"No problem. I'll call the Disc Vault and set it up."

"Great," Miles said.

"Just let me see your Form Twelve," Bluestein said, smiling down at Lanahan.

My what? thought Lanahan, and began to panic.

"How long now?" asked Chardy.

"Only about twenty minutes," said Leo Bennis.

"It feels like hours."

"You were supposed to be Mr. Cool."

"That was years ago. Even then I was never any good at waiting. I always wanted to do something."

He put down the binoculars with which he had been studying the western facade of the Langley complex. The buildings looked like computer cards, six stories tall, the windows a latticework of irregularly lit slots. It looked like the cover of a '50s sci-fi novel, some dream city, some clean future glinting in the night. Government theater: floodlights poured glare up across the skin of the place, hyping up the drama with stark shadows. It was difficult to read the architecture from here, the relationship of the buildings, even with all the lights, but he could see all that he needed to see; for on the other side of the road from the parking lot where he waited was a broad walk that led into the base of the building, to two quite common-looking glass doors and a lighted corridor. It was the Computer Services entrance in the C Wing, and it was through this entrance that Miles Lanahan had so recently disappeared. All the rest—the hulking buildings, the elaborate landscaping, the canopied public entrance on the south side, the central courtyard—was pointless for now. Chardy stared at the glass doors through the trees.

"Well, it's going to be a long one," said Bennis. "He's got to dig through a lot of stuff."

"If he gets in."

"He'll get in. Miles will surprise you."

"This isn't the parish hall."

"He knows what it is, Paul."

They sat in the front seat of a van inside the Agency parking lot. It was a warm summer night and rain had come, spatting against the windshield.

"I wonder if it's raining in Baltimore," said Bennis. "I hope the Oriole game isn't washed out."

"Twenty-five minutes now," Chardy said.

"Paul, if you see him now, he's screwed up. He's been kicked out and the whole thing's messed up."

"Yeah, yeah," said Chardy. He did not like being here, so close, inside the fence. He'd never been a headquarters man to begin with, and now they were practically parked on the roof. Yet there had been no other choice. They had brought Miles to the very door—they had him covered the whole way, a team of three units, radio-linked to each other and the hospital, each carrying the Bureau's favorite new toy, the .380 Ingram MAC-11 machine pistol, complete with silencer.

Now it was the altar boy's show; now all he had to do was get in there and fish the name out. Then they'd bust the man, and roll it all up and it would all be over.

Chardy looked at his watch again.

Thirty minutes.

Come on, Miles. Come on, priest's boy. You're on the bull's-eye now.

A buzz. Chardy jumped, disoriented. Bennis picked the radiophone off the dashboard.

"Candelabra Control, this is Horsepipe One," he said. He listened.

"Yes," he said, "all right, I understand. Can you get units onto the street? And call metro. Sure, I agree."

"What's going on?" asked Chardy, hearing the urgency in Leo's voice.

"It's Danzig. They just intercepted an Emergency Code off Miles's security channel. He's bolted. Danzig's taken off. He's out on his own."

"Form Twelve?" said Lanahan. "Aw, Christ." He tried to look hurt.

"Miles, it's the rule. They had a security shake-up recently. All kinds of new games."

"You mean I have to go all the way back to Building A?"

How do I play this? he thought. What the hell is a Form 12?

"I'm sorry, Miles. I really am. It's the rule."

"Jesus, you got a Russian in here or something?"

Bluestein laughed. "You know how they like to brace us up every so often."

"Sure. Three years ago they tried a fingerprint ID device. It kept breaking down though. Okay, back to Building A.''

''I'm really sorry. You can see my position?''

Is he giving? Miles wondered.

''It's not your fault,'' Miles said, not moving an inch. ''I should have checked on the new regs. No problem. The hike'll keep me humble.''

''Christ,'' Bluestein said bitterly, ''it's not as if they do anything with the Twelves. They just sit in Dunne's office until he throws them out.''

''It's okay, Bluestein. Really it is.''

''It's such a stupid, stupid rule,'' Bluestein said. ''They think them up, up there, just to justify their supergrades.''

''It's a good rule. You can't be too careful. Ninety percent of this business is security.''

''How long you figure you'd be on?''

''It depends. Real short—or maybe an hour. I don't know.''

''Just hustle, okay? It'd be my ass if somebody makes a stink.''

''Don't you worry about it,'' said Miles. ''Nobody's going to make a stink,'' and he leaned back, waiting for the man to punch the entrance code.

''Miles. You're back.''

''I am. Relax, Jerry—not for good.''

''Ah.''

''No, I'll just be in your hair for a minute or so.''

''What is it?''

Lanahan was in an office off the dark pit called the Disc Vault and the man he addressed was the Disc Librarian. Over the shoulder of the DL he could see the racks of discs, their plastic purity blinding in the brightness of this clean and odorless room.

"I hear you're doing real well, Miles."

"Not so bad, Jerry."

"I never thought you'd do it. I still don't know how you did it. You just kept pushing and pushing."

"I'll teach you my secret some day. I'm looking for a 'seventy-four disc."

"Fighting somebody's old war?"

"Something like that."

"That's when we were just gearing up on the system. I think it went on-line in late 'seventy-three. That's so long ago *I* wasn't even here."

"Can you help me dig it out?"

Jerry was florid and bitter, a reddish man of fierce ambition who'd never gotten anywhere. He stank of disappointment. He was plateaued out down here, his career aground in Computer Services. He looked down on Miles with something less than enthusiasm.

"The little priest. You really brought it off. You really got lucky."

"I never missed mass when I was a kid. That's why I'm smiled on. Come on, Jer, help me, okay?"

"Christ, Miles." He fished through some bookshelves behind him and came at last to a metal notebook, the disc index. He opened it, flipping through the pages.

"There's a lot of stuff here."

Miles nodded.

"You'll have to be more specific. Miles, there's a hundred discs here from 'seventy-four. From Operations—I think they called it Plans back then—from Economic Research, from Cartography, from Satellites, from Security. I assume you want the Operations stuff."

"What was the first disc archive set up? The very first?"

"Operations—Plans. That was the heart of it. Then later, other divisions and directorates went on-line."

"Yes, Operations then."

"Ahhh—"

Goddammit. He'd told them it would never work. A dozen discs—that's still nearly the entire New York Library system.

"Well?"

"Am I breaking any laws if I ask you how it's indexed?"

Jerry looked at him.

"It sounds to me like you're just fishing, Miles."

"Come on, Jerry. Give me a break."

Jerry made another face. "Whenever an item is transmitted, it's automatically recorded in a master directory by slug line. When the master directory reaches a certain level, all the stuff is automatically transferred to tape. But when that happens, at the same time the Extel printer generates this"—the metal notebook—"printout. Then later we index by months of the year."

"So it's chronological?"

"Yeah, but the machine gives you other breakdowns too. The idea is to be able to get your hands on something fast."

"Sure, I realize that."

"It's got a listing by target, by geographical zone, by—"

"What about alphabetically?"

"You mean by the code group?"

"That's right."

"Yeah, it does that. Let me—" He flipped through the thick notebook.

"Yeah, here it is. It's—"

"Jerry, look for *shoe.*"

Jerry looked at him. "You've got something exceedingly strange going on, Miles. I never heard of—"

"Jerry, when a Deputy Director tells you to check

something out, you don't exactly tell him he's full of shit.''

"Well, I've been here a long—"

"It might not be shoe, S-H-O-E. It might be H-S-U, a Chinese word of the same pronunciation. Or it could be, well, I suppose it—"

Jerry pushed through the printouts. He halted.

Miles bent forward, over the desk. He could smell Jerry's cheap cologne and the plastic, oceans of plastic, in the calm air. Jerry's finger pointed to the middle of the page and had come to rest at a designation for the ninth disc. It said, CODE SERIES P-R-O to H-S-U.

"I don't like it. No, I don't. I don't like it at all," said Leo Bennis, driving tensely through the late night traffic as they turned off Key Bridge onto M Street in Georgetown.

Chardy agreed by inserting the magazine into the grip housing of the Ingram. He'd already checked that the bulky silencer was screwed on tight. He unfolded the metal stock, then folded it again, purely to familiarize himself. The entire weapon weighed less than six pounds, yet it could spit its load of thirty-two .380s in four seconds in almost absolute silence. The Bureau people loved it; Chardy hated it and would have given anything for an AK-47 or an M-16, a piece he could trust.

"There are really only two possibilities," Leo said tonelessly. "Either Danzig just flipped out and bolted on his own, in which case he's walking the streets like a madman and will be picked up by morning; or, more likely, the man inside got to him somehow and has lured him out. In which case we'll find out soon too—find the body."

"How does the safety work?"

"There's two. A lever in the trigger guard, just in front

of the trigger. And the bolt handle: by twisting it a quarter turn you put the piece on safe."

Chardy cocked the weapon.

"Be careful with that thing," Leo said.

"They kick much on you?" he asked.

"Not hardly. There's not enough powder in that pistol slug. Paul, I think you're going to have to re-join the operation. You tell 'em you're out of the hospital, you're okay. You go back to Danzig's and see what the hell is going on. You could put some questions to the Security people. Sam'll probably be there too. Shit, it just occurs to me they're going to raise hell looking for Lanahan. We can—"

"What's the trigger? About fifteen pounds?"

"No, it's much lighter. They vary: some of 'em go off if you look at them. That's why I said to go easy with it. But it should be about ten pounds unless some hotdog has messed with the spring. I wonder how long he's been gone? He could have been gone *hours* and they only noticed forty-five minutes ago. Paul, I'll head back—"

A Pontiac jumped into the lane ahead, then careened to a halt at the light and Leo had to pump his own brake hard.

"Jerk. Goddammit! Look at this terrible traffic. You can't drive in this city anymore."

"It's okay, Leo," Chardy said. He opened the door.

"Paul!"

"See you, Leo." He hung in the door as a car swooped by them.

"Paul, they need us back there, they—"

"They want *you* back, Leo," Chardy said. "You work for them. I don't." He smiled, and stepped into the dark, the machine pistol and a radio unit hidden in his gathered coat.

54

After a long drive they dropped Ulu Beg at a Metro station in a suburb of Washington. It had been a silent trip, through twilight across farm fields, then over a great American engineering marvel, a huge bridge, and then into the city, but now Speshnev turned to him from the front seat.

"You remember it all?"

"I do."

"It will be easy. The killing is the easiest of all. He'll be alone this time. You'll shoot for the head?"

"The face. From very close. I will see brains."

"May I tell you a joke?"

The Russian and his jokes! A strange fellow, stranger than any of them. Even the young man who'd done the driving turned to listen.

"The man he expects to meet," Speshnev said, "is Chardy. Delicious, isn't it? This war criminal flees his own protection to meet the one man in the world he trusts; instead he meets the one man in the world who has willed his death."

These ironies held little interest to Ulu Beg; he nodded curtly.

The driver climbed out and walked around the car and opened Ulu Beg's door.

"All right," said Speshnev.

Ulu Beg stepped into light rain. The street teemed with Americans. Globular lamps stood about, radiating brown light to illuminate the slant of the falling water. They were at a plaza, near a circle of buses. People streamed toward the station; he could see the trains on a bridge above the entrance. It was all very modern.

"You must not fail," said the colonel.

"As God wills it," said Ulu Beg.

The door closed and the car rushed off through the rain. He stood by the curb for a second, watching it melt into the traffic, then pushed his way through the crowd to the station. With the exact change he bought a fare card from a machine and went through turnstiles to be admitted to the trains. He carried his pack in his left hand; inside it was the Skorpion.

Danzig left the theater at 11:30. His brain reeled from the imagery: organs, gigantic and absurd, abstract openings. He thought of wet doorways, of plumbing, of open heart surgery. It had given him a tremendous headache. He'd had to sit through the feature three times. As a narrative the film had an inanity that was almost beyond description: things just occurred in an offhand, casual way, contrived feebly so that the actresses could drop to their knees and suck off the actors every four or five minutes. The acting was amateurish—organ size was evidently the only criterion for casting on this production—and film technique nonexistent. The music was banal; only the photography had been first-rate.

At last he breathed in the air, cool, made clean by the rain which had now stopped. He cut quickly across M Street and headed down a street that he knew would take him to the river's edge. Then, really, he had but to walk a mile along the river—away from the police, who surely sought him now, away from prying eyes. It could be dangerous, the bleak streets of the city down by the river. Still, what choice had he? He loved the sense of danger in one respect: he approached it rather than letting it approach him, like an animal in a slaughterhouse pen. He walked on, a pudgy figure, pushing into the night.

At last Lanahan was alone with the machine. In its unlit screen he could see the outline of his own figure, shadowy, imprecise, bent forward with monk's devotion. Around him he could hear the hum of the fans and the strokes of the other operators.

The Model 1750 Harris Video Display Terminal was twice the size of the earlier model he'd worked with in the pit. It looked to the uninformed eye like a cross between a television set and an electric typewriter, clunky and graceless. But it was his access to the brain, the memory, of Langley.

If he had the codes.

He flicked the machine—curious, in the jargon they'd never become known by their proper designation, VDT, or by anything reasonable. Rather, to them all, atavistically, they were simply Machines.

The machine warmed for twenty seconds; then a green streak—the first stirring of creation—flashed at lightspeed across the screen; then a blip, a bright square called a cursor, arrived in the lower left corner: it was the machine operator's hand, the expression of his will.

Miles stared at the rectangle of light gleaming at him in the half-dark. His fingers fell to a familiar pose and he felt the keys beneath them.

He typed:

Fe Hsu, meaning, fetch the directory coded HSU.

Immediately the machine answered.

Directory Inactive

All right then, you bastard.

He thought for a moment. He'd taken the easy shot, and lost. But let's not panic. Let's dope this thing out. We are looking for something hidden years ago. Hidden, but meant to be found if you knew you were looking for it. And meant to be found if you were Paul Chardy. This guy Frenchy Short was said to be smart. And he must have known the machines, the system, if he'd been able to tuck something away.

A play on *shoe*. The shoe fits. Chinese spelling. He'd tried it, it hadn't worked. But let's not forget shoes altogether; perhaps one still fits.

Fe Shu, Miles tried.

The machine paused. No answer.

Christ, suppose it was a secret directory, and when tapped it signaled a security monitor? Such directories were rumored to exist, yet no analyst had ever found one.

The screen was blank.

Then:

Improper Code Prefix

Damn, wrong number.

He had a headache now, and an eruption on his forehead throbbed. Miles rubbed at it with a small finger. Already his back ached; it had been a long time since he'd made his living in a machine cubicle. He'd been in daylight too long, ruining his machine vision.

Think, damn you, think.

FE SHU, he tried again, making certain to leave only one space between the command and the code, for in a moment of rush or confusion he thought he might have left two—or none—the first time through, and the machines—this is why he loved them so—were monstrously petty and literal and absolutely unbending and would forgive no breach of etiquette.

The directory began to scroll up across the screen.

Danzig could see it now—ahead, along the water, beyond the neo-baroque mass of the Watergate buildings. He was alone on an esplanade at the riverbank. Across the flat calm water lay Theodore Roosevelt Island; above its trees he could see Rosslyn skyscrapers. He looked ahead; could he see a flicker on a hill that would be Kennedy's grave site, a *memento mori* for the evening? Or was it his imagination? He hurried through the night, on a walk by the water, among trees.

The rain had stopped and back where the river was wider, near the arches of the Key Bridge, the lights from a boat winked. Danzig could not but wonder who was out there. He'd patrolled the Potomac occasionally with a neurotic chief executive—much liquor and endless, aimless, righteous monologues, lasting almost until dawn. But Danzig's thoughts turned quickly from history to—for the first time in many weeks—sex. He had an image of a beautiful blond woman, elegant, a Georgetowner of statuesque proportions and great enthusiasms—just the two of them alone aboard a mahogany yacht in the Potomac, setting the boat to rocking with their exertions. He paused; from behind a shredding of the clouds came the moon, its satiny light playing on the river. A scene of astonishing allure for Danzig: black bank, black sky, silver moon on the water—a Hollywood scene. He paused, then halted.

He had many years ago abandoned all belief in the unearthly. Man was too venal, too evil. Reality demanded fealty only to the here and now. Yet this sudden image of sheer, painful beauty, coming as it did immediately after visions of the sexual and the historical, placed before him at the ultimate moment of his life: surely now, this meant something.

But even as he paused to absorb it, it began to fall apart. The clouds reclaimed the moon; the glinting sea returned to a more authentic identity as a sluggish river; the yacht under the bridge resolved itself, as he studied it, into a houseboat.

Danzig checked his watch. He had plenty of time. Chardy was probably already there.

He rushed through the night. On the other side of Rock Creek Parkway he could see the white edifice looming up, something on the Egyptian scale, arc-lit for drama, like a monument. Its balcony hung almost to the river, over the road. He hurried along, amazed at how dark and silent it all was.

He passed under the balcony, and felt indoors. He continued to the midpoint of the building where a door had been cut in the blank brick of the foundation, recessed in a notch in the wall. Danzig crossed the parkway and climbed three steps to the door. He paused.

Suppose it was locked?

No, Chardy said it was open.

Danzig's hand checked the handle.

He pulled it open and stepped inside.

Their efficiency never astonished Ulu Beg. They could do so much; they *knew* so much. He took it by now as second nature, simply accepted it. It was as if he were operating in their country, not in America.

He had gotten off at the Foggy Bottom stop. But he had not left the platform, hurried up the steps to the way out with the other passengers. He paused, on a stone bench. He was in a huge, honeycombed vault that curved over his head. It blazed with the drama of lights and shadows. Shortly, another train came along. A few people got out; a few got on. That was the 11:45 from Rosslyn; it was the last train. Ulu Beg took a quick look through the vaulted space. People paraded out. Nobody paid him attention.

He walked quickly to the end of the chamber, to the sheer wall into which the tunnels were cut. He looked back and saw nothing. A few people lingered on the balcony above, but they were a hundred feet away and moving out toward the door.

In the train tunnel there was a walkway, gated off from the platform with a No Trespassing sign. Ulu Beg climbed quickly over it and began to walk the catwalk along the tracks into the tunnel. The darkness swallowed him. A few lights blinked ahead. He reached a metal door set in the wall. It said, 102 Elevator.

It was padlocked. He removed the key from his pocket and opened the lock. He stepped into the corridor, found the ladder, and began to climb down to the tunnel.

Keeping the Ingram securely wrapped in his jacket, Chardy walked for a block or two until he was sure he had lost Leo Bennis. Then, certain, he stepped again into the busy street to snag a cab. He stood in the brown light until one at last halted for him.

He climbed in.

"Where to?"

Chardy had a great advantage over Leo Bennis and the others of the Bureau in the matter of Danzig's destination.

He knew now the secret of it. Since the object of the Russian operation was to protect the identity of a highly placed CIA officer working for them, it followed that the Russians operating in Washington did so with the special benefit of this man's knowledge. In short, they would be aware of and could take advantage of CIA arrangements.

So Chardy did not have to penetrate the Russian mind, on which he was no expert, but only to consult his own memory. He knew, for example, of five crash safe-houses, in the jargon, where an agent in trouble might head for safety if a D.C.-based operation went badly wrong. He reasoned that if the Russians wanted to lure Danzig into circumstances where the killing could be accomplished with a minimum of interference, a maximum of control, then certainly they would select one of the five.

But which?

Two were houses—old estates out in NW, spots private enough, except that both were heavily wired with recording devices so that nothing could transpire without leaving its traces. Clearly no good here.

Of the remaining three sites, one again was a sure no-go: the basement of a strip bar in the smutty Fourteenth Street area—its purpose was to offer refuge to an agent should some sex-related burn blow up in his face and necessitate a place to hide from the cops fast. But Fourteenth Street would be jammed with johns and hustlers this time of night.

This left, really, only two choices.

The first was an apartment on Capitol Hill—but chancy, chancy: the Hill always had lots of people roaring around, and this was a Saturday night anyway, party night up there, with horny aides and pretty women and drunken congressmen all over the place.

It was a possibility. The apartment was on an out-of-the-way street and had a separate entrance—but . . .

"Where to, mister?" the cabby said again.

The last possibility was the fourth level, the lowest, of the parking lot under Kennedy Center. It was a deserted arena, unwired, with three or four no-visibility approaches, reserved for VIPs so they wouldn't have to mingle with the common people. He knew that even six years ago when they were building the Metro system there'd been a plan to run a tunnel from the Foggy Bottom Station a half-mile down New Hampshire Avenue through to the fourth level.

Chardy looked at his watch. It was nearly midnight.

"Kennedy Center," he said.

"You must be wrong, mister," said the cabby. "It's dark by now. The shows are all over. It's all closed down."

"I think I'll go anyway, if you don't mind," said Chardy. He could feel the cool grip of the machine pistol under the coat. His show was just about to begin.

It was a short directory. The codes fled by Miles's eyes in a green blur. Suddenly he hit an end.

No Mo, the machine said: no more.

He went uneasily up through what he'd already slid down through. It was all nonsense, random letter groupings.

ABR..............2395873
TYW..............3478230

Codes, all codes, letters and numbers, in all maybe fifty of them. He could call each one up and see what it said, but that would take hours.

One of them meant something.

Twice, security monitors had wandered by to peer at him.

Miles stared at the letters. It was gibberish. He was guessing.

He hunted for a *shoe* of some sort in the three letter groupings—a SHO or a SHU or even another HSU.

Yet there wasn't any.

He stared blankly at the letters.

Come on, think, he told himself. Frenchy wants it found, wants Paul to find it. He tried to guess how Frenchy might have gamed it out. Frenchy was off on a job that involved the betrayal of his oldest friend, his brother of a hundred narrow scrapes. Frenchy for some reason felt he *had* to do it; the offer was too good to say no to. Frenchy was getting old; he was worried about losing his job, about ending up on the outside at fifty with no marketable skills, no resumé, no anything. So, yes, he'd sell Chardy out. But the loathing, the guilt, must have chewed him up. So he decides to hedge his bet. Chardy at least deserves that. He passes to Chardy the clue that will bring him here, to this chair, to look at this directory. It's a funny thing to do, isn't it? Or is it? Chardy had said only, "It's a thing an old agent would do." What did he mean? Then Lanahan knew what he meant: if Frenchy got fouled up on this job, if the job came apart, and Frenchy with it, knowing that he'd left his message back home for Paul would be helpful. To Paul? Not really. To Frenchy. It would help him die.

Lanahan saw now how Frenchy had doped it out. It was a way to face the chopper with some measure of peace.

He wants you to find it! He wants you to find it!

His eyes scanned the letters.

BDY...............578309
BBB...............580093
REQ...............230958

Come on, Miles thought, come on! He felt his limbs boil with a tremendous restlessness. He wanted to walk, to run. If only he could get a drink of water.

Shoe? Would Frenchy stick with the shoe gimmick? It had gotten him this far, hadn't it? Or would Frenchy have switched to something else?

Think, think!

Frenchy wants it found. Frenchy Short, all those years ago, sick with grief at what he's about to do, probably not understanding it all himself, but imagining reaching out to Chardy with this last gift, this expiation.

Was Frenchy Catholic? He certainly had the Catholic sense of guilt, binding and cruel, and the huge need to confess.

Lanahan was Frenchy's confessor. He sat in a dark booth and listened to Frenchy through the screen.

Forgive me, Miles, for I have sinned.

Make a contrition, son. Confess your sins.

Yes, Father, I will say a hundred Hail Marys.

No. Tell us your secrets. Your deepest, your darkest secrets.

But Lanahan drew back. He was no priest. He was an ex-computer analyst who'd bluffed his way into the pit and was trying to dig out a traitor.

Maybe *I* ought to say a hundred Hail Marys, he thought, for he had no other plan.

He looked at the codes.

Frenchy wants Paul to see something. Frenchy has planned it so that Paul will look at this list of letters and see something. Yet what? There are no words, for if there

were words, *anybody* could see them and Frenchy's
worked it out so that only Paul can see them.

What is there about Paul that's unique? What would
give Chardy an advantage, looking through this list of
codes? What would Chardy see that no other man would?

He felt he was getting close. He sat back, tried to concentrate on Chardy, call up and examine his components.
Chardy, hero, special-operations cowboy, toting guns and
gear around the dusty corners of the world. Chardy,
athlete, banging through jump shots and driving lay-
ups. Chardy, fool, cuckolded and used cruelly by a
woman. Chardy, suicide, tendencies toward self-destruc-
tion. Chardy, Chicago boy, coming off the same streets
Miles came off of, attending the same parochial schools,
going to the same churches. Chardy, Irishman, moody and
sulky and brutal. Chard—

Then Miles had it.

Danzig stood at the bottom of the stairwell. He opened
the door and looked into the parking garage and felt a
sudden, suffocating loss of confidence. Enormous weight
seemed to crush down on him; he could not breathe and
just for a moment he thought he might be having a heart
attack.

Yet it passed. Still, he felt almost physically ill with
fear, in a blasphemed place. He could not go back; he was
terrified to go forward. He could feel the sweat damp and
heavy in his shirt and was aware with what great difficulty
the air came into his lungs. At last he stepped through the
final door.

It was so simple. Frenchy, you're smart. No matter
what you did, Frenchy, no matter what you became in
your weakness, let no man ever say you are not smart.

What would Chardy see that no other man would?

Chardy would see Hungarian. Chardy was half-Hungarian and had grown up with a mad Hungarian doctor for a father, a raving anticommunist with a failed practice and a one-bedroom apartment on the North Side of Chicago.

Lanahan swiftly ended the directory. He looked behind him, down the rows of cubicles in the dark space. At last he saw a free machine on a different system. He rose, walked through the darkness to it. He could hear the other operators clicking away, each sealed into his machine, each fighting his private little war.

Miles sat at the empty machine, which was linked into a different computer system, and quickly punched:

Fe Lan

There rose before him a language directory. He filed down through the listings until he reached HUNG.

Fe Hung, he ordered.

A concise word-list and phrase catalogue of Hungarian—placed in the machine's memory in case an analyst who didn't speak the language came across a word in it and needed translation fast—sailed up before Lanahan. He looked at it quickly, then clicked the machine off.

He walked back to his own terminal. Why did he feel he was being observed?

He was so close now; if he could just bluff it through another two or three minutes.

He sat back at his own terminal, called up the SHU directory and looked again at the code groupings.

Fe Egy, Miles ordered.

Egy: one.

Another directory rose.

Miles glanced through it until he found the proper code.

Fe Ketto, he ordered.

Fetch two.

Another directory.

Fe Harom

Another.

Fe Negy

Another.

FE OT

One, two, three, four, five. He was in the fifth directory now. Where would it end? He was within a directory within a directory within a directory within a directory within a directory. Was this a Möbius strip of a code, an Escher drawing of a code, that would go on forever, twisty and clever?

The screen went blank.

The machine stared at him, mutely stupid.

Long moments lagged. Had the whole thing collapsed? He knew he'd have no time to dig this deep into it again.

The screen's emptiness mocked him.

Then a message with a long tail dragged into view:

This material will appear only on your screen if searched for. It will be stored with service level designators priority code a (advance) category c (standing

item). It cannot be destroyed or altered. We will begin
transmission upon receipt of six-letter security code.

Enter six-letter security code here

In all his hours before the screen, Miles had never seen
a communication like this one. Service Level Designator?
Now what the hell did that mean? Priority Code, Category
Code?

But he knew he'd tapped the mother lode.

Enter six-letter security code here

He stared at it. Another hurdle, a last one. Oh, come on,
Frenchy, Jesus, Frenchy, you hid it so good. God,
Frenchy, you must have been a clever bastard. Miles
reached across the years to love Frenchy Short, who was
so smart. Burying it so deep, so well; and now there was
only this last obstacle.

Enter six-letter security code here

Oh, Frenchy. Miles stared at it. Six letters between himself and Frenchy.

He tried to concentrate.

Was it SHOES, or some variation on the HSU-SHU
axis? No, not enough letters, unless you rolled them up
into one.

He instructed the machine:

Fe Shuhsu

His fingers stroked the send command button, but he
did not depress it.

Do it, he told himself.

But he could not.

If he was wrong, he might lose the whole chain, he might be back up top, back up at HSU again. He might be forced to dig through all the levels. And also, suppose—it was a good supposition—suppose there was some sort of alarm mechanism built into the system? That is, if you tried to penetrate this final level and displayed a kind of tentativeness, an awkwardness, a hesitancy, suppose the machine was programmed to recognize these inadequacies for the profile of a thief, recognize your guilt? The machine was notoriously literal-minded: it had no imagination, no capacity for sympathy; its ethics were coldly binary. It would blow the whistle on you.

Sitting there, Miles knew the machine would betray him if he disappointed it.

This awareness almost paralyzed him. He suddenly hated the thing. He stared at it and was afraid.

Enter six-letter security code here?

"Mr. Lanahan?"

He looked up, startled.

It was Bluestein.

"How are you coming?"

"Ah, oh, all right. Surprising how long it takes you to get it back, though."

"I'm afraid we're going to pull that disc pretty soon. The other systems are beginning to top up and the stuff from upstairs is really pouring in. We need the system space. You know how it is."

"I see," said Miles.

"It's not that I want to play the hard guy; it's that—"

"Sure."

Miles thought: Come on, altar boy. Come on, little

priest. Come on you stinking pimply suck-ass: *Do something! Say something!*

"Just a minute more, okay, Mike? I just have to wrap this."

"Miles, people are waiting and—"

"I'll owe you one. I always pay off. I can help you. A lot. You know what I mean? I can help you upstairs. Cover for me."

"Miles, I just can't. I gave you a big break and—"

"Mike, just let me say one thing. I appreciate what you did for me. I really do. You're a decent guy. I won't give you any trouble."

"Thanks, Miles. I really appreciate your co-op—"

"And I'll go to your supervisor first thing Monday morning to tell him you violated security procedure, Mike."

Miles smiled at him evenly.

"Form Twelve, Mike. I'm in here without a Form Twelve, Mike. You could be in big—"

"Goddamn you. You little—"

"Just back off, Jewboy. Just back the fuck off, and you get your career back. Otherwise, you're on your way to Siberia."

He glared at him in smug triumph. Miles could really be quite evil—he had the capacity for it—and he watched the tall young man buckle under the pressure.

"Five more minutes, Miles. Goddamn you, they said you were a prick!"

He rushed off into the dark.

Miles turned back to the screen. He could not escape it.

Enter six-letter security code here

Frenchy, you son-of-a-bitch. You old bastard.
Old Frenchy. Smart old Frenchy.

Then it arrived, from nowhere.
He commanded:

Fe Cowboy

He could see a labyrinth of pillars and acres and acres
of the rawest space under a low ceiling. It was an abstrac-
tion too, an infinitely open-ended maze. Tunnels and
chambers and warrens spilled everywhere in gloomy subterranean abundance. Every fourth or fifth pillar had its
own lighted EXIT arrow, stenciled orange, three-quarters
of the way up. Did Borges invent this place? Did Kafka?
Did Beckett? No, of course not. It was any underground
parking garage anyplace in America any time in the '60s
or '70s or '80s.

No trace of human motion met his eyes as they probed
the aisles and ranks, though in any of a hundred or a
thousand dark places, in shadows, in vent openings, in
ducts, in stairwells—in any of them—a man could hide.

Danzig's fear blossomed anew, exotic, an ice-blue
orchid inside his chest. It seemed a phenomenon of his
gastrointestinal system, crippling and weakening his own
interior ducts and vents. He wanted to be sick and could
feel bile in his throat. His heart was running hard. He
fought for air and found it foul with ancient auto exhaust.
He steadied himself. He wished he did not have to be so
brave.

The first theory of modern statecraft—so basic, really,
it never saw print—was that you paid people to be brave
for you. A class of man existed for just such exigencies.
Yet here was Danzig, no longer bold by surrogate, required himself to step into the arena.

I am not brave; few enough are. Soldiers sense this
intuitively, as if they can sniff it. Civilian, they sneer in
contempt, meaning: coward. Meaning also, in his case:

Jew. Kike. They were the elect: courage was their election. They held themselves apart, arrogant, hard. He'd seen the look in their eyes, in Chardy's too; he'd been reading it in a certain Gentile set of eyes for half a century now.

Danzig stepped out, hearing the door hush closed on its pneumatic pump and click (lock?) behind him.

He stepped forward. His shoes echoed under the low ceiling.

"Chardy? I'm here, Mr. Chardy," he called.

Ulu Beg could see him. He had a shot of close to one hundred yards, through a dozen sets of pillars, long for the pistol round that the Skorpion threw.

"You must be close," they'd said.

He began to draw nearer. This was not difficult. The fat man was very frightened and kept yelling for Chardy and it was easy to stay in the shadows and yet feel the voice growing louder and louder. He began to count. He would count to one hundred.

55

A sheen of images rose to fill the screen.
Numbers.

Service Level Directory
3839857495............2094875903
2884110485............0594847324

And on and on and on.

He hit the scroll button and the numbers rolled up, a rising tide of integers that climbed to the top of the screen and then disappeared.

He kept the button down until the numbers didn't move.

MO, it said. More.

He commanded more:

Fe Mo

Yes, more, more. I want MO. Give me MO.

He descended through a sea of green numbers.

He felt he had to hold his breath. He dreamed he was swimming in math.

Am I going insane?

The marine imagery continued to dominate his imagination as the numbers gurgled past, and he had to FE MO into three more segments of the Service Directory.

And then it began to slow on him.

The numbers rolled sluggishly. The system was going to crash on him. The warning light would flash on, high on the wall: sorry, brain temporarily out of order. And it would all be over for Lanahan; he'd never find his way down here again.

Move, you bastards, move, come on, damn you. His finger on the scroll button was white-knuckled and taut with pain as he pressed. The numbers moved more slowly. They moved so slow he thought he'd die. He'd never make it.

No Mo

Touch down. Sea bottom. He was way, way down and he saw nothing.

Nothing, he'd gone too far. He'd missed a line, the last line from the bottom.

784092731............Shu

The shoe fits.

Miles stared elationlessly at it. A tremor raced through him.

FE he instructed, and sent the line and the screen blanked out.

He waited for what seemed the longest time. Had he lost it? Had he fucked up, blown it? Had the Security people been alerted? Yet all was silent. No, it wasn't. It seemed silent because he was breathing so hard, was so exhausted. Yet now, concentrating, he heard the tapping of other operators on their terminals, the whine of their fans. Nobody stirred.

Words rose from the bottom of the screen, a slugline and then the message.

PAUL YOU BASTARD, said Frenchy Short, horribly dead these seven years.

> *I'M GOING TO GIVE YOU TO THE RUSSIANS. BUT THEN YOU ALREADY KNOW THAT IF YOU'RE READING THIS BECAUSE IT'LL MEAN I'M DEAD AND YOU GOT BACK AND YOU'RE TRYING TO PUT THE PIECES TOGETHER.*
>
> *PAUL, Frenchy continued (and Miles could see him: hunched over a terminal, typing quickly, typing desperately, watching his own words traipse across the screen; he'd be terrified; he'd be almost shaking with fear, the discovery could happen so easily), HE'S OFFERED ME A DEAL. IT'S EVERYTHING. THE UPPER FLOORS. SECURITY.*
> *EASY STREET. PAUL I'M SO TIRED AND THEY'RE GOING TO GET RID OF ME. SO I'VE GOT THIS JOB AND I'M HOME FREE.*
> *PAUL HE EVEN SAYS IT'S FOR THE BEST. BEST FOR THE AGENCY BEST FOR HIM BEST FOR ME. HE DIDN'T SAY ANYTHING ABOUT YOU. HE SAYS THE COWBOY DAYS ARE ALL OVER.*

Miles read on, to the punchline, and found out who ordered Frenchy Short to blow Saladin II and why.

Miles stood, clearing the screen, sending Frenchy's message back to the serene depths where it would be safe forever. He knew he had to reach Chardy now—and fast.

———

Danzig thought he saw something move.

His heart jumped.

"Chardy! Chardy, I'm here!"

He ran through a set of pillars, through a shadow—to nothing.

"Chardy! Chardy! Where are you, Chardy?"

His echo boomed around the chamber and back at him. His breathing was rushed and hard. The pillars offered a hundred crazy perspectives, each yielding a wall, a far-off duct, a doorway, a ramp, a shadow. Yet no human form stirred. The smell of combustion was rich and rancid and the atmosphere seemed to burn his skin. He fought for more oxygen.

"Chardy! Chardy!"

Then Danzig saw a figure half-emerge—freeze—pull back into a shadow.

At that moment the scope of his betrayal became evident. A great hate filled him—the urge to kill. Kill with his hands. But kill whom? He didn't know. Then came the terror. It was total and almost annihilating. And next: a suffocating self-pity. He had so much to *do*, to *give*, to contribute. If only he could tell the man, make him see, reason with him.

But Ulu Beg stepped fully out of the darkness. He wore jeans and was fair and tall and seemed—strong. Danzig had no other word. The man stared at him. He had his pistol.

Danzig began to run. He ran crazily from pillar to pillar, back into the chamber, through terrific heat.

"Help me," he screamed.

He looked back once and could see no one, but he knew the man was there. Ahead the world tipped precariously, spun out of clarity as tears or sweat filled his eyes. He sobbed for breath and the air would not come. He ran for the door and knew he'd never make it. But he did.

He was there. The door was locked. Danzig slid weeping to the floor, clinging to the warm handle, pulling weakly, and the man came out of the shadows and stood not far off. He stood straight and pulled the bolt of his gun.

"No, please, no," Danzig cried.

Then the lights vanished. Danzig cowered in the darkness. A thousand red EXITS glowed.

"Ulu Beg," cried Paul Chardy.

Ulu Beg answered with a burst of gunfire.

Bluestein looked at him sullenly.

"All right," he said. "Now get out of here."

Miles didn't even see him.

He rushed down the corridor, and turned in his necklace to the guards. He had to wait a century for the elevator. Finally it arrived and he stepped in. The trip up was swift and silent.

He headed down the last hall, moving swiftly, keeping his eyes down, passing guards. But just before a turn, he heard footsteps. He recoiled in panic, backing, testing knobs. One gave—there was always some careless bastard, you could count on it—and Miles slid in. A dark room, some kind of office anteroom encased him.

Outside, the steps grew to a clatter. He recognized the voices—men from his own operation. Now what the hell were they doing here? What was going on? He knew he could not face them, and let them pass, hearing their excited jabber. When they'd gone he bolted, raced through Badge Control, signed out, and bounded into the parking lot. The air was cooler now. He shivered, looking for the van. It was supposed to be right here. What the—

The van was gone.

Oh, Christ, he thought.

But a car wheeled up to him and a door flew open and he recognized some of the Bureau people.

"Where's Chardy?"

"Get in, for Christ's sake," somebody commanded.

"Where's Chardy?"

"Get in, goddammit. Danzig's flown. There's a flap."

The news staggered him. He could see Danzig having finally broken; he knew he should be there. Danzig alone, confused, walking the streets. There'd be a huge mess-up at Operations.

He jumped in.

"I've got to reach Chardy. Is he on a radio net or something?"

"Everybody's on the net tonight," somebody up front said, and reached back to hand him a microphone. "You're Hosepipe Three. Chardy's Hosepipe One. Our headquarters is Candelabra."

Miles snorted. The Bureau's idiotic games. He pressed the mike button and, feeling silly, said, "Hosepipe One, this is Hosepipe Three. Do you read? Are you there? Paul, are you—"

The response was instantaneous and furious.

"Hosepipe Three, this is Candelabra, get the hell off the air, we need this channel!"

"Screw you, Candelabra. Hosepipe One, this is Hosepipe Three. Chardy. Chardy, it's Miles, goddammit!"

But there was no answer.

Ulu Beg waited for his eyes to adjust to a dark that was less than total. Signs glowed on pillars; one far door was ajar, throwing a long slash of light through the chamber. Shadows fell away from this streak of light across the cement and he knew that to step into it would be to die.

But he did not care. Only Danzig mattered.

"Ulu Beg, listen to me." The voice rang through the low space.

But Ulu Beg did not listen. Instead, lying flat on his stomach, the silenced Skorpion in the crook of his arm, he slithered ahead like a lizard.

Had Danzig moved? Ulu Beg guessed not. He wasn't a man for much motion, no matter what the circumstances. He looked for a sign of the man but could pick nothing out in the dark.

"Ulu Beg," Chardy shouted, "it's a Russian game. This fat man means nothing."

Ulu Beg slithered ahead.

"Ulu Beg. The Russian, Speshnev, killed your sons."

Ulu Beg crawled ahead. He would not listen. But a memory of his sons came over him again, now at this ultimate instant. His sons: their smell, which he had loved so, gone. Their delicate lashes, their perfect fingers, their soft breathing, their quickness and boundless energy—gone. The memory convulsed him. He heard Speshnev instructing him in Libya: "Danzig killed your sons, betrayed them, made them die." He'd had a photograph of the bodies. "Look. From an office in America ten thousand miles away he decreed death to the troublesome Kurds, death to your boys."

Let me be strong just another minute, he thought. Then kill me, Chardy. Kill me.

"Ulu Beg. Don't make me kill you," Chardy called.

"For God's sake"—Danzig, sobbing from nearby—"save me, Chardy, oh, God, save me, please."

With a scream that was a sob, Ulu Beg rose and fired a clip at the voice. The hot shells poured from the breech and the stench of powder rose and he could see sparks where the bullets struck. Ricochets whined about. Then the bolt locked back: he was out of ammunition.

He jammed in a new magazine.

He searched around in the darkness and could see nothing. He looked back and heard sobbing ahead. He swung the metal stock over the piece, locking it in place. He rose and walked to Danzig. He found the fat man next to the door, weeping softly.

"Naman," he said.

"Don't!"

It was Chardy, so close behind him he could almost feel the breath. "Don't. Please don't."

The van pulled up.

"Colonel, are you sure?"

"Oh, yes," said Speshnev. "It's quite necessary."

"We have technicians," said the younger man. "Men of great skill and experience."

"Stepanovich, you always think of me, don't you? I'm touched. But I've some experience myself. And I've been looking forward for some time to this."

"I wish you'd let me send some backup people along."

"Oh, no. Too cumbersome. Wouldn't think of it."

"You're sure, Colonel?"

"No, I'm quite fine," Speshnev said. He smiled. The damp warm air had somewhat disarranged his hair. He turned in the cab, opened the door, and stepped out.

"You've got the device?"

"Of course," Speshnev said. "Right in here." He tapped himself just under the arm, and the young man knew it to be a standard KGB silent killing device, a tiny CO_2 pistol that fired small pellets of a traceless microtoxin.

"And just in case?"

"Of course, Stepanovich. The Luger."

He smiled, and the younger man marveled at his calmness. His whole operation hung in the balance and the old man himself was going to push it the final step. The younger man, by temperament a sentimentalist, wanted to weep in admiration. But he controlled himself as he watched the colonel head for the building.

"Don't! Please don't," Chardy heard himself urge with insane civility. He had the Ingram trained on the Kurd from a range of about fifteen yards. It seemed, in the passion of the second, immensely heavy. It was hot to his touch. He could feel his fingers on it, sense its weight, its warmth, its cruel details.

"Don't," he cried again. He could feel his voice quaver, grow phlegmy. It was so dark; the seconds seemed to be rushing past.

The Kurd was absolutely still, frozen against a pillar, his own weapon before him.

"It's a trick," Chardy began to argue. If he could just explain it all. "It's a Russian trick. It goes way back, it—"

He wished he could breathe. He could feel the perspiration forming on his body. It was so hot down here; it smelled of cars, of gas.

"Speshnev," he thought to say. If he could get that part out, make him see that part of it. "It's Speshnev—"

"CHARDY KILL HIM!" Danzig screamed. "CHARDY STOP HIM!" The voice echoed in the chamber.

Ulu Beg's head moved just an inch in the darkness.

"CHARDY! OH CHARDY SAVE ME JESUS!"

"Speshnev killed—"

"CHARDY KILL HIM KILL HIM JESUS!"

"It's the Russian, it's Speshnev, it's—"

"CHARDY GODDAM—"

Ulu Beg brought the Skorpion to his shoulder and Chardy heard a weapon fire a long burst. The Kurd fell to the pavement, the machine pistol clattering away. Blood ran from his mouth and out his nose and his eyes were open.

Chardy looked down at the Ingram and pretended to be amazed that he'd fired. It had just happened, almost accidentally: a twitch, the slightest, faintest tremor of nerve running from a secret part of his brain down his spine and arm to the finger, and the weapon, its orchestration of springs and latches and chambers and pins set in motion, had fired eleven times in less than two seconds.

No.

You did it, Chardy thought.

You did it.

Chardy walked to the man. He searched for a pulse, found none. He reached and closed the two eyes and the mouth. He set the Ingram down and tried to roll the Kurd to his right side. But it would not work; the man kept slipping forward sloppily. Chardy was trying to get it right.

"My *God*," said Danzig, suddenly just behind him. "He could have *killed* me. You stood there for an hour. Chardy, you *bastard*. Do you think this is some kind of a *game?* My God, Chardy, you *bastard*."

Chardy at last stood, gripping the Ingram. He put it on safety. A terrible grief and rage filled his head. He swung and hit Danzig across the face, under the eye, with the heavy silencer, driving him down. The man lay on the floor among spent shells. It occurred to Chardy that he might have killed him and it occurred to him he didn't care.

He looked back at the Kurd, who lay untidily, half on his side, half flat, legs twisted, face blank.

He explained to the corpse:

See, they have this way of putting you in a jam where you have to do the only thing in the world you don't want to, but you *have* to. It always works out that way. That's how it worked with Frenchy and Johanna and with . . .

At last he backed away. He could smell the burnt powder from his last burst. It clung in his nose and seemed to work through his capillaries as it climbed into his head.

He tried to figure out what to do next and after some effort remembered he'd taken a radio unit. He fished into his jacket, pulled it out and snapped it on.

"Candelabra," he said without emotion, "this is Hosepipe One."

The unit crackled. It wasn't receiving down here. He looked at it with disgust and almost threw it against the wall.

Do your fucking job. I did mine.

But then it spoke in a burst of grating energy.

"—dy! Chardy! Chardy!"

Another voice cut in.

"Hosepipe Three, this is Candelabra. I said get the hell off the air."

Chardy spoke quickly.

"Hosepipe Three, this *is* One. It's Chardy. Do you read?"

"Paul? It's Miles."

"Hosepipe One, this is Candelabra. Request position. Can you give your position. Chardy, where the fuck are you?"

"Paul, listen. Listen, Jesus—"

"Is he there?" the man in front said.

Miles tried again. "Hosepipe One? Hosepipe One? Goddammit, Paul?" He turned to them. "I can't raise him. He's off the net."

"Hosepipe Three, this is Candelabra. Did you get a fix on Chardy?"

Somebody grabbed the mike from Lanahan. "Candelabra, we've lost him."

"Did you get an acknowledgment?"

"He was there," Miles said. "He heard me."

"Candelabra, this is Three," said the man up front next to the driver. "We didn't get a fix either. We were barely receiving him. He must have been under something."

They drove on in silence.

"What's he up to?" Miles asked nobody in particular as the car raced down the parkway toward Key Bridge and Washington.

Nobody answered him.

Yost Ver Steeg was the first to arrive. He walked from the elevator across the cement, coming out of the light, his feet snapping on the pavement.

Chardy, leaning wearily against the pillar with his headache and his grief, watched him come.

"Hello, Paul. My people are on their way."

"Hello, Yost. I expected Sam."

"Sam can't make it, Paul. Well, you tried. But you couldn't quite bring it off."

"No. No, goddammit."

"It's a pity too. Because the Soviet operation had already come apart."

"I know it had."

"I figured you did, Paul. I thought something was going on in that head of yours. I wish you'd come to me, Paul. I wish you'd trusted me. It would have saved a lot of trouble."

"It's Sam, isn't it?"

"Yes, Paul. Sam has been working for the Russians since nineteen seventy-four. One of the consequences of the Kurdistan thing. Sam is an insanely ambitious man,

Paul. He was terrified that Saladin Two would be a big success and Bill Speight would become the next Deputy Director for Operations. So he sent old Frenchy to Vienna to blow the op. But Speshnev was too smart, too fast. Speshnev is very good, you know, Paul. He's just about their best. He nailed Frenchy and he broke him, broke him wide open fast. And then he owned Sam. He just had Sam so tight there was no getting out of it. I guess it wasn't long before they saw how their interests coincided. They've been helping each other along all these years.''

''Jesus,'' said Chardy.

''I guess there's some good news here for you, Paul. You didn't betray the Kurds. You really didn't.''

''That's just a technicality, Yost,'' Chardy said. ''A minor trick of timing. If I'm off the hook, it's not because they knew one day before I told them or one week or one year. It's because there was no hook. I tried; I failed. I did my best. I can't ask much more from myself and nobody else has the right to, either.''

''Now that's a healthy attitude, Paul. That's very healthy. I'm glad you see it that way. We knew all this some time ago, and believe me, the temptation was enormous to let you in on it. But I'm glad you worked it out on your own, Paul. We were just getting closer and closer and we couldn't risk anything. And when it turned out Danzig had duplicates on the Saladin Two files, we knew Sam and Speshnev would have to cook something up. We used it: we thought we could get Speshnev as well as Sam. Now that would be a catch, wouldn't it? A Soviet double and his Russian case officer? Damn, that would have been something!''

Chardy lay back against the pillar. This headache would not go away.

''The poor Kurd,'' said Yost. ''He's the tragic figure in

all this. He's the most innocent of all. He was used and used and used. The poor bastard.''

Chardy shook his head in pain.

''And Danzig. Oh, I wish we'd been a little smarter, a little sooner. It's such a dirty business, Paul. People just keep getting in the way. Sometimes you have to wonder about it all.''

''Did you get them? Did you at least get Sam and the Russian?''

''We arrested Sam an hour ago. When Danzig escaped. It was finally time. I wish you could have been there. He had no idea we were onto him. But there's no evidence Speshnev ever came into this country. Sam will tell us, though. Eventually.''

''I'm quitting, Yost. I'm getting out of it. Everything I tried to do I fucked up.''

Joseph Danzig moaned. He rolled over and put his hand to his face.

''My God,'' said Yost. ''He's still alive. We better get some medical people here, Paul—''

''Oh, he's fine. He's not shot. I hit him. I have a terrible, terrible temper. Did I ever tell you about the time I punched Cy Brasher? It was like that: I just let go. Oh, Christ, I'm in trouble. Jesus, he could have me sent to jail. It was so stupid of me. Why do I do these stupid things?''

Chardy looked over.

Yost had picked up the Skorpion.

''Be careful, Yost. It's loaded; it's cocked. Those things are very dangerous.''

''I know about guns, Paul. I was in the Delta during Tet.'' He pulled the bolt back a hair and looked into the breech. ''I can see the gleam of the brass cartridge in there.''

''Put it down. You could hurt somebody. Jesus, I hope Danzig doesn't press charges. Do you think you could put in a good word for me when he comes to? I'd really appreciate it.''

Yost had the Skorpion pointed toward Chardy.

"Sorry, Paul," he said.

"Hosepipe Three, this is Hosepipe Nine—do you read?"

The man in front picked up the mike.

"I'm reading, Hosepipe Nine."

"Who the hell is Hosepipe Nine?" Lanahan asked.

"One of our other cars, out looking for Danzig," somebody said.

"Three, I'm on Rock Creek Parkway by the Roosevelt Bridge, and I received that transmission loud and clear. From Hosepipe One, I mean."

"Thank you, Hosepipe Nine. We copy."

"What's that near?" Lanahan asked.

"State Department. Lincoln Memorial. Watergate. Kennedy Center. It's right in the middle of—"

"Kennedy Center!" shrieked Miles. "It's an Agency safe-house—the lower floor of the parking garage. You got a siren on this thing? Come on, hit it."

The siren began to wail and a portable flasher was clamped atop the sedan as it began to accelerate down M Street.

"Come on, hurry," Lanahan urged them again, and licked his lips out of fear. For now he knew what Chardy was up to.

"He's playing cowboy again," he told them.

Chardy looked at Yost. Yost wore his pinstripe suit and glasses. He was about fifty. He had sandy thin hair. As always he was controlled, quiet, calm. He betrayed no unsteadiness.

"It was just like you said, Yost," Chardy said. "Sam's

ambition, Frenchy's betrayal, Speshnev's fast footwork. Except all the way there was one other character. It was you. You were Sam's brains.''

"He's not very bright, Paul. He doesn't have a first-class mind. He's very smooth and charming, but he's just not very bright.''

"You sold him on blowing Saladin Two. And you went to Frenchy. And you sold Frenchy, offered him the big upstairs job. And when Speshnev cracked Frenchy, it was *your* name he coughed up. And it was *you* Speshnev nailed.''

"What could I do, Paul? He had me.''

"And when I'm in the cell and Speshnev can't break me and he's getting desperate until he tells me he knows about Johanna and he'll lay her head on the table, it's *you* he learned it from. And when Sam crucifies Bill Speight and me at the hearing, it's because you've done his staffwork for him. And up he goes, and up you go. And all those years you've been working for him and everything he knew you knew and it went straight to Speshnev. And when you set Danzig up in Boston and everybody thinks you've fucked up, he finds you a new job in Satellites. But Satellites are ten times more important than anything in Operations. You're right in the center. And if Sam should make DCI, he'll take you along. And if something goes wrong, if somebody thinks there's a double, and they begin to backtrack, the trail leads straight—to Sam. Sam takes the heat. Everybody watches Sam, not you. And during all this, it's Sam I hate, Sam I'm trying to screw, Sam who drives me crazy. Not you. I don't even know you. I never even *heard* of you.''

"Paul, it's time. Speshnev had planned to do this himself. It's time to end it. Sorry.''

He held the machine pistol in both hands and fired.

The bolt jammed halfway forward.

"I turned the first shell around in the clip," Chardy said. "You should have looked more carefully."

Chardy took the Ingram out from under his coat.

"This is how you fucked up. Because you underestimated everybody. Each step of the way, and by only a little bit, you underestimated everybody. You thought we were such losers. Old Speight did pretty good down in Mexico. That dreamy kid Trewitt did even better. And Miles, even little Miles came through when we needed him. Everybody was there when we needed them, Yost. And Frenchy: Frenchy was there too. You underestimated Frenchy the most. Frenchy left me a message, buried in an old computer disc, because he didn't trust you. Miles bluffed his way into the pit this evening and dug it out. A minute before you arrived he reached me on *this*"—he pulled out the radio unit—"with your name."

He paused.

"Yost, I ought to blow you the fuck in half for all you've cost me."

At the far end of the garage, a vehicle careened down the ramp and sped to thm. Before it had even halted, tiny Miles was out.

"Good work, Paul," he called. "We'll take him now."

Another car arrived in the next second, and then several others.

A team of medics had taken Danzig off, bleeding, his face swollen. He had not looked at Chardy. The body of Ulu Beg, too, had been removed, after a ritual of crime-site photography that Chardy could not watch.

Miles meanwhile moved among the various groups of officials who'd arrived at the scene and took it upon himself to represent the Agency's interests until a higher-ranking officer was located. A Deputy Director was due shortly—Chardy guessed it would not be Sam Melman—

and the DCI himself had been awakened and briefed and was now on his way to Langley for an emergency session. It was also said that the President had been awakened, as had members of the National Security Council and the Senate and House Intelligence Oversight committees, each of which had dispatched a man or men to the fourth level.

Chardy stood apart from all this. He drew on a cigarette deeply—he had not smoked for years and at first he coughed. But now he had it down again. He finished the cigarette, tossed it away.

"Got another, Leo?"

Leo Bennis handed him another.

Miles was suddenly there, and as Chardy lit up, Miles whispered to him, "Paul, we can really run with this. You and I, if we play it right. All right?"

"Sure, Miles. We'll be big heroes. I'll tell 'em you were in on it from the beginning; you were calling the shots. I'll tell 'em you were the guy who caught the double."

"Paul, I'd really appreciate—"

"Forget it."

"Right."

Miles bobbed away, disappearing among a group of men in suits who were asking questions.

They were about to lead Yost off. He had been weeping. His face was ruined, his hair messy, his eyes swollen. He could not control himself and nobody had thought to give him a handkerchief. Yet now, sensing Chardy's gaze on him, he looked over.

It was hard for Chardy to feel anything. He thought he'd see Sam being led off; he'd hated Sam all those years. Yost. Who was Yost? He felt he'd been denied something he'd earned. Ulu Beg was dead. Johanna was dead. And somebody he'd never heard of, or really even known, was behind it all.

They took Yost to a van, surrounded by FBI personnel. Miles had tried to get him released to the Agency for debriefing, but the FBI pulled rank. Still Miles insisted on knowing exactly where they were taking him, who was in charge, and began to establish groundwork for the future.

"Maybe you'll be big in the Agency now," said Leo.

"No," Chardy replied. "I never wanted that sort of thing. I just wanted—"

He stopped suddenly.

"I know where Speshnev is," he said.

"What?"

"Yost said, 'Speshnev had planned to kill you himself.' He did. Leo, get a car, get it fast. Clear these people out of here. Where's that Ingram? Come on, Leo."

"Paul!"

Chardy found his weapon—it had been impounded by the FBI and Chardy unimpounded it with a quick threat of violence—and ran for the car, inserting a new magazine as he ran.

He leaped in and turned to Leo as the car peeled out of the garage.

"There's a last wrinkle. There has to be. To bury Saladin Two forever, to seal it off from living memory."

"Paul—"

"At the hospital. Speshnev. He has to go for me."

The car squealed as it accelerated up the ramp, up four levels, and turned onto the parkway, siren wailing.

"He'll get in too. He'll find the wing, the room."

"All our people are gone now," said Leo. "They all hit the street after Danzig."

"God help him," said Chardy, for now he saw what must happen. "God help Ramirez."

56

It was a strangely quiet night, the strangest, the quietest since he had come north. It was a night for escape, but Ramirez felt so tired. They were putting something in the juice, he figured. His limbs weighed a ton; his vision was blurred, his mind working slowly.

Or maybe Reynoldo Ramirez is slowing down with age. All men must. Why would the dark angel spare you, Reynoldo? You do not even pray except when somebody is shooting bullets at you and in this hospital in the far north among pale, bloodless, calm *norteamericanos,* nobody would fire bullets at you.

He lay in the shadows, watching and not watching the television through his swollen eyes. The bulky bandage on his nose somewhat obscured his view, but it didn't matter. He felt almost asleep, but not quite. Certainly there was a drug in his bloodstream. The whores! But he had no energy left to hate them.

He was dreaming of escape and food and women. Mostly women: young women, Indian women, virgins to be exact. He had not done anything with his organ in months. It was worse than prison, where for a price a whore would accommodate you.

Then a blond doctor came in.

Eh? A new one.

He stood silhouetted in the doorway. Ramirez waited. So they had not forgotten him, then. A new doctor even. Should he say something to the man, who just stood there? It was clear the man was not sure whether Ramirez was awake or not, for the Mexican's bandaged face was hidden in the shadow. Ramirez puzzled over this irregularity of etiquette. Should I say something or not?

But they checked in on him often like this, he knew; he'd caught them at it before: peeking in at strange hours to see how their "guest" was doing. So Ramirez was not surprised and not alarmed and decided to lie quietly until the doctor went away.

Yet the doctor did not go away. He looked quickly up and down the quiet hall, then stepped in, pulling the door softly closed behind him.

Most curious.

Ramirez, lying still, watched the doctor slide along the wall. He came to the television, which was mounted on the wall, and reached up for the knob.

Did he want a different show?

But the doctor did not want a different show at all. He turned up the volume a bit, then a bit more.

Ramirez didn't like this at all. No doctor had ever done this before. Were they going to get rid of him? He was an embarrassment, after all, was he not? Had he not also been responsible for the death of that stupid young boy on the mountain?

Mother of Jesus, help me.

Holy Virgin, give me strength.

I pray, Holy Catholic Mother, for your forgiveness. I have sinned and am a bad man, many times bad, many times, I've killed and whored. Forgive me, oh, Holy Mother. He wished he had some strength. He wished he could move; he wished he didn't feel so doped, so logy.

The doctor came over to the bed, reaching into his jacket. He pulled out a small pistol.

He came closer, as though he could not see, and reached with one hand as though to find the soft throat that must have been in the shadow.

Ramirez felt the man's fingers at his skin.

Mother of God, help your sinning son Reynoldo.

The doctor brought over the other hand with the pistol and was going to fire straight down into the throat, but as he brought the thing close, the Virgin, in Her kindness and great forgiving love of the sinning Reynoldo Ramirez, rewarded him with a great spurt of strength which he invested in a short, upward, pistonlike blow into the doctor's looming chin, knocking the stunned man backward, and Reynoldo rolled to his right, out of bed, all his quickness and cunning restored as if by religious miracle, and as he dropped off the edge of the bed, out of the line of fire, the man sent a shot whistling past to shatter on the linoleum.

Reynoldo hit the floor and bounced off it to shove his shoulder into the bed in almost the same tenth of a second, moving it with growing acceleration until it slammed into the doctor furiously, knocking him against the wall with a yelp of outrage. Ramirez rocketed to his feet, lifting the heavy bedframe as he rose, and flipped it on the pinned man. He heard another of the strange shots. He turned to look for a weapon but could see only the television set with a cowboy firing a gun on its screen, and he plucked it with both hands off the shelf and heaved it across the room to where the doctor struggled to free himself from the mess of bedding. The set hit the wall above and fell to the doctor's head and again he screamed in pain.

Ramirez did not pause to investigate, only turned and fled. He found himself in an empty green corridor, unlit, and saw the door at one end marked EXIT and ran for it, his gown flapping wildly, his ass and organs bounding in his sprint. He reached the door and found the whore snugly locked and lunged for the door across the hall. It opened, admitting him to a dark, quiet room.

Had the doctor seen him enter?

It didn't matter. Ramirez looked about, desperately, for a weapon.

Speshnev could see the footprints—the mark of a sweaty foot—leading down the hallway. He followed. His head was bleeding from the blow struck him by the television.

Trust Chardy for the genius of improvisation: television as a weapon. How American.

The blood ran into his eyes. He halted to wipe it away. He'd have to stanch it, and throw this doctor's coat away before he tried the lobby again. Damn Chardy. He'd grown fat in the years, but not stupid.

I should have fired instantly. Yet sometimes they screamed as the microtoxin froze up their respiratory system, so the precaution had been advised.

Speshnev put the air pistol away. He pulled out the Luger from under his other arm. He snapped the toggle, chambering a shell. The silencer made the pistol a bit front-heavy. He knew he had to hurry—surely sooner or later someone would arrive at this far wing. But to rush stupidly could also prove tragic.

The footprints led to the exit door and then away, to the door opposite.

Chardy had to be in that room. He touched the door, pushed it open. It showed a black crack. He knew where Chardy would be: just inside the doorjamb, left side, crouched low. Chardy would punch for throat or temple.

Speshnev moved the Luger to his other hand. He poised—then drew back.

He did not have long to wait. Chardy, driven insane by the tension, was like all men of action without the gift of patience. Speshnev knew he'd come and he did.

The door burst open and savagely the man came at him, low and so fast.

Speshnev caught the plunging head with an upthrust of his stout knee and knew from the solidity of the impact that the blow was a rare masterpiece, perfectly timed, perfectly placed; he sidestepped adroitly—he was still fast himself—and clipped Chardy hard on the back of the skull with the pistol barrel, opening a terrible gash. Blood spurted everywhere. The man was driven to his knees, where for just an instant he fought the concussion until he yielded, collapsing forward with a smack, face down.

I have you at last.

Excitement raced through Speshnev's widened veins. He leaned over and held the pistol six inches from the back of the head, and Chardy flopped about, twitching, then turned with great sluggishness half over and Speshnev could see for the first time that it was not Chardy at all, but some stranger.

Where was Chardy?

He stood. He felt violated by an immense betrayal.

Where was Chardy?

The answer to his question came as the door at the other end of the corridor opened in a burst and Chardy, among others, spilled into the green corridor, and if someone yelled *stop* neither he nor Chardy heard or cared to hear it. He raised his pistol, thinking that he still might have a chance, even at this late moment, but as he brought it up he knew he'd never make it, for he saw that Chardy had a machine pistol of some sort and the bullets arrived to cut through his chest and push him down.

57

In the wake of Sam Melman's resignation and the subsequent Agency shakeup in the awareness of Yost Ver Steeg's treachery, there was a considerable power vacuum in the Operations Directorate.

Danzig had no official influence, of course, but he still knew important people and he still had favors owed him in the intelligence community. He made some phone calls and drafted several memos and even lobbied one or two influential men personally—difficult, because the swelling had not gone down, and his eye was gaudily discolored. His efforts were partially rewarded.

It was agreed to bring back one of the Old Boys, a retired officer of experience and judgment, to serve as interim Deputy Director of Operations until a suitable permanent tenant could be found for the job; but it was also agreed to appoint Miles Lanahan assistant Deputy Director in recognition of his brilliant service of late. Miles was twenty-nine; he was the youngest to reach that position by nine years.

In the aftermath, Danzig suggested that Miles join him for lunch at an excellent French restaurant in downtown Washington. Miles agreed quickly, and on the appointed day arrived in an Agency limousine, and walked in wearing a new gray chalk-stripe suit of conservative cut. His shoes glittered blackly; his hair was cut crisply. But he was still a little nervous; he'd never been to a French restaurant before and he wasn't sure what to order.

He stared at the menu in the strange language.

"A young wine, a Bordeaux. How does that suit you, Miles?"

"Fine," said Miles to the older man. "It suits me fine."

"The Margaux, please," said Danzig to the wine steward. "The *boeuf bourguignon* is very good here," he said to Miles.

"That's what I'll have then," said Miles.

"And the usual for me, Philip," Danzig said to the waiter, who disappeared as quietly as he had arrived.

"Well, Miles, you're looking prosperous."

Miles blushed under his acne, then smiled modestly. His teeth gleamed; he had brushed them that morning.

"They're treating you well at the Agency?"

"I'm a hero," Miles said. It was true. He was. In corridors, in conferences, in a hundred small ways he could feel it: he was a man who counted. He was the man who nailed Yost Ver Steeg.

"You're only getting what you deserve," said Danzig pleasantly. He reached to adjust his dark glasses, which were not quite big enough to obscure the purple blotch that even yet surrounded his eye. Chardy must have really whacked him, Miles thought. Jesus, Chardy, you really are a piece of work. Hitting Joe Danzig. Jesus!

Danzig's injury had quite naturally inspired a great volume of rumor, made worse by the fact that at an unguarded moment a free-lance photographer had gotten a good close-up of it, and subsequently sold the picture to *Time,* which printed it in their "People" section over the caption "Danzig and pet mouse." Danzig had issued soon after a statement that referred to a minor automobile accident in which no serious damage had been sustained. Of course nobody believed it. Danzig's reputation as a man of outsize ego and libido and taste for young married women was widely known and it did not take much imagination to concoct a scenario by which he could acquire such a wound.

"You'll do well, Miles, I know you will," Danzig said.

"Thank you. I'll work hard, I know that."

"I know you will."

"I was very lucky I didn't go down with Sam."

"You are a survivor, Miles. I could see it from the start."

Miles nodded. He was. It was true. Miles's true gift: landing on his feet.

"Look, I wanted to thank you for the help you gave me," Miles said.

"It's nothing. Please. You embarrass me. Ah, the wine."

It was served. Miles watched as Danzig was offered a sip, took it, and approved.

"Very nice," he said, without looking at the steward.

Miles's glass was filled; he took a sip. It *was* good. His delight must have showed on his face.

"It's a Chateau Margaux, a 'seventy-seven. A very good one."

"Boy, it's *terrific,*" said Miles.

"Miles, I have been thinking. These last several weeks have been a real test for me. They've made me confront a lot of important issues. Namely, do I want to spend the rest of my life doing nothing except living comfortably but pointlessly?"

"I'm sure you don't," said Miles, wondering where this was going.

"I'm a relatively young man, after all. I feel I've got a lot to *contribute.*"

"Yes, sir," said Miles, taking a little sip of the wine.

"I might want to be actively involved at some level—either officially or unofficially. Do you see?"

Miles did not. But then he did. Yes, of course he did. Miles suddenly realized an alliance was being offered. So that was how these things worked: you help me, I'll help you. But what could he—?

He could do a lot. He saw it now: a lot.

"Yes," he said. "I agree, Dr. Danzig. I·just want you to know you can count on me."

Danzig raised his glass, and paused for just a second. He seemed to consider the meal that lay before him, and perhaps the afternoon as well, or perhaps even beyond.

"Miles," he said, "to the future. It's really ours, you know."

There was a counterpoint to this tête-à-tête, a somewhat less swanky one, which took place on the same day nearly two thousand miles away and involved two other participants in the affair of the Kurd.

One of these, Reynoldo Ramirez, much recovered in health and glossily attired in a shiny new polyester suit, leaned forward and peered squint-eyed through a filthy windshield aglare with heavy sunlight and declared, "There! There it is!"

His companion, Paul Chardy, merely nodded.

The drive through the desert, down from Tucson, had passed swiftly and the town was upon them with a suddenness that almost drove the pain from Chardy's head. He could see it: the hills beyond the wire fence littered with the shacks of the poor, in blue and pink and other hopeful colors. Over the automobile-inspection booths and the pedestrian turnstile hung a bulky green bridge of offices. Cars were jammed up in both directions and a hundred people loafed on either side of the wire.

Chardy gazed on the scene without interest. It had all begun here months ago: so what? The sense of circle, of completion, of ending, held no magic for him. Yet, still, he'd wanted this job: to take the Mexican back and set him free, another survivor.

Chardy pulled the car over to the curb eighty yards up the slope of the avenue from the border.

"Okay, chum. It's all yours. Go on."

Ramirez lurched from the car. He must have had a thousand stitches in him. He was like some old, dented Mexican '52 De Soto, rusty and scabby, beaten to hell, with a gray fender and a blue door and a bumper wired on, but running smoothly after 300,000 miles. He moved ahead toward the gate and seemed to slow, as if he felt dizzy or nauseous. He stopped to gather himself.

Chardy got out.

"You okay?" he called, reaching for the trembling arm.

"Sure, sí. Reynoldo's fine."

"You've got your money?"

"You bet."

In his pocket Ramirez had a nice stake for the future, courtesy of the American government.

"Go on. What are you waiting for?" Chardy asked.

"Nada," said Ramirez, straightening. He must have been fifty; he looked a hundred. He walked ahead swiftly and reached the gate. He halted, his fingers touching the cold metal of the turnstile, then plunged through.

Chardy sat on the fender and watched him go until he lost him among the crowds of pimps and Indians and souvenir sellers and Exclusivo cabdrivers and young girls.

Chardy tried not to think of another man he'd hoped to take to a border and tell, Go on. You're free. Get out of here. He also remembered a woman—and a dreamy young man. They'd all gotten fucked trying to get across borders.

The sun was bright and the wind blew loose sheets of newspaper through the air, whipped up eddies of dust, swirled girls' dresses up to show their white thighs, but Chardy could not see the Mexican at all. He was gone. He was definitely gone.

Chardy turned back and climbed into the car. He thought he might find a bar and kill a few beers, a few hours. There was no hurry.